See my other books!

Trials of an Archmage series:
Book I - Discovery
Paperback ISBN: 9-595-25758-5
Hard Cover ISBN: 0-595-65313-8
Available from www.iuniverse.com

Book II - Pern and the Giant Forest
Paperback ISBN: 0-595-30229-7
Available from www.iuniverse.com

Book III - The Mystic Library
Paperback ISBN: 1-905166-40-0
Available from www.amazon.com

Book IV - Ascension/
Circle of Darkness
Paperback ISBN: 0-595-41898-8
Available from www.iuniverse.com

Other Fantasy Books:
Long Live the Queen
Paperback ISBN: 0-595-27449-8
Available from www.iuniverse.com

Balance lost/A Strange Friendship
Paperback ISBN: 978-1-4401-0693-4
Available from www.iuniverse.com

Science Fiction Books:

The Conquest of New Eden/
Sins of the Father
Paperback ISBN: 0-595-37561-8
Available from www.iuniverse.com

Droptroopers: Gauntlet of Fear
Paperback ISBN: 978-0-595-47591-9
Available from www.iuniverse.com

Other titles in the works:
The Last Wizard of Earth
Fade to Gray (Book and Music CD)
Chronicles of the Mystic Towers

A Watery Crash

Larry W. Miller Jr.

iUniverse, Inc.
New York   Bloomington

iUniverse books may be ordered through booksellers or by contacting:

iUniverse
1663 Liberty Drive
Bloomington, IN 47403
www.iuniverse.com
1-800-Authors (1-800-288-4677)

Because of the dynamic nature of the Internet, any Web addresses or links contained in this book may have changed since publication and may no longer be valid. The views expressed in this work are solely those of the author and do not necessarily reflect the views of the publisher, and the publisher hereby disclaims any responsibility for them.

ISBN: 978-1-4401-8180-1 (sc)
ISBN: 978-1-4401-8181-8 (ebook)

Printed in the United States of America

iUniverse rev. date: 11/17/2009

Dedication:

This book was written a few years ago. I was working at Preh electronics. So the list of people to thank is different this time. First of all, we have Kathy and Kurt Braun. The other members of the team were Ben, Violeta, and Laver. I have since lost track of all of these people, but they were inspirational at the time. I hope that they are all doing well. The current economy has been somewhat of a strain and it was uncertain whether or not this book would be published. However, if I did not publish it then the economy would have won. And I could not in good conscience allow that to happen.

Next on the list is my family. Without their care and support, works like this would not happen. I look forward to the next project; and the next with eagerness. I would also like to thank all of the people that read my stories. You are the ones that make the writing worthwhile. So from the bottom of my heart, thank you.

1

Lieutenant Quinn Ramses had waited for the ship to dock for over three hours. His neatly pressed, finely tailored uniform was the picture of perfection, right down to the old-fashioned brass buttons on his jacket. His last assignment ended in glory. He had received the Golden Starburst medal for a smooth and profitable new alien contact. He had personally negotiated the entry of a new species into the fleet. Many of the higher brass knew who Quinn was, and his superiors were quite jealous of that fact. He knew there would always be a period of adjustment, but his ego was not a major problem. His ability to blend in and follow orders saved him more than once. There would always be time to shine; it didn't have to happen every day. He admitted to himself that he did like the adulation. It was also quite a huge benefit that he felt like he was doing something useful for his people, and the peoples of other races. Now though, his assignment seemed to be almost a punishment. He was a survey officer after all, and survey was their primary job, but this ship was going to look at uninhabited worlds and survey them for colonization. He was a professional though, and he would not let his disappointment show at the new orders. He knew he could do the job. That was, after all, all that mattered to Fleet Headquarters. He continued to watch as the gray hulking ship drew nearer to the Solarian Fleet's own *H.M.S. Waverly Station*. The *S.S.F. Abraham Lincoln* made the final turn and began its approach.

As was protocol, the ship turned on its exterior lighting while making the final approach to the station. This allowed proper navigation, and also allowed the people waiting for the ship to see it in all of its glory. The Lincoln was not the newest ship in the fleet. However, its four hundred and fifty-two meter length and its sleek lines made it beautiful to him. He read the ship's registry number and the name as the ship slowly worked its way by his window. The lettering was obviously meant to be seen from a very far distance off. The writing was nearly ten meters high. As he looked, he could see closed hatches for armament, and sensors. The young man took it all in and he felt a sense of pride. He watched it creep forward and engage the clamps. The umbilical feed tethered out to the hull and automatically sealed to the receptacle on the ship's side. The maintenance crews were anxious to get the servicing underway. Fleet credits, the standard monetary unit of the fleet, were good spendable credits, and this was a non-military station with concerns all its own. Plus, there was always the chance to milk the job for extra credits with overruns and labor costs. Yes, this was a celebrated event at the station. The quartermaster smiled as he saw the numbers on the imaginary spreadsheet in his head. The lights turned from bright amber to green and the hatchway swung into place. Like the airplane jets of old, a boarding ramp was then extended out to the craft and a clean and safe entrance was provided for the passengers and crew to disembark. The overhead speakers were playing the fleet anthem and the officer of the day was waiting with a crisp salute for the Captain of the *Lincoln* to come down. The man was sure to be disappointed though, the Captain did not leave the ship. Several of the crew did, however, and the duty-free shop was soon selling everything they could to the eager crewman that had been out in space for over six standard months. As usual, the bars would do well this night too. Unfortunately that meant that more than one spacer would end up in the brig tonight as well. Of course they would pay their hefty fines and be released. It was just another way the economy thrived when spacers were in port.

Quinn watched as the crewmen scattered out into the station and disappeared into one amusement or another. He shook his head and entered the walkway to board the ship. His duffel bag was over his shoulder and he presented the officer on deck with a salute. The man smiled back, and then regained his composure and asked for Quinn's orders. Quinn handed over a data wand, a glass cylinder with data stored in it in complex protein chains. It was like a living computer disk. It had long ago replaced the fallible magnetic media that used to be commonplace on board space ships. In fact, those same magnetic disks had replaced the antiquated paper orders. Now it was only at the rarest of occasions that actual paper was used.

The data wand slid into the reader slot and the orders were displayed on the tiny screen. The officer was used to it and he squinted to read the tiny writing. Then he grumbled something that Quinn didn't catch and he handed the data wand back. "You are to report to the billets officer on 'C' deck before doing anything else." The man pressed his thumb into the access port and the door slid open to allow access to the ship itself. Quinn nodded his thanks and stepped through the doorway and into the artificial environment like a pro. He compensated for the tiny gravity shift that threw off so many crewmen and crewwomen when they boarded or left a docked ship. There was more grumbling just as the hatch slid shut and resealed. Quinn listened a little closer, but the only word that he heard was survey. It was enough to get the gist of the message, but he let it slide and then he oriented himself to the ship's layout and proceeded to the 'C' deck. There seemed to be no one else on board. The corridors that were usually cramped with bustling personnel were free and he made good time to the lifts. He set his duffel on the lift and sent it down to the 'C' deck, and then he stepped onto the ladder and descended the shaft next to the lift. He had developed this habit to keep physically fit in the cramped environment of shipboard life. He actually got to 'C' deck before the lift arrived and he was standing at the entranceway to the lift when the doors opened. He grabbed the duffel and swung it over his shoulder.

The 'C' deck was small, even smaller than the 'E' deck he had just left. The shape of the hull caused the decks farther from the center to be smaller than the inner ones because there was less space in the oval design. It probably didn't help that the *Lincoln* was also considered a war ship. It had heavy redundancy in all of its systems and the rocket launching system took up most of the outer spaces of the vessel. He made his way through access corridors and terminal junctions. The duffel caught on one obstruction or another a few times until he finally reached his goal. He shook off the momentary flash of anger and frustration at his own clumsiness and pressed the entrance chime. The door slid up into the ceiling and he stepped through the opening. He had just entered the personnel section of the ship. There were racks and racks of data wands on a bulkhead wall. It was all color-coded in an elaborate filing system that few could understand, but was also standard learning in the survey service. The clerk was a tall thin man with razor stubble on his chin. His armband suggested that he had seen a lot of combat. Although the fleet was not actually at war with anyone, there were always skirmishes here and there. If someone wanted to fight, there was always a place to send them. His uniform was cleaner than he was and he leaned heavily on a synthetic leg that looked as if it were meant for someone else. His name patch said Masterson.

He looked up at the sound of the door sliding closed again and he sighed at the man in front of him. "Fresh meat for the grinder, eh?" He said with very little humor. Quinn presented his data wand and the man didn't even bother to put the wand in the reader. "I'm sure you are who you are supposed to be, it's just damn inconvenient to have to process you while everyone else is down on the station having a good time." He said candidly and Quinn nodded. Then the man reached back and grabbed a portable computer. It was the standard model hand-comp except that it was extremely outdated. He handed it over to Quinn and waved the new man over to a metal chair bolted to one of the bulkhead walls. "Fill in these forms and get back to me for your billet assignment." He said and his attention wandered back down to the periodical he was reading on his own personal hand-comp.

Quinn shrugged his shoulders and took the offered seat. He had seen the forms before; he filled them in quickly and set the hand-comp back down on the clerk's desk. It was a few long moments before the clerk looked up from his comp to note the new man's paperwork. When he did, it was like it was a major inconvenience to lift a finger for anyone. Quinn held his anger in check with no visible signs to set off this miserable excuse for a soldier. The man further reduced Quinn's opinion of him by snorting derisively at a couple of the entries, and then tossing the comp back to Quinn. "Yeah, that's good enough; go and get a briefing from the XO when you get your room squared away. You're in B21 on the port side of the ship. If you found this place, you can find it just as well. It's kind'a part of the test to see if the crew know the ship properly when they report in." He finished and Quinn nodded and thanked him for his time. Then he felt a wave of relief upon leaving the compartment and that seemingly brainless man with the responsibility of personnel. This ship probably had other problems to worry about. He wondered how many stations that man had been incompetent in before he had gotten shuffled to that spot.

Quinn made his way to the Port side bays quickly. It was really a matter of backtracking and taking the other access corridor. He found the 'B' bay and he counted the doors until he found 21. There was an access port and he stuck his data wand into it and the door opened obediently. So no matter what he thought of the man he had just left, at least the computer had been updated for his access. The room was small, and tight, but it was all his. Survey officers usually found that they were alone. Most of the regular navy chose to steer clear of the survey people. They were viewed as the prima donnas of space. They always got the best stuff. They even got the best pay. But their job had a low life expectancy too. It was all too difficult for the average navy man to understand. They felt that everyone was risking their lives the same. On a ship, that was mainly true. A hit to the ship could explode anywhere and kill anybody equally. Survey crews were usually down on the planet and on the front lines. They were used for first contacts and more often than not, it became fatal over misunderstandings and cultural problems. The survey personnel were a breed apart; the sturdier part of humanity, and most other people resented them for their arrogant attitudes. Quinn had done his level best to not appear superior to his crewmates, but the survey service stigma had followed him most of his career.

He unpacked his duffel and put everything in its required space. He had always followed protocols when storing his gear and he always knew where everything was. It was just a part of his nature to crave order in all things. There were so many things out there that one couldn't control; it was refreshing to have something that he could. He finished stowing his gear, and then he sent a quick letter off to his folks informing them that he had arrived safely and that everything was fine. Then he freshened up and resealed the quarters. He had a briefing with the Executive Officer to get over with, and waiting would not help the situation any, so he sighed and headed for the bridge. He had to take the forward lift up to the top and there, he first laid eyes on the Captain. The man was not impressively built. He looked like a hunched over throwback to an earlier society that allowed human weasels to gain vast power. He was huddled over a diagram of a planetary body. He could not tell which one from here, but the data was precious to the little man as if he had his arms around it, cradling it for security.

But this was not the time for Quinn to meet the Captain; he was here to find the Executive Officer. He didn't know much about the man except what his public record allowed. He could tell that the man was efficient and a hard worker, but his medals list was locked away. Quinn had found that curious, but not a big problem. Usually, survey crew had access to almost everything. He found it relieving that he had not been granted free reign of the computer. It meant that they were treating him just like every other member of the crew. The thought brought a smile to his face and the XO caught sight of him on the bridge.

The XO approached Quinn and held out his hand in the old-fashioned gesture of a handshake. Quinn had not had that pleasure for quite some time and his smile beamed as he shook the man's hand with a firm grip. "You must be the new guy?" He said almost needlessly. The XO's hands were rough and callused; he was definitely a hands-on kind of guy who had done a lot of work personally.

"Yes sir, I just came aboard." Quinn answered. They told me in personnel to reach you and get a briefing. I've already logged in and am ready to go with whatever you need sir." He said helpfully.

"Good to hear it soldier." The stocky man said. His uniform was a bit worn and it looked like he had been wearing it for over a week, which was probably close to the truth. When all was said and done, the XO spent the better part of three shifts on duty and only one or even half of a shift down. The general feeling among the crew was that the man was a machine that never slept. It was commonplace to find him at his station when you reported for duty. He would still be there when you went off duty, and miraculously, he would still be there when you came back for another shift.

Quinn decided right away that he liked this man. Pretty much anybody with that kind of work ethic impressed him. It took a great dedication to duty to accomplish that level of professionalism and a strong devotion to discipline, and he felt that quality was everything. Quinn was almost a fanatic about the subject and he respected and enjoyed others around him who were like-minded.

The XO eyed Quinn over and a quirky smile crossed his face. "I suppose you'd like your full briefing now then?" He asked in an almost impish tone. Quinn felt that there was more here than met the eye.

Quinn nodded and added, "If it's not too inconvenient, that would be nice sir." He replied.

The Xo stood up and slapped Quinn on the shoulder. "I like a man who wants to get down to business. Let's use my office and get you squared away." He suggested and then led the way from the bridge to his adjoining office. The office was a tiny space with barely enough room for two chairs along with the computer terminal. A bunk was furnished in the room and it folded out of the wall to conserve precious space. There were no windows, which was common in smaller ships, but the ventilator duct seemed to dominate the ceiling almost completely. The XO stepped to the terminal and he waved Quinn to the other seat. "Well, let's just pull up your file now shall we?" He asked, not really expecting a response.

Quinn took the move as a good sign, this man not only did a lot of work, but he also did it by the book. It showed promise that this assignment might not be as bad as it first appeared.

The XO was reading the file quickly before beginning, and Quinn waited patiently for the man to get up to speed. Of course, the XO knew everything in that file. He had memorized the thing before requesting Quinn for this assignment. It was just customary to make this show for the men; it made them think he was truly interested in them personally. Of course in Quinn's case, he was. "I have been spacing since before you were in the academy, but I have never seen such a short and impressive record in the same file." He said and Quinn nodded his thanks at the praise. "In fact, it is the reason that I requested you for this post." He said and Quinn's eyebrows rose at the comment. He was unaware that he had been requested out here. He had assumed that it had been a random assignment by the computer at Survey HQ. His mind started churning on that piece of information and he listened intently for the XO to continue.

"You also know how to handle yourself with upper brass. That could be useful if this mission is a success." He said and Quinn started to fidget. The XO continued on. "We are to survey for colony planets. The area we are to search in is designated as a green spot. In other words, no trouble is expected, and the worlds look hospitable from the original surveys. However, those surveys are several years old and we don't know the systems' status now. I'm sure you can handle the survey work fine." The XO pressed his fingers together in a steeple in front himself as he looked away from his terminal. "The real problem will be the Captain." He finished and Quinn's eyebrows shot up again as alarms went off inside his head. It was almost unthinkable for the XO of a ship to discuss the Captain with a new crew member in this manner, and it bothered Quinn immensely that the subject came up in his initial briefing.

Quinn cleared his throat, and hoped his heart would slow

down a bit. "Sir, do you think that the Captain does not want the mission to succeed?" He asked with trepidation on his breath.

"No, no it's nothing like that." The Xo replied. "It's more the way the man thinks that will be the biggest obstacle for you. You see, he was born in a poor province. His family was important enough to get him into the academy, but they were not well off. He had several years of lean times, and he will not tolerate bankruptcy at any cost. His only wish is to become wealthy enough to give up the ship and retire someplace nice." The Xo shifted in his seat, and Quinn did not fail to notice the tension in the room. It was obvious that the XO was as uncomfortable with this subject as he was; maybe even more than Quinn was.

"Sir, do you think he would drop mission parameters if the opportunity for profit presented itself?" Asked Quinn incredulously.

"I can't say for sure, but my feelings lean towards grabbing the money and going. I don't know why they put him on this ship, but they did. I have to live with that. And now, so do you. But we can still make sure that this mission gets done, and done right." He made eye contact with Quinn and he nodded at the commitment he saw there. "I knew you were the right man for the job. I will get you the original surveys of the planets we will be visiting. If all goes well, we'll find some good planets to land farms on and then get our butts back to civilization. The captain hates being stranded out here doing missions when he could be among the wealthier well to do's. It is part of the life he has always dreamed of, and one that he would probably kill to achieve. Any questions?" He asked, and it was obvious that none were expected.

"No sir, I can start on the reading right away, and I'll be ready when we hit the planet." Quinn promised and then he got up and saluted. "It will be an honor to serve with you sir." He said and about faced and left the cramped compartment.

The XO nodded after the closed hatch. "Good man, I just don't know if he's good enough." He thought to himself. Then he shook off the notion and dove back into his reports. Any ship of the line ran pretty much solely on paperwork. Even though there was no paper anymore, there definitely was a trail of forms to be filled out. Personal computerized notepads provided the medium for most forms. They were easily recyclable into the next form and they could be linked to central databases, making them useful for pulling up data as well. The data transmission could be echoed to other terminals with the correct identifier, and they could also be encrypted to prevent anyone viewing essential data that they shouldn't be. They had evolved the data industry into the mighty information conglomerate it was today.

Of course with all of that data to be saved and categorized, classified, stored and archived, there had to be someone entering it. Thus the XO was usually the one that the duty fell to. First of all, the Captain could not be bothered with the day-to-day operations of his own ship, and no one else had the clearance to see most of the messages. In fact, the Captain had even fallen to the position of allowing the XO to view *Captain's Eyes Only* messages to weed out the unimportant ones to save time. The only messages that the captain looked at himself, were the ones concerning the finances of his family fortune. As it was, there was a stack of paperwork waiting for someone's attention, and that was something that the XO could not stand for. He dove right in and started filling in the blanks. Before long, the stack was considerably smaller and he decided to finish it up before returning to the bridge.

Quinn was reading in his room when the call for lights-out came. He felt that it was a strange custom to have a *downtime* like this, but he was not the one in charge here. It seemed ridiculous to him that some of the crew had to be manning duty stations while the rest of the ship slept. In fact, during wartime, the *downtime* rule was generally dropped. There was no need to put most of the crew out of action at a predictable time of the duty cycle. It had been originally instituted to allow for the air filters and cleaners to recycle. They needed to recycle and have maintenance performed every so often and it was a good opportunity for everyone to relax. However, the more modern systems were self-cleaning and required no down time to maintain the environment in the ship.

The psychological benefits of down time were exaggerated and it just seemed better to have three separate duty schedules like on most any other vessel he knew about. On the bright side, though, it cut down on the crowd that formed in the gym during his off-duty shift.

The information he was given on the planetary survey was sketchy at best. He cursed the incompetents that had made the original survey more than once. The report only hinted at things that needed to be known to properly assess the value of the planet. There were traces of minerals and even a hint of precious gems. There was breathable atmosphere and the gravity was almost a match for Earth's, which was the shipboard standard. The planet seemed to be mostly covered by water though. There was no PH test on the water itself, so he didn't know if it was salt water, or fresh water, but there was plenty of it to go around. There was only a thermograph picture to suggest that life existed anywhere on the planet. That picture was taken on the only continent. That means that the survey crew had completely ignored the vast oceans for life studies. He shook his head at the incompleteness of the report. If he had turned in a report like this in the academy, he might not have passed at all. He decided quickly that more information was needed before the ship could recommend landing a colony on the place. He decided that the only way to get this information was to drop in himself and complete this damned report. He checked the byline at the bottom and it was empty. Quinn came to the conclusion that anyone willing to submit this shoddy of a report would not want to leave identification. The damning report would have been like committing career suicide. Fully disgusted, Quinn tossed the pad aside and lay down for his down time. He still thought it was ridiculous, but orders were orders. The sooner he adapted to the new schedule, the easier life would be here.

The morning chime came and the bunks emptied as the crew got up to start their morning routines. Quinn was among the few that stayed behind, as he did not have a particular duty station to report to on a specified schedule. He waited to let the more urgent personnel shower and dress. It was just a common courtesy, but it was one that tended to soothe the nerves of personnel who resented the new guy. He didn't know who would be the ones he would have trouble with yet, but survey crewmembers usually had problems with the regular navy people. It seemed inevitable. He made sure to keep his most friendly smile firmly in place as the bustling bodies moved through the outer compartments. After about half an hour, the bustle had calmed down considerably and he had the opportunity to see the mess area. The food was standard rations. A protein enhanced paste that somehow failed to please the palate. There was also concentrated juice and purified water that had a metal aftertaste to it. He knew from past cruises that any ship that was headed out for long term space duty only served standard rations so that the crew would not miss other food while out in the great expanses of space. Anything that could hurt the morale of the space crews was generally avoided, at least on most ships.

Quinn sat opposite a sergeant in a technician's uniform. It didn't even look like it fit him properly. They ate their rations in peace and the other man began to get up to go wherever he was heading to next when Quinn waved at him. "I'm sorry, but what function do you have on this ship?" He asked and was surprised by the answer.

"Hi, I'm Conners, Duane." He says. "I'm a linguist and a history buff. They got me here on loan from Headquarters Operations where we have been trying to crack some ancient codes found by other survey missions. Now I am just waiting for a planet-side mission to get my hands dirty on the real thing. I guess that makes me a modern day archeologist, but I grow tired of computer simulations. They can net us some serious information, but they are so cold and impersonal. The earthy feel of the soil has so much more zest." He said, shaking Quinn's hand.

Quinn smiled and gestured hello. "I am interested in planetary duties as well. I am a member of the survey crew and I am also anxious to get to some real search and investigative action. My name is Quinn." He finished.

Duane's eyes widened, "Quinn Ramses, the commendation toting Quinn from the Admiral's own survey crew? It's an honor to meet you sir. I have seen some of your early findings, and I have even read the transcripts of one of your first contacts. You seem to feel your way through languages like an expert. I am impressed." Duane finished and it was Quinn's turn to be surprised.

"I didn't know any of that information was available to the general public. I really didn't do much more than what we were taught at the academy. Most of the rest of it was simply being in the right place at the right time." Quinn finished and Duane shook his head.

"Whatever you say. All I know is that if they needed you here, we are liable to find something I can finally sink my teeth into. I have been stuck on this boat for over a year waiting for a big break." Duane turned in his empty wrappers into the recycler. "You don't mind if I consult with you every once in a while as you uncover more data on alien technologies and languages?" Duane asked and Quinn nodded.

"It would be my pleasure. After all, it is easier to decipher something when you get more brains wrapped around the problem." Quinn replied and they parted company. Duane headed back into the bowels of the ship where his computer lab was located. Quinn decided to check out more of the library files in the main computer, so he headed back to his room to reload his pad. He had many more hours of reading to do before he could safely tell the XO he was properly prepared for the mission. He did decide that he would only read up on the next target planet though. The others could wait for this survey to be completed. Then he could read up on the next one while the ship moved towards the next target world.

2

The XO was a busy man. He had personally overseen the refit of one of the shuttlecraft and he was watching the initial take-off like a nervous father as it edged its way out of the docking bay of the ship. The small craft cleared the doors and began the pre-calculated maneuvers that were the proprietary test flight program from the manufacturer. It didn't help matters much that the test program was one of the most intense rides you could ever fly through, but it was also maddening that the pilot had nothing to do while it was going on. The shuttle would be taken through the course on computer control. The pilot was only there to provide the proper weight distribution during flight and to take over if anything out of the ordinary happened. This program had a knack for shutting down and aborting part way through the mission, so the pilots involved usually held onto the controls. They were ready if the thing let go and started doing something bad.

This ride was like no other test flight, and the ship responded with eye-blink swiftness to the computer's commands. The shuttle completed the course exactly where the pre-programmed course was set. The pilot took over the controls and brought the ship back into the bay. The XO watched intently and didn't let his breath out until the shuttle lightly touched down in the docking bay. The doors sealed and the shuttle showed green lights when the pressure equalized. Then the pilot stepped out of the shuttle and smiled at the crowd of maintenance people that had gathered to watch the flight. A small cheer let out and then they split up to return to their duty stations. The pilot, a seasoned veteran named Margaret, waved at the XO and he smiled back. His mind could rest at ease now that the refit was complete. The paperwork would be on his desk in a couple of hours. He expected a full report on the performance and status of the new drives. He could count on Margaret for that, he was sure.

He turned back to the lift and headed for the bridge. He always felt uncomfortable leaving it to the Captain. He felt a nervous twitch whenever the man committed another blunder of command. He still wondered where the man got a ship from if he couldn't handle people well enough to maintain control, but that would all have to wait. Duty demanded that he help maintain the ship under strict guidelines of function. He thought about the duty rosters and the mission briefings he had delivered and he smiled again. He had run this ship like a Swiss watch, and this young Captain was not going to prevent him from continuing to do so. The men and women under his command were loyal and hard working. That was enough to allow him to do his duty even if the going got tough. Sooner or later it always did, and he was ready for it.

The new man seemed to fit in nicely with The XO's goals, they would reach a successful conclusion to this mission and then he would get this Captain reassigned to another ship, or better yet, he could be *retired* to some backwards world where he could cause no one any further trouble. If only they could find something valuable enough to make the Captain quit, he could get rid of the man all together. After all, the ship did not need the incompetent fool to operate smoothly. The XO thought for a moment and he hoped that his vision of the future was somehow not skewed by the fact that he hated the man in charge. He had had to work around almost every rule to maintain his control, and thus maintain the flow of this ship. The Captain was merely a puppet now, the command decisions were made without his knowledge, in fact they were made without him even caring about what they were, or who was deciding things. The XO saw this as another in a long list of character flaws the man carried with him everyday. His duty bound loyalties forbade him from taking any direct or indirect action against his superior, but that didn't mean the man had not been flayed alive in the XO's dreams. It was perhaps for the better that the Captain was not aware of his second in command's feelings and thoughts. The lift reached the bridge and the XO stepped off into the crowded space that was the nerve center of the ship. He smiled at the Captain and the unknowing man smiled back and then proceeded to flip through his video channels, looking for only God knows what on the monitor. The XO showed no outward signs of displeasure, as he normally did not, and sighed to himself as he took his regular seat near the incompetent fool in the command chair. The readouts he had had rerouted to his terminal told him that the ship was not in any danger. The status boards all registered green. He knew that this kind of bypassed security was in violation of several fleet standing orders, but he was convinced that the only key to the survival of this ship and the successful completion of this mission was his direct involvement in all things. He smiled again at his own wisdom. He knew that the mission was soon to come to a head and he also knew that he would be ready when the time came. His pulse quickened a bit at the thought of really commanding this vessel, and a bit of a quirk crossed his lips as he somehow failed to hide his emotions completely.

Margaret had completed her logbook entries and had recorded all the relevant flight data from the test flight. She was glad that it was over with. She did not like to deal with the higher-ranking personnel aboard the ship. They all seemed so smug and superior and it stuck in her craw that she had to grovel to these idiots. She had known some brilliant officers in her long career, but she had been discarded from the front lines and placed on this vessel as a punishment for striking a sleeping man in the field. She protested as they busted her rank down and that cost her even more on the career path. It is true the man had been on guard duty and should not have been asleep at his post. It was also true that the enemy nearly breeched the gates while he was lying unconscious on the floor after being struck. It was also true that the sleepy whelp had been the nephew of an important civilian dignitary.

What was probably worst of all for Margaret was the simple fact that her military career hung by a thread and she was forced to endure these other cast-offs from honorable service. In fact, she had been wondering about the new arrival. Of course any personnel changes were posted on the boards of the inter-ship communications, but on this ship, very few people ever read the posts. She had been surprised to learn that a decorated survey man was coming aboard. She hoped it would be the sign that things were turning around for her. She couldn't possibly spend her whole career in the armpit of space with this ship of bilge rats, but maybe a star could shine even here. She was hopeful, but not overly so. It was quite possible that the man had proven to be a disappointment and that he deserved this exile to what amounted to a slave ship. Each man or woman aboard had done something that had relegated him or her here. They were trapped within their own fleet like prisoners of and unseen war. It was a war of political expedience, not of hatred. It was like being in prison. Nobody knew as well as she did what would happen to this man if he showed any weakness here.

Margaret brought her mind back to the current task and she started typing her report on the test flight into her terminal. She knew that the XO would demand nothing less than a full report, and she was not about to disappoint anyone. At least she would let no one down that had a hold of the reigns to her future. The typing went quickly and she was soon finished with the standard report. She saved the file and then transferred it to a portable hand computer. She would deliver this to the XO and then retreat from his sight. She knew she was currently in his good graces. The best way for her to stay that way was to simply remain unnoticed when something bad happened. Something bad always happened, and she had avoided more than her fair share of the trouble by not being around while the nit picking man vented his anger. It was a survival tactic she took to early on in this voyage. She wondered where to go when her task was complete; she thought that maybe a trip to the gym could help her burn off some of her anxiety. It worked for her before. She threw on a fresh shirt and grabbed the hand comp. There was no time like the present and she had no wish to prolong the task anyway. She pressed the door switch and it slid out of her way and she was off into the corridor and away to the XO's office.

The Captain had noticed the new man on the bridge, but he had been pulled over to the XO right away. Even though he was the second in command, the Captain found the man to be quite a nuisance. In fact, the man seemed to block almost every avenue of profit that this ship approached. This new man was supposed to be a professional at finding and exploiting natural resources so the Captain rubbed his hands together greedily at the prospect of the newfound wealth. He decided to go and see this young fellow and make sure that they were on the same page. He wanted this to be his last mission aboard this practically derelict vessel. His Captaincy was supposed to afford him opportunities for financial advancement, not allow him to die in paperwork. He couldn't imagine how other captains had done the same tasks with real paper. There must not have been room on the ship for anything else. He nodded to the XO and left the bridge. The XO breathed a sigh of relief at his departure.

The corridors were all clearly labeled, but the Captain was not terribly familiar with the layout of his own ship, so he consulted his hand comp and brought up the schematic. In moments, he was back on track and he arrived at the non-descript hatch where this new man was being billeted. He knocked on the metal hatchway door and it slid into the ceiling to open the entranceway. The man inside spotted the rank insignia and immediately came to attention. The Captain smiled. At least this man knew where respect was due. "At ease soldier." The Captain said and the man relaxed a bit, although he still looked stiff as a board. "I suppose you're wondering why I've come to see you like this." The Captain prodded and the young officer in front of him nodded.

"Yes sir, the question had crossed my mind." Was the response and the Captain sat on the only chair in the compartment.

"Well son, I've come to see you because I believe you are the key to my future. You have the power to find what I am looking for on the survey missions." The Captain took off his hat and fidgeted with it between his fingers as he spoke.

Quinn still stood bolt upright and the fidgeting was getting on his nerves, but he didn't let it show. "Sir, what do mean by that? Are you planning to settle down on one of the surveyed worlds?" He asked and the Captain laughed aloud.

"No, no my dear boy." He said between chuckles. "I need wealth. Mineral resources or crystals, or even crude oil would be just fine. I want you to look for any possible profit on these planets. Keep them out of your official report, but make sure that I know about them. I would recommend a separate log book to tally my rewards." The Captain finished and Quinn tried to hide his astonishment.

"Sir, I will do my best. That is my duty as assigned by charter. My commission demands nothing less. I would be happy to see you get wealthy, as long as it does not interfere with the successful conclusion of the mission." He said hoping that would placate the Captain and his lust for treasure. It was one of the most dangerous situations Quinn had ever faced. The Captain was basically ordering him to violate several fleet regulations for his own personal profit. Quinn would have to be careful about what he would say and to whom. For his part, the Captain seemed to be pleased with the talk and he put his hat back on and straightened it in the tiny mirror on the wall.

"I'm glad we had this little talk, and now I'm sure you have more studying to do before we reach the first survey target. I will leave you to it then." He said and he exited the compartment without any further discussion.

The hatch slid back closed again and Quinn noticed that he was trembling. He found it hard to believe that a man like that could actually get to the rank of Captain. Worse yet, the XO had been right on the money when he had complained about him. The two men were a combined pitfall that Quinn had to avoid at all costs. The only way out seemed to be to complete this mission and get reassigned as soon as possible. He picked up the reading material, but his nerves were too unraveled for him to concentrate, so he

decided to let off some steam in the gym. He grabbed his workout
bag and headed off down the corridor.

Margaret had reached the gym and was busily stretching when
the new guy entered and nodded. She noticed he was in good
shape as he went through his stretching routine. She had tried
not to be too obvious as she watched him. She was working out
on one of the resistance machines that worked the lower body.
She had checked her pulse twice, unconsciously trying to impress
this younger man. She glanced at him again and they made eye
contact. She turned away embarrassed and he didn't seem to
react at all. 'This was going well.' She thought to herself and she
threw her momentary anger into the workout. She must have
pushed it a little too far because her leg locked with a horrible leg
cramp. She dropped off of the machine and grabbed her leg. The
knots of her muscles were visible through the skin and she gasped
at the fury of it all. She closed her eyes and tried to will the pain
away but it continued. The sound of a muscle relaxer buzzed and
she opened her eyes. It was the new man, he was soothing the leg
and the muscles obediently relaxed and ended their assault on her
brain. She stood up but the leg was going to be sore for a couple
of days.

Quinn told her to take it easy for a while. She had been
pushing a bit too hard. Margaret cursed herself for a fool. She
was a veteran, not some schoolgirl trying to ogle the new boy. She
sat down on a workout bench and rubbed her leg. The new guy
stood next to her. She felt uncomfortable under his gaze.

"I am Quinn Ramses, new man around here." He said needlessly,
then he cleared his throat. "But then you already know that don't
you?" He asked with a knowing smile. He was jovial even with the
situation he was currently in. He remembered an old story about
a rock and a hard place and he chuckled at the ridiculousness of it
all. Then his attention returned to Margaret and he held out his
hand. "And you are..."

Margaret blushed but recovered quickly. I am the chief shuttle pilot around here, but you can call me Margaret." She replied and he bowed.

"Nice to meet you Margaret, but I have some more exercise to do if you will excuse me." He said and she nodded her ascent. "I'll keep an eye on you, if you need anything else, just wave and I'll come running." He said with a level of sincerity that surprised the seasoned officer.

She smirked herself at his flamboyance. "My night in shining armor is it?" She asked and he bowed again as he backed away from her towards a rowing machine. She shook her head and stood up. Walking seemed to help her leg so she walked around a bit trying to work it all loose. Further working out was out of the question, but maybe she could lessen her limp before reporting for duty. Her supervisor would probably ground her if she weren't fully operational when she reported in. She had to admit though, this new guy certainly made a good first impression. She headed off to the showers and when she got out, he was climbing the artificial wall. He was remarkably good at it; he had scaled some 20 feet while she approached. He was nimble of hand and foot. He was using cracks and crevices that most people would have considered to be too small. He kind of looked like a human spider walking up a vertical surface almost effortlessly. He used the final ledge to vault himself up onto the top and Margaret clapped at his success. He looked down, surprised that anyone had been watching. He flipped over the edge again and climbed down the rock even faster than he had gone up. She watched as he re-traced the same path flawlessly and stepped off onto the deck plating. He turned around and she could see that he had not even worn a safety harness. This man was either remarkably confident or he had a death wish. That metal deck flooring is rather unforgiving from 70 feet up. She decided not to find out which just now. Instead she smiled and led him over to a rest area.

"I'm afraid that I didn't get the chance to thank you for your rescue." She said and he just smiled.

"Think nothing of it. Someone was in pain, and there was something I could do about it. No harm in that is there?" He asked and she shook her head. "Besides, all the better to meet you."

He said and he looked away, perhaps trying to avoid further eye contact. "I need to finish my mission briefings before we arrive at the planet." He finished lamely. "If you will excuse me?"

"Sure." Margaret responded. She was a little confused. She was wondering what she had said that made him bolt like that. She shrugged and decided to worry about it later. She still had a letter home to write, and that was in addition to getting her new shuttlecraft online with the upgrades. She headed back to her quarters to start the correspondence.

Quinn had been reading for a while when he noticed that the end of the file was near. He rubbed his eyes and got some water. Then he cleared his head and finished the documentation. One look at the ship's chrono and he knew that rest was due. He had been up for two duty shifts already and the third one was mid-way now. He had even worked through the downtime shift. It was true that he had no regular duties aboard the *Lincoln*, but he always liked to maintain a regular schedule so that he could stay in sync with the ship's time. Of course all bets were off when he was planet-side. The natural rhythms of a day and night always took over his mind and body. He lay down and switched off the reading lamp. He knew that they were still moving forward towards their goal. The ship was only a couple of days away from the first target planet. That was good enough to ease his mind for now.

3

The Captain returned to the bridge at his pre-selected time. The *Lincoln* had reached the edge of the system containing the planet in question. He had not read the survey reports on this hunk of rock floating in space, but he knew that he had professionals to do that kind of work for him. All he had to do was to collect his just reward for getting them here. He was well prepared to do just that. The view screen next to his command chair showed a graphic representation of the system and he liked the way the computer simulated the tiny star this system revolved around. The planets were uninteresting for the most part, but a blue jewel hung in space waiting for him to come and claim its prizes. This planet was remarkably close to that of old Earth. It had water in overabundance and it had good temperatures and a breathable atmosphere. Furthermore, it was a likely prospect for colonization. The colonists would be short on building materials, but such materials could be imported. The Captain got bored with the computer rendering of what should be outside. He shook his head and ordered the external cameras brought on line. The main view screen on the front wall of the bridge lit up and the planet below was displayed. On the large monitor, the scene was breathtaking. He could see that water covered most of this planet. Of course further detail could not be reached until they got a bit closer. They were still only at the edge of the system. Survey code stated clearly that all reconnaissance was to be taken in stealth mode with enough distance from the target to prevent accidental discovery by possible indigenous species. It was for this reason that the *Lincoln* did not simply barrel in and orbit the planet directly. The Captain dispatched for Quinn to be alerted and readied for his survey mission. He smiled at himself for he knew this man was working to better his financial situation. This mission was sure to net him enough credits to quit this damn fleet and settle down somewhere nice.

The communications officer relayed the request and the personal communications unit in Quinn's quarters buzzed for attention. The orders were direct and to the point. "Be at the docking bay and ready for launch in one hour." It read and Quinn hurriedly got up and dressed for the mission. He had flown these missions before, but his stomach always seemed to develop a case of the butterflies until he actually got underway. It was as if he was using up all his fear and anxiety during the final countdown. He headed down to the docking bay and a small fighter was ready for launch. He nodded at the maintenance man who undoubtedly got the heads-up earlier than he had and prepped the plane for flight. Quinn strapped himself into the seat and started the pre-flight checklist. There was a checklist pad with the itemized checks under the arm of the chair and he pulled it out and swung it open. The list was relatively short because it was such a small craft, but he took each item seriously and it was done before too long. He powered up the engines and set them to stand-by. Then he radioed in for clearance.

The flight officer checked the read-outs and confirmed the ready status of the small survey craft. He tapped his ear mike and acknowledged the request for departure. "You are cleared to undock and follow the projected flight plan." He said coolly and the pilot of the survey ship, Lieutenant Ramses, winced at the absolute cold that could be broadcast while maintaining regulations. Regular fleet officers always hated the survey crews. The survey men and women put themselves in danger with each mission. First contacts usually resulted in lost lives. There was always some trivial misunderstanding, or just the dreaded fear of the unknown. Most survey personnel were projected to survive for between ten and fifteen missions. Lt. Ramses had been on forty-nine so far. He was the most decorated junior officer in the survey service. Still, he would prefer a little more respect from these navy people. After all, they benefited too by the survey crew's efforts to recruit or settle a new planet. The empire would get larger, and their power would grow. It even helped the economy, which on an interstellar basis was a complex mechanism of dangers and pitfalls that could make the most seasoned investors cry like a baby in his sleep. All of that would all have to wait, for this mission was about to begin.

Quinn collected himself and braced his stomach for the lurching drop. "Understood, undocking in three... two... one... Mark!" He hit a switch and the docking bolts released with a metal on metal sound that always sounded like it hurt the ship. Quinn could see the outer hull of the *Lincoln* as panels and access ports whipped by with his descent.

The survey ship dropped away from the *N.S.S. Lincoln* and fell away into the void. The pressure of the releasing docking hatch propelled the tiny craft away from its big brother. The lieutenant flipped a switch and the maneuvering thrusters fired in a pre-programmed sequence stabilizing the ship and directing it towards the orbit that was needed to enter the atmosphere. Quinn had done this type of mission a dozens times before, but caution was a watchword in survey. He took the checklist one by one. Verifying everything from cabin pressure to landing gear activation, he went through the numbers and signed off on the log by imprinting his thumb on the data pad. Then he turned his attention to the slowly approaching planet. It was a vast blue ball hanging in space like a jewel. The color blue has always meant life to survey and this world was a promising target for colonization. If he could get this job under his belt, then maybe he could settle down onto one of these luxurious planets himself. He steadied himself for the transit into the atmosphere and when it came, he let his nerves relax. The tiny ship careened through the atmosphere and was arrowing itself on a predetermined path that would end up on the only continent on this world. He had a few moments before pilot intervention would be needed, so he watched the water below. There were no huge waves, and he could see the planet's sun glistening off of the reflective water. Visibility was temporarily reduced as he hit a patch of clouds.

Just as his vision was clearing from the white puffy clouds, a blue flash of lightning hit the ship from below. It ripped through the stabilizer and then arced into the engine. It danced around the engine for an agonizingly long few seconds, and then it dissipated. Black smoke began to fill the compartment, Quinn choked a couple of times and then hit the vent switch and the smoke was pulled outside. Then he tried to activate the communications system only to get a shock from the electricity that was dancing across the switchboard as another bolt of blue struck the helpless ship. His grounded flight suit was probably all that saved him from electrocution. He heard one system after another fry from the massive electric shock. The Lieutenant veered the craft, which was bucking badly, into the wind trying to compensate for the destroyed stabilizer. He could not see clearly because the clouds had returned. He just wanted to get sight of the landmass so he could hit near it somewhere. The ship cleared the clouds and plunged into denser air masses. The jolting turbulence became fierce. Another shock blasted the ship and this time there was no time to notice the damaged systems. The entire dash was dead. No systems were working. Quinn gritted his teeth as he was being bounced around the compartment like a rag doll. Pieces of metal from the hull were being ripped off by the wind. The sounds of rushing air became louder with each new missing piece. The black scorch marks from the lightning were evident in the pieces that flew off.

The broken turbine in his atmospheric thrusters screamed its last cry of pain as the engine seized up entirely. The smoke was billowing out as the tiny ship entered its death throes. The small craft began to drop like a rock. Unfortunately, it was also a rock with about 1400kph of momentum, and a torn stabilizer. Quinn fought frantically to right the craft, but it tumbled helplessly over as it dropped. His hands were sore from the shaking of the controls. The hydraulics had gone out and the forces outside were pulling the yoke hard to one side. He used all of his strength to try to right it. The planet below was approaching fast, but the lush blue water seemed to call to the broken craft. The canopy was intact, so there was a slim chance of survival. Sweat beaded on Quinn's forehead as the muscles in his arms began to knot under the strain of the controls. Just before impact, the ship did a miraculous maneuver to flatten out and skip the surface for about 250 meters before the water clutched and held onto its prey. The tiny ship lurched to a stop, bobbed twice, and then slipped below the surface, heading for the bottom of the ocean. Quinn fought the urge to panic as he released his seat straps and punched the seal button on his helmet. Then he pressed the button to pop the canopy. Blue fire erupted in the water around him as the explosive charges did their work. The canopy flew up and back out of the way and the sinking survey man kicked off the craft and shot up towards the surface. The helmet had maybe ten breaths of air in it, so he tried to breathe really slowly. He shot through the surface into open air after the fourth breath and was instantly exhilarated by his success. Quinn checked his wrist chrono to see if the ship's automated distress signal was activated, but the chrono had been destroyed in the crash. Its digital readouts could help him no more; they had been smashed into uselessness.

From the brief seconds before impact, he knew that there was no land in sight. In fact, the only continent on this wet world was 1200 kilometers to the west, and he knew that the swim would be way too much for him. The water was sweet smelling, and he remembered something from the survey files that it could be a freshwater ocean. He took in a mouthful and was relieved to find it refreshing. His emergency pad in his pants leg could provide him with food enough for 3-5 days depending on exertion. He would try to minimize his efforts and aim for that far-distant life saving landmass. His already tired arms were aching at the effort to keep him afloat.

First thing he had to do was to raise his buoyancy so that he could save his energy. He kicked off his boots and let them drop away into the water. Then he removed the pants of his flight suit and tied the pant-legs together, sealing off the leg holes. Using his belt, he drew the open end of the pants shut and sealed it with a single fold. Then he blew up the pants to form a makeshift floatation device. He put his head and shoulders into the opening between the tied legs and rode the current. He kept his face to the west, basing his direction on the local sun. He was amazed at the variety and sizes of wildlife in the fresh water. He could see into the depths for quite a ways and the thought chilled him. Huge gray things were in the waters far below him. They were swimming slowly, casually around. He tried to estimate the size, but not knowing how far away they were, his best guess was larger than a drop boat on a stellar class starship. That would put the beast about 22 tons and nearly sixty meters long. He tried to calm his nerves because fear could be transmitted to any predators and bring them to him.

Telling time accurately was impossible without his wrist chrono, but the day was winding down as he watched the sun drop into the violet sky. The hues blended with the surface of the water as he drifted up and down on the gentle waves. The sparkling waters created a mesmerizing effect on the lone pilot. He felt content, the winds were blowing him in the direction he wanted, and he could even feel a slight current beneath him that also seemed to be heading west. He was making better time than he would have thought possible. There were floating plants in the sea too. Some smelled nasty and he paddled around them to avoid contact. Others were of varying colors and smelled most fragrant, even over the sweet water. Biting into one of them resulted in an explosion of bitterness in his mouth. Quinn spat out the offending plant and paddled away in disgust. As hunger loomed, he tried to catch a fish, but the little beasts were way too fast. They could react to his movements with eye-blink swiftness and his hand always came back empty. He finally gave up as the light faded into the utter darkness of night. He took a food bar from his leg pack and ate it slowly, nibbling a little at a time to spread out the effects of the little amount of food that he had. His arms and legs were tired, and soaked to the bone. The bobbing survey Lieutenant was weary and his spirits faded with the coming of the stars. He wondered if he would ever be among them again. Self-pity started to invade his consciousness, but he drifted off to sleep as exhaustion overtook him.

Sleep brought dreams to him that were not really helpful. They were filled with swirling waters stocked with huge murky creatures that could swallow him whole, electric eels large enough to pull down those antique galleons he had read about, and even smaller bugs that skittered across the surface and crawled into any orifice they could find to start their new homes in his body. He would have awakened several times that night, but the exhaustion he was feeling let his body drift along until the first light of dawn began to touch the horizon. The water maintained a moderately warm temperature, so there was not much of a difference between the night and day temperatures in the water itself, the winds were biting though. He tried submerging as much of himself as possible to keep out of the chill that could cut right through him. With the light, came the realization that he could see birds, or whatever passed for birds here in the distant skies to the west. A spark of hope ignited within him. If these birds could fly to and from the land, maybe he could make it there too. He began with another food bar from the packet and gulped down some of the water. He checked his aim and verified that the birds were where he wanted to be. Then he started paddling. He kept his eyes on the birds, they swirled around and around in huge circles as they searched for prey. Occasionally he would see one dive for the water and come up with some sort of creature he could not identify. It could have been some kind of snake, but it could have been a slim fish too. The wildlife around him awoke with the dawn too. The huge things below him were still there, following him mostly out of curiosity he guessed.

After about an hour or so, the birds all flew away. He continued his paddling, even more determined in their absence. They hadn't flown by him to get away so they must have flown away towards the land he so desperately sought. His paddling became a rhythmic cycle of boredom. His mind was barely conscious of the action. He just kept going and going. The sun had climaxed a while before his arms cramped up with the effort. He laid back his head and waited for the muscles to release their iron lock and he cursed himself for not paying more attention. He took the moment to look around and noticed smaller creatures in a greenish gray blob off to one side of him. The animals were so thick in the water that he could not see through the school. He decided to steer clear of the pool, but his arms wouldn't behave yet. They cramped up immediately when he started to paddle again. He thrashed around a little, and the pool seemed to close in on him. He froze, fear striking deep into his being. Quinn could feel the motion in the water, as the blob of color became a school of individual beings, swarming around him. They were tracking to the movement and they seemed confused at his sudden stop. They prodded at his legs and slithered around him until they became disinterested and then the whole swarm seemed to pick a direction and eased away from the terrified pilot. He was still terrified when he saw the huge gray monster come up under the school of beasts from below. A huge gaping maw cleared the surface and he could see the entire school of serpents was inside it as it clacked shut. Then the giant of the sea eyed him and dove down under the surface. It continued to dive and was quickly out of sight below those cavernous depths. Quinn gulped and found the strength to paddle some more. There were a couple of inches of sun left on the horizon, so he figured he could rest again soon.

From the south, a dark smear crossed the sky. It was insubstantial at first, but it grew in intensity as Quinn watched. Water was being pulled into the air by swirling winds beneath the massive cloud system which was growing wide and tall. The top areas capped and the rain started pouring underneath. From his vantage point, he could watch the whole thing form, and it filled him with dread. Then bolts of lightning began to dance around inside the cloud. The first breezes of cooler air reached him and a shiver rolled down his neck. The moisture was evident in the air too, and the waves began to pick up in size. They soon were raising and lowering him with their steady rhythm as he bobbed helplessly in the vast contoured seascape. He blew more air into his makeshift floatation device and braced himself for the crash of the front. The water was showing the signs of rain and the front moved relentlessly closer. Then, like a solid wall of water, it swept over him. The initial force shoved him under the surface. He could see the water's surface ravaged by raindrops and wind from underneath. It was quiet and peaceful under the raging storm. He held his breath and tried to stay under as long as possible. There were no fish around now, all the wildlife had left and he was alone. He bobbed to the surface and felt the blast of the wet wind as he took another deep breath and plunged beneath the surface. Lightning flashes showed him the bottom, the water was not so deep here, and the bottom appeared to be only about 30 meters down. His eyes followed the ground west and he saw the bottom sloping gradually shallower. He had not seen land anywhere close, but he became excited at the prospect. He surfaced for another breath and then he began to swim under the waves.

Breath after breath, he drove himself farther. The storm still raged on and more than once he caught a mouthful of water when he surfaced. He choked and fought back the anger and frustration and dove again. The bottom was getting much closer now. It was only about 9 meters away now. He swam along it, ever faithful to his westerly course. The storm was proceeding almost directly north, so he could see the end coming when it finally swept by. He popped up again, and took a few cleansing breaths. His clothes needed serious work. His makeshift life vest needed refilling so he blew it up again, and pulled the belt tighter. Then he took his bearings. As far as he knew, he was still on course. He really couldn't tell until night fell. He had memorized the local stars for his safest form of navigation. After all, he had all night to look at them. He was sorely tired now though. There was still no sign of land anywhere on the surface. He was uncertain why there should be this shallow area with no islands in sight. He decided to stay here for a while and rest. A couple of hours later, the alien sun was just touching the horizon and he watched as the stars started breaking through the haze to show him their heavenly glory. First one, then another appeared.   After a short while, the sky was full of them and he traced the patterns he had seen the night before. It didn't seem possible, but they were shifted to his mind by more than they should be for a day's travel. He realigned his directions and determined west again. Then he nodded off to sleep amidst the dreamy waves of warm water.

The pilot awoke in the early morning to his grumbling stomach. He had skipped the previous night's meal in order to preserve his rations. Now his fatigued body was crying out in alarm. He knew this was not a good sign. By the fresh daylight, he inspected the horizon and found it to be as he remembered; there was no sign of land anywhere but down, and water everywhere else. He decided to investigate the bottom in this shallow area. He let the air out of his pants and dove. He reached the bottom in no time and he reached his hands into the sand on the bottom. It was warm and gritty. He saw clouds of it that he had disturbed. He dug a little more, and it kept going. He worked around for about a minute and a half and then resurfaced. He stayed at the surface until his breathing was slow and relaxed, and then he took a few deep breaths and dove again. He followed a ridge in the bottom and found something metal on the bottom. It was nearly covered in the sand. He tried to grasp at it, but it wouldn't move. He had to resurface again; his lungs were burning for air. A few more deep breaths and he dove back down towards the metal piece, bracing his feet on the bottom and pulling with all of his might, it still didn't move.

He anchored himself to the metal piece and floated above it for a while, while he rested his weary body. He ate one of his food bars and drank some more of the plentiful water supply. It was nearly mid-day now, and the sunlight shone brightly through the shallower water. He could see that the shallow area extended for quite a ways in three directions. It appeared to drop off sharply to the north. He decided to try to dig up the object, so he followed his line back to the metal piece and began to dig the sand away from the interesting artifact. He had dug for several dives when his mind clicked in recognition. This was a communications antenna. It was like the one he had seen in the docking bay once when two ships had run into a navigations mishap and collided. The sensor arms and the communications equipment had been torn completely off and had had to be rebuilt from scratch. His heart fluttered at the thought of a ship being here. He surfaced again to think about it. His line was still connected, and he had freed up about 4 feet of the antenna from the sand. He estimated that there was at least twelve feet more hidden beneath this sand. His hands were scratched from the digging, and little wisps of blood trailed off into the water. He gave up the idea of digging until hitting the hull, if there was one down there. He decided to explore more of the shallow area for other signs. He had killed most of the day in his digging, and he ate again to try to keep up his strength. It was only about an hour to dusk now and he was determined to find something more before he had to abandon the search for lack of vision.

He used a circular pattern from the antenna, but the water became too dark before he could find anything useful. He resigned himself to trying again in the morning. He re-inflated his pants for floatation and drifted off to sleep, tethered to the antenna to keep from drifting.

Aboard the Heavy cruiser *S.S.F. Lincoln*, the bridge is tense. The metal bulkheads of the cramped compartment house the 6 members of the vessel's command staff. Metal ladders lead out at the rear of the cabin. A continuous ramp of metal mesh circles the various station chairs and ends up in front. Nothing in or on the bridge is there by chance. Everything has a purpose, and right now, none of it is truly being used. The multitude of readouts and buttons reflect off the polished aluminum consoles. The captain sits in his command chair behind the five staff workers. His elevated chair offers him a good vantage point over the tense crew and also hides his own readouts from those who don't have a "need to know". Right now, the captain is looking at the flight path of a survey ship that has gotten lost. The red light flashed, indicating the loss of contact. The communications officer was still trying to reach the small ship, but his efforts were going unrewarded.

The survey ship had disappeared from the scopes almost as soon at it had arrived at the planet. Maybe there were some anomalous readings to check on, maybe not. It was always best to let the surveyors have plenty of rein to perform their jobs fully. The Captain had always believed this to be true. Still, the radio silence for three days now did nothing to steady his overwrought nerves. They were deep into enemy territory here, and he had personally briefed the young pilot that this was to be a fast in and out sort of mission. The long-range scope showed a peaceful enough looking planet. It was a blue ball in space. The surface was mostly covered in water, and the radiation readings were almost non-existent. This was a good prospect for the company to set one of their colonies on and thus broaden the borders of the fleet before the enemy even knew this little ball of mud existed. His ship was in stealth mode, so he had only passive sensors to read with. He knew his tension was feeding into the command crew, but he just couldn't help it. His fears, and indeed his nightmares always centered on a vast armada of enemy ships dropping out of warp next to his little ship with guns ablaze. It was not a settling thought. Of course there had been no enemy activity for over two hundred years, but the briefings had been clear enough.

He idly tapped his fingers on the console in front of him and stopped when he noticed his Exec glancing over at the distraction. Of course the regular space navy men and women all had things to do. The captain would not be needed unless something happened. He felt himself dragging into depression and he sternly reminded himself that he was the captain. This was his ship and his mission. No matter what the little hotshot on the planet thought about it. He decided to give the survey tech two more days, and then he was going to bring the ship into the system proper. He'd be damned if they thought he would sit out here the whole time, twiddling his thumbs in stealth mode. His ship was doing its best to look like a hole in the vast blackness of space. To all observers, it was doing an excellent job. Passive sensors had no chance at all of noticing the *Solarian Space Fleet heavy cruiser Abraham Lincoln*, and active sensors only improved the odds about 20%. Unless a captain got very overconfident, or very stupid, the ship would pass unnoticed just about anywhere. Of course, it still didn't help to relieve the boredom of just hanging out in space. It felt ironic that of the 235 people aboard, he seemed to be the only one with nothing to do but wait. He slouched in his chair and sipped his coffee as the buzz around him continued on.

The choppy waves awoke Quinn just before sun up, and his weary bones were complaining. He hadn't eaten properly, and his rations were gone. If he did not find something to eat, his strength would ebb away even faster. He decided to make a last check of the shallows, but reality told him this search was not really helping him. He dove a few times and checked the sands, but came up with nothing more. He left his helmet tethered to the metal antenna and continued west. The birds were in the air again, and he was surprised at how close they were now. They were circling practically above him now. He paddled onward, trying not to lose sight of the marvelous birds as they ate. He envied them their freedom of movement and the fact that they were being fed. His stomach knotted a couple of times, but he gulped down some more water to keep the urges down while he continued his paddling. The birds continued for over an hour and then, as if on cue, they all turned and headed northwest. He was confused, but decided to follow them. They were leaving him behind but he continued on with renewed urgency. In a few more moments, they were out of sight. His spirits left with them. He stopped and floated in the warm waters, beaten and tired. After a couple hours of simply floating with the current, his stomach began to complain again. He resigned himself to continuing westward. He paddled until he felt his arms would fall off. Then he paddled some more. Midday came and went; his only thought was of continuing the ceaseless rhythm towards his salvation. He was hoping beyond hope to find it before he could go no farther. The first sign of land caught him by surprise. In fact, his mind told him it could not be true. But the mirage did not go away as he neared it. Soon, he could hear the waves lapping the shore and his mind felt the pull of reality. He began to paddle his exhausted muscles towards the very real shore. When his feet hit the sand at the bottom, he trudged forward and spilled out onto the moist sand on the beach. He felt exhilaration like he had not felt in quite some time. He decided to rest away from the water a bit. He forced himself up and poured the water from his pants. He hung them over a tree branch at the edge of the beach. Then he lay down in the grass and leaves and fell asleep.

The *S.S.F. Lincoln* had gone through three more shifts. The tension was wearing on the crew and the captain was probably the worst of the lot. The exec was not sure what the captain was waiting for, but he knew that the crew was losing faith. On a star cruiser, that could be dangerous, sometimes even fatal. He decided to check on the Captain and hopefully nudge him into some sort of action the crew could focus on.

"Captain" said the exec clearing his throat for emphasis. "What do you think the planet has in store for us?"

The Captain turned his head and his eyes were blank. He was in a daze. Then they focused and he regarded his first officer as if he had just materialized in front of him. "What did you say?" He asked, a little bluntly.

The exec was momentarily frozen. This was not the man he had signed on to this ship for. These outer rim missions were killing this fighting man and dulling him to uselessness. He steadied himself and drew a breath. "Well, sir. I was just wondering what you thought the planet has in store for us?" He asked and he saw a spark of thought as the Captain considered the question. The exec inhaled inwardly. This one is not dead yet, just asleep.

The Captain glazed over again then snapped back. "This miserable planet has probably nothing to offer us." He said matter-of-factly. He then shifted in his seat and the creak it made caused the entire bridge crew to turn to him. "Still, we should go and see for ourselves shouldn't we?" He said and the crew seemed to agree. The Captain stood up and straightened his uniform. "Helm, take us in for standard orbit of the planet. Communications; keep checking for our missing bird, I want an update as soon as you've got it."

The crew snapped to their tasks with a cumulative "Aye sir." The exec smiled and strolled back to his station. The captain noticed the change in demeanor and smiled back himself. He hadn't realized the funk he was in, and the exec was right to intervene. He mentally noted that he "owed him one" for the assist.

In space, the ship began to move and the stars shimmered off of the reflective hull. The planet loomed before them and soon there would be more answers. That is what the captain wanted most of all right now, answers.

The Lieutenant awoke to near dusk and his stomach was clenched with hunger. He fought down the urge to dry heave and staggered up to the beach. He looked around and soon he was picking up small water creatures and popping them into his mouth. The hearty crunch was music to his ears, and the tastes were tolerable. He had eaten about ten or so of these small, many legged creatures when he saw a huge one moving through the sand, picking them up. He raced away towards the brush line as fast as his sore legs could carry him. The creature moved to where he had just been standing. The pilot got a good look at this new foe. It looked like a giant centipede. It had feelers that were testing the sand. He couldn't tell how they worked. They seemed to making a circle around his footsteps. The creature was mostly the color of rust with deep red accents at the joints. As it moved, the clackety-clack of an exoskeleton could be clearly heard. The thing had no eyes to speak of but its overall length of 4.1 meters was enough to make anyone pause. It was nearly two thirds of a meter wide and probably a good 3 decimeters thick. He decided to wait out this thing. It continued its scan of the sand. Occasionally it would grab a smaller version of itself or some other washed up creature, and the front pincers would feed it into the gaping maw at the front. It moved slowly at first, as if testing for a predator in the area, and then it sped off down the beach. Its legs worked in unison to bring food to the mouth and propel the beast at incredible speeds. The tracks it left in the sand were rows of tiny dots, as if the creature were walking on porcupine quills. Quinn noted the tracks and left them well alone.

He returned to his rough campsite and he collected his meager belongings together. The plan was simple, move to where the food supply was. He decided to follow those birds again when the next day came. His uniform was a tatter, except for the pants, which had been his floatation device. They were wrinkled at the leg holes, but they worked fine. He was now shirtless, as the shirt had been employed as a fishnet with no success. After the cutting and stringing he did to the shirt, it would never serve as clothing again. He still had the crushed chrono on his wrist, he wasn't entirely sure why, but he left it there just the same. He wore socks that were of the finest wool the military could buy. That meant that they were easily wet, but also that they dried well too. Now they were covered in sand. They also afford little protection from anything but temperature changes, which this world didn't seem to experience. It was all a little surreal, but he vowed to see it through. He had estimated that a possible pick up from the main ship would take just over two weeks. This was based on standard protocols for survey missions. However, it was also protocol to signal back to fleet when he landed. Since he had no communications equipment after the crash, that had become impossible. In fact, after hitting that atmospheric cloud which disabled his ship the entire mission had been anything but by the numbers. He was well trained, but just how much potentially hostile world could one man face? He brought himself out of the funk and focused his mind back on survival. After all, there was still a job to be done here. He decided to head inland a couple of miles and then setup a more permanent camp with a fire pit and some form of shelter. He looked up and gauged west, then he picked up all his gear and trudged into the foliage.

The trees were remarkably like the holo-pics he had seen of

old earth, before the full industrialization of the planet. They were unbelievably tall, and had a good size to their trunks. He might consider a lookout vantage point in the tops of them if he can manufacture the climbing gear he would need later. Right now, he wanted some distance from the beach and the monsters that inhabited it. Survival being at the top of his list, a signal fire would be in order, and a good clearing would be required for it. He would prefer a spot near some natural shelter too. He ventured into the woods, looking for rock outcroppings and caves. His legs were still sore, but the strength was returning to his arms. The steady food supply was helping his mood as well. His mind began to think back on that antenna in the water. Surely it could not have been too far out in the ocean. Maybe he could find it again when he had some better gear made up. He had studied well in the academy of the surveyor's guild. He knew how to make rafts and floatation devices. He could even construct rudimentary diving gear including air tanks and masks if he could find the right materials. But all of that was secondary to finding a safe place to sleep tonight. Flashes of the original survey raced through his mind. Mostly ocean was the highlighting factor of the planet. The land masses had hardly been touched by the original crew. There were no reports of indigenous life and certainly no mention of any predators. That didn't mean they didn't exist, it simply meant that no one had spotted them from the air in a shuttle or smaller craft. The shuttles had poor sensor arrays, and probably had never been used in a survey capacity except to ferry personnel about a particular planet. He hadn't seen enough open land, except the beach, to set one down here yet anyway.

Several small things skittered from the shadows, seeking to evade him as he moved through the underbrush. He was feeling better about his possible position on the local food chain when he stumbled across an opening in the tree line.

The area before him was vast. The clearing was patches of dirt and fields of tall grass with tangling brambles. The greens and browns and yellows of the waving grass was somehow soothing in the breeze. It was probably some 1,800 meters across and the monstrously tall far wall could be seen. Wall seemed to be the best term for the sheer cliff face this opening ended up at the bottom of. The hard lines of the rock face were in stark contrast to the flowing fields of tall grass below. Of course, that hardly caught the pilot's attention. What his eyes were riveted on were the statues. They were monstrous as well, even at this distance. They appeared to be carved out of the cliff itself. They were roughly humanoid, with bulbous heads and six arms. They were obviously warriors, for the statues were armed and four of their six arms were holding curved swords with serrated edges carved out of that same stone. The pilot estimated that the statues had to be sixty meters tall, and the workmanship was amazing. Every detail was perfect in fact it looked like they were alive. How could anything so monstrous in size have been missed in the original survey? This was somewhat of a puzzle although he suspected it was simple incompetence. He looked around the clearing and saw nothing threatening the whole way across, so he ventured forth for a closer look.

He let out a whistle, as he got about halfway across the expanse. His shoeless feet had troubles with the brambles so the going had been slow. It was now obvious that the two statues were guarding a doorway. It was also intricately carved out of stone, and stood some sixteen meters high. There were strange symbols carved into the border of the arched doorway, and he decided to scribble them down in his checklist pad in case they could be translated later. He stepped to the door and found that it was indeed carved out of the native rock face. The precision was remarkable. It was as if the door had grown there like a crystal grows. There were no marks of hammer and chisel. The surfaces were totally smooth. He touched the door, and the cold rock face trembled. He jumped at the feeling. He passed his hand around the seam of the door, but nothing happened. He touched the door again, and this time it didn't move. "Had he blown his one chance?" He thought to himself. A movement of shadow in the distance caught the corner of his eye, he whirled around and his mouth fell open involuntarily. The statues, the solid made of stone statues, had knelt down and were holding their impossibly long arms out in a series of graduated platforms, like giant stairs. He looked on in amazement for a moment; shock prevented him from taking immediate action. Then he realized he must look pretty silly there, and he jumped onto the first platform. He was looking at the carving of the hand he now stood upon. It was very detailed. He could even see fingerprints etched into the stone giant. He jumped for the second hand and made it easily. The pattern of hands made a spiral back up to the cliff face. They didn't seem to reach quite near the top of it though. He didn't care, curiosity was the reason he had gone into the survey business, and this was a find like no other he could have possibly imagined. He continued his ascent, occasionally looking down to see how far he had come. He was quite high now. He was certain a fall from this height would be fatal. He tried to gauge the distance of his next jump and made it. He felt a little shaky, but he was still quite motivated. Two more hands to go and he would be at the top of their reach. He eyed the next one and started to leap. The hand in front of him shifted and he froze in place, nearly falling forward off the hand he was riding. They were both moving up now, and he could feel the air pressure change from the altitude difference. He swallowed to equalize the pressure in his ears. The hands came to rest on the ground at the top of the cliff. He stepped off of the hand, and onto the other one. They did not move further. He jumped down to the ground and both hands retreated. The pilot peered over the edge and saw the impossibly large statues resume their original positions. The entire activity took about 18 minutes, and during that time he had completely forgotten about the door.

The dense foliage at the top of the cliff was in stark contrast to the patches of dirt and waving grass below. He wondered how such a natural landform could have happened, but his tired bones reminded him of their exertion to this point and he looked for a place to lie down for some sleep. There were no trees here, but the shrubs and vines were plentiful, and soon he was wrapped in vines and suspended from one of the larger bushes in his makeshift hammock. Up here, the afternoon breeze was pleasant, and he drank it in as his eyes closed. The hammock rocked him gently to sleep and he dreamed of summer shores and wonderful gardens from his home planet. When he awoke, the stars were out in force. They were even clearer at this altitude, and his mind absorbed them like old friends. He had used them for guidance more than once, and they were twinkling merrily to him now. Sleep took him peacefully again and his mind drifted off to luxurious dreams.

4

In orbit above the water world, The *Lincoln* settled in for a final pass before deploying its drones into the atmosphere. The drones were the mechanical version of the human survey crews. They would report data on almost every facet of the planet's environment. The effectiveness of their data, however, was limited by the search pattern they were programmed with. Once the launch was accomplished, the data would be relayed to the automated colony ship that was on standby just out of system. The captain stood on his bridge; the main view screen was now filled with the watery blue of the new world. Overlaid on the planet were the bright green icons of the drones. They were making a circular pattern of the surface, checking everything they had been programmed to check. As he watched, one of the drones took on an amber hue. That meant that it had discovered critical data on the surface and was requesting a data query from the host ship. The Captain nodded to the communications officer, and the drone fed its data into the main computer. The area of the world map enlarged and details began pouring in. It was on a small landmass almost in the middle of a gigantic ocean. It was two unbelievably large statues made of stone. This meant the survey mission was over. If the planet was inhabited, they could not plant the colony here. The captain sat back down and rubbed his chin. The XO was eyeing him curiously and the Captain knew that meant he was supposed to do or say something.

Comm., note in the log that we have discovered evidence of intelligent life, but we are going to investigate to see if it is still present on this planet before proceeding to the next target." He said and let out a heavy sigh. The XO nodded his approval.

"Aye sir, entering it in the duty log as we speak." She trailed off, as if something more was to be said, but protocol would not allow her to voice it without provocation. The Captain, for a change, didn't miss the opening.

"What else do you think is going on down there, Lieutenant?" He asked and her shoulders rose at the greeting. "Well sir, we have scattered life signs on the planet, but most of it is very small. I am reading humanoid life signs near the statues. It could be our lost pilot, or maybe an indigenous species." She turned to face the Captain directly. "Should we dispatch a shuttle to investigate?" She asked, possibly overstating her position.

The Captain didn't even recognize the slight, and considered her question for its true merit, not with anger. "Yes, send out the shuttle. I would like to get some answers. If that is our lost pilot, we would have recovered our personnel and gotten his report for colonization. If it is not our pilot, then whoever it is will prevent us from colonizing anyway. Either way, if the shuttle gets us an answer, we can leave this pathetic rock and get on with our assignment." Then he turned to his XO. "Get me the mission briefing, will you, I think there was a clause about finding ancient cultures in there. We may all be up for a bonus." He said and the crew perked up at the possible news.

Moments later, the shuttle undocked and veered towards the blue ball of a planet. The pilot at the controls, Margaret Manning was one of the more seasoned. She was determined to get to the drop off point without incident. She steeled herself against the atmosphere and the shuttle sliced its way into the turbulence of entry.

The sounds of heavy rock shifting on rock brought the pilot out of his restful sleep. The statues were moving again. He got out of his hammock and went to the edge of the cliff and peered over. The statues were holding their hands skyward, pointing to something in the sky that he couldn't make out. He watched with fascination until arcs of blue lightning danced from the outstretched fingers into the open sky. There was a brilliant flash as the tiny object was struck. He wailed in surprise and the statues turned to look at him. Their faces were blank, no emotion registered. But the eyes contained intelligence. He wasn't sure how that could be, but it felt creepy and he was instantly afraid. He held up his hands in supplication and backed away from the cliff. The sounds of shifting rock continued, and even got louder. Then he saw two pairs of giant stone hands grab the cliff edge and begin to pull the statues up. He began to run. He knew in his mind that there was no way he could get enough distance between himself and them to save his life, but his legs hadn't gotten the news yet. They were still trying with all the newfound strength he had. Adrenaline can be a good motivator. The distance he ran in the few moments he had would have made a track star cry. But it was still desperately shorter than the statue's eyesight. The statues were nearly onto the higher elevation now and were starting to stand up. He estimated that it would take them only two strides to reach him and then this mission would be over. His lungs hurt with the effort, and he stopped bothering to look back. He simply ran. He kept running even when he heard the first footstep land way too close for comfort, and then he ran out of space. He came to another beach. The sick realization struck him that he was on an island. It was a small island too. He was dead now, he knew it, and his legs knew it too. They buckled and he plopped down into the sand, mentally and physically defeated. The next footstep was further down the beach in the sand, and he could feel the tremors it created in the planet's crust. He looked up and he could see the statue reaching down for him, even as one of its arms flew off. The arm became solid rock again and it flew end over end and crashed into the sea to the north. The statue stopped, and looked at the stump. The Lieutenant could hear the sounds of a roaring engine and then the laser blasts came. Another arm was lopped clean off by special charges usually used for mining. It was the shuttle from the *Lincoln*! Quinn was elated as he watched the shuttle dart around and dissect the giant statues. A final slice across the upper thigh and the statue on the left fell over backwards and to the side. The resulting tremble shook the pilot and the creatures in the sand darted into the water in surprise and fear. In a desperate effort, the remaining giant reached for the offending shuttle, but its grip wasn't working when the arm became severed halfway through the extension. The arm crashed loudly to the ground as well. Then the shuttle circled around and landed on the beach. Margaret stepped out of the hatchway and signaled to Quinn and he jumped up to get aboard. Pleasant as it may be, he did not want to spend the rest of his life here.

The pilot climbed aboard and Margaret strapped him into the passenger chair. Then she headed for the command chair and powered up the engines from standby. She was just taking off when the normally brave pilot shrieked. She lifted off at full military power and soared into the sky.

"What did you see?" Quinn asked now that they had a couple minutes.

"The arms were crawling back to the statue. The thing was regenerating."

Margaret set the controls to escape orbit and rendezvous with the *Lincoln*. Then she turned back to the scared man. "I say we go back and report this, then let the big dogs come and pay those things a visit." She winked and turned back to the command station to monitor the computer's progress on their trip.

"When I saw the statue shoot the lightning, I thought you were toast. That's what happened to my ship. It went down in the ocean. It took me days to get to land." Quinn said and he slumped back in his chair as the memories flooded back to him.

"Then you'd probably not turn down one of these." Said Margaret and she handed him a rations pack. She smiled as he reached out and took the packet and tore into it hungrily. "You do look a bit thin." She turned serious for a moment, "Actually, that lightning fried half of the systems on this heap, but it was meant to handle ion storms, so the backups worked fine." She checked the boards for messages in the queue, and found several from the Captain. "It seems like you have some explaining to do to the old man, but at least it looks like you got lots of sun." She turned away again so that he could eat unobserved.

The survey man was eating furiously and he managed to squeeze in a thank you between mouthfuls. "You know, I actually look forward to writing the report up on this one. The survey mission has only begun though; there is a doorway that leads to some underground cave. My gut tells me that is where we will find the answers." Then he looked back out the window towards the planet. He could not make out the statues anymore - they were simply too far away. "That is if we can get past those stone monsters." He finished the food and shoved the empty packet into the recycler. Then Margaret handed him a drink pouch. He nodded his thanks and plunged a straw into the pouch. The sweet punch had been designed as a survival food. It was packed with nutrients and helpful enzymes. He could almost feel the healing effects as he felt the chilled liquid go down to his stomach. The sensation was almost magical.

Margaret had yet one more order of business for the pilot. "You seem to be out of uniform. Here, this won't be your size, but at least it will cover you better than that thermal blanket." She said and the pilot smiled and got dressed. He had just gotten seated again when a small chime sounded on the control console.

A small light flashed on the console and Margaret took the controls. The computer assist had disengaged due to a proximity alert. Since they were about to land in the *Lincoln's* docking bay, this was perfectly acceptable. Margaret used her steady hands to expertly maneuver the small shuttle into the docking pod and she manually released the clamping mechanism that grafted onto the side of the main ship. They both heard the hissing sounds as the pressure equalized. Then the hatch lights turned green and they were both away. The corridor was filled with personnel on their own duties. No one even spared the two new arrivals a passing glance. They emerged into the main corridor and were met by the officer of the day.

Quinn's scruffy look caused the lieutenant to raise an eyebrow, but he had them sign the log and then he turned away as if they had ceased to exist. The two pilots shrugged their shoulders and went to their cabins to freshen up before reporting to the Captain. After all, one did not report to the captain with almost a week's worth of beard.

☆ ☆ ☆

It took about forty-five minutes to reclaim a semblance of social dress and behavior. The time in the wilds of a new planet had changed him somehow, and now he felt the closeness of the metal bulkhead walls as if the ship were a monstrous cage designed to keep him in. He shook off the feeling and gathered the notes he had scribbled while on planet. They were mostly a log, and the glyphs from the archway. He hoped they were accurate enough to decipher. It would be awhile before he could get to records to try to match the symbols. He was on his way to the Captain's quarters now.

The pilot reached the door to the captain's office, and Margaret was already there. She was in a clean uniform and the polish on her boots would make glass envious. Still, she didn't look completely sure of what was to come. Of course they both knew that the captain was not a man to cross, but he was also a man that was difficult to predict. He had a history of making decisions that were questionable. However, he was a Captain because there were times when he was the clearest seeing man on the bridge. He had made some crucial decisions early on when the ship was in danger. His hot and cold demeanor was nerve racking to his subordinates. But he still was the Captain, so everyone treaded lightly around him and did the best they could with his reactions.

Margaret spared the pilot a glance and smiled. "You clean up pretty well." She mused and his blush shined through the tan he had recently gotten. Then Margaret turned serious. "I already sounded the chime. I expect we'll probably go in together on this one. Least ways that's what I would prefer. What about you." She asked and she made longing eye contact with the pilot.

"Yes, that would be best. If one of us gets too much attention,

the other can chime in and divert the Captain from his rampage."
He said and she visibly relaxed, until the door opened. Then
they both entered the office and saw a huge tapestry of a battle
cruiser fending off a horde raiding party. The designation of
the battle cruiser was the Captain's last ship. The needlework
was exquisite, but of course it had been done by machine. The
Captain's background had been part of the mission briefing when
coming aboard the ship. So both of them were familiar with his
last command.

The pilot spoke first. "Sir, Survey Pilot Quinn Ramses reporting
as ordered." Margaret stood by his side and added her name to
the report with a click of her heels.

The Captain was not a big man. His presence did not fill the
room; he was a timid specimen of a beaten animal. Something in
his past had made him nervous and fussy. No one knew what was
going on in that mind of his, and this moment was no exception.
The Captain stood up from behind his desk and stepped around
to the two individuals on the carpet. "Am I to understand that you
had no choice but to break with protocols on this one Ramses?"
He asked with dangerous authority in his voice.

Quinn took a breath and then responded. "I could not maintain
radio or subspace contact because I no longer had a wrist chrono
or the ship anymore. It had been struck repeatedly by lightning
and crashed into the sea." He answered and the captain stood less
than inch from his face.

"So you think that's an excuse?" The Captain asked, raising his
voice.

"Sir, there are no excuses. There is only fact, and the fact is, I
was unable to follow written protocols on this mission." And then
Quinn did something the captain would never have expected. He
saluted with parade ground precision and shouted loudly, "Sir!"

The captain was surprised by the outburst, but he recovered
quickly. "Fine, then what is the story with this planet son." The
captain asked, the anger bleeding away from him as suddenly as
it had erupted.

"Well sir, the original reports of it being uninhabited are most
likely false. There is a monstrous construct down there. It would

have taken a pretty high intelligence to manufacture something like that. I would like to investigate further with the proper tools sir." He said and the captain swung on him quickly.

"You mean you wish to waste more of my time here?" He asked with a dangerous tone of voice. "You just told me this planet is inhabited. We cannot plant a colony here according to the regs. Do you have a reason why we should remain here where there is no profit?"

"Sir, I found some writing on the large door and I think we can gain access to the underground structure through there. It is possible that the inhabitants are no longer here. I saw no sign of them at all, just their statues. I believe they are some kind of automated watchdogs. The technology necessary to produce them would be staggering. I think that is where the potential profit lies on this mission." Quinn replied and the captain leaned back onto his desk.

"How long would you need to get into that thing and assess the situation, and our *potential profit*?" He asked a little sarcastically.

"I think we could probably get inside the doors within a couple of days, provided the guards haven't reassembled and drive us away. The last reports were that the pieces were returning to the statues even as we speak. I would like to take these sketches down to the computer lab and set Conners on them. After all, he's the linguistics specialist around here."

The Captain considered his options for a moment. Everything considered; the potential profit won out. He might be able to offset the cost of sitting out here so long. "Okay, go ahead and let Conners sink his teeth into those glyphs. I want regular status reports this time. Commander Manning will take you down there and fly cover in the event that the statues pose a threat. I don't want to risk firing anything heavy from up here or we might destroy your chances to get in there with an errant shot. We need that profit to justify our existence here, so don't let me down."

"Yes sir, I'll get on it right away." Quinn replied and he and Margaret were dismissed.

They left the Captain's office at a brisk pace and as they parted for their respective duties, Margaret winked at Quinn and her smile was warm. He was caught a bit off guard by her advance and his own face simply reflected a stupid grin. As they rounded far corners, he cursed himself and his emotional instability. Sure she was nice, he thought to himself, but he was on a mission here. The pressure was on, and he was not one to accept failure, or to even admit that it was an option. He brought his mind back to focus and headed for the computer lab. He used the comm. panel on the wall and paged Sergeant Conners. Then he spread the glyphs he had sketched out onto the scanner and the computer obediently copied the information into its memory. He punched the save button and the data was secured by the protected housing inside the computer core. Then Quinn decided to start the search himself. He pulled up a query on language files and started the computer crunching on possible matches for the images on file. It was still crunching along quietly when Conners entered the room.

Sergeant Duane Conners is a slightly portly man with a passion for the subtle nuances of language. His standard sized uniform was a little snug, but he kept it regulation clean and pressed. He had polished the brass on his outfit to a high degree and his boots had the type of shine that would make a new car buyer happy. His eyes were seeking all the time, like something unnoticed might just be important. His eclectic habits had been cause for concern in some of his previous assignments. He had also done well with textbooks. He had doctorates in Ancient languages, Archeology, and Alien relations. He had been assigned to the *Lincoln* because of an unfortunate event with the niece of an actively serving Admiral, but his uncanny knack for identifying language use and extrapolating the commonalities of complex speech should prove invaluable. His work so far had always been planet side and he had found that ship life was rather confining. The cold metal walls gave off no signals that his brain could interpret. It was like living inside a giant robot. The computer could talk to you, but it couldn't feel anything. He was almost always edgy and uncomfortable when on board. He saw the ship as a means to an end, he always longed for the open air and solid ground of a habitable world. He enters the room and sees Quinn staring at the screen. He notices that the computer was crunching on some images and he steps up like a predator, waiting to pounce on the unsuspecting data and turn it into a decent meal. Quinn gets up out of the chair and let's the expert at the equipment.

Duane sat down in front of the keyboard and flexed his fingers. "What do we have here?" He asks to no one in particular. Then he smiles and cuts the search short. Then he starts entering an algorithm to search all the databases more precisely.

Margaret reached the docking bay and she changed into the greasy coveralls she used when she was working on her shuttle. The maintenance crew was already hard at work on her ship, but she preferred the hands on approach. She grabbed the clipboard of projected repairs and noted the ones that were already checked off. The crew was doing well; they had almost completed half of the list already. She started by double-checking the completed projects, and then she took to replacing the hydraulic dampening system on the control servos. She was always happiest when she could keep her hands busy. She was so busy that she did not even notice the buzz about her. The tales of her flying and exploits on the planet had fully circulated, and many of the men were just happy to be around her. As was usually the case, she was oblivious to the attention. No one had ever really attracted her, and these hopefuls honestly stood no chance at all with her. She was in all-business mode and that was simply that. In fact, the buzz continued on unabated. No one directly asked her any questions, perhaps out of respect, but more than likely out of fear. Margaret was intimidating when she was working.

The bay foreman, Captain Casey Fulsom, came by just as the repairs were being finalized, and he nodded to Margaret and dismissed the rest of the crew. He was a tall, thin man with only moderate personal hygiene. His uniform was clean enough to be within regulations, and he had long ago opted to carry the sidearm that the officers were allowed. Most of the navy men did not choose to observe this tradition, but Casey was an expert at small arms and was a fleet champion at the gunnery finals. In addition, he had once seen a mutiny on a small courier vessel. He had vowed never to be caught unawares and unprepared again. However, he had a pleasant face and his blue eyes tended to prevent anyone from arguing with him. He maintained a sensible tone even under the most extreme circumstances. He considered himself a steadying force in the docking bay and his superiors felt the same way. It probably had prevented him from being promoted away from his assigned duties. But if that made him bitter, he never showed a sign of it to his work-mates.

"How are the new specs, Marge?" He asked and Margaret smiled back to him. She held up a clipboard with so many figures and calculations on it that he couldn't make heads or tails out of it. "The specs look real good, I think I can increase thruster efficiency another twelve percent if the preliminaries work out as projected." She replied with a calm self-satisfaction.

Casey's eyebrows rose. "You can get 12% after just some small adjustments? I thought the engineers had tweaked it already?" He asked incredulously. Then he held up his hands in surrender. "No, don't try to explain it to me, I trust you. Just write up the procedure in the log so I can recommend it to the other crews. Then run some computer simulations on it and add those findings to the end of the report. We'll see if fleet tech central will publish you again." He said and grinned at her as she rolled her eyes at him. She started to protest and he cut her off with a gesture. "When you do good we all look good, you can't blame me for pushing for it a little bit, can you?" He asked and he put his best innocent boy face on.

Margaret saw the face and felt a bit betrayed, he knew she couldn't resist that face. "All right already, I'll write the report. Just give me a little time first. The survey mission isn't done yet, and I can't afford not to be ready when they need to do the drop." She looked at him with the unspoken words, *"Is that Okay with you?"* In her eyes.

He resigned himself and took the repair log from her. "Of course, that would be just fine." The innocent face turned into an impish grin and Margaret marveled at the man's ability to manipulate his and everyone else's emotions. Then he turned towards the lift and waved good-bye. "Catch you after the excitement is over." He said as the lift carried him up and out of the docking bay.

Margaret finished putting away her tools and changed back into her regular uniform. Then she headed off for some rest. She wanted to be fresh when Quinn commed her, and the next adventure would surely begin. As with most competent professionals, she was always worried about the details. She was resolutely determined to be ready. The team would be counting on her and they would not be disappointed.

The computer had been steadily crunching numbers, comparing the images of the symbols to those on file. Some rudimentary progress had been made as two of the symbols found a match almost immediately. But it had been working for a couple of hours more without any further advancement when Quinn started to get edgy. Duane was still typing away, trying to narrow the search parameters. He knew that the database was huge, even by fleet standards. He had dumped his own personal files into it when he came aboard. The system administrator had had to requisition extra memory modules to accommodate the additional data, but Duane had carte blanche when it came to computer resources. His computer clearance level was higher than many of the lesser admirals, so when a request came through with his name on the tag line, it was immediately approved.

The screen froze a second and a new match popped up on the screen and Duane's jaw dropped at the possible implications. Quinn did not understand what Duane was shocked about, but he was startled when the new image was presented. He put a hand on Duane's shoulder and brought him out of his temporary paralysis and asked him what was going on.

"That symbol is one I personally added to the files, it is from a common ancient language from old ruins on many planets across this and three other explored sectors." Quinn's face showed that he did not understand just what Duane was getting at. Duane sighed and turned to Quinn. "That means that it could be a lost section of the Jeng you've found here!" He said in desperation. His voice trailed up at the end of the sentence with tension.

Quinn had a small recollection of the term *"Jeng",* but it obviously did not hold the significance that Duane was putting on it. "Who are the Jeng?" He finally asked and Duane let out a deep sigh, it seemed to deflate him for a second.

Duane sat upright and got his mind into lecture mode. "The Jeng were an advanced civilization that roamed the stars about 400 million years ago. At least that was what the scientists say. We have encountered artifacts from them before, but they had always been ransacked or just outright destroyed. From what the historians have been able to piece together, they were a space faring race that mapped most of this galaxy. They had outposts almost everywhere. But one particular artifact depicted the final days of the Jeng. They were caught up in some kind if civil war. It was Jeng versus Jeng in a battle that cleansed the race from the history of the galaxy. They were utterly destroyed in the cataclysm that followed the release of some kind of doomsday weapon. The inhabited worlds were left bereft of life. Even the foliage was destroyed. Only their massive stone constructions remained. They had the ability to command the very essence of stone. Buildings weren't exactly built; they were grown from living rock. A building would evolve from a single piece of habitable stone. Many of their remnants fell into disrepair over time and many have crumbled away entirely. But it sounds like you may have found a working set of statues. Maybe there is more, this door you described could contain some kind of vault. Or maybe it contains some kind of bunker. Due to its historical significance, the profit in this journey could be immeasurable, even by the Captain's standards. I'll set the computer to crunching away at the door lock symbols. I'll bet we can get inside this thing." And Duane turned back to the screen and began typing in those magical equations with lightning speed.

Quinn just sat there; there was simply too much information to absorb. Or maybe there was too little to understand what was truly going on. He was excited at the prospect of redeeming himself with the Captain. But he was even more excited at the chance of becoming a prominent figure in history. His ego had always insisted that he had been born for greatness. Somehow, that attitude did not endear him to the various crews to which he had been assigned, but he did not care. Now it seemed like those doors down on the planet held his future behind them. He was anxious to get a look at that. Even if he had no control over the future, it still mattered to him. He was determined to gain entry and solidify his position.

Duane simply saw the current activity as a quest for knowledge. It was his brain and the computer against the mysteries of the unknown. He knew he was up to the task. This puzzle was on-the-ropes in his mind. He was looking forward to the elation he got whenever he solved a particularly hard puzzle. He was certain that moment was coming soon here. His fingers were flying across the keyboard as he entered logic level after logic level, picking and scratching against the arduous task before him. His mind raced ahead of his typing, figuring angles and approaches, even as he was denied one after another on his previous approaches. That's the way encryption work always was, try and try again, and all of a sudden, success will erupt for the vigilant, or the lucky. Duane hoped that he was both.

Quinn was lost in his own thoughts when Duane cried out in exultation. "That's it!" he yelled. And then he pushed back from the monitor to see it from a distance. The patterns of symbols were displayed on the screen. The translations were below each symbol and Duane rubbed his tired hands as he soaked in the simple message.

The symbols read, "choose retold". Neither man was sure what it meant by that, but they were both anxious to go and find out. They buzzed the captain, and he authorized the departure. Then Quinn called Margaret on the intercom. She was instantly alert, and her reflexes saved her from knocking over a lamp by the desk as she jumped out of bed and keyed the mike on her end.

The speaker crackled to life and Quinn's voice was dripping with excitement. "We're ready to continue the investigation on the planet." He announced and Margaret could just see his smile in her head as she envisioned him on the other side.

"We're ready, the pre-flight has been completed. Just tell me when you want to leave, and we're off."

"Great! I was hoping you'd say that. I'll see you in the docking bay at about 0700 then. He said and Margaret checked her chrono. That was only forty-five minutes away, but she had done her homework and she knew she was ready. A quick shower and change and she would report right on schedule.

"0700 confirmed." she said politely. Then she closed the comm. link and headed into the shower. Her mind was too busy to contemplate what they were going to see when they got down there, but she knew that they could handle whatever it was.

Margaret finished and hurried to the docking bay, only to find that not only was Quinn there already, but he had assembled a small team to go planet side. Duane was there for further translations, and there were two archeologists there too. Margaret thought that it all made sense, so she just nodded and then she smiled at Quinn.

Quinn cleared his throat and Margaret's eyebrows rose in attention. "These two need to stow their gear, it is sensitive equipment." He said and Margaret escorted them to the underside storage compartment. Everything held within it would be unmovable inside a stasis field. Both archeologists nodded their approval, loaded their gear and boarded the shuttle. Margaret did not really care what they had with them. It wasn't the technical side that interested her; it was the adventure. She winked at Quinn and they too boarded the shuttle. Quinn stepped over to the secondary command chair and strapped himself in. The four-point harness was always uncomfortable, but he had seen the training film of drops before the straps were installed, and he was glad they were there.

Margaret strapped herself in too, and her hands were now flying through the quick pre-flight routine. She knew the procedure by the numbers, but she was in the habit of reading the checklist also. It prevented people, even her, from making mistakes. Mistakes, especially mistakes in aircraft procedures, usually ended up causing lost ships, dead crews and mournful letters to families. Margaret would never allow that to happen while she was on watch. The last of the switches was flipped on, and the signal board showed all green lights. She nodded out the side window of the canopy to the maintenance crew and they breathed a sigh of relief. She gave the signalman the universal thumbs up, and put the radio headset on. The bridge flight officer was already feeding her coordinates for the drop. She could have calculated the figures herself in a few seconds, but she thanked him for the effort anyway. In moments, the clearance came and Margaret handily pulled the shuttle out of the parking slot and into the docking bay proper. Then she tapped the thrusters, and the craft nimbly exited the bay doors with equal clearance on both sides of the tiny ship. Margaret allowed a small smirk as she felt the artificial gravity envelope slide through them and then they were in zero-G.

Now she could use her in-system drive. Of course that was the best that a small vessel like this had on board. The drive system was useless inside the mother ship. Its magnetic signature would cause catastrophic imbalances in the drive and inertial dampening systems of the host ship. Now that they were clear, she kicked them in and felt the pressure of acceleration. The drives, although small, still had quite a pull on the occupants of the shuttle. They were thrown almost violently into their seats during the acceleration period. The small shuttle darted away from the *Lincoln* and headed back to the bright blue ball. The archeological team had not yet seen the planet first hand, and the dazzling light reflecting off the massive ocean drew a couple of gasps as the main view window was rotated to facilitate a good view of the water world. Quinn had spent his share of time in that water, but it still looked beautiful from orbit.

Margaret had plotted the course in her head. It turns out the coordinates were correct, and she smiled at the thought of the young man in operations. She pulled the ship around and watched the land race ahead of her. She would catch the small island on the next orbit, and she was adjusting her system clock to a countdown to atmospheric entry. She glanced back and saw the archeologists and Duane gripping their seats. Their knuckles were white from the strain. She figured they would be quite happy to land after this drop. Then she glanced over at Quinn. He had been relaxing on the drop, and he was lightly snoozing now. She knew that the survey crews usually were fearless, but she had never seen anyone taking a shuttle drop this peacefully. It was yet another facet of this young adventurer that fascinated her. She watched the clock hit 10 seconds and then she rotated the ship around so that the engine could help them slow down for entry. The rockets fired, and the turbine screamed as the first air hit it. The in-atmosphere thrust system did require something to "push against". The rushing air became a dull roar as the speed started to spill off the metal bullet racing towards the planet. Then the engine fired in full and the craft lost speed rapidly. Margaret engaged the airfoils and the shuttle began to glide down towards the island and the possible answer.

She decided to scan ahead and see if the statues were going to be a problem. They were standing beside the door as they had been before. She gritted her teeth as she hit the alert signal and dove the craft towards the water. There was a loud crackling sound outside. The air around the shuttle came to life as the blue energy slapped it from the ground below. Arc after arc, the statues were not letting up on the assault this time. The controls were acting sluggish and the computer was fried again. Margaret smirked at the devastation the dash was undergoing. She wondered how many of her academy classmates could pull off a landing in these conditions. She did not have long to wonder though; the water was rushing up at the ship as it plummeted towards the waves. In an almost impossible feat of piloting, she leveled the craft and skipped it along the surface of the water. The occupants were tossed about; their faces were white with fear as the craft skipped a couple more times on the higher chops of waves. The final skip brought the shuttle up onto the beach where it skidded to a stop. She turned around and took a mental inventory. Everyone was busily unbuckling themselves from their seats. The shuttle still had power, so the sensitive gear would still be secure underneath the shuttle. She took a last look at the dead instruments and she felt a pang of sorrow for the loss of her shuttle. Still, they could complete this mission and get another shuttle down to pick them up.

Quinn was the first to recover. He had grabbed the field rations and two cases of equipment and he popped the hatch on the shuttle and it flew clear. He looked out and the actual landing began to sink in. He turned back to Margaret. "That was some nice flying." He remarked and she simply nodded and grabbed her own gear.

Duane was nervous, like a freed laboratory mouse in an enormous lab. Looking around like someone was going to scoop him up and plant electrodes in his brain. He grabbed what he could and then scurried out of the shuttle and over to the tree line. He cowered there in the shadows as the rest of the occupants abandoned their transportation. The archeologists started to look at the sand and it seemed that they would get distracted when one of them picked up a rock from the beach. He held it up and observed it from several angles and then handed it to his partner for evaluation. Quinn decided right then not to allow distractions to derail this mission.

"Get over here you two; you don't want a visit from giant centipedes, do you?" He asked and they dropped the rock and ran to the tree line. There was a little bit of grumbling, but none of it loud enough for Quinn to hear it. "Well, let's get over to the site, I want a good look at those runes again." Quinn said and the group gathered their gear on their backs and headed into the vegetation just as a trio of huge explosions went off in the distance shaking the ground beneath them.

5

Aboard the *Lincoln*, the monitor showed the shuttle as it entered the atmosphere. The arcing blue lightning from the statues danced across the tiny ship and it fell like a stone towards the ocean. There were gasps around the bridge as the spectacle played out before them. The captain ordered his reserve to be deployed. On the far side of the planet, beyond sensor range, three tactical fighter craft had been waiting for orders to proceed and destroy the statues. Now that the shuttle had the statues busy, it was the perfect time to launch their surprise attack. With a nod the order was given and the XO hit a comm. switch and informed the pilots. The fighters screamed to full attack speed and raced along the surface towards the contact point. The water flew by below them as they covered the ground at just under six times the speed of sound. It only took the fighters a couple if minutes to reach their goal and laser target locks were almost instantaneous. Missiles that normally were used to kill ships were sent screaming in on the stone behemoths. The statues looked up as the first missile struck. The entire area was scattered with debris as the statue blew to pieces in the explosion. Finishing the job, two more missiles screamed in on the second statue and blew it to dust even as it raised one of its arms to attack. The area for about a quarter of a mile was layered with a fine dust from the impacts. Their mission complete, the fighters arced skyward and headed to rejoin the *Lincoln* in orbit.

The monitor on board the *Lincoln* showed the tactical elimination for what it was. It was a surgical strike of the most professional sort. The cliff wall had been practically untouched, and the targets had been completely eliminated. It was a shame that the shuttle had had to be disabled to allow the operation to take place in the first place, but it was a minor loss, considering that the crew had disembarked safely due to some of the most miraculous flying anyone had ever seen. The Captain smiled and the bridge crew breathed a collective sigh of relief. The XO sat there, showing no emotion at all as the news brought some relief to the tension in the bridge. He had worried that the young man would die out there and bring a crew of investigators aboard. That would be both good and bad for the XO. First it would be good because he would be rid of this incompetent captain and the ship would be available to a new commander. The bad part was that his mutinous activities would come to light as well so he would not be that new commander. His emotions had to be shunted aside or he would not maintain his control of the ship at all. Meanwhile the unaware captain took the opportunity to refresh his cup of coffee. He congratulated the crew on their performance and left the bridge with a spring in his step.

A dispatch went out that a replacement shuttle would be required and crews down in the docking bay began to preflight another one from storage. When the call came, they would be ready to launch. It seemed to be the motto down there in the docking bay's crew quarters. Satisfied that the crew was motivated enough, the captain turned away from the monitor and began to contemplate the steps he had just taken. A pair of potentially priceless statues was just destroyed in the chance that the so-called experts can get inside the mysterious doorway and find profit within. He wondered if it was really a sane course of action. But he decided to hold out for the potential wealth behind the door. Now all he could do was wait, and worry that his gamble will pay off. On the bright side though, without the statues in the way, colonization could now take place on this ball of water and he would still reap rewards from the percentage he would claim on the survey mission. As far as he could see, there was no real wrong move here. His mind wandered to how he would spend all those credits when they started pouring in.

The ground rumbled for about twelve seconds. Then the sky was filled with powder and ash. The crew pinned themselves to trees to keep from being hit by any sizable debris. Margaret and Quinn made eye contact, and both of them realized what must have happened. The statues had been attacked. The Captain must have had his own plan for how to deal with them. As long as the door was still undamaged, Quinn could probably care less what the Captain had done here.

They waited a few minutes more until no one heard anything falling into the treetops anymore, and then they headed off at double time towards the doorway. If the opening did exist, they were determined to get to it and open it before the statues could return. Margaret was carrying a portable radio to make contact with the *Lincoln*, she had not had time to use it so far, but she decided to wait until they could see the doors themselves to check in. The grumbling of the archeologists continued as the terrain was now littered with rocks of varying sizes in addition to those tangling brambles. The footing was now more treacherous. More than a couple of times, they nearly dropped their sensitive equipment due to a slip or turned ankle. Quinn let them grumble, they had a job to do and they were professionals. They would get the work done, or he would see to it that they never worked again.

The trip went pretty much without incident. The equipment was being set up in front of the doors. The statues were mostly gone. There were giant feet here; they were motionless, much as Quinn had seen them originally. The tops had been broken off by the blast and the rest of the bodies were nowhere to be seen. Duane was looking at the glyphs around the door and he noticed a possible problem. At least his face showed concern as he checked his notes. Quinn noticed the change in demeanor and stepped over to the troubled man.

"What is it you've found out?" Quinn asked and Duane puzzled through the notes and then looked up at Quinn.

"The symbols are not in the same order as you had drawn them." He said and it was now Quinn's turn to look confused.

"Are you sure, I copied them exactly. At least to the best of my limited artistic ability." He added but he could see that they were different too. "Is it possible that carved stone symbols can change their order?" He asked, not really expecting an answer.

Duane startled him with his response. "Yes, they could be moved now. The Jeng had the ability to mold stone like modeling clay. Some automated process may have altered the runes on the door. Using the database I made to recheck the writing, it now says 'echoer so told'. He said and both men puzzled as to the meaning of the words.

Margaret finished her checking in with the Captain, and then she stepped over to the confused looking men. "What seems to be the problem gentlemen?" She asked with a hint of amusement. She took the 'I'm waiting' stance and both men looked at her, being startled out of their train of thought.

Quinn recovered first. "What did you say?" He asked and Margaret put on her best 'dejected' look.

"I asked what the problem was." She repeated and Quinn pointed up at the runes on the door. "These symbols have changed their order. It has changed the meaning of the words and we understand the new message even less than the last one." He replied simply.

Margaret looked at the two messages. She scratched her head and then looked up at the door. "I don't know what they mean either." She admitted. "But I bet the scan will reveal something for us to go on. It must, we cannot have come this far to be stopped by this ancient slab of stone." She kicked a small rock and it skittered up to the door and bounced off, leaving a mark.

All three of them raced towards the mark and began to take a closer look. There was a small door there, almost like an access panel. It was made of thin stone that was only a couple of millimeters thick, but it looked just like the rest of the rock on the cliff face. Pressing a finger into the mark, which was actually a small hole, Quinn pulled and the access door flipped open. It was just a flat box, carved out of the rock inside. There were no markings to speak of, but there was a recessed square shape in the bottom.

Meanwhile the archeologists were scanning the doorway itself. The scanner was taking readings through the very stone and they quickly determined that there was a chamber beyond. The distance inside was too great for their instruments to detect, but they were both excited now about the possibilities inside. They continued to search the door itself and they found a seam in the lower middle of the door. It was as if a child's block had been used to finish the otherwise solid stone door. They turned to report their findings to see the other members of the group on their knees in front of the rock wall. They marked the spot where the block was and went over to see what the others had found. Duane looked up and the glyphs had changed order again. Now the message read, "echo sole trod". He scratched his nose and puzzled about the seemingly indecipherable messages. The archeologists stepped over carrying their scanner.

"What did you find here?" they asked and Quinn stepped back from the little opening. The two knelt down and scanned the new doorway. They both saw the dimensions of the space and the square in the bottom, and then they both looked at each other in shock. The move was not lost on the rest of the party.

Duane was the first to speak up. "What is it, what did you see?" He asked and the two nearly fell over themselves trying to get up and face Duane.

He held his hand out and admonished the two to settle down and explain. Neither man seemed ready to be calm; they were almost too excited to speak at all. They passed Duane and headed back to their mark on the wall. As one of them picked at the almost invisible seam, Quinn and Margaret cornered the other for an explanation.

"Okay, tell us what you found, and why he is scratching at the door." Said Quinn, trying to keep his patience.

The man pointed at the area where the block was. "There is a cube shaped block that is of different stone than the rest. Our scanner detected the density shift. If we can remove it without damaging it, it looks to be a perfect match for the recessed area behind your access door." He said in a flurry, stopping only because he was out of breath.

Quinn's mind was sharp. "You mean it could be some kind of key to this bigger door?" He asked and the excited man nodded enthusiastically. Quinn looked at Margaret and then back at the fidgety man in front of him. "Go on and help him get it out then." He ordered and then he sat back with Duane and Margaret while the two anxious men tried to pry the stone free. It did not seem to budge. Even with their micro-tools, they could not get the stone block to move.

Margaret looked at the runes on the doorway. She also did not get the message it offered. What did it mean? She saw that Quinn was working on that question too. She decided to watch him as he worked. It was no small thing to solve ancient puzzles. She figured that it might give her some insight into the creative mind.

Quinn paced about, trying to fathom the cryptic message. Then he seemed to stop in his tracks. He looked around on the ground. Most of the vegetation had been swept away here. There was just a layer of fine dirt in front of the door. He dropped to his hands and knees, looking for something. Margaret watched him with acute interest. His mind was working on some theory here. She would just have to wait to see what it was. He continued to root around in the dirt until his hands caught on a piece of stone underneath the top layers. He began to brush around the stone, looking for the edges. There was a second stone next to the first one. Margaret stepped closer.

"What have you found here?" She asked but Quinn was still excavating the two stones. She stood there, with her hands on her hips while she waited. Her patience was running thin, but her curiosity had been fully aroused. Okay, tell me what they are." She commanded and Quinn looked up as if she had just appeared there in front of him.

He shook his head. "Sorry, I was lost in thought." He replied weakly. "These are possibly the key to the stone block. Think about the message 'echo sole trod." He said and Margaret still looked confused. Quinn caught the confusion and sighed. "Look, sole trod must mean footsteps. If we assume that, then echo must mean repeat, or something like that." He said and she suddenly recognized the stones for what they were. They were footprints carved in stone. Her heart raced at the prospect of getting a step closer to a solution.

"So what you're saying is that we should stand on these, and see what happens?" he asked and Quinn nodded enthusiastically. Then he stood up and stepped onto the two rocks. The archeologists jumped back as the block suddenly slid out of its hold and dropped to the dirt in front of them. They turned around and Quinn was standing on two rocks, smiling at them.

Quinn waved the two men to the door. "Put the block into the slot, so we can see if this is all going to work." He ordered and they scooped up the artifact and gently carried it over to the small door. With a supple turn of the wrist, the block negotiated the doorway and came to rest in the square slot. It was an exact match, much to everyone's delight.

Everyone turned around when they heard Margaret gasp aloud. She was pointing at the doorway. Sure enough, the runes had changed again. Duane looked up and checked his personal computer for the unbelievable results. He addressed the group. "It now says 'close the door' on the runes.

Quinn pushed the door closed, and it latched shut. The seam disappeared in front of him and the rock face looked solid. Then the big door began to seam out. The rock slid out towards the group and they backed up a few steps in reflex. The door came out about 18 inches and then split apart. It opened before the eager eyes of the adventurers. Dust and stale air rushed forth and nearly gagged them.

Quinn stepped forward and waved his hand in front of the opening. Nothing happened. He felt the hot air from the inside. Then his eyes began to adjust to the inside of the vast room, and shock almost overtook him. He stepped forward, partially out of curiosity, and partially because the rest of the group was pressing him in with their curiosity. The floor was polished stone inlaid with gold and silver. The cavernous room stretched as far as the eye could see. There were workstations along the giant walls and the center held a circular stone artifact. It was a sphere about forty-five feet across. The inlaid patterns on the floor suggested that this was the focal point of the room. He looked back at his companions, and they were staring in amazement at the vast chamber. He brought their attention back with a clearing of his throat. He waved the two archeologists over to the workstations and he set Duane to a wall of glyphs for translation. The deeper chambers were calling to his imagination and he just started walking. He decided to find the far wall of this thing. He flipped on a small helmet light. Maybe there was another door on the far side. His sense of wonderment was in overdrive as he perused the ancient room with awe and respect. Everything was dry and dusty. The artifacts were everywhere. Surely a fortune was contained within this chamber. The Captain would definitely be pleased. There was more here than material wealth. This was a piece of history. This find was one of the most important ever recorded because this equipment was still functional. At least he thought it was. After all, the statues outside had still been working. The door mechanism was still working. The layer of dust on the floor showed that no one had been in here for several centuries. He was willing to bet it was substantially longer than that.

Duane whistled as he got the translations rolling. His personal comp was already filled with the database he had brought with him, so he was left with manual dictation for his additions. His pen was flying over the notepad he had brought with him. His personal computer was spitting out whole verses at him and he was doing his best to take them all down. There was a lot to retrieve.

Margaret stood by one of the consoles. The rock seemed to have been formed into the various pieces she would have expected to be made out of metal. There was a stool-like bench in front of one of the stone cabinets. She sat in front of it and a panel of rock separated to reveal a polished stone. It was black obsidian. At least she guessed that it was. She knew of no other substance dark enough to look that shiny. Then she gasped as the display lit up. It showed the statues outside as they had been. The door was in the frame as well. There were several beings in front if it. They looked a lot like the statues. The slender bodies and elongated heads were evident. So were the multiple arms that characterized the statues. She couldn't believe the quality of the picture she was seeing. It was as if a camera were pointing at the doorway when the image was taken. She tried to raise someone's attention, but they were all equally engulfed in their research. Then something unexpected happened. The beings moved. They stepped into the door and it closed. She would not have believed that moving images would be possible on a piece of rock, but there they were. So lifelike, she could make out the rise and fall of the chest of the closest alien on the screen. The camera, if that was what it was, moved rapidly towards the door and slipped in just before it closed completely. Inside the structure, it was well lit and everything was clean. Margaret marveled at the clarity again. The dials and switches and plates were all there. Much as they were here now, only everything was active and looked new. The alien procession continued on into the chamber and headed towards the far end. They were approaching a large door with black runes around it. They looked afraid, if the body language was similar to that of humans. They approached another group of aliens who were injured and struggling to control a black beast of immense size. It was like a cat, but had 8 legs and razor sharp teeth. It flicked its tail and another alien was swatted aside. The newcomers brought out short sticks and held them up to the cat-thing. It yelped from the strike and bounced back from the small devices. The group closed in and they drove the cat through the doorway and it automatically sealed behind them. Then the injured ones sealed the doorway back to a solid piece of rock and then they erased the runes from the doorway. It was certain that they did not want the doorway to be opened again. Margaret watched as still further, a new wall of stone was grown over the doorway as an added precaution. Then the base was being evacuated. Hundreds of the strange alien creatures were leaving and they sealed the door and put the now familiar block into the stone where it was held fast by standing on the trigger stones that Quinn had uncovered. Then the image faded back to black. She stared at the black stone a moment, and then she realized that Quinn had gone deeper into the cavern. She jumped up and ran down the center of the room, shouting after him.

Quinn had reached the far end of the vast expanse and found that the other end did indeed contain another door. The lock on this one looked perhaps even more complex than the one to get into the cavern itself. He quickly found the runes and with the help of a personal computer from Duane, he had the symbols translated in no time. They appeared to be a warning. The translation was not complete, but It said something about a mythical beast that ravaged the entire planet. Quinn laughed at the unbelievability of it all. People with the power and ability to build this cavern could not have been ravaged by some kind of animal. At any rate, it would be long dead by now if it were enclosed inside this room he rationalized. He found a keystone inlaid into the rock wall and turned the lock. The now familiar look as door seals formed in the very rock marked the beginning of a door opening. He heard some screaming behind him and he had just turned to see what the excitement was all about when a giant paw clubbed him on the head. He was thrown away from the door and lay there, splayed out and defenseless. Margaret stopped in her tracks. Her mouth fell open as the huge black beast stepped smoothly out of the prison it had been held in for so long. Quinn was certainly about to be killed. The beast probably had not eaten for some time. That is, if it did at all. Margaret drew her pistol and pointed it at the beast. It locked eyes with her and a snarl crossed its features. She paused in fear and shock. It reached out a clawed paw and slashed her hand, throwing the gun away to skitter across the floor.

Duane was running behind her, when the commotion started. Now he was almost caught up to the melee. He saw Quinn get tossed aside, and now the gun was just out of reach. Margaret let out a scream and she held her hand to her stomach. The flesh was cut to ribbons and dangling loose on her hand. She began to back away from the ravaging monster. Its fangs dripped saliva as it stepped closer, its haunches lowered in a pouncing pose. Margaret saw her life flash before her eyes. The giant black cat's haunches rocked from side to side in preparation for a leap and then it hurtled into the air. The powerful legs propelled the beast at incredible speed. It would tear Margaret apart in its first strike. But just as it was about to hit, a blast from the side threw it to the wall. Quinn had recovered the gun and was leveling the pulser for another shot. The handgun fired small metal blades using a chemical charge to accelerate them. The clip held about forty of the deadly blades. Quinn pumped about ten into the beast as it lie writhing on the stone floor. Its blood was soaking into the stone and Margaret screamed for Quinn to stop.

Duane stepped forward and wrapped his jacket around Margaret's wounded hand. He tied it tight with his belt and they headed back towards the exit. Quinn nodded to them both and then he continued to watch the monster for signs of aggression. It seemed content to lick its wounds at this point. It had pure hatred in its yellow eyes, and it all seemed to be directed at Quinn. The two archeologists had gone back to their work on the control surfaces. They did glance back at the animal though from time to time. The communicator beeping at his waist startled Quinn. The cat jumped visibly, but otherwise made no moves at the strange sound. Quinn picked the device off of his belt and pressed the answer button. "Quinn here, how can the Survey team be of service today?" He asked, his tone dripping with sarcasm.

The voice on the other end did not seem to be amused. "Cut the chatter and give me a status report. What's going on down there?" asked the captain. His patience had been pretty thin at the onset of this mission. The constant delays and the fact that they could no longer see the group had simply added to the tension. "You'd better not disappoint me." He reprimanded and Quinn grimaced at the volume in his ear.

"No sir, we have found the genuine article. Why, with the artifacts alone, you should be quite wealthy before this is all over.

In fact, many of these devices seem to still be functional. I think we will need some more time, but it will be worth the wait. He finished, hoping that it would be enough to appease the man upstairs in orbit.

"Operational you say, what kind of things did you find? What can they do?" The captain asked. He could see the captain in his mind's eye. The man was the image of an impatient child waiting to see what's new in the toy store. Quinn felt his neck prickling up. The cat was on the move.

"Sorry sir, I'll give you a full report later, I've got a situation to deal with down here first." He said and switched off the device. There was a pool of blood where the cat had been, but the great cat was not there now. Quinn cursed his own inattention. If he had not allowed the Captain to distract him, the beast would not have slipped away.

A scream from down the great hall caught his attention and he ran towards the sounds of distress. He had the pulser in hand. He got to the sight of the two archeologists. There was nothing but a smear of blood on the console they had been working on. The trail of blood looked like they had been dragged off towards the exit. Quinn followed the grizzly trail and exited the cavern. The beast had been through here all right; the trail was obvious. It led off towards the downed shuttle. A twinge of rage mixed with dread as he imagined Margaret being caught unawares by the nasty beast. He ran across the open field, towards the tree line. The trail stopped. He found what was blood soaked tattered rags. He turned away, feeling his stomach clench. Then he continued his run for the shuttle. Taking no notice of his own personal safety, he barreled into the trees at a full sprint. A stitch in his side told him that he could not keep this up much longer, but his brain reasoned that it wasn't that much farther to the shuttle anyway.

Quinn broke free of the trees and burst onto the beach. The downed shuttle was there in front of him. The black beast was scratching at the closed hatch. He could only assume that Duane and Margaret were inside. Why else would the creature want in so badly? He panted a few times then he raised the pistol up to eye height to properly sight the creature. Somehow, the cat realized what was about to happen and it bounded aside as he squeezed the trigger. The blade struck the door and stuck into the metal. The cat continued its bounding and rounded on Quinn. It was like black lightning, the creature was so fast. Quinn pulled the trigger again, and this time, the cat caught it squarely in the chest. Unfortunately, Quinn only had time for one shot and then the beast was upon him. Raking claws were everywhere, Quinn was too dazed to register the pain. He brought his fist down onto the thing's head, and then he brought the pistol back up to its belly and held the trigger until the blades were exhausted. The horrible sounds the thing made will echo in Quinn's memory for years. The blades cut through and nearly severed the beast in two. It fell off of him as he tried to get up. He was bleeding from many wounds. His legs would not support him. It was as if his whole body was one big nerve ending. Everything hurt. He fell back over into the sand. Amazingly, the beast was still alive. It appeared to lose the ability to move, but its yellow eyes met with Quinn's and the hatred was almost a physical thing. Quinn was powerless to move away from the thing, so he just stared back horrified at the venom in that stare.

Margaret opened the hatch just in time to see the black cat thing launch itself on top of Quinn. She gasped in horror, but otherwise she was ready. She held a second pulser taken from the shuttle's stores. She waited for an opening in which to fire. With the two so closely mingled, a clear shot never surfaced, and she saw pulser darts cutting the beast at the midsection. She dropped the weapon and grabbed the first aid kit. Impossibly, Quinn tried to stand. She could see that one of his legs was broken, but she marveled at his strength. He fell back down into the sand and she noticed that the cat twitched. It was possibly still alive. She hollered back to Duane to warn him, but he had also seen the twitch. She had also picked up her discarded pistol and had it trained on the beast. If it moved again, it would be toast.

"Just lie still, you have several extensive injuries here." Margaret admonished and Quinn laid back his head and sighed. "You are lucky to be alive at all." She continued. She began to tend to the less serious wounds. She was patching and bandaging here and there. She decided to wait on the broken leg until she could get help. There was also the matter of the cat still lying there too close to her patient. She worked feverishly. She was rewarded with grimaces or gritted teeth at the more painful parts. Quinn otherwise took it all in stride. She again marveled at his internal strength. She checked to make sure Duane still had a good handle on the situation. He nodded that everything was okay, for now. She left to find a suitable branch for a splint. Field expedient medical facilities were all they had. They would have to do. Margaret checked the ground and soon found a long enough stick. It would need some work before it would be a proper splint, but she was not concerned about the work. She headed back to camp with her prize.

When she got back, Duane had moved Quinn. Quinn had passed out from the pain and shock. Margaret stared daggers at him. Duane could sense the anger. He held up his hands in supplication. "Now hold on." He stared. "I had to move him before the cat got to him again." He said and Margaret whirled around to see where the cat had been lying before, it was gone.

Margaret looked at Quinn and then at Duane. "Well, at least we can get this splint on before he comes to. It will save him some pain anyway." She surmised and Duane nodded partially in relief. Margaret was not a person to anger. He pitched in and set the leg as Margaret cut the stick down to the size and shape she wanted. They used pieces of cloth to tie the splint in place. If only the shuttle had had power, she might have been able to use the regenerator on this wound. But now that would have to wait until they were evacuated to the ship. With the immediate problem solved, she turned back to Duane. "So, where did the beast go?" She asked and Duane looked away, as if to avoid her stare. She prompted him again. "Come on now, out with it." She said and Duane drew in a deep breath and let it out slowly.

"Okay, after you left to get the wood, I decided to check our rations to see what kind of food we have left. I was making sure to keep Quinn in my line of sight. Of course, looking back, I should have done the same for the cat. Anyway, I was counting the eleven meals when the cat got up and Quinn shouted an alarm. I dashed to his side and saw the cat limping towards him. It was still badly wounded, but it must have healed enough to get up on its own. Its eyes held such hatred. I had never seen anything like it before. I raised the gun to shoot the thing and it recognized the gun as a source of pain. It growled at me and then left. It headed down the beach a bit and then it actually bounded into the tree line down there." He was pointing south, down the beach.

Margaret followed his finger and her eyes plotted the course to the tree line he had spoken of. She experienced a flash of hate of her own. Still, they were alive and they had a shelter of sorts in the form of a downed shuttle. She could defend this space if she had to. She finally resigned herself to the situation. "I need a temporary defendable position here. See if you can get me some sort of deterrent here. An electric fence or a force shield would work. Maybe you can get the battery from the shuttle to work. It took some damage, but it may be salvageable." She ordered.

Margaret saw Duane set to the task and she went over to Quinn. She saw his communicator on his waist and took it. In her mind, things were looking up. "Pilot Margaret Manning to *Lincoln*, come in." She spoke into the pickup and she was instantly rewarded with the communications officer's strained voice.

"What is going on down there? Where is the survey officer?" The gruff voice asked and Margaret shook her head. A gesture lost completely on the audio only communicator. "Never mind that for now. We need a medical evacuation for three party members. The rest are dead. There is a predatory beast loose on this planet. Recommend that no one else land on this planet until it can be dealt with."

Margaret drew a breath and waited for the response. She expected an explosion for her insubordination. She was surprised when the communications officer replied calmly. "Yes ma'am we will dispatch a pick up shuttle immediately."

Margaret took the response as a good omen. "Understood" She replied into the communicator and switched it off. She replaced the unit to Quinn's waist and he stirred. He had looked pretty bad before. He looked worse now. Somehow though, his smile still brightened up her mood.

"I suppose that EVAC is on the way?" He asked and she nodded. "Damn, I wanted to crack this planet before anyone else could get into harm's way here." He complained and Margaret was taken by his passionate plea.

Aboard the *Lincoln*, emotions had ridden the roller coaster as it were. First there was the elation of landing the team safely onto the planet, despite the giant statues in the way. Then, the loss of contact and subsequent loss of some of the party members dropped the hopes of the crew, and that of their captain into the crapper. Now, there is the report of a fierce beast roaming loose on the planet. This trip just seems to have taken one bad turn after another. The captain sits on his command chair, watching the screen scroll the water world beneath them. His fingers rap the console and the executive officer just shook his head. The bridge crew is on edge. No announcement had been made, and the rest of the ship was circulating with rumors. Something had to be done, but the only one with the power to act is content just sitting there, watching the pretty blue water.

The XO stepped towards the command chair, and then decided against action. He was walking a fine line between morale damage control and undermining the captain's authority. That was a line he hoped never to cross. Executive officers that did tended to have very short careers. He decided instead to text message the captain on his data screen. Maybe he would notice it, and maybe not. Either way, he was afraid the ship's crew would spiral into uselessness with the rumor mill cranking out horror stories about the planet and the survey mission. He sat back down at his terminal and typed the short message; "Talk to the crew." Then he hit send. He hoped that the captain was at least marginally aware of the crew around him, and that he would do the right thing with this small amount of prompting. If not, maybe he could suggest something a little stronger.

The captain sat, still gazing at the screen when the cursor on his personal screen flashed. It meant that a new message was in the queue for him. He lazily reached over and pressed the 'accept' button. The short message displayed on his screen. The words were small, but they were demanding. The message read, "Talk to the crew." He thought about it a little while. Just exactly what was it he needed to talk to the crew about? He thought to himself. Well, he had better figure out what or he was certain that something bad would happen.

The captain startled everybody on the bridge by standing up, handing control of the bridge to the XO and leaving. No one knew where he was off to, and actually no one cared. He was gone, and the XO would now call the shots. Maybe life would be looking up, but doubt was apparent in the faces of the startled crew.

The XO stepped up to the command chair and sat down. He made a log entry assuming temporary command. Then he smiled. "All right people, we have a job to do. First of all, I want a report put together as soon as the survey crew is aboard. We need to diffuse the rumors with actual facts about what is going on down there. Speaking of that, I really need to know what IS going on down there. Get me as much information as you can. I believe we should be finished with this world soon. Let's do our jobs and get moving again. This sitting around waiting is not proper conduct for a fleet vessel." Then he smiled at the crew and many of the faces smiled back. A message alert popped onto the display at the communications station. The communications officer hit the receive button and the message displayed.. "Get that shuttle on the line, I want to talk with whoever is still in charge of this blasted mission. I'll take the message in the conference room." The officer hopped to his commands and within moments, the terminal in the conference room beeped to life with a message alert.

"This is the Captain speaking, who is on the line?" He began gruffly. The static on the signal did not help his mood when the reply came in.

"Sir, this is Pilot Margaret Manning, we are en route to you due to some casualties we have suffered on the mission. We have, however, discovered a functional base of the Jeng. Preliminary scans show the entire complex to be active, or at least activatable. In fact, the problem we discovered was from within the complex.

The beast had been imprisoned inside a holding cell of some kind. When it was released, we had nothing to stop it. Conventional weapons damage it, but it regenerates or heals at a dramatic rate. My best guess is that it is already back up to one hundred percent after being nearly cut in two by our hand weapons." She finished and took a deep breath to calm her nerves.

The Captain took a moment to digest the information. "Do we need to abort this mission and quarantine the planet because of this predator you have down there?" He asked reasonably.

It was Margaret's turn to think for a moment before speaking. "No sir, I saw some video inside the complex that suggests that they had a non-lethal weapon that could drive the creature back into the holding cell. I believe that such weapons may be found elsewhere in the complex if an exhaustive search is permitted." She finished, crossing her fingers about the man's response.

When the reply came, his tone was stone cold. I understand what you are asking for Margaret, but we cannot afford to lose a lot of personnel over this find. If you can find a way to keep the thing at bay until it can be captured, I will approve the continuation of the mission. After all, the profit should be substantial. However, if personnel start disappearing or dying down there, I'm pulling the plug. My responsibility to the crew is a serious matter. I don't like writing letters to families, and it seems I already have to write at least two of them by your preliminary report. I need a more detailed report right after you get out of the infirmary. I need more information to justify our delay to the next survey target." The Captain paused for dramatic effect. "Is that clear?" He asked in a tone that applied his full authority. Margaret gulped at the sound.

"Yes sir; understood perfectly sir." She answered and closed the communications channel. She looked around the small shuttle at the wounded men around her. The crew was light because of the loss of the archeologists. She felt the lump in her throat forming but she forced it back to focus on the task at hand. The mission so far played back in her mind as her hands expertly went through the docking pre-check list on memory alone.

☆ ☆ ☆

6

The archeologists, Tom and Roy found themselves in a cave. Both had been bloodied until they ceased to resist the creature's pull. Neither man knew why they were still alive, nor did they know where they had been taken. But they knew they were not out of the woods yet. There was a lot to do if they were going to survive. Not the least of which was to contact either the survey mission crew or the ship in orbit. Since neither one of them had a strong radio, the ship in orbit was probably a lost cause. The survey crew could possibly pick up their weak signal, providing they were monitoring for it.

The cave itself was rather small. They could not fathom why such a large creature would employ such a small cave, but the closeness of the walls pressed in on them over time. It was cooler in here though. It was a refreshing contrast to the blazing sunlight outside. The walls were damp and musty. There was standing water on patches of the floor, and the two men found that some of the fungi were edible. Not tasty, but analysis told them there were sufficient nutrients in them to warrant stomaching the bitter spongy growths. The cave walls were lined with them. It seemed that anywhere there was water the fungi were present. They continued to search the cave, being careful not to leave it. The creature had marked the entrance somehow, and they could feel the pull to stay away from the opening. It was like an impenetrable wall of force that stopped them. For now they were content to explore here. They would work on escaping later, when they understood more.

Aboard the *Lincoln,* tensions were high on the bridge, again. Upon returning from his conference room, the Captain had paced around agitated. Whatever he had heard from the shuttle obviously had not appeased him. He almost stormed around the tight spaces. The bridge crew was doing their best not to be noticed by the ranting madman they served under. The infirmary reported the arrival of the new patients and the Captain decided he could do nothing more here.

"Report to me when the mission party members are released from medical." He ordered and the XO nodded to him affirmative. He stormed out of the bridge and went to his quarters to try to calm down. "These morons will screw up my fortune." He thought to himself.

Everyone on the bridge drew a deep sigh. They had escaped the bullet again. It did not help ship's morale much to be on guard like this all the time. The XO wondered how the Captain had risen so high in rank without recognizing the basic human needs around him. He shook his head at the thought and then returned his attention to the planetary scan. He had some sort of animal to find. He would hunt until exhaustion for it so that the Captain could do something positive about it when he returned.

Quinn was in pretty bad shape when he hit the gurney in the medical facility. His leg was broken and had to be set again. He had scratches and gashes over most of his body. A rib was broken on one side and one eye was closed with a swelling knot under it. It appeared to the nurse as if he had gone several rounds in a prizefight. Of course that wasn't too far from the truth. Margaret was in better shape, but not by too much. The staff brought the gurney into the intensive care ward and the doctor made a cursory inspection. Then he nodded to the nurse and they continued on into the pod chamber. There were several regeneration tanks in the space. They were eight-foot long cylinders of metal and glass.

They had the new ergonomic design, which meant that they were harder to use. Panels with dials and wires of all sizes on them surrounded each tank. They rolled the gurney up to pod five and transferred Quinn into the pod. The doctor administered a painkiller and then set his leg and locked it in place with a clamping device. Then he closed the pod and the seal lights all went green. The doctor pressed a large green button and the tank filled up to neck level. The warm fluid simulated the sensation of being back in the womb and the body naturally relaxed a bit. The restraints kept Quinn from sinking into the fluid. He floated there, completely relaxed. One of the agents in the fluid was also a muscle relaxer. Quinn was soon snoring as the nano-bots and the healing fluids worked on his body. Margaret had held a fear of the pods for quite some time and she was much relieved when she discovered that she was not going into one of them. The doctor used a dermal regenerator to re-grow the skin of her hand. It was another example of nano-technology being used to further medical science. Her hand felt better almost instantly as the nerve endings were repaired by tiny robots that were small enough to repair individual cells. Duane was receiving similar attention and soon he and Margaret were released. Margaret went directly to her quarters and logged into the computer. She made her personal log and her mission log so the Captain could peruse it before she got to him to let him ask questions. She was hoping that Quinn would be up and around before she was forced to report to the captain. Unfortunately, the doctor didn't know exactly how long Quinn would take to heal in the regen tank. All she could do was to check in every once in awhile to see it he was nearly done. She found that there was another batch of forms to be filled out. She had lost a shuttlecraft. There were accident report forms, there were equipment scrap forms and there was a new shuttlecraft requisition form to be filled out by the senior pilot involved. She knew that these were all standard forms, but she was still quite tired and she resented having to deal with them before she could get some proper rest. Still, duty was duty and she obediently filled out the forms to the best of her ability. At the bottom of the accident report, she recommended better electric shielding for the key systems aboard the standard shuttlecraft.

Duane went back to the computer lab. He had so many new scans to enter into the translation matrix. He knew that he should be more worried about the surface, and what was still going on down there, but his curiosity still had the better of him. He decided to try to decipher all of the runes he had gathered. He scanned one after another into the computer and began a concentrated search and match routine to look for possible cross matches. After a flurry of typing, the computer began its search and Duane leaned back in the chair to watch the results as they came in.

The Captain jumped a bit when the chime sounded. It was the executive officer, making his usual watch. The Captain had sent him away when it was time to do the daily paperwork. He just wasn't in the mood for paperwork. He wanted more in life than his current post allowed. He was miserable here. He was stuck in the middle of nowhere, with belligerent survey people and a totally uninteresting crew. His ship spent more time just hanging out in space than actually doing anything. The Captain was lost in his self-pity when the chime sounded a second time.

"Captain, are you in there?" The XO asked nervously. He was worried that something had happened to the man. In his heart he knew that that would not necessarily be a bad thing, but he wanted to earn his captainship, not simply inherit one. "Sir, we need to go over these reports before the watch changes in an hour." He said to the closed door and it opened with a hiss. The door slid into the ceiling and the XO breathed a sigh of relief when he saw the captain leaning back from the control panel. He came into the rather spacious compartment and plopped himself down into one of the overstuffed chairs the Captain so favored. He had his clipboard in front of him with a relieved, expectant look on his face. "You had me a bit worried there sir." He continued when the Captain refused to start the conversation.

The captain rolled his eyes a bit and then sighed in resignation.

Okay, what do we need to go over in your precious book before the watch changes?" He asked and the XO overlooked the hint of sarcasm and dove into the subject at hand.

"Well sir, you see this duty roster has some changes on it, and I need you to initial them." He produced a small document and the Captain placed his initials in the required blank. The XO continued on undeterred. "Next, we have a supply issue; the cook has been complaining of reduced stock quantities. The computer shows them at full stock. One of them must be wrong, or someone has been removing food stuffs from stock without updating the stock quantities properly." He said and then waited for the Captain to respond.

"What do you want me to do about that? Am I supposed to wave a magic wand and make the food reappear? Adjust the computer to reflect the actual counted stock value, and then secure the food storage facility. If more comes up missing, then charges will be filed. In the meantime, inform the crew that stricter methods will be being used in conjunction with food storage. It is most likely that the culprit, if there is one, will give up his or her grabbing of food and rely solely on the furnished meals for sustenance. Does that solve your problem?" He asked and the XO wrote down the recommendations and smiled.

"Yes sir, that takes care of two of these papers. The rest just need your signatures on them. I'll leave them with you and not take any more of your valuable time here." He said and got up to leave.

"Wait a minute." The Captain ordered. The XO came back over and sat back down into the comfortable chair. "I have been watching you with the crew." The Captain stated plainly. "I want you to get on their good side and tell me what they are up to." He said and the XO got a look of confusion that seemed to set his features out of whack on his face.

"What do you mean, up to?" He asked and it was the Captain's turn to look confused.

"You mean they are not planning something? He asked a little defensive. I would not be happy to learn of a possible mutiny without any prior warning." The Captain stated blandly.

The XO's mouth dropped open in shock. "Mutiny! Who ever even breathed a sigh about mutiny?" He asked, flabbergasted. "I think you may be watching too many holo-dramas on the cube. I have heard no words of dissention among the crew. It is true they are feeling a bit put off by your stomping around the bridge, but no one has even suggested doing anything about it sir. They trust you to keep them alive and to help them along the way to the next posting." The XO stood up and pointed a finger at the Captain's face. "Keep those goals in mind and you will never have a problem with the crew." He said and then he leaned back. He picked his clipboard back up off the floor. "Now, if you will excuse me, I have real work to do. I hope to see you at dinner sir." He said and left the room. The door slid obediently shut behind him and the Captain was left to ponder the outburst, and to weigh the XO's words in his own mind for their validity.

Margaret had taken a rest and was now about ready mentally to face the Captain. She hoped beyond hope that Quinn was healed up enough to accompany her. She so hated to go in alone on this mission. Still, she was a professional; she would adjust and overcome as was required of her.

She swung by the medical center and was surprised to find Quinn sitting upright on a hospital bed. He saw her and his face lit up. Hers blushed in response, the tension in the room doubled between them. The doctor watched the whole display and smiled to himself. He said nothing to either of them though; he simply looked at his pad and pronounced that Quinn was well enough to leave the facility. He would, however, have to take it easy for a while. The repairs to his body would not hold if he went into strenuous activity or combat again. Quinn thanked the man and hopped down gingerly from the bed. Margaret watched him dubiously and was ready to catch him if he fell over. He held onto his dignity and recovered himself.

"I have been ready to leave this place for a while, but they wouldn't let me go. They kept muttering things about rushing into trouble again. I don't understand their problem though. If this mission goes well enough, they will all be rich. Some of them may even become famous from working with the objects and data we collect down there." He finished and he found he was almost winded from the short speech.

Margaret gave him a stern look. "I believe you are under orders to take it easy. I was hoping you could face the Captain for the briefing he is pestering us for, but if you are truly this weak, I would rather you were in your bunk recuperating. I intend to be sent back down there as soon as possible. It would not do for you to have a relapse and have to miss your own opportunity to become a part of history." She admonished and Quinn held up his hand in surrender.

"I see your point. I should go to the briefing with you though. I let that thing out; it is my responsibility to get it put away again. It is obvious to me that we cannot kill the thing. I certainly gave it a good try, but it just healed at a phenomenal rate and came back for another attack. I promise to rest as soon as the mission briefing is over. In fact, you can escort me to my quarters if you think I will stray or something." He put on his charming smile and Margaret felt a twinge of self reprimand coming on for listening to this man with her heart instead of her head.

"You make sure you are in your bunk no less than ten minutes after the briefing ends." She ordered, pointing a finger at his chin to emphasize her point.

"Yes Ma'am, It will all be as you say." He said with a mock salute. Then they headed to the Captain's quarters together. The sooner this meeting was out of the way, the better.

The beast was tired. It had mapped the area around it and found it to be an insignificant island. It was not happy. There were no cities of victims for it. There were no temples to sacrifice beings or animals to it. Its dignity was heavily tarnished by the affront. The cat was eons old; it had been worshipped on several occasions throughout history. Only against those vile slender xenophobic people had it been defiled. It felt the rage at the imprisonment it had suffered. It had spent a seeming eternity inside the dark and foreboding room. Now it could taste the air again. It could feast on flesh again. It could run, but not the great distances it desired. It could also think. Right now, all it could think about was getting out into open places. This island limited it too much. The water was fresh smelling, but how far did it go? The thing could swim well, but only for a limited time. What if this was the only piece of ground on this forsaken planet? If that turned out to be true, then it would need another planet to dominate and rule. These new little ones were amusing, but they possessed no real power. They had vicious weapons, of that it had experienced first hand, but they had no other redeeming qualities. They didn't seem to communicate with each other efficiently, like the multi-limbed ones had. They had shinier toys to play with though. This metal box thing they must have come in provided a few moments of protection from even its formidable claws. This was something of a puzzle for the ancient creature. Now the little beings were gone, except the two it had put aside for study. The being's powerful sense of smell verified that they were nowhere on this island. Where had they gone? When it found out, it would leave this place also. For now, all it could do was wait. After all the centuries of waiting, it could handle a small amount longer. After all, what is a year to one who lives for eternity? It knew that someone was coming and it could see the line tracing from the prison to the sky. They would be here sooner or later. The thing settled in and waited for the return of the little ones from the box.

The Captain was getting angrier by the hour that he had to wait for his briefing. Those untold riches were still down there waiting for him. He was getting impatient, waiting for results from these incompetents that seemed to want to stand between him and his fortune and his future. If he could prove that they were trying to hold him back, he would ruin them both.

The door chime sounded in his quarters, and he sighed as he

called "enter." Quinn and Margaret stepped into the compartment. It did not seem so vast to Margaret with both of them before the Captain like this. She could see the man had been fuming. His smirk was completely gone. He had issues she could probably not begin to fathom, she thought to herself. They stood there on the carpet for several uncomfortable moments. A side glance at Quinn showed nothing to her. He was completely composed. She again marveled at his strength, how could he go under the gun this calm?

The Captain sat there, his ire rising as he watched the two people before him. He held his temper back for a moment longer. It was a moment that seemed to hang in the air a lifetime of heartbeats. Then he spoke, so softly that Quinn heard the danger in his voice. "So, you have managed to release a dangerous animal on the planet. There are deaths concerned and now there will be even more delays in accomplishing our mission." He took a deep breath and his volume began to rise. "Furthermore, I have no real update on what the findings were down there. Not to mention the loss of the shuttle. Do you have any idea how much one of those costs?" The Captain continued. His voice was now the volume of a loud speech, but it seemed he was not done yet. "What have I got to do to get some decent work out of you two?" He screamed at them. "The review board will have my hide for letting you continue this far into the mission. Do you realize you have jeopardized my career as well as your own? If I had my way, we'd be leaving you on that planet, chained to a rock wall so the beast down there could devour you piece by piece as it saw fit." The steam seemed to leave the Captain and he visibly deflated. His anger spent, the Captain's true color shone through brightly. The man stood up and brought his face forward to lean over his desk. "Well you two, what profits do you have to report for me?" He asked with that same danger in his voice.

Not a good start to the conversation thought Quinn, but he had prepared for this. "Sir, we have uncovered a lot of new artifacts. The profit margin will exceed your expectations by about three fold." He said like a salesman trying push a lemon onto a prospective client. He brought up a data pad and punched a few keys and showed the display to the Captain. "This is a partial inventory of the items we found inside the stone chamber. There is probably more there, but we were under attack and thus in a hurry to depart." He finished and Margaret wondered when he had made an inventory. She had not seen him do anything but open the fateful door that released the creature. Surely he did not have more time than that.

The Captain read the list, and he even had to press a key for the next screen. He nodded at several items and then he surprised Margaret. He produced a huge smile. "Well, my boy, I didn't think you had it in you. I will be pleased to read your final report when we have the loot stowed in our holds. Do you think we can still plant a colony here after that has been completed?" He asked.

Margaret's mouth dropped open at the sudden change in demeanor and familiarity the Captain was now displaying. Quinn looked thoughtful for a moment and then he nodded. "Yes, I think we should be able to do that if we can contain the creature that is loose down there." He replied and then he smiled back at the Captain. Sir, this will be some of the easiest money you've ever made." He finished and the Captain smiled again. He now looked at Quinn almost father-like.

"I need you down there as soon as you are able. I understand from medical that you are to be resting. Rest well, and we shall all wait to see what you discover next." The Captain stepped around the desk and put his hand on Quinn's shoulder. "Keep up the good work, and you and I will leave the service wealthy men." Margaret was doing her best to hide her shock and amazement. Some of it was slipping through her guard though. The Captain noticed it and winked at her. "You are dismissed now. Just get me what I want and everything will be fine." He said and waved them out of his quarters.

Quinn lead the way out and Margaret followed closely on his heels. When they were safely out of earshot from the Captain's quarters she grabbed his shoulder and spun him around to her. He grimaced at the pain it caused and then he had a look of surprise at the interruption. "What did you tell him you found down there?" She asked and he pulled out the data pad again and showed it to her. Most of the entries were normal stuff except for item twelve. "Diamonds! There are diamonds here?" She asked and Quinn nodded his head.

"Yes, and fossil fuels and all the elements to make starship hulls and drives as well. There are even crystalline structures here that can produce vast amounts of energy underground." He said and she shook her head in disbelief.

"How can you know this? Where did you go that no one else went? Do you have some kind of sixth sense about alien worlds and their energy properties?" She asked challengingly and Quinn raised his hands to forestall her tirade.

"Look, what we have here are the basic building blocks of a successful colony right? He queried and she nodded in agreement. Well then, where could I have gotten all this data on the planet?" He asked and she scratched her head.

She came across a few ideas and dismissed them. Then her brain hung on a particular possibility. "Did you read the original survey report?" She asked and Quinn smiled warmly at her.

"That's how it all started anyway. He admitted but she wasn't convinced of his intentions. "You see; we have two surveys of this planet not to include mine. The simple fact is, this planet has been reviewed and rejected by the mining guild and the corporate offices have passed over this planet as well. According to the several surveys to land here it would be too difficult to harvest this planet's wealth from an industrial viewpoint. When the colony plants on this planet, they will prosper without any additional aid from off world. That self-reliance is the foundation that will bring this world into power in the universal government and when it is, the founders will be spoken of with reverence. But of course that is still a long way off. The first part is to get that beast under control. I found out that it could be hurt, but not killed. The words above its door were talking about a mythical beast. My guess is that this thing is somehow immortal. That little tidbit of news should interest the medical community. It is quite possible that the planet will be exporting much of its wealth to keep the Captain happily wallowing in wealth the rest of his life. If we are to keep this unplanted colony healthy, we must hide most of this from the greedy old man so that he doesn't steal it away from the future generations that could desperately need it to become sponsored members in the government. We still have to get the survey filled out completely. We also have to catalog the partial list for the Captain and get the colony ship ordered in. There is still so much to do here."

Margaret eyed Quinn and then she nodded. "Okay, I can get started on some of those points, but you promised me to get some rest before doing anything else. I intend to hold you to that promise. You can't help us if you collapse of exhaustion before we can get everything done here. Go to sleep and we'll touch base later on just how far I have gotten. Then we can check back in with Duane. He was anxious to get to work on those runes. My guess is that he will have a lot of them deciphered by the time we are ready to ask him. They may hold a clue as to how the beast was contained in the first place. There was also a video that played down there in the control room. It showed them driving the beast back into the room and then they locked it closed. We may be able to glean a clue from that recording as well." She finished, taking a huge breath.

It was Quinn's turn to be amazed. "You mean you actually got some of that weird control console to work? That was some pretty impressive work there, Margaret. There may be more that works down there than I had originally believed." She could see that his mind was turning over possibilities and she decided not to just let him go.

"Oh no you don't; you go and get that rest now. Or do I have to call someone from medical to sedate you?" She asked. The look on her face showed that she meant every word.

Quinn held up his hands in surrender. "All right, I'm going doctor." He said and his smile lifted Margaret's spirits again. He left to go to his quarters. He fully intended to rest. The wounds ached even now, and he was certain that some decent sleep was the ticket to enhanced productivity.

The *S.S.F. Lincoln* had been in-system for a while now. They were behind schedule at least a couple of weeks. There was no longer a chance that they could simply push their drives faster to make up the lost time. There would be reports to fill out and questions to be asked. The only real solution now was for this planet to pan-out and provide enough distraction to merit the lost time. The Captain was driven completely by finances, but the rest of the crew was still focused on reaching their goal. The *Lincoln* was to find not one, but three habitable worlds in which to plant colonies. This had been their first choice. Now it was looking as if they would have to skip this planet due to some sort of predator on the surface. Morale was now at an all-time low for the ship. The XO knew that this was a dangerous time, but he saw no solution to the Captain's one-track-mindedness. The man did no damage control when it came to the intangibles. It frustrated the XO beyond belief. He had rotated the schedules so that everyone on board was with new people. It was a little less efficient, but it prevented any combination of individuals taking the time to plot and scheme. Perhaps he was a bit paranoid, but as the XO's record would show if the Captain had even checked it, he had seen a mutiny in action first hand. He desperately wanted to prevent another. He had been an ensign when it happened the first time. He had been knocked out early on in the fighting, and was nearly spaced when the wrong side came out on top. He would be dead now if not for the intervention of the Colonial Marines. He still had nightmares of ships floating, burning in space, and crewmembers floating behind the wreck in the frozen void of space. It was not a pretty sight.

His mind snapped back to the present and he looked around his terminal. No one was looking over his shoulder so he set up the next set of schedule changes and posted them on the network. There would be grumbling, but he could always hide it as a training exercise. After all, each man or woman aboard needed to be familiar with every job on board. He wondered why the planet below had not turned out to be what they needed. He had not been authorized access to the survey records, but he knew something was up down there. He decided to hitch a ride with the next down shuttle. Maybe he could see for himself what was happening. It was a stretch of fleet policy to let him go, but there were precedents that supported his decision. He made a note of some of the particular ones for when the Captain called him in for his transgressions. After all, he couldn't really be that out of it not to notice his second in command leaving the ship. At least he hoped the man was not that far gone.

He signed off the terminal and headed for his quarters, leaving the Lieutenant on duty to take care of the bridge for now. He had to pack some personal gear for the trip. He hoped they would be embarking soon. His mind was all a flutter with anticipation. It had been quite some time since he had gone dirt-side during a mission, and he was looking forward to it.

Margaret went back to the hangar. She wanted to inspect the new shuttle that was being provided. It was one of the older models she noticed right away. I guess she had ruined a new one; she would have to settle until a replacement could be acquired. It was all just fine with her, she had trained in one of these older shuttles and she was quite the expert at making them do things other shuttle pilots would never attempt. She smiled at some of the memories, and some of the white-as-a-sheet faces of her instructors whenever she sprung one of her surprise maneuvers on them. She walked straight up to the hull and placed her hand on the panel. It was cold and solid. She could feel tiny imperfections in the hull plating. These were the result of strikes by debris in space. She knew they were normal, and they were also an attest to the reliability of the vehicle. The more time it spent in operation, the more pits it would have. This was one reliable ship based on the plate she felt. Still, there was nothing quite like flying, and she was happy just to still be doing it. She was never truly happy on the ground. As a child she had watched the giant birds of her home world. They would gracefully take in the rising air off the cliffs by her hometown. They could remain in flight for hours. Some of them could even do it while they slept. She learned later it was a survival technique to prevent being attacked by predators while sleeping on the ground. She had dreamed of flying. Her parents had never allowed her to do anything they considered to be dangerous. That might explain her attitudes now. She smiled at the self-reflection and walked over to the rear hatch. This truly was an antique as fleet craft went. She sat in the command chair and felt right at home. The old seat fit her like a glove and she relaxed quite a bit just sitting there. She checked the gauges and found that they were still fueling the vessel. She made a mental note to check on that before they left. Still, she went through the rest of the checklist and was pleasantly surprised to find out that the craft was in great shape. She powered down the battery systems and exited the craft. Taking a look back she gave a thumbs-up to the maintenance crew that had kept this old vessel in such good shape. She would make sure that they got this one back.

7

Duane was getting eyestrain from staring at the screen. None of the usual calculations were working on this last passage. He had uncovered a lot of data, but a vital key was missing. The glyphs did not even look like the rest. It was as if someone had added another language to the wall just to throw him off. He gritted his teeth and dove back in. The computer was working hard to process his requests. The files were displaying at inhuman speeds, and Duane was watching them scroll and taking key bits here and there and re-trying them in other ways. He started to get woozy. Looking down at his hand, he was surprised at how much it shook. He would drop if an answer were not found soon. Maybe a step back was needed. He tried to stand up but he was unstable and he fell over and hit his head on the table behind him. He lay on the floor, looking up at the ceiling and then, as he felt an answer looming close, his vision tunneled and he passed out.

Duane awoke to a bright light. There were people around him. He could sense them but he could not focus his eyes. Blurs of shape continued to pass through his vision. He tried to call to someone, but his mouth had something in it. He tried to raise his arms, but they were held fast to the table. His mind was trying to figure out the puzzle as he began to panic. He found that his legs did not respond either. He was trapped within his own body. He raged and screamed mentally, but no sound came to his ears. The sounds of the outside world were muffled and incomprehensible. His vision was a cloudy vision through wax paper. There was just no solution his mind could grasp. The table beneath him felt cold. It was metal, of that he was certain. There was something crinkly on it, like a paper of some kind. He tried to shake his head, but it would not move. Then, as if turning on a light, his eyes cleared and focused on a single figure above him.

The doctor hovered over him, and he made eye contact. The light was starting to hurt a bit. And he hurt in other places as well. He couldn't explain why as yet, but he intended to find out. "Can you hear me Duane?" The doctor asked.

Duane felt the thing pull out of his mouth and he tried to talk. A weak squeak came out and he tried to swallow to help the system get back on line. Pain met with the swallowing attempt. He tried to talk again and this time he managed a weak sound. "What happened?" He asked and the Doctors, for there was more than one there now, congratulated each other on their fine work. Duane asked again and they stopped to look at him. Then one of them, he could not tell them apart anymore, stood over him and met his eyes.

"You have been attacked by something we do not fully understand." The man looked around uncomfortably, then he sighed and continued. "We found you under a table in the computer lab. You had been infected by something. Whatever it is, it seems to destroy nerve tissue first. You may have noticed some trembling in your hands first. Then the virus, or whatever it is, spread. If you had managed to call in instead of simply collapsing, we might have gotten to you sooner. You have lost the feeling in your body. For a while, you had lost even autonomic functions. We had you on life support until we could battle this thing. It is probable that you have been cured now. The virus is retreating from the anti-toxin we created to battle it. The return of your breathing and speech are definitely good signs of remission. With luck, the rest of you will return to normal function as well. There is something down on that planet that is just toxic as all hell. We will be inoculating anyone else who goes down there." Then the doctor turned back to Duane. "Your main concern right now is just how far the virus will recede. I believe it will be eradicated from your body. If so, you will regain nearly all of your functions again. There is always some damage with a case like this. Anything that attacks the nervous system this violently always does, but the results so far are encouraging."

Duane moved his head a little and looked around the room. There were machines everywhere. He could recognize only a couple of them. They must have pulled out all the stops to try and save his life. He felt grateful, but also a bit confused. He didn't remember touching anything bad, or having any problems that the others had not had. Yes, that beast had scratched him, but Margaret and Quinn had each been attacked worse. The wall of runes was just that, a flat wall of stone. Odds were not good that a virus that lethal could have survived underground all that time. There wasn't even a lot of moisture for one to culture in down there. It had been dry as dust, and dark too. Then he remembered the computer was still searching. "How long was I incapacitated?" He asked and the doctor shrugged.

"We don't know, they found you when you didn't report to three meals in one day. That's not healthy you know. They sent a watch officer to check on you and he found you on the floor. Based on your level of dehydration when you came in, I'd say it had been about two days since you had eaten or drank anything. Other than that, it's anyone's guess how long you were down." The doctor noted the medical chart, and then shook his head. "I see that you have visitors. If you feel up to the task, they'd like to have a word with you." He said and Duane nodded that it was okay.

Margaret and Quinn entered the room and Duane's face lit up. He had been worried that they had been struck down as well. It was obvious that they were quite healthy now. He let the sense of relief flow over him and comforted himself in the warmth. The doctor cleared his throat as if uncomfortable and then left the room. Quinn stepped up first.

"They told me you had gotten a nasty bug there." He said and he looked Duane in the eye. "We don't think that is the problem here." He continued and Duane's eyes opened large.

"What do you mean? The doctor just told me that they had the virus on the retreat." He said and Quinn and Margaret glanced at each other and then looked back to Duane.

"They got it in retreat all right, but we did it. You left the computer displaying glyphs in your room. It was something you read that started this thing in your body. Those runes have some kind of power. When I read the one's over the door to the creature, the creature was formed. When Margaret scanned the ones over the display screen, the movie played. They have locked some kind of power into the writings themselves. I don't understand how, but I doubt that anyone truly knows how it works, unless someone can find a Jeng and ask them." He finished and Duane thought about the theory.

"Okay, let's say that you are right and the thing came into existence when I read the runes. How did you come up with an antidote for it?" Duane asked and Quinn smiled, if only thinly.

"Well, we found the translation you were working on. It had completed while you were out of it. We knew that or you would have turned it off. The last line read '*beware the words of death*'. I puzzled over that for awhile, but there were several other phrases that were equally cryptic and I soon discovered that some of the phrases had powers. I used a line from your translation in my personal computer and it produced light. I could see no visible source, but the room was lit up whether the ship's lights were turned on or not. In fact, I don't know how to turn it off yet, so I won't be sleeping in those quarters for a while." He finished with a chuckle." Quinn sat down next to Duane and Duane was surprised to find that his head could track to him and keep him in view. Quinn noticed the surprise. "Don't worry, if the words are correct, you will be up and on your feet again within the hour. Now, where was I? Oh yes, the words of power. There were many examples on the board you translated. Most were ordinary things like produce water, or suspend stone. But one passage told of the words of death. We believe now that you read those words and started to die by the most hideous way you could imagine. You feared dying of a disease, and so one was created to oblige you." Duane started to protest, but Quinn waved him back down to silence. "Furthermore, you were anxious to get back down to the planet, so you were a motivated reader. Most people would have started the death words and stopped when they got hit with an eerie feeling of mortality. My guess is you read straight through them, not even understanding what it was you were reading. The warning had three words at the bottom of it, and that was the key to bringing you back. The three words were '*death is reversible*'. On a long shot, we decided to try to read the death chant backwards. Within a few moments, you were already regaining consciousness. The rest you know already about the doctors trying things while we experimented behind their backs. Now they will be upset because a solution was found for a medical problem that was a bunch of superstitious nonsense to them. It may be an advanced technology, but it looks like magic to them and that is something that they just cannot face or fathom."

Quinn took a deep breath. "To extend this discovery further, I think it is possible to put the cat back in its hole if I read the glyphs above the door backwards. I think it's definitely worth a try. There is still so much to learn here, but I believe that the Captain will not give us the chance. As soon as it is profitable for him, I think he'll head us back to civilization and start spending his loot." The trio looked at each other with worry lined on their faces. "I also think we are about to be split up. I don't know how long the man will risk having us work together against him. He is the profit seeking type and they tend to be pretty paranoid about anything that can affect their bottom line." Quinn slammed his hand down on the table next to the hospital bed. "We are so close to making history here." He exclaimed through frustration. "There has got to be a way to continue this mission and keep the promise of profits alive for the man in charge." He stood up and looked like he was going to pace, and then he caught himself and sat back down. "Do you think we can get anything else out of the computer, or do we need to be back down on the planet?" Quinn asked Duane.

Duane thought about it for a moment, and then he startled the others with a curse of his own. "I can't believe I almost killed myself with a magical phrase from the ancient past. There I was, looking at the answers and not seeing them all the time. What would have happened if I had accidentally stumbled across another potent combination during the search that you could not reverse? These things are obviously dangerous. I should have seen the patterns though. I must be losing my touch." Then Duane turned thoughtful. "I think we need to be down on the planet to get any further. It should also be recognized by now that no one should work alone on these glyphs. Without someone there to reverse the damage, it can only get worse in the case of a mishap." He tried to raise his arm and was pleasantly surprised when he saw it lift off of the bed and he let it drift back down. "Well, at least the effect is wearing off now. When can we get back down there?" He asked and Quinn looked at Margaret and they both shrugged their shoulders. "What is it? What aren't you telling me?" He asked.

"You have been quarantined. We have been too for coming to see you. No one from here is going down to the planet until the quarantine is lifted. As it looks to me, the Captain is going to use this opportunity to replace us on the dirt-side missions. He wants to cut us out of the profits on this one. His greed may well be his undoing here. If the new crew doesn't go in with the knowledge we now possess, they may fall victim to the glyphs like we did. I'll bet the archeologists are still down there somewhere as well. They could benefit greatly if we could just get down there. There are armed guards holding this section of the ship off limits to everyone else though. We couldn't get to the shuttles if our lives depended on it. I just hope that no emergency situation arises. We could well be stuck here until the Captain docks somewhere and a decontamination crew can get to us. We could be in for a long wait."

Duane let out a heavy sigh. "I didn't want to ground you two from flight. There was no way to get a decontamination team from on board? You're sure of that? He asked and they both nodded their heads.

"It wasn't your fault that we came in here; we just couldn't let you die in here while they fumbled around for an answer in the wrong places. It was a matter of honor. Don't think on it any further. Instead, see if you can get access to any systems on board this ship. We need to create a diversion if we are going to grab a shuttle and head down to the planet undetected."

Margaret saw a flash as her mind replayed her career in her head. Would she really go that far and jeopardize it? She didn't know, but she knew that being trapped here was possibly worse than losing her job. She only hoped that history would record her as a freedom fighter and not a criminal. However, she reflected that history didn't always care one way or the other as it recorded the smaller events. She wanted to be remembered. This was probably her best chance. There were obstacles still to be overcome. She steadied her nerves for the attempt and looked to Quinn for direction.

Quinn noticed her moment of self-reflection and he smiled knowingly. "You will be fine; we just have a few small tasks to perform to cement ourselves into the history books. I think everything will be fine." He pulled out a personal computer and plugged it into the wall socket. As expected, the socket had been deactivated, but survey crew training was pretty extensive. In a few short moments he had the plug working and churning out false reports all over the ship. He fully expected the security men to smash through the door and try to take them as he worked, but nobody entered the compartment. "Okay, if they believed that those calls were real, then there is nobody left to answer anything else from security. We need to setup a small charge to knock out the guards. Can you do anything for us here?" He asked Margaret and she nodded.

"Yes, there are sufficient chemicals in this lab to make a small bomb. But you would have to use it sparingly to keep it from killing the guards." She warned and he held up his hand.

"Please, spare me the morality. I agree that they shouldn't be killed. How can we be the good guys if you can still think otherwise?" He mocked and she blushed. She threw herself into the work to help shrug off the momentary embarrassment. Margaret felt a little more than embarrassed about the affair but she let it slide while she tried to figure out Quinn's next move. He had something cooking and she was always excited at the prospect of his daring plans. Whatever they were, he wasn't going to tell now so she just decided to bide her time and see.

The Captain had returned to the bridge. The good news about his financial prospects had him walking a little quicker and stepping a little lighter. The feeling radiated around him and the bridge crew felt the difference right away. By the time the Captain sat in his command chair, he was actually whistling. He was greeted by smiles on the bridge and he felt the reaction rise up inside him. He was happy. This had not happened to him in a while and he liked it. He would soon be free of these idiots and the space navy all together. He would settle down in some remote province and retire wealthy. The locating of diamonds can change a man like that. He just sat back and envisioned his future. He was so entranced, that he barely noticed the proximity alarm when it went off.

The communications officer was watching over the plotter's shoulder when the huge blip appeared right in front of them. The view-screen showed a moon forming in front of the stealthy *Lincoln*. The image of a shimmering planetoid brought gasps from the various bridge crew and the next assault on their senses was sound. A crack like a thousand lightning strikes echoed through space. Sound cannot travel without air to carry it, but force can. The wave struck the side of the *Lincoln* and tossed it around like a child's toy. Collision alarms were ringing and the bridge lost power and switched to auxiliary lighting. No one was dislodged from his or her seat; there were shock frames on all of the bridge stations. However, the ship was reporting damage and injuries on all decks. Then the most amazing thing happened, they were being electronically hailed. The bedlam settled down as the communication's officer shouted for quiet. She recorded the message and routed it to the Captain's station.

The Captain looked at the message, and his heart sank. It was a warning that the planet below was the property of the Jeng, and they were not to venture down to the surface again. The Captain saw his fortune turn to vapor and blow away on the solar winds, and then his mind clicked on the potential of that short message. *The Jeng were alive!* This was almost too good to be true. If he could just make peaceful contact here, he could be wealthy forever. He thought about it for a moment, and then he returned a message to his communication's officer. She looked at him in surprise and he nodded to send the message out.

She broke the shock and turned back to her terminal. In moments, a response signal came back and it left nothing to the imagination. "Do NOT go down to our planet. Anyone who attempts a landing will be eliminated. You will be tolerated in our space only until a reasonable amount of time to make repairs has elapsed, if you have not left by the end of that time, you will all be eliminated. Message ends"

The Captain felt his heart jump up into his throat. "You heard the message, get on those repairs right away. He barked at the crew and they started coordinating their reports with the damage control department. There was real bustling all over the ship for the first time since the Captain had come on board three years ago. He had lost his vision of profits, and now he could lose his life over this damnable planet. Someone was going to pay for this. Maybe he could somehow pin all of this on that uppity survey lieutenant. It would be rewarding to watch that man finally squirm on the hook.

Quinn was working on the door latch when the general quarters sounded. Now he had real reason to worry. General quarters had not sounded before aboard this ship as far as he knew. They were never in any danger with the Captain more interested in money than fame or glory. Still, they were locked into this small compartment and they had no space survival gear. No masks, or pressure suits. They were vulnerable, and they all knew it. Margaret's eyes turned wide at the warning sound. They also had no news from outside of their tiny space to know what danger the ship was in. They had felt an impact of some kind. They had been thrown from their feet by the sheer force of it. It didn't feel like any conventional weapons Margaret was familiar with. It was most puzzling. Quinn redoubled his efforts. He was working on interfacing a small hand comp to the door lock. A software-driven artificial intelligence matrix pod protected the lock. He was trying to convince it that there was no one in the room and that maintenance wanted in to clean the room. He had tried a couple of approaches with no success. He gritted his teeth and typed again, clearing the old request out. He pressed the send key and was rewarded with the swishing sound of the door sliding into the wall. Both he and Margaret dove through the door before the computer detected them and re-closed the door. It swished shut behind them as the servos kicked in. Duane had not been fast enough because he had been too far from the door when it opened, he was still trapped inside. The two adventurers were now in the hallway of the quarter's wing of the aft deck. There was not much they could do from there, but they managed to secure a couple of pressure suits from a wall locker. At least they felt a little better. The computer terminal at the aft station was down; in fact it was in pieces. Some major repairs were underway, and they were going fast. He had never seen this crew moving so fast. Quinn grabbed a stunner from the station's locker and felt the weight in his hand. The stunner was a rod about 30centimeters long with a bright red tip. It delivered a jolt upon contact that would incapacitate a foe for a couple of hours. There was also a tiny needle on the end that would inject a mild sedative. They decided to head to the docking bay and try for one of the shuttles. They had to get to the surface. It was even more important now that the ship was in danger somehow. They needed to get the archeological site locked down before looters came and destroyed the historical evidence. It seemed that everyone was involved with the repairs. Whatever was going on, the Captain wanted the ship fixed in a hurry. It was the first thing the Captain did that Quinn actually approved of. He nodded to some additional maintenance personnel and then they were off at a trot towards the docking bay. Several of the corridors had buckled from the damage to the ship, and so the course they eventually took was quite intricate. They used an access panel here, a service duct there. At long last, the sealed docking bay doors finally rewarded them with a red pressure light. The pressure seals were in place, so it was possible that the bay had been depressurized. They checked the readouts, but the reading made no sense. One told them the temperature in the bay was over a million degrees, which would have melted the metal to slag long ago. And another instrument read the temperature as absolute zero, the dead null of space. They hoped for a happy medium and they sealed up their pressure suits and kicked on the heaters. The zero reading was much more likely if they lost pressure in the gigantic bay. They opened the inner hatch and swung inside and sealed it behind them. The tell-tales on the inside hatch were all green. That didn't make sense with the readings they had gotten earlier. Still, they opened the hatch and started to descend the ladder to the main docking bay floor. Shifts in the artificial gravity made the trip treacherous. More than once they would be weightless, and they had to hold onto the rails tightly or drift off into the open space above them. That would have been unfortunate when the gravity came back on. As it was, they completed the descent without too much trouble, but progress had been really slow.

Margaret found the maintenance schedule hanging from a wall locker and she pointed to the most likely target. It was the old shuttle that had been prepped for departure. It was ready to go according to the paperwork. She made her way directly to it with Quinn in tow. They decided to skip the entire pre-flight and just center their attention on the vital systems. Within moments, they were off the hangar deck and easing forward. The docking bay doors were closed. Margaret gave the automated signal but they remained fast on their huge mechanical treads. The shuttle eased even closer, close enough to start collision alarms screaming aboard the tiny craft. But the doors still refused to move. They turned to the radio and static answered them. There was either no one at the communications board or nobody was going to answer a rogue shuttle trying to take off.

Quinn took the gunner's seat and aimed the lasers at the door. From the outside, they would have had no chance to penetrate the shielding and reach the metal doors. But from the inside, it was relatively unprotected. They sliced a clean hole into the doors. They took the time to make sure they only damaged one of the doors so that it would cost less to repair them. Then Margaret aimed the tiny craft at the newly formed hole and they were free and clear, out into open space. The planet still loomed below them and they both breathed a sigh of relief. If the ship had left the system, they would now be stranded in the middle of only God knew where. Now they were certain that their goal was in sight.

The shuttle shot out away from the ship and they both gasped when they saw the new moon, looming over the tiny ship they had just departed from. They both knew that it hadn't been there before. Fear quickly gave way to curiosity and they turned the ship back towards the moon, rather than go land on the planet itself. The moon was vast and it looked as though it had an atmosphere of its own. There might be life on that big hunk of rock, and life was what Quinn was the best at dealing with. They started to actively scan the surface as they passed close to the moon. The gravity signature suggested that it might not be a real moon, but rather a construct of some kind. The thing read as if it were hollow. They relayed the telemetry back to the *Lincoln* and someone was on the communications board now. An acknowledgement came back of receipt of the data. Then Margaret spotted a black square on the surface, deep into one of the ravines. She nosed the craft down towards the spot and as they got nearer to it, they could make out more detail. This was a construct of enormous complexity. The black square they were heading towards was nearly a quarter mile wide, but they had guessed right, it was also a landing strip. Now that they were closer, there were flashing lights, leading them into an opening in the rock face to the north of the landing area. Margaret took the message and brought them in for a landing right in front of the lights and veered around them into the dark entrance beyond. Lights from an unknown source lit up as they entered and they were shocked by the sheer size of this place. This one vast room dwarfed the grand cavern on the planet below. The general structure was the same, but it was so much larger.

The shuttle looked like a fly landing on an open table. It gently touched down on the granite floor. They checked the atmosphere and opened the hatch. Quinn gingerly stepped out of the shuttle and Margaret was right behind him, almost gripping his shoulder for support. They had just flown into this cave, and there were no doors or seals, yet the air in here was breathable and stable. They marveled again at the size of the place, and then Quinn wondered aloud. "I wonder what we do next." Lights in the floor lit up and directed them to an opening in the wall about 200 meters away. Margaret and Quinn looked at each other in amazement and then they shrugged their shoulders and followed the lights.

Aboard the *Lincoln* was not so peaceful. The damage control teams were working at a furious pace. The ship was nearly ready to depart, but there were personnel issues all over the ship. People were not where they were reported to be. They were being drawn into every handy repair, regardless of where they were actually sent. Authority had broken down into localized team leaders who recruited any talent that happened by. As a result, the repairs were continuing, but not at full efficiency. Almost everywhere, there was a state of panic. Not the least of which was the Captain himself. The bridge was on full alert. The moon had just sat there ominously in front of them and it was showing no sign of backing off. In fact, they would be doing so if they could, but repairs to the guidance system were still underway, and they couldn't be sure they wouldn't go forward into the moon if they made the attempt to back away. The computer systems were overloaded with maintenance requests. The ship had degraded into an assembly of autonomous sub parts, none of which could see the whole picture, and none of which were actually helping to squelch the din of panic that was raking its way across the ship.

The XO was doing his level best to keep the bridge under control without undermining the Captain's authority. It was a tightrope of power and responsibility he was walking, but he was an expert at this sort of diplomacy. For the most part, things were going forward, just not in the way he would have liked, or that he would have expected and demanded if he were in charge. But the Captain was not getting personally involved in the operations. He was simply complaining that progress was going too slow and barking useless orders at people who knew their jobs better than he did. A slight glimmer of contempt for the man entered his mind, and he forced it aside to keep it from getting in the way of doing his duty. He had just dispatched security to break up a maintenance crew that was interfering with the drive system while trying to fix a sub system that was redundant and non-essential. He shook his head at the ridiculousness of the situation, but he refocused and forced his mind back to the task. There was still much to do, and nobody knew how much time they had. He wanted to back the ship away as soon as possible, and his goals were in line with the task at hand.

What was probably the worst thing was that the crew knew that the XO was really the one in charge. They also knew that he would get them out of this mess if anyone could. The authority was switching away from the man in charge, and that was dangerous aboard a ship out all by itself like this. The XO did nothing to encourage this attitude except to be competent and relatively efficient. He wanted no part of the glory, and he wanted no part in any subversive action. But the facts were still the facts, and he kept the ship running as smoothly as he could.

The security team reached the maintenance personnel and shooed them away from the problem area and headed them off on another repair that the XO had put on a waiting list. At least the men were going to be too busy to wonder what was going on. The ship began to move in small spurts as the reaction drives tried to pull power and only partially succeeded. It was like trying to drive a stick shift without the benefit of a clutch pedal. The ship would lurch rearward and then bounce back, and then lurch again. The compensators were working overtime to try to keep the crew from being tossed from wall to wall. But there was movement and the important maintenance crew was busily fixing the drive system even as these small jerks and stops were tossing them around the unprotected drive bay. Using tether harnesses and magnetic boots, they were doing their best to repair the ailing drive. When the final connection was made, the ship threw the crew into the bulkhead as the ships engines came to life at full power. The bridge crew was thrown to the deck as well. Several injuries were reported across the ship, but at least they were backing away properly now. The helmsman got back into his seat and reduced the power to the drives and the ship idled down a bit and backed away at a much more reasonable rate. The XO was still radioing crews here and there to complete the repairs. He did not know precisely what system would be needed first in their encounters, but he was determined to get them all back up and running as quickly as possible. The effort across the ship was enormous and focused. The moon was falling away from them as the *Lincoln* backed gracefully away from it. The tension was bleeding out of the bridge crew and the Captain looked rather relieved as well.

The XO finished his batch of re-routing and sat back with a deep sigh of relief himself. He nodded to the Captain and found that the man actually nodded back. The thought of the man developing a knack for command seemed unthinkable, but it could happen. He decided to test it out later. Right now, he was too weary and there was still too much work to be done to rock the boat with doubts and tests.

***

8

Quinn and Margaret had been walking for quite some time. They were both footsore and they decided to stop and rest a moment. The lights had gone off into the distance as far as they could see for their entire journey. For all they new, this path went on in a grand circle that they could not detect, but that led them to nowhere. Of course why would someone take the time to light an endless corridor? After about ten minutes, they got back up and headed further along the path. It appeared to be some sort of test. Maybe the inhabitants wanted to see how the two humans would react. Quinn kept getting the white mouse in a maze feeling but he kept it to himself. Margaret looked pretty nervous and he didn't want to alarm her unnecessarily. They finally reached a doorway that stood some thirteen meters high and arced across a ten meter opening. The lights led them straight to it and they both looked at each other, and then back at the door. Quinn took a deep breath and stepped forward. Margaret followed closely behind him. This whole ordeal seemed to be weighing heavily upon her and she wanted the added security that Quinn seemed to provide by proximity alone. They crossed the threshold and the door sealed behind them. The rock just seemed to melt and slide down from the ceiling to seal the gap. It reformed almost immediately without the feeling of heat. Quinn marveled at the technology that he could not understand as he looked back at the door, and he turned at a sound from in front of them. A tall figure stood there, hands out stretched from its body. Quinn hoped it was a greeting. The being was obviously the type that the statues had been patterned after, only it had two arms instead of six.

Its bulbous head tilted towards the humans and a voice as smooth as silk seemed to fill their heads. "Welcome to our little piece of a once mighty empire." It said and there was a hint of amusement in the tone. Neither person had heard anything; it was planted directly in their minds. Margaret found the technique to be a bit unsettling, but Quinn took it all in stride.

He stepped forward and held his arms out at his sides as the creature had and nodded to the figure before him. "I thank you for your hospitality." He said, hoping that the being could hear his speech and understand it.

"I do hear your speech, but it is nonsense to me." The creature replied. "But your thoughts echo your voice and that I can understand. To be less confusing, please think your words instead of orating them." It instructed and Quinn nodded again.

Quinn looked at Margaret and wondered if she had heard the instruction as well, but she nodded to indicate that she had. He then turned back to their host. "I thank you for your advice. We are unfamiliar with your customs and we were hoping that you would enlighten us about yourselves as much as possible. I am an explorer and a diplomat for my people. I represent my people's government in matters of contact with other species or peoples like you. I bring greetings from the human race and I offer peace if you'll have it." Quinn thought as loudly as he could and the creature stepped forward and touched his forehead. Quinn flinched back a second but it was only a reaction of shock. There was no injury or damage, only surprise.

The being before him smiled as it read through his thoughts. "I can see that you are telling us the truth or at least the truth as you know it. It is good to know that there are such specimens of humankind like you who honor your words and back them up with actions if necessary. You see; we are a dying race. Our kind once ruled this galaxy, and several others, but now we are few and scattered. Our essence is but a ghost of its former glory. Still, we are bound by our laws to uphold some of our territories. I must admit that we have become lax without the manpower for fleets such as the one you belong to, but we endure through our technology and our gods. On the planet below, you have awakened

one of our gods. You already know the folly of trying to kill it.
That just makes its hunger all the more insatiable. We stepped in
to halt whatever activities you were involved in on that planet and
secure it for the god for all eternity." The thin alien man turned
and pointed to a wall and it became a glass-like substance and
then images displayed on it like a screen. It depicted the beast
being driven into the sealable room with short sticks that burned
when they touched the black cat. "We have remained vigilant
about our responsibilities to our gods and we are rewarded with
you. Somehow I don't think that's what the gods had in mind
for you, or us, but we have to follow the ancient texts to find out
what to do with you next." The thing turned back to Quinn and
the hapless human got the impression that the judgment had
just been decided against him. His nerves pulled taught as they
strained to contain his fury.

"You would condemn me for having released a beast from your
ancient past and you think that I am the one with the problem?
Boy you guys are messed up on this one. I can save you here, if
you will let me." Quinn said and the creature took a moment to
consider the comment. Quinn didn't wait for an answer. "Give
me the proper tools, and I will put that thing back in its cage. I
can handle the problem for you and everything will be as it was."
He finished and the creature craned his neck towards him trying
to determine what he was thinking.

After a moment it nodded again. "I see, you feel responsibility
for the creature's release and you think recapture is a proper
course of action. We agree that you hold responsibility for the
release, but the problem is ours, and ours alone. Once freed,
we do not think that the creature can be contained again. It has
grown much during its imprisonment and we may not be able to
hold it anymore. Your effort would be in vain. What is worse is
that the god seems to have centered its rage upon you. It has tried
to kill you more than once and we had not seen such devotion to
a single target like this before. It would be unwise for you to go
back down to the planet."

Margaret stepped up and added her thoughts to the
conversation. "He is right Quinn, I saw that thing looking at you

while you were unconscious. It had the red fire of hatred in its eyes, even while it appeared to be dying of multiple wounds. It could not wait to get up and attack you again." Margaret thought to the group. Surprising to Quinn, he heard her thoughts too. They must have been relaying her message to his mind as well as broadcasting their thoughts to him.

Quinn turned to her and smiled. "I believe that the creature, or god or whatever it is wants me dead because as the one who released it, it can sense I am the only one who can imprison it again. It is willing to destroy me to prevent that from happening." Quinn paused to let that sink in. "I really have to go down there and finish what I started. It is quite possible that no one else can do it. I sense that even you fear this god and it cannot be allowed to roam free, killing everything it comes across. Something must be done and I appear to be the only one to do it." Then Quinn thought about the archeologists who had disappeared down on the planet below. "Plus we have two missing men down there. The beast may have killed them, but if there is a chance to get them back, I owe it to them to make the attempt." He finished and the being before him stepped back a bit. It looked around and seemed to be talking to the walls. Within minutes, several more of the thin and graceful beings entered the room through doorways that melted open in the walls and then resealed after they had passed through.

"These are members of Gold squad. They are an elite force for violent problems. They will help you to find your friends. If you can put the god back in the room, they can reseal the vault and imprison it in there again. The god cannot be killed, but these warriors have the closest thing to it, they can paralyze the creature for a short time." The alien being pulled a baton from its waist belt and handed it to Quinn. "This is a driver. It is a high frequency device that will repel the god. It somehow causes the beast pain without actually damaging it. The team will be similarly armed, but they will also have protective shields that they can employ. Unfortunately they operate by broadcasting a wall of force from their minds, and you have demonstrated that your mind cannot perform this action so you will not be outfitted with one. It is probably for the better since the god would know you had it and may not come to you as bait. You will perform the given task more efficiently without one." The being rationalized and Quinn shook his head.

"Okay, have it your way, but we need to get down to the planet rather soon so we can save my men. Putting your god away should be the first priority and I think it will not take long to find it. As you say, it has a special interest in me. I plan to use it as well as I can to get the task over with quickly. Any delay could spell doom for those poor men down there. Is your team ready to go?" He asked

The group of aliens came to attention; at least it was the closest thing that Quinn could call it. He heard all of their thoughts at once as they announced their readiness to proceed. It was confusing, listening to all of those voices at once, but he got the general feel of the emotions behind it and he was satisfied with the resulting message. "Very well, then we should leave now then."

"We might have trouble fitting your team in our shuttle, but they are welcome to come if you do not have transport for them." Margaret offered.

"We have our own means of transportation; we do not require the metal boxes you use to get around in. Please follow our warriors and they will lead you to the transport device." The being said and it gestured towards a section of wall that was currently melting a new opening.

Quinn and Margaret looked at each other. Then they shrugged their shoulders and followed the warriors into the newly formed doorway and stepped into a semi-round chamber with quartz walls and a shimmering floor that looked like a pool of mercury. The beings stepped out onto the floor and it supported them so the two humans followed suit. Sure enough, the surface was liquid, but it was not very deep and they all stepped into the room. The wall sealed up behind them again and then the warriors drew a knife each and held it in the air. "To success and honor" They exclaimed and Quinn and Margaret echoed their sentiments. Quinn held up the driver device and Margaret just held up her fist. She had a standard issue sidearm, but she felt it would be a problem if she drew it here. There was no sense in provoking these aliens when they appeared to be on the same side at the moment.

The floor shimmered and the wall before them took on the image of the doorway with the destroyed statues. The image was high resolution and the colors looked so real that you felt you could reach out and touch the rock-face. Then the startling thing happened. The warriors stepped into the image! Quinn quickly recovered and stepped after them, pulling Margaret with him. They stepped off of the wet floor and out onto the patchy grass and dirt they both recognized as the entrance to the cavernous Jeng base. The warriors looked around and found nothing threatening around them so they entered the complex. Quinn decided not to enter just yet. He had his driver in his hand and he was ready to draw this god of theirs back to his prison lair. Margaret stood by his side, slightly back, waiting for the beast to appear too. It wasn't long before they saw it bounding towards them. It was covering a lot of ground quickly. It had grown in size and was nearly twenty meters long now to the tip of its tail. Its massive muscular legs thrust it forward like a freight train. Small trees were blown apart as the creature ignored them in its hate-crazed run. Quinn held out the driver, but he doubted that it would really help the situation much. Margaret had drawn her pistol and she was busily adjusting the power settings up to their maximum setting. She leveled the gun and waited until the target closed in. The driver device in Quinn's hand began to vibrate. It was a smooth tingly feeling at first, but it grew in intensity until he could feel his forearm falling asleep. He had trouble keeping the thing in his grasp as his hand went limp. He ripped a piece off of his shirt and tied his hand closed around the vibrating baton. The creature could feel the pain that was being transmitted to it, but its maddening rage empowered it to continue towards the target of its hate. The cat hit a clump of bushes and uprooted them as it started the final pounce onto this puny man-thing. With his arm out of commission, the device thumped against Quinn's leg and it fell asleep. He toppled over without its support and the cat sailed over his head as Margaret let the full energy pack loose into the creature's side. The howling god screeched and slammed into the ground rather ungracefully. It had an open wound nearly 120 centimeters long down its side and it was losing a lot of blood. But they had both seen this creature in this condition before. The hating red eyes were still locked on Quinn. Margaret untied the driver from his hand and dropped it to the side. The feeling began to return and she helped Quinn into the complex. The warriors were inside, destroying the many control panels in the great complex.

Quinn shouted at them and they all froze in place. All of a sudden the situation clicked in his mind. Duane had told him that all they had ever found was destroyed artifacts. The Jeng were not a dead race, they just cleaned up their messes so that no one could get a hold of their technology. The betrayal ran deep and Quinn was ready to attack when the beast limped into the doorway. The warriors swung towards it and brandished nasty looking blades on long pikes. Neither human could tell where they had gotten them. Or for that matter, where had the bizarre hammers come from that they had been smashing the equipment with? Quinn and Margaret were both forced to face the beast and they readied for an attack when they saw the beast cower away from the pikes. It still had that gaping wound in its side and it was losing blood at a catastrophic rate. But its hatred kept it trained on Quinn. Margaret popped in another battery pack and leveled the gun at the beast again. But before she could pull the trigger, a Jeng warrior leapt into the fray and sliced a paw off of the beast with its razor sharp blade. The staff swung around in a fluid motion as the merciless fighter lopped off another front paw and the beast collapsed forward onto its face, howling in pain and surprise. The beast was only partially helpless though. It grabbed the Jeng man with its middle paws and its rear claws raked the warrior mercilessly. The cat tossed him aside and he went down with a scream of his own. His innards spilled out onto the floor, as his abdomen had been ripped open from side to side. The weapon fell harmlessly to the floor and the creature writhed again as the paw began to retrace its path back to the cat. Quinn knew that the thing didn't have much of a chance if the other Jeng attacked in unison, but they didn't. He was confused at first, but he watched as another warrior jumped into the fray and singly battled the beast until he had also been killed. The cat was in pretty bad shape though. Its pitiful moan and curses were difficult on the ears to say the least. Margaret looked at the equipment and she saw that most of what they had found was now in crumbling ruins. She leveled her gun at the remaining Jeng warrior and fired. The blast caught the unsuspecting man under his right arm and he fell over with a noisy flapping sound as he hit the cold stone floor. The Jeng tried to claw at the wound, but shock was setting in and his movements became slow and meaningless. He passed out on the floor, glaring at the human woman with those same red eyes that the beast had used for Quinn. Quinn walked back into the cave and stopped just inside the doorway to the stone cage. Margaret got out of sight of the beast and waited. She popped in her last battery pack. She dropped the power to half to allow her an extra shot. She hoped it would not be necessary.

It wasn't long before the beast pulled itself into the cavernous room. It was still bleeding profusely, but it had reattached its paws now. The cat had a will of iron and it was determined to kill this small creature before it could put him back in that detestable prison. Killing those jailers had only been a bonus. The beast was only focused on maintaining his freedom. What was one more life to the eternity of carnage he would cause over the ages? Surely no one would miss this little one. The scent was near and his prey was very close. He could sense the fear too. There was more than one source of the addictive smell of fear. He maintained his focus on the target. The male creature must die. The hatred welled up inside the god cat and his eyes fired up red again. The rage gave him more strength and each step was easier than the one before it. The hate built even higher and now the walk was almost pleasant. The wound in his side was healing, and he had already tasted blood this day. This was going to be a day he long remembered. He would win his freedom and bring the galaxy back to submission under his will alone. The dark god would sink his sharp teeth into any who opposed him. It all began with this insignificant human creature. It was almost laughable to the god, but still the facts remained. The moment of freedom was at hand. Just through this small portal and the death would be swift, almost anti-climactic, but he would savor the moment just the same. A few steps more and…

Quinn saw the beast entering the room. It was focused on finding him. He guessed that it would be using the sense of smell to accomplish its hunting goals. The small fan had blown his scent into the room, even though he was just outside of it on the far side. This was Quinn's ace-in-the-hole, and it was almost his last card in this deadly game of cat and mouse. He did not misunderstand his role in this thing as the mouse. The fear he felt was real. He hoped that Margaret would be able to remain calm and collected. He had guessed that she would. The moment was close and then the beast realized where it was and it wailed. It turned to bound back out of the hated chamber but Quinn had finished reading the runes backwards and the stone began to melt back together. Quinn tossed the driver into the remaining hole and it struck the beast and dazed it for a moment. But it was a precious moment that Quinn needed to complete the seal. The door formed in front of the god and it hissed violently. Its worst fear was realized in that instant and just before it was totally trapped, it let out the most hideous and pitiful howl. That tortured sound would haunt Quinn and Margaret probably for the rest of their lives. Then the runes disappeared and the wall was once again solid. After the echoes of the sound died away, Quinn's breathing was returning to normal. Margaret came out of the shadows and holstered her pistol. She was looking a little ragged, but it was mostly from worry. The beast had not even noticed her, or at least if it did, it did not show it.

There was a groan and Quinn and Margaret rushed over to the fallen Jeng warrior. He was still alive, and maybe it was time to get some answers. Margaret put a patch on his wound, it would not make it heal any faster, but it would prevent some of the blood loss that was killing the alien man. Quinn started formulating his questions while the man recovered somewhat.

Aboard the Jeng moon, the commander watched the team as they entered the complex. As he had ordered, they immediately started destroying the equipment so that it could not fall into the wrong hands. Then, as he watched, the humans came into the chamber, and the male was hurt. Could it be possible it had already made contact with the god? Of course the humans were not happy about the destruction and the commander ordered a temporary cessation of the activity. Then the horror began. The god had entered the chamber and the honor-bound warriors began to challenge it for supremacy. Each man caused its own share of damage to the god, but in the end they failed to contain its rage. The foul human female struck down one of our warriors and he would now be denied his chance at honor. It was a pity, but how could these savage beings understand true honor. At least the man would die and no Jeng secrets would be revealed. Then the unheard of happened. The humans lured the god into the capture vault and then they sealed the god inside. It howled in rage and agony as it was re-condemned to a life of solitary confinement. Part of the commander ached at the injustice to such an exalted being brought down by these backward savage people, but he also saw it as a necessary evil. The dark god would have killed everything on the planet if it had been allowed to run free.

The commander watched as the doorway opened before him. Reinforcements had been called for when the god entered the cavern. Now they would not be used to contain the beast, instead they would eliminate the security threat the humans posed. He opened the portal room and sent the ten new warriors through. They were each outfitted with a blade and a shield. It was the honorable configuration for a holy warrior. The humans might disable one or two, but there was no way they could best the entire group. This planet would soon be re-secured and the Jeng would move on to the next one and set up their new base.

Life aboard the *Lincoln* had calmed down somewhat. The repairs were completed and the ship was now more operational that it had been almost since it had first been launched. The maintenance crews were able to stand down and get some much-needed rest. The XO was positively gleaming with the condition of the vessel. The Captain was in a fit of depression over the loss of the planet that had held the profitable diamonds he longed for. He was almost lost to it, but a spark still remained. The spark was a small fire that burned inside him and ignited the depression and turned it into hatred. He sought vengeance on these Jeng and their damnable moon, obscuring his view of the planet. It was *his* planet after all. He had brought this survey mission here; they had abandoned it and left their toys behind. It was not his fault that they failed to find the wealth inside their discarded property. He was an ambitious man and he had dreams of striking it rich with planets just like this one. The colony would just be butter on the toast. His future would be secure with a few like this one under his belt. It was not fair that the nasty beings still existed. They were supposed to be just myth or legend. He made a decision and he startled the bridge crew with his decisive orders. "Plot a course back to HQ, I want to get a strike fleet and come take this planet back." He said and the crew jumped to comply with his order.

The XO was shocked for a moment. This man wasn't capable of such directness. He never shared his intentions with the crew either for that matter. Maybe something inside was waking up after being buried in financial dreams and political fervor. The XO decided that this man might become dangerous. He started making plans of his own.

Meanwhile on the XO's terminal, personnel lists were coming through and he noticed that the survey man Ramses, and that blasted pilot woman were missing. He checked the logs and noted that the older shuttle was missing. He easily put two and two together and came up with trouble. That lieutenant from survey was a master at first contact situations and he could bring the Jeng around to their side if this Captain did not bring a shooting match down on them first. There must be some way to delay this violent lunatic before a galactic war broke out. He had to order those maintenance crews to get back up and start slowly sabotaging equipment under the guise of scheduled maintenance requests and planned outages. He had better weave this web of delay and deceit carefully lest the quarry get wise to the trap and avoid it somehow. He was not comfortable enough to smile just yet, but he saw the potential if this Quinn came through with another miraculous treaty. Surely the risks he was taking were completely justified. High command wouldn't fry him for insubordination if he were pivotal in the success for this mission and a benefit to the fleet as a whole. He mentally crossed his fingers that the rationalization would hold under court conditions and he sent his next batch of orders over the computer to the terminals of the personnel they involved. It was amazing how quickly things could develop on a modern day starship.

Margaret had stabilized the Jeng warrior and Quinn was just about to start thinking questions at the man when the strike troops arrived. Ten warriors stepped into the room and they had business on their minds. They advanced with weapons drawn and each held a predatory stance as they eyed the two humans. Quinn stepped back from the fallen man and Margaret drew her pistol with startling speed that would have made Wyatt Earp proud. She brought the weapon up and fired. The shot struck the lead warrior in the chest and it exploded out his back, spraying gore across the face of the second man. With weapons drawn, the sword-wielding aliens advanced in an intricate dance of death. The humans looked to be done for. Margaret had only one shot left, and Quinn was busily trying to access his personal computer to get a transmission to the *Lincoln*. He knew they could not get here in time to save the two unfortunate humans from slaughter, but they could possibly get here fast enough to recover some of the Jeng equipment before these warriors could smash it all to uselessness. Quinn was prepared to make that kind of sacrifice for the good of mankind. But Margaret wasn't, she fired at the ceiling and brought down a huge chunk of rock. Three warriors were caught unaware and were crushed by the falling debris. The warriors looked at each other and the six remaining men reformed into another formation, a kind of a V and they advanced again. Margaret threw the gun, it was empty and useless now, and it bounced harmlessly off of one of the warriors' shoulders. She ran back towards the rear of the cave and she stopped at the doorway that held the cat beast inside. She could not read the runes, so she could not open it, but Quinn could. She called to him and he abandoned his attempts. The *Lincoln* was not answering. It was possible that they were still having technical difficulties and they didn't receive his message, or maybe they did get it but couldn't reply. He hoped it was one of those situations, because the alternative was that they were not there anymore. They would either have left, or they would have been destroyed. He did not like the odds in either of those choices. He ran to catch up with Margaret and was surprised to see her at the cage vault. The runes were back on the doorway and he could hear the blades behind him singing through the air as the warriors marched slowly forward each carving their intricate patterns in the air before them. He had seen these types of exercises in the past. Martial artists often performed these rituals before a fight. Sometimes it was to appease the gods for their wisdom in giving man the art form that they practiced. Other times, it was purely a matter of honor and protocol. In either case, he was pretty sure that they were going to die here. But that is when the survey crewmen were at their best, when life and death was on the line. He quickly scanned the runes and started reading them aloud.

The warriors halted their steps at hearing their language from the human's lips. They knew that something was amiss, but honor dictated that they complete their ritual before they can slay these intruders. They continued their slow advance. Although it seemed they were executing the moves a little faster now. It would still be another minute or so before they could charge and cover the rest of the ground to their prey.

Quinn finished the phrase and the stone melted away the door again. The dark cat god stood there, watching him. Its hatred had returned, but now there was surprise as well. He had not expected release. At least if he was released, he did not expect it to be this same creature. The beast stepped forward out of the hated prison and the warriors froze again. They knew they were in trouble. They switched formations so that one man at a time could advance on the beast and then they did as the others before them had done. They each died against the beast in a one on one fight. The cat was wounded in a couple of places, but it had had that before and it had always lived. It would do so again.

Quinn and Margaret watched the cat as it finished off the last warrior and then lay down next to the bodies. It was some sort of ritual that the cat's instincts told it to perform. There was much about this culture that Quinn failed to understand, but some of it was coming to the surface of his brain now. They were linked, the god and his people. They were both caught up in some sort of code of honor that they valued even more highly than their own lives. Quinn understood honor, it was linked in his mind with personal integrity. He valued that in any being, and he was sorry to see these Jeng were killed for doing their duty even though their defeat had been to the benefit of the humans. He looked at the cat lying on the floor, lamenting for the lost souls it had just killed and he felt sick to his stomach. He stepped over to the gruesome scene and sat down on a clear patch of floor. He locked eyes with the beast and thought two words to it. "I'm sorry."

The cat raised its head and its eyes lost the red glow of hatred and a beautiful yellow shone through like gold in this low light. It really was a majestic beast. It was also in pain. The physical wounds didn't seem to bother it at all, but the emotional scars cut deep. It had killed some of its subjects. The bloodlust had been brought on by pure hatred and vengeance. Now it was calm and full of sorrow. Quinn realized that this animal, or god, or whatever it was would have to live with this emotion for an eternity. His grief was mounting and the large black cat inched forward and placed a massive paw on his thigh. It was an act of comforting and tears formed in Quinn's eyes as he stroked the muscular neck and listened to the low rumbling purr of the giant beast. It was a moment of shared pain and the bond was thick and deep. Margaret was amazed at the whole spectacle but she remained silent. She was afraid that to break the moment would spell the end of young Lieutenant Quinn Ramses, and she liked him a bit too much to watch him die because she couldn't keep her mouth shut. The moment continued to stretch out and it was just over an hour when the two stood up. The huge black cat and the tiny human stood side by side and they stepped from the cave and out into the sunlight. It was almost sundown. The hues of the amber light mixed with the clouds making a whole spectrum of violets and oranges painted across the horizon. It was breathtaking as the sun finally touched the water and Quinn imagined that it sizzled. They watched it together until the sun disappeared and the darkness spread across the small landmass. The stars came out one by one and soon the entire sky was dotted with the mystical lights. The cat felt good. The ocean breeze was slightly chilling, but its fur only felt the pressure, not the temperature. It thought a message to Quinn and his mouth dropped open at the statement.

"Follow me to your comrades." It thought and then headed off across the grassy field. Quinn jogged behind and the cooler air was quite refreshing. He could hear the surf in the distance and the powerful animal before him would make sure that nothing sinister got in his way. He was practically carefree, except for worry over the two archeologists they were going to meet. He had considered them lost forever, it was a great relief when he entered the cave and saw the two men cowering from the cat. He stepped alongside the great creature and stroked its back. The cat nuzzled its massive head against Quinn's side and he stroked it approvingly. The two scared men turned from fright to shock. Then they were all smiles when they realized that they were being freed. The whole group headed back to the Jeng base and Margaret was waiting for them with some food packs. It was some of the stuff that they had abandoned before and she had recovered some battery packs as well. Maybe their communications equipment would work a while longer. When all of the humans were safely back to the base, the cat broadcast a good-bye to them all and left, heading out into the grass. It made amazing time as it bounded for the trees. When it got there, Quinn felt a deep satisfaction. He wasn't sure if it was his own feeling, or one from the cat itself. He decided he didn't care which. They could share this emotion and he would savor it for a long time.

She reported that the wounded Jeng had died, and that the equipment had all dissolved into solid stone again. It must have had some kind of remote destruct sequence or even a self-destruct that had somehow been triggered. These Jeng really valued their secrecy. She wondered what Duane would have made of it all, but she may never know. Duane was back on the *Lincoln* and they were not in contact with the ship now. In fact, they were without their shuttle as well. It looked like they were going to make their new home on this world. Margaret looked around and decided that there were definitely worse places to be marooned. After all, they had shelter in the form of an impregnable cave, and the natural surroundings were bound to supply a food source somehow. It was only a matter of time before someone would come along. The *Lincoln* did know that this planet existed. The Captain also knew that there were gems here. As long as the ship survived, they would surely get a ship sometime to pick them up. That wasn't too much of a problem in her mind. It looked to be more of a problem for Quinn. He was pacing the cave entrance. His hand was rubbing the stone, as if he could feel something in it that no one else did. She decided to just let him have his space for a while. They had plenty of time together; she could afford to wait a bit.

The *Lincoln* cruised through space and entered the home system on the outer rings of the traffic cycle. Communications were immediately established with the planet and the helmsman was directed which course to take into the system and what orbit to assume once they had arrived. The Captain stood on the bridge. His seat had become uncomfortable for him and he was ready to order it replaced. Of course, the seat itself hadn't changed, only the recognition of responsibility made it seem hard and unforgiving. He was still ready to have it replaced; it was a vain hope that somehow the change would restore his comfortable ignorance. The Captain was at a point of growth that he had avoided for a long time.

The XO was ready for whatever the Captain was planning. He had plans within plans, and backup plans for even these. But he did not know what was going on in the man's mind. He seemed to have been changed by recent events and it seemed that change was a good thing. The man was focused and alert. There were fewer things delegated to the XO. It all caused a murmur of panic as the XO felt his grip on the control of this vessel slip. If the Captain came around and became a leader, he would no longer be needed here. Or at least he would have a lot less power here. He was comfortable with power. He enjoyed it. He sucked it up like a liquid candy that was addictive unto death. "That crazy Captain had better not find a heart now." He thought to himself. He would just have to sit back and watch this man. If he had become dangerous, there would be additional plans to make. He was so good at making plans. He just needed someone to carry those plans out and life would be perfect.

The Captain left the XO in charge and headed to his quarters. He had started preparing a report of what was found, and the apparent solution to the fleet's trouble. If there was a situation out there that could help him, he hoped it would surface. He wanted that planet, and he wanted the Jeng to know who had defeated them. It was mostly an issue of vanity. He was convinced that the planet could be colonized, and he would also like some of the profit from the Jeng discovery, but he recognized that the existence of the Jeng only complicated matters as far as the fleet was concerned. If the race was truly around after all of these years, then they were sharing space with them. The unstoppable technology would interest high command and he was ready to get a report to them about exactly that. He was just getting his last notes down when the chime to his door rang. He called out "Enter."

The communications officer stepped into the cabin and saluted. The Captain weakly returned the salute and took the pad that was offered. It was a transcript of all the communications between the *Lincoln* and the small moon that materialized in front of them. He would add pieces of this document to his own report, especially the stuff that supported his arguments to colonize the planet. If the aliens did not want them there, then there was something there that they wished to hide. There was more to that ball of water than what met the eye. He was certain there was something there to sink his teeth into, and thus expand his bank accounts. This situation was salvageable yet. It was too bad he had not yet heard from that blasted Lieutenant before having to leave the system. An update might have proved invaluable in his report. They would be returning to the system without the reconnaissance that Quinn could have provided if he had been a team player. It hadn't been reported until after the repairs were completed that the two crewmen had escaped. He expected something wild from the survey crewman, but Margaret's defection struck him hard. He knew that she had been under the wing of the XO. This sort of thing reflected badly on the commanding officer, and he was sure to push some of the blame onto the XO for this betrayal. Still, the situation was salvageable. If they turned out to actually find something or be beneficial, he can always say that he had sent them undercover into the heart of the Jeng forces. One never knows when it will be important to be observed taking risks in the name of the fleet. He was sure to pounce on anything that might further his career and thus his opportunities for profit. The Captain looked up from his thoughts and noticed that the communications officer was still standing there. "Thank you for this report; you are dismissed." He said and she snapped a salute and withdrew with military speed and precision. After the hatch had closed behind her, the Captain wondered what made officers act like that. She was too perky and somewhat too efficient. He had seen the type before and it always made him wonder what inspires one to act that way. Life was too precious to waste it running to and fro in the name of duty. He simply shrugged his shoulders and went back to his notes for some last minute data. He can let those *motivated* fools do all the work.

The admiralty had always liked to station men close to them that they did not trust until they proved to be harmless and then they tended to send them far away. They could keep a closer eye on them until that determination was made that way. Just such an officer was Sherman Ratledge. He was an aged man by most standards. He had served in the Fleet for more than forty years and he had never been stationed more than a system away from headquarters. He was passed up for promotion more than once for not being placeable by the upper echelon of the military service. Of course they had not been bold enough to come out and say that. There was always a legitimate reason to keep him close under the watchful eye of his superiors. He had commanded smaller craft and he was a good pilot himself. Unfortunately, he was not good with personnel problems. It seemed ironic that he was put in charge of personnel when he was elevated to his present post. He took the job with trepidation for he knew that it was not his specialty. He was an organized person with some mathematical genius, but no social skills whatever. There was never a tactical or organizational problem that he could not overcome. He felt that he was being wasted in this capacity, and it was turning him bitter. Three years he had spent looking over compatibility charts and selecting people to put on ships so that they would not cause problems with the rest of those ship's crewmembers. It was a tedious task, and to his credit he was doing a remarkable job. But he wanted to command a fleet in space. He wanted to bask on the glory of a true military hero. He wanted, well it didn't matter what he wanted. The admirals around him were not going to let him do those grand things. He would continue to write reports and throw darts and assign people across the galaxy. Each time he wished he was reassigning himself. But here he has stayed for over three years. Now he was sent to meet with some Captain about possible alien contact. It would be something if this alien race existed, but the one mentioned in the report had to be a joke or a mistake. The Jeng were long ago extinct. They had found countless artifacts and ruins scattered across the quadrant to prove that they had once existed. But there was not even a thread of evidence to suggest that they were still around and active. He prepared to meet this man and at least find out which one of his superiors had set him up like this. He sat in the transit corridor and waited for the prankster to arrive.

९

Quinn had settled down after a while and then he switched over to business mode. He was making plans and diagrams. He was using an old fashioned pen and some paper to make his diagrams for the others to follow. When he finished, he asked for the two archeologists to inspect his work. Both men were surprised at the depth of the plans he had envisioned and they were instantly excited at the prospects before them. Quinn had laid out a plan for rescue. They were to make a beacon to radio into space. They had some small battery packs and his wrist radio. They would need to supply more power than that to accomplish the goal. Next he had laid out plans to make a wall to protect the island from other Jeng attacks. He wanted alarms and sensors installed everywhere on this island so that if they came, there would be some notice before they were at his throat. Finally, he had come up with some rudimentary weapons designs and he wanted them manufactured last. He felt to focus on the weaponry before the security of their defenses might disenchant his people and that they could not afford right now.

The first problem was power. They decided to check out the ruined shuttle and see what they could scavenge. They had a really short shopping list, so it was not too difficult to find some useful stuff. They broke apart some basic metal plating for noise making devices in manual alarm systems. There was cord and Margaret found a basic tool set. There was even a handheld cutting torch inside it. They began taking the shuttle apart systematically and soon there was nothing left but the inner skeleton. The exposed ribcage of the cargo section of the once proud little ship shone in the sunlight. It was almost sad, but they hauled their booty back to the cave. Once there, they started categorizing the parts and soon the two archeologists were busily manufacturing a radio set from one that had been damaged aboard the shuttle. Quinn decided to just let them go with that project. He was more interested in getting the alarms systems in place. The Jeng could turn up at any time with that teleport wall of theirs. He wanted to have some rudimentary systems in place before they had to break for sleep.

Fortunately for Quinn, he had logged some mission time on a backwater world that had an aboriginal native species on it. He knew how to make spiked sticks and rope into lethal traps. He started a staggered ring of traps around the complex. He set snares and spring traps and the edge of the forest would get a whole set of specialty traps based on the wooded coverage. The sun was in the mid-afternoon position when he cut the final tie on the inner ring of traps. He was never one to shrug off work, but he felt exhausted to the bone. The others were looking pretty worn out too. Margaret had gathered vines and sticks and she had been using a survival knife to cut and whittle them into whatever Quinn needed next. Here hands ached with the effort, and muscle cramps were plaguing her. She never complained though, but Quinn could tell she was hurting. With the inner ring in place, he was ready to let them sleep, at least in shifts. The archeologists were still working on their radio, and they were not ready to quit just yet, so Quinn and Margaret picked spots away from the entrance and they laid down on the survival blankets from the shuttle. They were thin, but they would maintain body temperature with minimal effort. As tired as they both were, it was not long before they were both out cold. The two men hardly even noticed them in their excitement at the task before them.

There was still a lot to do, but with progress being made everyone felt a little better. After a few short hours, the two scientific men felt the fatigue catch up with them. They strolled into the main chamber and saw their comrades asleep. They lay down near them and drifted off to sleep themselves. It was not what Quinn would have wanted, and they somehow failed to realize that. Darkness had swept over the countryside, and a cool wind was blowing from the shoreline.

The beast looked at the cave and its mind raced with the possibilities. Was the little creature going to try to recapture it, or was it truly free at last? There was no way to know for sure. The cat-god decided to check out the small creature and ask it what its intentions were. One could not be too careful when eternity was involved. It crept up to the cave and the sounds of sleeping reached its sensitive ears. The cat smiled in spite of itself. "This was going to be easier than it should be." It rumbled in its own language. It leapt up into the opening and slid to a stop. No one attacked it, nor did anyone even notice the big cat as it padded its way into the compound and up to the small creatures. It breathed heavily as the danger level was high and its nerves were sending spasms of panic into its system. It ignored the prompting with an iron will and advanced over to where Quinn was lying down. It felt his breathing as his chest slowly rose and fell. The thing was so peaceful the great cat did not want to disturb it, but it also had a purpose here. It nudged Quinn with its nose and he reflexively pushed the head away from his arm and rolled over. Then, amused, the god-cat put its heavy paw on Quinn's back. Quinn's eyes opened as he realized what was happening. Fear took him as he slowly rolled over to see the yellow eyes of the great cat mere inches from his face.

The mighty cat sent its thoughts into Quinn's brain. "Relax, I am not here to kill you." It said in that silvery voice that could not be heard. Quinn sat up and it was obvious that he was confused. The cat tried to explain. "I need to know what you plan to do. Do you plan to seal the chamber where I am kept?" It asked and Quinn shook his head no. The beast was a little surprised. "Do you plan to seal the main chamber and leave?" and this time a shake or nod would not do.

Quinn considered his position and finally he thought the answer to the cat-god before him. "I hope to be rescued and to leave this place. But we will probably not seal the chamber unless you ask for it to be sealed. There is much we can learn from its creators and we would like to plant people on this world for ours is too full and cannot hold everyone on it." He replied and the cat thought about it for a long moment before continuing.

"If you plant your people here, then you must seal this chamber first. If the Jeng find out that you are here, they will be back. They are extremely xenophobic. They will destroy anyone or anything that does not belong and they will protect their own secrets without regard for life and limb. The only way to ensure they do not come for you is to seal the chamber." The cat lay down next to Quinn and its eyes were level with his. The creature had grown again. He didn't want to know what it had eaten this time. He admitted to himself that the thought of not having anymore of those giant centipedes at the beach sounded good to him.

"Does this require us to lose all of this possible technology?" He asked. "We need this stuff in order to defend ourselves from the Jeng. My people would regard this information highly and if we seal it off, it would not go good for us back at home. We could be cut off from the fleet entirely and without their assistance, our future here is uncertain at best. If the population grows beyond the landmass's ability to support, we may not have the capability to colonize the oceans without the fleet's help." He turned to the cat-god and smiled. He saw it thinking about his words.

The cat lowered its head onto its paws and thought for a moment more and then responded with a question of its own. "Why would humans decide to colonize such a hostile environment as the oceans? You are unsuited for life underwater. Your frail bodies will die easily in the pressures of the oceans depths, not to mention the problem of circulating air to breathe." It finished and its eyes showed concern.

Quinn laughed, but it was a good-natured laugh and the cat waited for him to finish for its response. "Living under the water is no more difficult than living in the vacuum of space. We must produce our own air and gravity there as well. It is just a minor change of equipment for the immense pressures involved. I think we could make this world thrive again." He finished philosophically.

The cat purred its low rumbling purr and its eyes closed. Then Quinn heard the cat's mind again. "I am glad that you have come here. Not only have you released me from my prison of many centuries, but also you have a different perspective than the Jeng about life and the workings of the universe. It is refreshing for me not to know what you are thinking all the time. I also find that I like you. I don't have a logical explanation for why, but I am comfortable around you and that is saying something for a being like me. I am usually feared and attacked by creatures such as you, but now I sense the curiosity and wonderment you harbor in your mind, and I like the flavor of it. These are qualities we share and I am happy to have you here. If you believe that this world can support large amounts of your people here, then I am sure it will be so. I only hope that my hunting grounds are allowed to persist, or I may have to turn to a less cultured means of sustenance. That would be unfortunate at best. It usually creates a social barrier between us, as hunter and prey are separate. But they are also linked in a tighter, more basic level that few can appreciate. However you decide to proceed, it shall be as you command."

Quinn stroked the massive back and the cat rolled a bit to turn a particular spot towards the attention. "I appreciate your support. I am sure that we can set aside a piece of land for you to hunt on. Anyone who would violate the reserve would risk summary eating by you, and thus we shall maintain control." He scratched the great cat behind the ears and was rewarded with an even louder purr. It was almost loud enough to vibrate a cup of coffee off of the table. "I like you as well." Quinn added and the two of them settled down for some quality bonding time. The other humans, the ones that were supposedly on duty, slept unaware of the welcome intruder. There was still a lot to do.

10

The headquarters conference room was empty today. Ratledge had reserved the spacious room for the entire day and he was bound and determined to use it to look important to this visiting ship's captain. He had the seats arranged so that he could sit higher than the rest of the attendees on a small dais in front of the main seating area. From there he would listen and decide the fates of these little people. It was so much of a burden to have to listen to them first before sending them away, but protocols were protocols and he was anxious to get this ordeal over with and get back to his favorite pastime, loafing around collecting credits for his inefficiencies. The chronometer on the wall told him that the man should arrive within the next ten minutes, if he were late then there would be a reason to flay a strip of his hide off for good measure. He contemplated the thought for a moment and then the door opened. He was a little disappointed to see that it was indeed this captain who was trying to gain a greater audience. The Captain crossed the expansive room and he didn't even glance at the lavish interior. He remained focused on his goal. He was staring directly at Ratledge, and he was ready for a direct intervention from his fleet government. Ratledge doubted that there was even a situation serious enough to make him advise this man about fleet matters. He almost forced a yawn, but that would have been too over the top. He instead kept a bored stare going as the man came closer and sat down in the proffered chair.

Ratledge began with a pompous attitude that dripped contempt as he rose and spoke. "Before you begin, I must inform you that you are in breech of fleet protocol demanding a meeting like this.

My schedule is quite full already without your sniveling demands for attention. Now, that being said, what is so important as to bring you back home during an important mission such as yours?" Ratledge glared at the Captain as if his very gaze could make the man burst into flame. After a brief pause, he continued, but he was already beyond his normal measure of patience. "Now, if you please, I haven't got all day."

The Captain cleared his throat and stood up. "Sir, if you will please, I have important news for the fleet and I believe you will find that I am quite justified in requesting this meeting. I do note, however, that it is a breech of normal etiquette and for that I humbly apologize. But I do stand by my decision to call it nevertheless." He paused for dramatic effect while Ratledge raised his eyebrows at the potential impertinence. "You are aware of the findings of ruins and artifacts from a long lost race called the Jeng?" He asked and Ratledge nodded that he had heard of such things. "Well sir, I have been in contact with a living representative of the Jeng. They ordered me to evacuate the planet that we were surveying. However, their warnings came after I had put a team on the planet and found a remarkable discovery. They have an active base with working equipment in place on that world. My reports are on file here sir." The Captain said while laying a data pad on the table. "I believe that you may want to consult with some higher authority about the possibility of deploying more ships to aid me in securing this planet. The possible ramifications could be astounding. We could potentially add to our own technology base, and we could also be alerted to a threat that has gone unseen for centuries under our own noses." The Captain sat back down, and crossed his legs. Then he leaned back in the chair to a more comfortable position. The very move dripped contempt back at Ratledge. "Perhaps you need some time to make your decision. I will wait here while you go and consult with your bosses over what to do." He finished and Ratledge actually flinched at the insult.

The Admiral took a brief moment to collect himself and then he brought that aristocratic superior attitude back over his face and left the room. His spine was ramrod straight, and his ego was recovering. He went to the adjutant's office and read the report in full. Line after line, the data was empowering. This lowly Captain had indeed discovered an outpost of this mysterious Jeng. When he read the particulars he noticed the name of Quinn Ramses and then it clicked in his mind how this had all been accomplished. Quinn was a star in the first encounters universe and he was surely guiding this imbecile to greatness. Who knew for what reason, but who cared. This discovery could change the whole of the fleet for either good or bad, they did not want to go to war with an unknown force, nor did they want to pass up this opportunity for learning and advancement. For all of his faults, that Captain had been right; this decision was too big for Ratledge to make. He commed his boss and requested an audience with the committee on Fleet Affairs. It was highly unusual, but he believed that the ends justified the shifting of schedules and other headaches this would cause. He was certain that this data was worth their precious time. He knew that he was not liked in the admiralty, but he felt that this was too important for them to be petty about such things now. Plus he hoped that somehow this could help him redeem himself among them. Maybe he would get to command a small fleet to go and meet these Jeng. He knew that the dream had been far-fetched, but he had not given any specific time to dreaming of late, and now that this one rose unbeckoned into his psyche, he felt it was a good sign. He was surprised when the replies back were all favorable. He had not expected a positive reaction. He had imagined having to drag them into the meeting, gripping them by the brass on their collars and shaming them into attendance. Now it was looking almost effortless as the meeting time was set up and he punched the confirm button on each one. Then he raced back down to the briefing room to catch up with this miserable Captain from the *Lincoln*. Just before opening the door, he straightened out the front of his uniform and then he regained his decorum. He strolled into the room with his dignity intact and smiled curtly at the lounging man in the comfortable chair. In the back of his mind he wondered if this had been the only man to ever sit in that chair the way the manufacturer had probably intended in the first place. The thought colored his opinion of the man a little rosy. Somehow the Captain felt the change as if a light had lit Ratledge's forehead.

The Captain did not even shift his weight towards any kind of good posture. He looked up and smiled. "Are they coming?" He asked and Ratledge looked surprised.

"What do you mean?" He asked even though he was sure that this captain knew what he was doing.

"The Admiralty, of course, you probably went to contact the committee and they have responded favorably; although the news has come sooner than I would have predicted. I'll bet that even surprises you that they agreed to come so readily. "The Captain mused and Ratledge was shocked at how perceptive this little man was. He found it hard to believe that he was so transparent. Then as if to mock his very thoughts, the Captain continued. "I don't expect you know why I know so much about you, do you. Well, our families go back a long way you and I. I know that they want you gone, but that they don't trust you enough to let you have free reign. I hope that this small event can get you in good with them. After all, our fathers shared a common uncle."

Ratledge was nearly floored. He had not even known who this man was, and now they were supposed to be related somehow. It was all so confusing, but this man knew too much to be dismissed out of hand. He stammered for a moment and then he sat down. "I'm afraid you have me at a disadvantage. But no matter, they are scheduled to come in just over an hour from now." He finished and he watched the man as he sat more upright.

"Don't worry, I won't do anything that will lower your image in their eyes. I just want to get back out there and finish what I started. You have read the report now I am sure or you would not have requested the meeting. They disabled my ship with basically a wave of their hand. I do not like the feeling of losing control over my command. I need help to resolve this crisis. I lost people on that world, and I need to go back and try to recover the bodies for proper burial as well. Quinn is still missing too and that will get these admirals in line if nothing else does. He seems to be their wonder child. I am hoping to get this resolved quickly so that if there are survivors, there is still a chance at recovery." He finished and Ratledge looked at the small man with a new respect. He had not believed this man to be so committed to his job or the fleet, but the evidence before him was irrefutable.

Ratledge folded a clipboard closed and set aside his personal hand comp. "It sounds to me like you have prepared for this meeting. To my chagrin, you have bested me at my own game. I will leave the rest to you then. If you can convince them to rally to your cause, I will not interfere. You have my word on that." He announced.

The captain looked at the man closely to determine if he were being sincere. His senses told him that the comment was genuine. He raised his opinion of this man a notch or two. It would not be long now, and he was saving the rest of his nerve to address the admirals that were on the way. He suspected that they were only coming because they wanted to see Ratledge fall. If he could prevent them from focusing on the man and keeping their minds on the task he had set before them, things should turn out okay.

When the moment came, the two men were practically unsettled. The wait had frazzled nerves and neither man was in the condition they had hoped for. There was only one saving grace. Ratledge had forwarded the report when he had contacted the committee. Now they all knew the same things and they had already discussed the possibilities before entering the room. That had saved the Captain from having to pitch it to them. They would now decide without his need to elaborate on the events. The two men fidgeted visibly as the committee took seats around them. It was almost like a trial in the vast room that now seemed a lot smaller. Ratledge felt his future hanging in the balance and he was decidedly nervous. The Captain looked pretty collected on the outside, but the butterflies in his stomach were tying his intestines into knots.

The group finally settled into their seats, and it was obvious they were aware of the tension they were causing, and also that they reveled in the feeling of superiority and power they shared over others. They may have been the high and mighty of The Fleet, but they were spiteful and shallow people that needed to reign over others to give their own lives meaning. It was sad after all.

The leader cleared his throat for attention and the room fell silent. He held up a data pad and perused it quickly and then set it down on the desk. The sounds of the plastic frame landing on the wooden table echoed in the vast, silent chamber. "We have read the report." He stated needlessly. "Do you have anything additional to add to this data?" He asked and both men shook their heads. "Very well, it is the decision of this committee that we cannot afford to go to war with the Jeng. Therefore, the request for a fleet to accompany you back to the system is denied. However, we cannot lose this opportunity to gain technological knowledge. We are advancing you a segment of ships for study. They are the latest stealth craft and they are not to engage the enemy. The orders are to strip that base for anything useful and leave the planet behind us. The stealth ships will stay as far from that moon as possible and still accomplish their goal. Even the shuttles on these new ships are equipped with stealth generators. There will be no battles here. It is understood that if confrontation cannot be avoided, you are to break off and flee. Let them take the upper hand and get the hell out of there. Be sure to record all data from the confrontation if at all possible. We need information here people." There were a series of agreeing nods around the committee. Then the speaker turned to Ratledge in particular. "You are to command the stealth wing. I don't want any slip-ups. If you fail for any reason, the commander of the flagship will assume command and throw you in the brig. Is that clear?" He asked sternly.

Ratledge couldn't believe his own ears, a command at long last. "Yes sir. I will not fail you sir." He answered a little shakily, but his chest inflated with pride.

"I believe that concludes this mission briefing. We cannot stress enough how important this mission is. Time is of the essence, so get on with it immediately. The stealth wing will meet with the *Lincoln* just outside of the system. This is to make sure that the Jeng don't see you leaving together. Since we do not know about their stealth capability, we must assume that they monitored you coming here. If you leave the system alone, they will assume that you could not convince us to support you. The chartered flight path for the *Lincoln* will take you away from the system. Then you will rendezvous with the wing and then circle back to the target. Good hunting gentlemen. This meeting is adjourned." The committee left the room in an orderly, practiced manner and the two men were left alone to ponder their words. Of course they did not have any spare time so Ratledge nodded and headed back to his quarters to pack.

The Captain smiled. He didn't get what he wanted, but he did get more than he had believed he would. Now this planet would still give him his profit. That meddling Lieutenant Ramses would not be able to keep him from his wealth. Maybe even the planting of the colony could continue. The successful completion of the mission would go far for him to reaching his goals. The Admiralty would also be impressed if working artifacts were recovered. They needed to get back to that planet as soon as possible. He commed the port authority and ordered his shuttle prepared for lift off. There was much to be done, but he had to do all this waiting before it could truly begin. The committee's plans to have him sail the other way and then rendezvous with this wing of ships seemed a little cloak and dagger to him, but who was he to argue with his superiors? Anyway, at least they would be leaving soon and he would be ready for them.

The ground transport took him to the port and his pilot met him and they both headed into the shuttle. Because he had commed ahead, the shuttle was coming up in the flight schedule and they were soon away from the planet and headquarters was dropping away behind them. It felt good to be back out in space as the tiny ship crossed the threshold of the atmosphere and entered free space. The Captain expected to see that Ratledge again, he didn't know which ship the man would ride on, but he assumed that the *Lincoln* would carry his flag. Either way, they were about to make history. Nothing can raise profit faster than fame. Opportunities would present themselves soon enough and he would get that retirement he craved. The images of wealth filled his mind and he smiled while the shuttle pilot arrowed them towards the *Lincoln* with his usual precision and grace.

Admiral Ratledge got to his quarters and his hands were shaking. "Finally he would get to see some action," he thought to himself. There was some light packing to do and then he would be off to the spaceport and his future. He had been there countless times before of course, but it had always been to greet others that were coming in. Now he was going to ship out and the elation he felt could not easily be contained. He felt like dancing around the room, or going to each of the men that said he wouldn't make it and blurting, "I told you so," into their faces, but that would not be proper. It might be appropriate, after all he had been stationed here most of his life. But it would have been petty. He decided to take the high road and ignore all the little people that had held him back and he would embrace his future. He would wrap it around himself like a protective blanket. He would be untouchable, and he would be successful. He had always dreamed of becoming a heroic commander. He would be one that could further the cause of the fleet and bring fame and fortune down upon his family and elevate himself to his proper status.

His meager belongings were quickly stowed away and he sent a message that he would no longer require the room, or the services of the staff. Then he took one last look at the room that represented his career up to this point and he locked the image in his mind. Then he closed the door and left it all in the past. He would start fresh and stride forward. He took an automated ground vehicle to the spaceport and he chartered a shuttle flight to the *Lincoln.* He knew that he would make a grand impression there. He had changed into his dress uniform. It was only proper to wear that when assuming command of a small fleet. He was ready, and he was excited. The only dark spot on the horizon as he saw it were these Jeng. What would they do? And how could he counter it? He would read the reports again on his way to the ship and hopefully something would come to him before he needed to make those critical decisions. The burden would not tarnish this moment in history. Of that he was certain.

Progress on the water world was progressing at an astonishing rate. The traps and alarms were all placed and food had been gathered and stored for prolonged use. The electronic signal was not yet operational, but the device was nearly completed. The two men were working feverishly on it. It was transmitting, but just not at a level that could be heard from space yet. They were trying to get their makeshift amplifier circuit to boost the signal, but so far they were coming up short. It was possible that if a ship were in orbit, directly overhead, they might catch this tiny signal, if the communications officer were not distracted, but they wanted more than that slim hope.

The cat-god had overseen the placement of the traps and had offered design assistance as the amount of building material had dwindled. Now all of the members of the party were tired. The work had been furiously fast, but still had taken them the better part of two days. Who knew how long they would be here, but they knew that the security was still the number one priority. Quinn had worked himself overly hard and his body was beginning to argue with him. He tried to force back the fatigue, but the warning signs were becoming more acute, and he knew that it would be better to simply rest and begin anew tomorrow. He called a small meeting and the crew, such as it was, sat down heavily in the Jeng cave. They had all been working harder than they had ever before. There were plenty of blisters and sore muscles. This survival was hard work. Fortunately, they were generally in high spirits. After all, they were each sitting in an actual museum piece of history. Of course that was colored a bit by the fact that the Jeng were still around and wanted them out of this place, but for now it was enough that they were here. Quinn looked at the weary faces and Margaret actually managed to smile at him. He took strength from her and then he sighed.

"We have all done some good work today." He assured them.

"But there is still more to do. I am sure that we are all beyond the normal feeling of tired, so the best course of action is to have everyone rest until morning. There is something miraculous about a good night's sleep, and I think we all deserve it." He concluded and he got no arguments from the assembly before him.

The dark cat-god swept by his shoulders. "I do not require sleep, so I will keep watch for you." It offered in that silvery mind-voice and Quinn nodded his thanks. The animal purred loudly and then left the cave. No one was really interested in where it would watch from, they simply trusted the being to honor its word. After all, what real choice did they have? They decided to find comfortable places and rest. Within minutes, the exhausted crew was asleep.

The Jeng commander stood in the transport chamber. He fidgeted nervously while he waited for reports. He was certain that something was wrong. He had not heard from his attack crew, and they were still getting signals from the base. This meant that everything had not been destroyed, as was the order. That meant that the team had somehow failed. It was inconceivable to him that those barbaric humans could best his warriors, but he had to consider the evidence before him. He wanted to know where the tin can went and he was waiting to hear the final word on its whereabouts. The wall before him shimmered and the feeling of "It's about time," flashed across his mind and he banished it away. The image formed and he could see the command room of a planetary body and another commander Jeng standing before him. The figure stepped towards him and entered the chamber through the mystical membrane. Then the wall faded and returned to normal. The new officer stood comfortably and made a gesture of greetings. The commander returned the greetings and thought one phrase, "What word do you have?"

The newcomer identified himself as Remmik49 and proceeded to fill the thought with a picture of the tin can in space. Then the commander saw the can launch a smaller metal box towards a planet. It was a busy planet with many metal boxes around it. "This must be the hive of this human race," the Commander thought and Remmik49 nodded that he agreed. The image continued on this way while the ball in space rotated about halfway around, then the tiny metal box rocketed skyward and rejoined the tin can. Then a second metal box shot up and also joined the tin can. The image added directional figures around the outside edge for clarity and then the tin can raced away from the Jeng at a high rate of speed and left the system. The Commander was shocked. He was certain that they would have returned in force to try and claim the Jeng's prizes. He had somehow overestimated these humans. They truly were a barbaric and unpredictable species he decided and thanked Remmik49 for his report. The greetings were repeated and with a wave and a few of the archaic syllables, the wall began to shimmer again. Within a few seconds, the image on the wall was the same as it had been and Remmik49 stepped back through the portal and left the Commander alone with his thoughts. The wall faded out again as the connection was cut at the far end. Then the stone returned to its natural state and the Commander was left to ponder the mysteries of these savages. Without reinforcements, these humans would be an easy target, he concluded. He would dispatch another squad of warriors and then he would be free of this human infestation. After all, their odd appearance gave him the creeps. He feared them almost to his very core. They were so different. He was ready to be free of them and then he could return to his comfortable existence. Once this base was behind him, he could start fresh on some other planet and be hidden from all things again. That is the way of the Jeng, and it was the only thing that made him happy.

Out in space, just out of long scan range of their last port of call, The *Lincoln* stopped at the rendezvous coordinates and waited. The preliminary scans of the area turned up nothing. This was not expected. They were in a hurry after all, and the Captain was going to lose his patience soon. The shuttle bringing Ratledge aboard had only just made it in time before they left orbit. He was now on the bridge and his chin was held high. The crew looked around a bit, but then they all concentrated on their consoles so as not to make eye contact. It was a case of not speaking unless spoken to. They waited in fear of being called out. It was, after all, uncommon to say the least, for an admiral to be on board such a small and insignificant ship as this one. They knew that the meeting with the Jeng was important, but they did not expect to go back to the system. It was generally assumed that some other, more important ship would be the one to go. The sensor technician spoke up first.

"Sir, there is no sign of the wing at these coordinates." He announced and the Captain looked at Ratledge, but said nothing. He slumped back into his command chair and sighed.

"All right, we're here, and we'll wait for them. I'm sure that the amount of brass behind them will get them here as soon as humanly possible." Engage our stealth cloak and keep passive sensors only. Let's see if they can spot us." He ordered.

"Aye sir, going to stealth." The helm answered unnecessarily. The outside of the ship shimmered and vanished into the blackness of space. The hull reflected the stars around it and the electronics emissions were down to less than 10 percent of normal operating levels. Even the drive signature would have been masked, that is if they had been moving. Still like this, it was one tough ship to find by normal means. The helm officer watched the status lights all go green and he updated the bridge of the status. "Now reading full stealth mode sir." He barked crisply.

The Captain leaned forward to watch the view screen a bit closer. "I hope they don't take too long to get here, I need to get to that planet as soon as possible." He murmured. Then he started as a voice behind him answered.

"We are already here." It announced and the entire bridge crew jumped and whirled around to see the man dressed in all black standing easily behind them. The man was in uniform, but all of the colors were black. Even his rank insignia was flat black on a black panel. This man outranked anyone on board, including Admiral Ratledge! "Let me introduce myself." He said easily. "I am

Admiral Vorn, Tyler Vorn. I am the leader of the black squadron. You are here to escort us to the target location where we are to begin maneuvers in an information-gathering situation. Am I correct?" He asked, fully knowing the answer was yes.

The Captain stood up and stepped over to the man. "Forgive my surprise." He started and the man smiled warmly. "I am sure that you already know the answer to your question, so I won't bother to answer it. We are glad to have you and your crew with us. I must admit that we were a bit taken by your display of stealth technology. I am assuming by your being here, that you were waiting for us in-system when we arrived?" The Captain asked with a gentle nudge.

The man shrugged his shoulders and raised his hands. "Of course, we have never been late to a mission. I am glad that your ship has a modest cloaking ability as well; it will make it easier for us to mask your signature in-system. I believe you will find our technicians can do wonders with your outdated equipment. I suggest you let them have their run of the ship until the upgrades are completed. It's more efficient that way."

The Captain nodded. "Of course, we will accept any help you can give us. It was quite unnerving to lose control of my ship to those aliens before we even knew that they were there." He scratched his head. "That brings up another point. How did you get aboard the *Lincoln* without triggering our security alarms?" He asked and the man put his finger to the side of his nose.

"Trade secret I'm afraid, but I can tell you that I teleported to your ship. As to the warning alarms, that is classified." He said and his tone suggested that further discussion on the subject would be impossible. "I'm sure that you will be pleased with the upgrades we provide, but we won't give you all of the toys. Something must be held in reserve for future confrontations." Tyler Vorn turned to Admiral Ratledge and smiled. "I trust that you have the report and the findings of the committee on file?" He asked.

Ratledge smiled back disarmingly. "Yes sir, we do. You are free to examine the files as long as you need." He offered and Vorn scoffed at him.

"I have access to everything, and that includes your pitiful database. I was only asking to make sure that you had the information available to update when the time comes." Vorn turned back to the Captain. "Make your best speed to this water planet and I will do my best to rid you of this alien menace; although technically we are supposed to avoid contact with the enemy. We should operate under stealth for most of the mission. It would not do to go in guns blazing and scare them off, now would it?" He turned around as if to leave. "I shall return to my ship now, and you can get underway. We'll follow you, don't worry about your stealth gear; we can still track you just fine. Leave it on so the enemy may not see your approach. I don't think they have a chance at seeing us. I look forward to seeing you on the planet." He said and turned away from the bridge crew. He raised his arm as if looking at a watch and then he shimmered and vanished. The Captain's jaw dropped. Nobody on the bridge had ever seen anything like that before. It was amazing what mankind had accomplished. They were able to transport matter from ship to ship without a physical connection. Clearly, there were many more questions than answers here. Then the Captain remembered that they were a fleet now.

He turned to the scan technician. "Can you see the others ships now?" He asked and the man shrugged his shoulders.

"No sir, there are no readings of any kind on our passive sensors. If they are out there, they've got better cloaks than I've ever seen." He said. Before anyone else could comment he added, "Of course I've never seen a man vanish before my eyes before either, sir." He finished in explanation.

The captain looked out at the stars on his view screen and he knew that there were ships out there, but he just couldn't see them. His equipment was definitely out of date. He knew that some advances were coming. He smiled and sat back down. The scan technician was still looking at him and he made eye contact. "My guess is that we are going to learn a lot on this cruise. When we can figure out how to sense them, let me know right away." He ordered and the scan tech nodded his understanding. "You know, it would have been nice if they had told us how many ships are escorting us." The Captain mused and Ratledge stood up.

"That information was not given us to know. Do you know how secretive this wing is? Well I'll tell you. They never breathed a word of it to me at headquarters, and I am in charge of personnel. They never went through my office to assign the people that are out there crewing those ships. They also did not go through normal channels to pay them or I would have gotten wind of it through that channel as well. Whoever ordered this was at the top somewhere. No one could circumvent so many systems. It wouldn't surprise me if they were above the government somehow. I suggest treating them with kid gloves. If you upset them somehow, they will simply disappear and no one will ever know that they had been here. Either that or you will disappear with the same finality." The Admiral looked around at the bridge crew to make sure he had all of their attention. He did of course. "We had better all concentrate solely on this mission. When the time comes, I am sure that we will be allowed some of this technology, but for now we must hold our curiosity at bay. The situation is much too tenuous. The mission must come first, and then we can worry about the rest."

The Captain looked around and his crew seemed on edge, but ready to do their duty. That was a good sign. He knew that the mission was of the utmost importance, but he also knew that the planet could provide him more than just technology. He was anxious to get back there and start earning those credits. The XO had been quiet all this time. He was still sizing up the situation. He was not happy that this Admiral was aboard. What if the man found out that the Captain did not truly run the ship? It was a burden he did not appreciate bearing. This man was important somehow to the mission though, and the sooner the mission was completed and the colonies were planted, the better. He also knew that Quinn and Margaret had gone out after the Jeng moon. He didn't know how they knew it existed while they were incarcerated, but he did not care. This young lieutenant was a master at alien contacts; perhaps he could remedy the situation on the planet before they even got back. It was an ambitious wish, but the young man had impressed him. Maybe it was not too far out of the question. It was not time yet to act openly, and he sent a few minor orders out across the ship to make sure that the reigns were seen as being held firmly. Appearances were always important and apparently, he was not ready to give up this ship to anyone.

11

A squad of warriors stood before the Jeng Commander, and he eyed them approvingly. They had the ritualistic marking of fire clan. It was one of the highest-ranking squads in this sector. The Commander knew that he was lucky that they had been sent. The earlier warriors had been of a lower caste, and they had all been destroyed on the planet below. They had faced a god in battle; there was no shame in their defeat. But it was inconvenient to say the least that the human scum had somehow survived the god's wrath. He hoped that it would not always be so, but for now he had to assume that they were still on the planet, and that they were still interested in acquiring some of the Jeng's secrets. He could not allow that. No matter how many squads he had to send, he could not allow the inferiors to possess such power. He strolled from one end of the line to the other. The men all faced front and held their gaze firmly forward. His chest swelled with pride as he prepared to send them in. He reached over to the controls and waved his hand over them. A few spoken rune words and the rock wall took on its formative state and the image began to clarify. The humans were asleep in the cave of the ancients. They were a damnable plague that had to be eradicated, and the Commander hoped that he was sending the right group to the planet. He believed that he was. The men all took their positions before the great wall and when the image finished, they all stepped forward fearlessly into the image and appeared on the planet's surface.

Alarms rang off immediately and the warriors braced for an assault. They looked around but nothing came at them. They kept their swords drawn and advanced towards the cave. They were only a few yards from the entrance and they could sense tension in the air. Step after step, the tension rose. These seasoned fighters were starting to tremble. They couldn't figure just why, but there was a strong sense of foreboding in the cave, and they were not eager to enter it. The tension rose remarkably higher within ten meters of the entrance and the warriors stopped in their tracks. The leader looked around and could see no threat, but he was certain that there was one there. He tried to step forward, but his legs would not move, except to shake involuntarily. He was immobilized with fear. He glanced around and saw that his men were in the same state. Fear had crushed their wills and they were paralyzed. One of the humans stepped into sight, just inside the cave, and the fear tripled. Several of them even dropped to their knees, their legs would no longer support them. The leader tried to focus on the enemy, but all he could see was a monster. This little creature was his doom, and the feeling rolled over his mind like a steamroller. The human came to within arm's length of the leader and the fear buckled him as well. The small man leaned over the fallen warrior and smiled at him. It was a normal smile, but somehow the fear twisted it into evil incarnate. The leader closed his eyes and threw his arms up over his head in defense. The swords were already lying on the ground where they had fallen from slack fingers. The dry stone ground was of no comfort as the mighty squad commander shook with inescapable fear.

Quinn had agreed to this security precaution by the cat-god. It was a non-violent means of defense that prevented anyone from entering the doorway. Quinn stood over the shaking man and he was feeling sorry for the tortured soul before him. He took a closer look to be sure that it was not an act. The creature looked terrified beyond all reason. Quinn backed off a step and spoke to the Jeng warriors. "You are free to leave this place, but do not return. Only death lies beyond this door for you, you are not authorized to enter this holy place. Tell your superiors that it is off-limits to the Jeng. Your lives will be restored to you upon leaving this sacred place." Then Quinn lifted the leader up to his feet, and the look of terror began to fade down a bit. Then he locked eyes with Quinn and his control nearly buckled again.

Quinn spoke in his most soothing voice. "Please leave now, I don't wish to see you die." If there was a language barrier, it was not evident now. The men all gathered their dropped weapons and exited away. They broke into a flat-out run a few meters back from the doorway and in moments they were out of sight into the tree line. Quinn hoped that they had the means to return home without the contents of the cave.

There was no way for him to know if they did or not; but he was secure in the knowledge that another attack had come and been thwarted. They reset the trap and backed back into the cave. The cat-god was there, and it stepped up to Quinn and nuzzled his side. The push nearly knocked him over. Margaret had spent some of her free time trying to make the equipment work. She was having a bit of success. The viewer she had used before had been smashed, but she had seen other similar objects and she had accessed some sort of library. In this library were all kinds of formulae. She didn't know what they were for, but they were definitely important. She was using her hand-comp to store as much of the information as it would hold, but its capacity was limited, and it was nearly full already. Quinn had stopped by once or twice to hear her progress. His almost natural grasp of the Jeng script came in handy. He had identified some of the phrases, and warned not to attempt some others because of warnings on the headers of the pages. There were phrases to shape rock, and others to warp air and water. They even found some references about time, but were unable to grasp the concept that was presented. Perhaps with more minds at work on the problem, they would decipher what that one was all about. They could not add Quinn's hand-comp to the data storage because it contained the Jeng language symbol structure and it was also nearly full. But many minor advances added up to a major one, and these phrases contained ancient power that was still beyond the human comprehension, but the ground was being steadily made up. Margaret had tried a couple of the phrases out and was surprised to find that they seemed to work exactly as they were meant to. Evidently the translations were quite literal, and the force was still available to perform the tasks.

The cat-god had stayed around the humans. It was attached to them now. It actually cared what happened to the brave young souls it had encountered. When one of the rocks moved and shifted, it thought that the Jeng had returned. Its senses were alert, but the smells were only that of the humans. The creature was confused at first, and then it was happy. The humans were using some of the Jeng magic. The cat god got excited at the prospect, and it gave moral support whenever one of the humans got discouraged at a failed attempt. One thing that the god had learned was that humans were able to adapt and assimilate new things quickly. They had taken over this base and they had quite a few of the mysterious devices working. The thought brought a dark haze to an otherwise bright picture. If they grew too smart, the Jeng would have to interfere. They had just sent the customary party last time. If things continued on this way, they would launch a full-scale invasion soon. It was only a matter of time. He didn't want to worry his friends overmuch, but the thought kept returning and the cat-god-creature-turned-protector worried on its own. It kept ever vigilant and it checked and rechecked the defenses. It hoped that Quinn would find what he needed so they could get out of here and disappear from the Jeng threat altogether. It seemed the only solution to the problems they faced. The humans had not forgotten about the Jeng, but they were continuing about their business as if the threat weren't anywhere close. That was the problem with the Jeng magic; they were never far away. Distances were inconsequential and the people could see everything. They had been the overlords for millennia, and they were still around due only to their ruthless fear of outsiders, and their conviction to secrecy. The cat knew in its heart that the humans' time was limited on this planet. It also knew that the human's transport had disappeared. The only solution seemed to be to get the Jeng devices working and transport off of this water bound world that way. It was all basically a race against the clock, and nobody could see the face to know how much time they had. It was yet another of the mysteries of the Jeng. The cat-god sighed to itself and lay down on the cold stone floor. It rumbled itself back to a calmer demeanor with its deep purr and waited for the humans to finish their tasks.

The *Lincoln* sped through space at nearly full power. It was actually full power available while cloaked. The sensor technician had tried many interesting things to try to detect the wing ships that were somewhere around them, but there was still no electronic signature, no sign that they were close. The only reason they believed that the ships were still there was the hourly reports the wing commander sent to them by a secure directional communications terminal. In fact, the scan techs had even tried tracing that signal back to its source and came up empty. The Captain was getting perturbed at the lack of success. At least they were probably right about the Jeng not being able to see them either. That was the bright side of the situation and it played on his nerves a bit. The smug attitude of the fleet man seemed to reflect in every report they received. He was playing some kind of game with them and the Captain did not like it. The man sat in his chair in his quarters. He was sipping on a bottle of whiskey and he was brooding over their situation. He had the distinct impression of a rat looking at an empty mousetrap, and wondering where the cheese was. He was leading the wing into enemy territory; that was obvious. But what was not obvious was what the *Lincoln*'s role in all of this would be. He had come so close to victory and financial freedom only to be pressed back to headquarters by those miserable Jeng. He had expected to lose some of his profits because of his weakness, but he had not expected to be chaperoned back into the system by guardians that he could not see on his screens. Invisible hands were guiding him and his ship like a puppet back into danger. He desperately wished he could sense those hands, and quantify their power. He wanted to feel secure and protected. They weren't offering him that. Instead, they were offering him only questions and doubt. His mind would replay disaster scenario after disaster scenario. There were so many ways this mission could go wrong. He was pretty sure that he had guessed just about every one of those ways in his mind, and the mission was still in its early stages. There was no way to foresee what was going to happen next, and he found that to be unnerving. The thought of profits turned aside to allow room for the thoughts of survival. He felt a deep fear in the pit of his stomach about not surviving to retire. Why had he taken this Captaincy in the first place? He couldn't remember now. He was sure now that he was doomed. The idiots on board would not be able to thwart the enemy and they were all going to die. He was sure of it. He might as well just shoot himself now and get it over with. No sense in prolonging the agony. Then his greed caught up with him again, and he was ready to strike a bargain with these Jeng and purchase bits and pieces of their technology. Maybe he could become rich through distribution of the vast knowledge of these ancient people. His future was looking bright. He wondered if that Lieutenant had gotten anything useful yet. He wondered if they were going to make a profit on the very landing, let alone the additional boon of a colony plantation percentage. Yes, these wing ships would get them through this. They were loaded with the latest technology mankind had come up with. The *Lincoln* would come out financially victorious with the Captain standing atop the hoard triumphantly. That would show his uncle the kind of man that he truly was. He was a pioneer. He was an adventurer. He was an opportunist, and most of all; he was a good businessman. His position in the family business would be secured. He could just sit back and count his credits while being waited on hand and foot. The thought brought out the best of him and it was rudely interrupted by the communications system buzzing in his ear.

"Yes what is it?" He said gruffly into the microphone. There was a pause while the speaker read the message off of the screen.

"Yes sir, the message says that we are to swing around the system and come up from the far side of the planet. They expect the Jeng moon to still be in place, guarding that settlement of theirs. They did warn us away from it. They have come up with a tactical analysis and they believe that we can take them out of the equation by hiding on the far side while they go in and recover the technology." There was a slight pause and then the operator said the customary words. "Is there a reply sir?"

The Captain thought for a moment. The message was like a knot in his stomach. *They* were going to go to *his* planet and recover *his* treasures. They were going to leave him behind and take all the glory for themselves. He was furious and afraid at the same time. If they got to the planet they might find the diamonds that he was keeping from them. After all, that Quinn fellow had found them right away down on the surface. They would not be happy when they found out he was holding out on them. How should he reply to this message? Should he rant and rave about being kept out of the technology loop, or should he accept it and be thankful that his ship would be safely out of harm's way? He decided to hold both emotions in check and respond in the most dignified manner he could muster. "Send the reply as follows: We acknowledge and comply." He finished and the communications officer read the message back to him for verification. It sounded so hollow even in his ears. He really wanted to send more, but protocol demanded this be short and sweet. He acknowledged his message and moments later, the reply was sent and a new message came in. It read only "acknowledged". The one word pretty much summed up the rest of the Captain's career, he would be known as a *yes* man. He was a patsy for the powerful. He was not a mover and a shaker; he was a pawn in a political struggle to control the future of technology fleet-wide. He felt sick at the realization and he was ready to give it all up again. But he had known yes men before and some of them said yes to the right people and became powerful themselves. It was true that they never overshadowed the powerful people ahead of them, but they did have plenty of lowlifes to boss around below them. So he wasn't a hero, at least he could still be well off. He could still make it into a family fortune. This wasn't over yet. He decided to be on the bridge when they arrived in the system, so he got dressed the rest of the way and headed out of his cabin. He would show them how a professional acts under pressure. His chin was high, and he thrust his chest out in pride as he made his way to his command center.

The elite squad of Jeng warriors returned to the commander with their proverbial tails between their legs. They were all shaken to the core. They knew that it meant summary execution to admit failure without even attempting their mission's goal, but that was not nearly as frightening as that place on the planet had been. The commander shook his head at the men. He was shocked and amazed that Jeng could be manipulated by humans so fully. He thought for a while and his shock turned to anger. He was ready to annihilate the humans and destroy that blasted wet ball of mud in space once and for all. Unfortunately, in order to call in that much firepower, he would have to explain what had happened so far. This episode of fear and intimidation would not look good on his record, but unfortunately he was powerless to change the past. He ordered the executions and started wording his reports to rid himself of this human infestation permanently. The fallen warriors were led out of the room. They stared at the cold stone floor as they were herded to their destiny. The commander barely even noted their passing. It was more of an annoyance to him. They were now insignificant and ineffective. He troubled over his own future much more and now he would try to save a little of this situation and free himself of these blasted human beasts at long last.

The commander of the black squadron sat back in his command chair and smiled. His tactical display showed the outline of the *Lincoln* on full stealth systems. His computer filled in the details from the last time they were in range without the stealth technology engaged. So now he saw a normal image of the ship. He was in position just 200 kilometers off their starboard side and from here he could listen in on the internal communications systems. He was pretty sure that they could not see him back. He was under the new cloaking device and he had masked his signature and displaced it as well. Even if their sensors could penetrate the new cloak, it would report the wrong location on the sensor reading. This prevented any ship from ever getting the drop on the black squadron. It also kept the fear firmly in place for space pirates. The wing had been used primarily to beat off the pirate threat and this was going to be their first mission outside of the system in which the ships were created. It was a momentous occasion for the crew and they were anxious to get out there and prove their mettle to the fleet.

The ship sailed on without a glitch as the pre-programmed course kept it alongside the *Lincoln*. The early scan data on the system was proving helpful. The Jeng moon was indeed where it was supposed to be. That was the first step in the plan. The planet was ripe for the taking, and they were there to do just that. Vorn had spearheaded this wing from the start. It took all of the clout he had to hide the credits that had been required to set up and operate the secret labs that had produced several big advances in technology. He had had these stealth ships built even as the breakthroughs were coming. The hulls had been modified again and again as the specifications changed. Even the government did not know how many ships he had, but he did. He had ten battle cruiser stealth ships. They were armed with weapons no one else in the fleet had ever seen. They had teleporters and a sensor suite that would make any navy scan man cry. They also had faster-than-light communications. This allowed them to get almost instantaneous information about the system before they actually entered it from drones they sent on ahead of them. The tactical advantages could not be overlooked. The enemy was still a big question mark though, so care was still required even with his impressive ships. Vorn mused to himself about what that silly captain's reaction would be if his ten ships de-cloaked around him as they were now positioned. Each of the stealth battle cruisers outweighed the *Lincoln* three to one, and their oversized power plants allowed for higher acceleration rates and quicker warp-jumps. They were one of the very few designs that could tow a ship at warp speeds. If only that imbecile could see these great wedges in space. Their hull plating was made from an emission-absorbing alloy that was one of the first scientific breakthroughs the black squadron had produced. If he had been able to detect their resonance somehow, they would have looked like giant spearheads on his screen. No images registered on the screens, so the image was lost. The power around him made Admiral

Vorn giddy. He wanted to test himself in battle. He only hoped that the situation would arise where he could flex his newfound military might. Another report crossed his personal display and he thumbprint verified it. This marvelous ship was practically running itself. There just was no substitute for great engineering. The self-replicating damage control robots made the ship appear to heal as the crew continued to battle the enemy. At least that was the theory. The system had not truly been tested. The crew was confident though, and they would eventually get their chance.

Aboard the *Lincoln*, hopes and expectations were not quite so high. The XO was busily routing people to the sections that had been damaged in the last Jeng attack. The general thought being that those would be the first areas hit if there was another skirmish. If that were the case, he wanted maintenance personnel on each of those locations to begin repairs as the damage was occurring. That should restrict the downtime considerably. Of course, all of this happened without the Captain even getting wind of it. However, Admiral Ratledge was not so unobservant. He waved the XO over to a corridor and the look on his face suggested that he would brook no argument.

The two men entered the corridor and it was empty of other personnel. The hatch to the bridge swished shut and they were cut off from the rest of the crew. Ratledge leaned in close. Their noses almost touched. His eyes were red like fire. "What are you doing over there? The Captain has not issued any orders and you are so busy the computer has logged your traffic use." He demanded and the XO felt a lump in his throat. He had forgotten about the computer usage logs. He had also forgotten that the communications system had been upgraded to share memory and bandwidth with the computer circuits running throughout the ship.

He thought quickly, looking for a way out that did not scream *mutiny*. He did not want any part of mutiny, but his actions could be viewed as little else. He decided that the truth was better than any lie he could come up with, so he took a deep breath and laid it out for the Admiral. "Sir, I have been running this ship from the secondary console for quite some time. The Captain is a good man and all that, but he is inefficient when handling this ship or its personnel. He originally asked me to help out with the logistics of the day-to-day operations. I turned out to be quite good at it, and now he doesn't even bother himself with the details of it at all. I was only trying to head off potential down times with my latest dispatch. I sent crews to the systems that were damaged last time. If we get hit again the same way, they will be ready to bring those specific systems back up as quickly as possible. If we get hit some other way, then the damage crews will already be distributed all over the ship and will be able to respond quicker than if they were all still sitting in maintenance waiting for the call. Everything I have done is in the effort to keep this ship running smoothly despite a leader who does not care whether it works out or not." He finished and he wondered if he had pushed things a bit too far. He knew that his career was hanging in the balance here. He hoped that this man would see things the same way as he did and allow things to continue until the danger was past.

Ratledge stood there, tensed up, his face turning red as the speech was delivered and then there was realization. It was indeed possible for the Captain to be completely out of the loop about the operations of his ship. The XO had laid out a pretty comprehensive defense strategy. It was also possible that the man was used to commanding this ship from the second spot. It was not protocol in any way, shape or form, but it may just be working. He knew that he should court-martial this man and make sure that the book was thrown at him for good measure to discourage other activity of this nature. This mission was too important to upset the power ladder at this time. He bit back the tirade he was about to deliver. It was with visible effort that he calmed down. The XO did not miss the change and he inwardly prayed that it was the good sign he thought it was. When Ratledge spoke, it was in a firm, even tone that icicles could hang from. "I want you to continue doing what you are doing. But I want regular reports of the activities you plan. I also want to a copy of each order routed to my terminal as you give it. If I find anything out of place, I'll hang your butt out to dry and then have the rest of you spaced. Is that clear?" He finished like the last nail being driven into a coffin.

"Yes sir. I'll get right on the link-up now." The XO replied and his relief was evident in the amount of tension across his back. He had knotted up while under the scrutiny of the Admiral, but now he was being given a bit of a leash to go ahead. He hoped it wouldn't be too tight so that it would allow him to do the job, but he really wasn't in any position to argue the point with the man who definitely held his career in his hands. He looked at the Admiral again and they both left the confined space. Ratledge went away to his quarters. The XO went back to the bridge. He set up the terminal echo and then checked his status boards. They were nearly to the system and his knees started shaking. It was one thing to risk your life in the line of duty, it was quite another to have someone standing over your shoulder while you did it, judging your every move. He would adjust, he always did, but he didn't have to like it.

Down on the planet, the work was progressing slowly. The runes were easily translated, but they were difficult to speak aloud. One misspoken word would change the results of the carefully laid out formula. They needed to get this down before rescue came to them. It was true that the cat-god had heard some of the phrases used, and its input was invaluable when trying to sort out some of the complex runes. But it was only a limited dataset. They needed to transcribe the entire language before some of the more bizarre combinations would make any sense at all. Margaret was logging information by hand, having filled her personal comp quite a while before. Quinn had filled his as well, but they were still busily translating and transcribing as much as they could get their hands on. These would have to be entered into the computer later when they got back to civilization. They had managed to scan the skies for ships a couple of times and found that the *Lincoln* was not in orbit. Wherever she had gone, she was not able to save them at this time. The two archeologists were sampling dirt and rock. They had dated the stone and they were happy with the soil samples. There were many trace minerals in the soil that would allow plants to thrive in it. They were still trying to justify this world for colonization. Of course all of their readings gave the planet a go. It was perfectly suited to human life and they were quite thorough in their analysis.

The cat-god had disappeared for a while after a particularly frustrating session of Jeng technology work. It had bound away and left the caverns completely. Quinn felt the creature's distress but he couldn't tell the cause of the problem. He tried to think after the beast, but it paid him no attention and continued on its flight from the area. Maybe it was hungry; he thought to himself, but the thought felt wrong even in his own mind. He would make it a point to ask the cat when it returned. There was a whoosh sound outside and the very ground shook as if from some major impact. The quartet of humans rushed to the entrance, stared up at the skies, and was frozen in shock at the sight. Large stone monoliths were dropping from the skies. One of them briefly crossed the sun and cast a shadow over the entire island. They were impacting the water with a fountain of spray and the crust of the planet was taking a beating. The large stone missiles had to be at least three kilometers long and who knew how much they weighed. It was certainly a lot. Tidal size waves swept out from the impact sites as the huge gray stones slapped the surface again and again. The waves were way too high and coming fast. The bewildered humans tried to close the doors before they got flooded on this little island. The great stone doors seemed to stick just before sealing shut. One of the runes was damaged and it would not function. The massive doors were open about half a meter and would not hold back the rising water. It was obvious that this whole place would be flooded. Quinn ran back to the vault followed by his wet comrades. He checked the entrance and he double-checked the runes. They were completely intact. He ordered everyone inside and then he spoke the words that had sealed the cat-god in before. The doorway sealed up with molten stone and then solidified. They were now safe from drowning, but they had no supplies with them, and they were all trapped inside a vault. There were no runes on this side to open the doorway with. All they had with them were their hand comps. It was time for some quick thinking. The thudding of gigantic monoliths continued for quite some time. Then the floor tilted and everyone got that *riding the elevator* feeling of falling as something outside went terribly wrong.

Outside, the hail of giant stone blocks had continued. They did not strike the island, but they were having a devastating effect. The Jeng had launched these weapons with a specific purpose. They were striking the fault lines of the tectonic plate the island rested on. The first few hits caused a massive crack and it circled the island at the ocean floor. Then the unspeakable happened. The tectonic plate dropped. It fell towards the center of the planet and plummeted into the depths, bringing the island with it. The Jeng base went the way of Altlantis and fell into the sea. The water crashed and churned in the wake of the large chunks of rock that had just passed by and the attack from the sky ceased. All that was left of the island were some of the monoliths reaching up to the sky from the water's depths. The humans had been officially dealt with. The Jeng moon started to move away from the planet. The Jeng commander watched from his wall and his satisfaction was complete. He had taken down those pesky creatures and eliminated the god at the same time. Now there would be no inquiry as to lost technology. His career had been salvaged. He was ready to move on to a world with open green grass fields and good sturdy rock underneath. He was tired of all that water. He closed the viewer and went to his cave for relaxation. The moon would take a little over a year to reach the next target planet; he could wait for it in peace.

From the bridge of the black squadron commander's flagship, the devastation on the planet below was obvious. They had been in-system for less than a day when the great pieces of rock started breaking off and plummeting towards the planet. Vorn considered his options and realized that there was nothing he had that could stop that many gigantic pieces of rock. His best move seemed to be to wait it out and race in to recover the personnel dirt-side. He watched the bombardment with military curiosity. They hadn't hit the island yet. It was one of the worst military raids he had ever seen. That didn't mean that there wasn't any collateral damage. The island was washed over by tidal waves that completely hid the surface from his sensors. Then the rocks stopped coming. The bombardment ceased. The moon held its position for about an hour and then started backing away from the planet. The atmosphere was pretty messed up and there were no good readings of the surface yet, but Vorn was confident that he would get a picture as soon as was feasibly possible. When the picture did pop up, he jumped out of his seat. "What?!" He exclaimed and the bridge crews of the ten stealth ships simply sat in awe of the destruction. The island was gone. There wasn't a crater or any scorched pieces of land. It was gone. It had been completely wiped off of the face of the planet. He fell back down into his chair and sighed. His first mission and he had failed it. Had they known his fleet was here? He started going over the various orders he had given looking for the error that had brought them to this point. He just didn't see one. The Jeng moon was backing away and leaving orbit. Incredibly, the pieces of rock that had fallen to the planet were being replaced as it backed away like some living thing healing itself. Vorn turned to his communications officer. "Better tell the *Lincoln* what has happened down there." He said and the com-tech nodded his acceptance of the order.

The *Lincoln* was sitting back from the planet about three diameters away when the first blocks began to fall. Normally they would not have seen the action on the far side of the planet, except that they had dropped spy satellites the last time they were in system. Now the stealthy and small device gave them a front row seat to the destruction of the Jeng base. The impacts seemed to encircle the tiny island and then the unthinkable happened; it sank into the ocean. The Captain saw his profits sink with it. The doorway of the base had been under specific surveillance and it had not closed as the water approached, so it was probable that the entire base had flooded. The odds of the survey team surviving if they had been down there were remote. Of course it was more likely that they were on the Jeng moon. That was where the stolen shuttle had gone. In fact it had gone directly over to the enemy when the conflict began. It was infuriating how chance could drop opportunities into your lap and then simply pluck them away like so much ripe fruit on the vine. The *Lincoln* dropped its stealth cloak and slowly moved towards the battle scene. The wing could be damned, he wasn't going to just sit back and let them dig though the mess of his lost fortune. Now that the base was gone, this planet could still be used for a colony. As long as the crust was stable enough to support the cities that would eventually form on its surface. A geological survey was in order. He was just beginning to order exactly that when the communications officer reported an incoming message. It was a log of the destruction of the Jeng base. But it was not from the great vantage point that they had had via the spy satellite. The Captain figured it out quickly. "They do not know that we saw where the island went." He mused aloud. It was as if opportunity kicked him in the side to give him a second chance. His first problem was how to get rid of his escort. There had to be an acceptable way to get them to give up and leave him here.

Ratledge eyed the Captain suspiciously. "What are you thinking?" He asked but the man was lost in his thought circles. He didn't even acknowledge hearing the Admiral speak. Ratledge stood up and strolled over to the Captain, choosing to ignore his first insult. "Tell me what you are thinking." He repeated.

The Captain started, as if noticing the man for the first time. "What? What are you asking me?" He stuttered and Ratledge grabbed him by the shoulder and pulled him from the bridge. The XO watched intently as the two men left the confused bridge.

Out in the corridor, the Admiral held the Captain against the wall and stared into his wild eyes. "You are up to something; you owe me an explanation of what it is." He said with finality.

The Captain looked back at him and his eyes reflected internal conflict. Then he shrugged as if coming to some sort of conclusion and smiled. "Well sir, I am trying to plant a colony on this world. In addition, I think we may be able to get to that sunken base. For those tasks, we no longer need the black squadron out there. If we succeed, the financial rewards will be great, and I do not wish to share them with those pompous able-bodied crewmen out there in those cloaked ships. Therefore, I must get them out of the system so I can get down to the planet and finish my original mission. If you would like to transfer your flag over to the other ships, I would have no objection. Unless I miss my guess though, you would probably rather stay here and reap the rewards with us. How would it look to the fleet if you came back triumphantly after the professionals left with their tails between their legs?" He finished and Ratledge was amazed at this man's ability to seek personal gain in almost every situation. He was also a master manipulator. A characteristic one only forgot at one's own personal expense. He considered the odds of recovering anything from that sunken island and his doubts were obvious.

"All right, I will give you two weeks to get this miraculous Jeng equipment or whatever from that base, and then we have to go back to headquarters empty handed or not."

The Captain thought for an instant, wondering whether he could push the time limit or not. He chose not to try just now. "Very well sir, now if we can just get these blasted black squadron ships away from our prize, we should be in good shape." He commented and the two men returned to the bridge. Ratledge was still wondering which man was the more dangerous, the XO or the Captain. In his mind, they were dead even.

The Captain turned away from the Admiral and strolled purposefully back onto the bridge. He was ready to embrace his future; he just hoped he had chosen the right path for it. He had god knows how many stealth ships to get rid of and he had only a shadow of an idea about how to do it. He faced the communications officer and nodded for attention. "I want a com-link to that stealth-ship out there, can you handle it?" He queried and the communications officer nodded affirmative.

"I'll get them for you in a flash sir; they are close enough that a wide band broadcast should reach every ship in their wing. We can page them and they should respond to complete the link sir." The man replied and then he pressed a few buttons and the antenna on the bottom of the *Lincoln* came to life as a radio-wave broadcaster. The man knew his job. The stealth ships were swept over by the broadcast and Vorn responded himself. The link was set up within seconds of that first broadcast.

When the link completed, the two ships switched to video mode and Vorn's picture appeared on the screen in front of the Captain. The man looked pretty dejected. His kind rarely accepted defeat well. "Well Captain, what do we do now?" He looked away from the screen for a moment as if checking something and then his gaze returned to the small image of the Captain before him. "That blasted Jeng moon is moving out of the system. We could give chase, but what can we do about it? I'll have to put this in the log as a complete failure. We did not recover any information and the Jeng won the only confrontation." He did not speak the next phrase that popped into his mind. That was "This will not look good on my record." But the Captain had the impression he knew what the man thought without vocalizing it. Admiral Vorn looked tired; like he had been on edge for a long time and now he looked deflated somehow. Ratledge was looking over the Captain's shoulder at the screen and he kind of felt sorry for the man.

"Admiral," The Captain began. "I need to collect some satellites we placed here on our last time out. We'll be back at base within the week." He lied. Vorn seemed uninterested in the *Lincoln*'s schedule. The Captain continued. "Did you want us to take headquarters any message for you? After all, you may be going somewhere else and need our services to file the proper reports." He finished and Admiral Vorn looked shocked.

"Are you suggesting that we run and hide to cover up our defeat? I should come over there and beat you to within an inch of your miserable life for even suggesting such cowardice!" He fumed and the Captain held up his hands in a defensive posture.

"No, no I meant nothing of the sort. I simply meant that maybe you had another mission to attend to and could not spare the time to return to base with the sad news." The Captain responded in a placating tone that did nothing for Vorn. "It will be pretty boring around here, docking satellites and retrieving useless telemetry reports and air samples from the planet below."

The Admiral knew that tedious tasks like that were a part of every survey mission. It was one of the reasons that he had not volunteered for survey service. He was a man of action. He was still upset that this action had gone on under his nose without him being able to do anything about it. These Jeng were definitely a mysterious lot. They destroyed their own base to keep it out of enemy hands. He could understand that, but how could they have been unnoticed for so long? They had been completely hidden before this insignificant Captain stumbled across an active base. There were many questions, and damn few answers. He was itching for another crack at them, but the situation here was dead. He intended to return to headquarters and request to search for the Jeng elsewhere. He would make it his personal quest to establish some sort of dialogue with these people. There had to be a way. He brought his mind back to the here-and-now. That miserable captain was waiting for a response. "No thank you, I will be returning to headquarters to file a full report. Recover your equipment; I do not need to wait here for you. There is no longer any threat in this system. I will file a full report and you can move on to your next assignment after cleaning up here." He said graciously and the Captain celebrated inside. This had gone exactly as he had hoped.

"Of course sir, we shall be on our way as soon as we've mopped up then. Thank you for your help here. I am sorry that we weren't successful. Maybe next time we can have more luck." He said and Vorn just nodded. "*Lincoln* out." He said and the communications officer cut the link and the Admiral's face disappeared from the small screen. Ratledge nodded in satisfaction.

"You did a pretty good job there. I knew you had talents

that were not in the files. Your ability to manipulate people was somehow overlooked in your official records." He said and the Captain looked at the man curiously. Was he jesting, or was this a warning sign of things to come? He decided to forget it for now. There was much to do as soon as those other ships left the system. He hoped that they would drop their cloaks so he could tell when they were gone. He didn't really expect them to though. They had kept their number hidden from him for some purpose of security. He did not expect them to reveal anything now.

He turned to his helmsman. "Set a course for our satellite and keep it nice and slow. I want to take a couple of hours to get there. Then orbit next to it for a couple of hours. Then contact me for your next move." The Captain ordered and the helmsman responded with a simple "Yes sir."

12

After falling for a seemingly endless length of time, the small group in the vault tumbled to the floor when the island impacted and stopped. No one knew how far they had dropped, but they knew it was not a good sign. They had some Jeng information in their hand-comps, but now it looked like they would not survive to get that information back to the fleet. Hopes were running pretty thin. Quinn was paging through his data, looking for anything that might be helpful. He knew they were beyond help with human technology. He hoped to pull a Jeng rabbit out of the sunken hat they were in. Margaret was also paging through hers. She had more of the corridor and cavern manipulation information though. She had been interested in the construction of the base. What she had was most impressive. She could duplicate many of the phrases that she had and had actually extended the base by several meters before it dropped. Of course the whole island was now beneath the surface, so the amount she had added was insignificant next to the destruction the Jeng had unleashed upon them. The archeologists were also busy. They had come across several unrecognizable runes and they had copied them down on special archeological imprint sponges. It was the modern day equivalent of casting fossils. They had captured runes from some of the deeper regions of the Jeng caverns. Of course, neither man had made any progress in translating the runes since the knowledge was locked in Quinn's hand comp, but they had hope that they had something worthwhile in those cryptic runes.

Quinn was coming up empty and Margaret had found something about a spire. It was hoped that a tall tower could be constructed that they could ascend and thus exit to the surface on. Maybe then they could contact the *Lincoln* if she was in orbit. It would take a lot of luck, but in desperate situations, any chance is better than none. Margaret started the process of reading the runes. She took her time and tried to pronounce them as accurately as possible. In the center of the chamber, a stone mound began to form and it started to grow. Quinn was just finishing his search and the archeologists handed him their data to search through next. Margaret was still speaking and her small protuberance was growing alarmingly. The base of the structure she was building was displacing the chamber they were in. The amount of available air was shrinking fast. She realized the situation and aborted the creation. They had lost valuable space in the attempt and they hoped that it would not be a fatal mistake. Margaret sat down exasperated. She had hoped beyond hope that her spire would be the answer. Now that it appeared to be the wrong answer, she was sinking quickly into depression. She began to realize her own mortality. It was not a pleasant thought just now.

Quinn was reading the rune-casts. He scanned one then another and then another. He was getting so familiar with the Jeng's rune language that he could just read them straight without the need for his translation software. Then he picked up another and froze. The change in demeanor was noted in the now tiny chamber immediately.

Margaret was the first to speak up. "What have you found?" She asked and her voice trailed up as her hopes dared to return. She trusted Quinn explicitly, and if he thought he had a solution, she was prepared to embrace it wholly. After all, what choice did any of them have?

Quinn looked at the anxious archeologists and smiled. "You two are either the most intelligent geniuses I've ever met or you are the luckiest SOB's in the galaxy." He proclaimed with satisfaction. Their faces reflected the confusion they felt at the mixed praise. This cast here contains the instruction for the Jeng transport wall." He announced to the group and faces turned up with beaming excitement. "There is just one catch." He continued. The two walls must be made of flat stone. We can go anywhere;

distance is irrelevant. But it must contain a wall like the one in here to receive us. That means we cannot go back to the ship. But we can go somewhere else, somewhere not at the bottom of an ocean. We need think of a place we have been, or that we have seen that has a flat vertical wall to accept our transport." He finished triumphantly. The group tried to think about places they had been that had walls in them. There was much discussion, but many of the locations were devoid of human life and thus they could not get transport back home. Home for Margaret was a space station, so there were no stone walls there. Home for Quinn had been a small colony. But the air around it had been unbreathable. They could not go there without breathing gear. Unfortunately that was something they just did not have. It was the same for the archeologists as well. They each wracked their brains for an answer and came up empty. Then Quinn's face lit up like a light going on inside his brain. "I know a proper wall, but it will be risky." He said and they all looked at him questioningly. "We can go to the Jeng moon. We left from there to come here, Margaret and I. We have a shuttle over there; we may be able to escape if we can manipulate the walls accordingly to get back to it from the transport chamber. It is the only place that I can remember seeing that would suit our needs." He concluded and he was met by skeptical looks all around. Then he drove home his final point. "Does anyone have a better idea?" He challenged. One by one, the team shrugged their shoulders and fell into line for Quinn's frightening plan.

He sat down in the small chamber and faced a good solid flat stone wall. It was large enough to accommodate them all at the same time, and that's just what Quinn wanted. He did not want to send one or two people through and then have the thing cut off at the other end. He wanted to save them all and return home with his finds. The fleet could definitely use this information, not to mention the Jeng's surprise at seeing these pesky humans again. As his mind went over the plan again and again to ensure that it was solid in there, all the things that could go wrong began to surface. He envisioned a Jeng welcoming committee with those honorable warriors and their blades. They could handle the four humans easily without the help of the cat-god. He spared a thought towards his feline friend but they were probably too far apart to communicate. Then there was the possible problem with his plan if the Jeng had destroyed the shuttle after he and Margaret had abandoned it in that moon. There was nothing he could do about that situation now, so he decided to put it aside and focus on the positive. He needed clarity to do what he had to do now. The air was already getting a little stale, and he knew they had better escape soon.

The first instruction told him to visualize the target wall. He brought up the image of the glittering wall in his mind and the wall took form in his mind's eye. It became more and more detailed as he concentrated on the image. He could see where the wall met the stone floor. He could see the control section off to the right of the main wall. He could see the image of the base that they had gone to when traveling through this wall. It became so real he could feel the fear he had had when he first saw it. Then he moved to step two. He spoke the words of the runes. They came out sounding garbled, but that was the Jeng way. His pronunciation was actually perfect and he heard a sharp gasp as the wall in front of him shimmered and formed the image of the Jeng transport chamber. In mere moments, the image clarified and the four humans were stepping though it and stepping out onto the Jeng moon. There was one guard in the room and he stared in shock as the humans jumped him. The element of surprise was all they had, but it was enough. The Jeng was subdued and lay unconscious on the floor. Quinn visualized their maze-like course into this room the first time. He was sure it had been done to confound his efforts now. He finally got through the whole sequence mentally and he pointed in a direction. "Margaret, make a tunnel that way." He commanded and she said the short phrase to make a simple tunnel. It expanded out before them and they started to run down it as it advanced. All of a sudden the end of the tunnel fractured and melted into an opening. It was with great relief that Quinn saw that huge chamber with their tiny shuttle in the middle of it. The enemy had not destroyed it, and now there was a chance for escape. The walls were quiet, no sign of all those lights they had seen the first time that they were in this chamber. They made their way to the shuttle at a run. They were all tired, but the chance of survival spurred them on further. They boarded the vessel and Margaret started the quickest pre-flight of her long career. Their luck had held so far, but no one was willing to push it any farther than they absolutely had to.

The Jeng commander heard the distressing sound of an alarm. The moon had never issued one before, and he was unsure of the meaning of the irritating noise. He got up from his bed and touched the information wall. The unconscious guard was displayed on his viewer. He jumped at the sight. "Who could have infiltrated his security like this?" He wondered to himself and the answer became obvious on the next sequence of images. The humans were here on the Jeng moon. They had overpowered the guard on station at the transportation chamber. They had somehow managed to activate the transporter on the submerged base. It seemed impossible that they could have advanced technologically so far since their last meeting. They had shown only moderate intelligence. Surely they could not have been able to decipher Jeng runes. Even less likely, they could not have determined how the technology works, but the facts now pointed to the contrary. These humans would have to be dealt with again. Their survival was becoming a bad habit. He was getting tired of dealing with these creatures. He was also worried that his ineffective handling of the situation so far had resulted in a security breach, the use of Jeng technology by alien hands, and the loss of a class two base. It was looking pretty grim as field reports went. The only solution that he saw was to eliminate these upstarts and return the moon to its normal operations as quickly as possible. A decisive move now could erase his earlier missteps. He ordered a complete lockdown of the facility and the activation of the drones.

The moon began sealing all of its openings and locking each individual chamber off from one another. The drones were automated sentries. They were made of some elaborately layered stone that had many unusual properties. One of the more useful properties was a medium level of artificial intelligence. They launched and spread throughout the moon. Each one had the ability to make a wall opening just large enough to fit their egg-shaped bodies, and then seal it up behind them again as one fluid motion. They were looking for anything out of the ordinary. They moved effortlessly from chamber to chamber. Then they found one of the things they were programmed to look for; an unauthorized tunnel. Within moments, the drones were screaming down the new tunnel and racing into the opening. The vast chamber had little in it, and the sensors began to scan quickly. The shuttle was in sight, but the drones did not recognize it as a threat.

The pre-flight was almost complete aboard the shuttle and the passengers were strapping themselves in when the new threat arrived. They were roughly egg-shaped pieces of stone that somehow floated along. They were making course adjustments and beams of light came out of holes in their sides. There were six of them now in the chamber, and they were methodically checking everything with their beams. A chill went through Margaret as she watched them. She didn't know what they triggered on, but she was certain that the things were looking for were four lost humans. The entranceway to the bay had closed up when the alarms went off, but Quinn had looked up the runes for a new tunnel. He was going to tunnel them straight out of the massive ball of rock and hopefully safely into open space. By watching the drones' pattern, Margaret calculated that they had about three minutes before those beams crisscrossed over the shuttle. The general thought among the crew was that they would not survive such a scan. Margaret brought the shuttle's engines on line slowly. The power eased up in almost undetectable increments over a period of a minute and a half. The drones seemed determined to finish their sweep. They paid no extra attention to the little box of metal in the otherwise empty cavern. If it was an error in their programming, everyone hoped it was a big enough error to allow them to slip by unnoticed.

Quinn started reading the runes and he pointed in the direction of the surface. The tunnel started to form and the walls of the chamber melted into the new form. The opening formed and the flying eggs immediately stopped their pattern and rushed over to the new tunnel. It must have been one of the things that they were meant to look for. That gave Quinn an idea. He continued the reading until the tunnel was formed and then he started again. This time he pointed at the opposite end of the tunnel and half of the eggs raced away to check the new disturbance. Now there were three eggs in each tunnel and Quinn started yet another one, this one straight up. The new tunnel confused the egg-shaped drones and they all left their positions to investigate the new tunnel. Margaret saw the opportunity and launched the shuttle forward at full power towards the original tunnel. The shuttle cleared the entrance and shot like a bullet through a barrel and out into the black void of space. The moon was beginning to fall behind them as they breathed their first breath since take-off. The tension broke almost immediately and there was a cheer in the small cabin. The cheer was cut off short though when the moon turned to follow them.

The runes could no longer help them, as they had no stone to manipulate. The Jeng, however, had a whole moon to work with. Spires of sharp rock began to break off and race away towards the small metal box that was darting through the inky void in desperate haste. Margaret tracked the first two and deftly avoided them with sharp turns and changes in acceleration. However, even as they avoided those first ones, even more of them were breaking off of the sinister moon. Now there were a dozen of the sharp spires shooting after the fragile little ship. Margaret was trying her best, but these new spires would track to her course changes. It was as if they were being controlled. Who knew the Jeng's capabilities? They were probably under some sort of mental control. She tried maneuvers that had not been seen since the old days of fighter combat and dogfights. The larges pieces of rock just kept closing in. A last minute move brought two of the rocks together and they destroyed one another in a shower of debris that made little impact sounds on the hull of the shuttle to let the passengers know just how close they had come. The remaining spires adjusted course to compensate for the loss and Margaret knew in her heart that they would not fall for that trick again. She decided to pilot in a straight line and push the engine as far as it would go. It was their last and only hope. The monitor showed the huge chunks of deadly rock growing steadily closer.

One of the black squadron stealth ships was observing the entire flight. It had been left behind to monitor the moon and make sure that no one else ran into it while the Admiral returned to headquarters to ask permission to engage the enemy. The stealth ship *Prometheus* tracked the shuttle and the spires. That pilot was good, but they just didn't have the velocity to get away from the attack. The commander, Captain Robert Durben checked his tactical display and ordered his weapons brought online. "I want a single spread to take out all of those projectiles. See to it so that we don't have to launch again." He ordered and the weapons officer responded with "Aye sir."

The stealth ship hovered over the shuttle, it synchronized flights paths with it facing to the rear of the shuttle's path and the gunner targeted each spire in turn and painted it for the computer to hit. Then he held his finger over the launching button. He turned and looked at the captain for the final order. It came right away. "Fire." It was spoken calmly and coldly. The missiles raced out of the cloak area and appeared just outside of the spires and they detonated in a relay pattern that shattered all of the stone weapons. The debris scattered across the sector, but the Jeng moon was falling further behind. The shuttle could probably escape now unassisted. Every time ammunitions were expended, a log in the daily report had to be entered. Durben thought about it for a moment. He could see the shuttle causing him a lot of grief. After all, they were escaping the Jeng moon. They might even have been the ones reported lost by the *Lincoln*. His orders were clear though. He was to monitor the moon and report any Jeng activity to his superiors when they returned. He decided to follow his orders to the letter. He brought the daily report up on his computer pad and entered the single line. "The Jeng launched spires of rock, but our missiles destroyed them handily." Then Captain Durben ordered his ship back to their position shadowing the Jeng moon. They had a mission to complete. He eyed the viewscreen one last time and smiled at the lone blip racing away from the moon. "Good luck people." He thought to himself and sat back down in his command chair.

Explosions rocked the tiny shuttle. They had not seen any other ships in the system, but there must be one out there somewhere. The giant spires of rock were about to overtake them, and then they were obliterated at short range by high-powered missiles. It took a moment to sink in, but they were free of the Jeng moon. They had succeeded in their desperate plan. Margaret started to plot their location. Quinn checked their supplies. The shuttle was fully packed for a mission, so they were in good shape. They had a good amount of fuel as well. Things were definitely looking up. Of course the shuttle was meant for short-range use. They could not get back to the fleet by themselves. They did not want to push their luck with their unseen benefactor, so they continued on in a straight line until a course could be decided upon. All four of them began to study the star charts in the shuttle's computer. There simply was not much out here, and the shuttle could not reach too far. The obvious choice came to Quinn and he cringed inside before he brought it up.

"The only place we have a chance to rejoin the fleet is at the water world we just left." He stated and the others looked at him in shock. The crew's reactions started to change from surprise into other, darker emotions. The archeologists were struck with horror. How could he even suggest that they re-strand themselves there? Margaret was thinking over the possibilities, but she was far from convinced that Quinn's reasoning was sound on this one. It was up to him to prove to her that he was right. Quinn noticed the changes and he discounted the two men completely. Fear could be overcome. No, it was Margaret's reaction that most concerned him. "Look." He began. "We know that we cannot reach a civilized world in a shuttle. Even if we spent all of our fuel and kept a straight line, we would die of old age before we made it back. Of course food, water and air would run out long before that. We don't know who or what saved us, so they are probably not a solution for us. If they were, they would have shown themselves to us when they lent their helping hands. The water world we left behind has a continent that we could settle on if worse came to worst. On the possible bright side, the *Lincoln* still wants to plant a colony there. Now that the Jeng moon is gone, there is really nothing from preventing them from doing so. Also, the Captain is interested in some of the mineral wealth of the planet. He won't leave it so easily. The *Lincoln* is bound to return to the planet sooner or later. With our new Jeng skills, we could construct a base suitable for the colony when it comes. As far as I can see, that is the only possible rescue we can hope for." Margaret watched him closely as he spoke. He really believed what he said. He still had those beautiful eyes that seemed to engender trust. She felt herself attracted to him again. Of course now was not the time again, but there could be a time soon if they followed the course of action he was suggesting. She reluctantly gave in to his idea and brought the shuttle around to aim for the water world. She really had no desire to go back there. It had cost her a shuttlecraft, and she was not about to forget the possible Jeng threat returning, but she was committed to a decision once it was made. It was one of the things that supervisors looked for at revue time.

The archeologists were flabbergasted. "You aren't actually considering following his insane plan, are you?" One asked and the other nodded his agreement to the question. Margaret just shrugged her shoulders and both men threw their arms up in the air.

Quinn thought that they were overreacting, but he could not voice that just yet without alienating them any more than they already were. He decided to study the landing report of the original survey crew again, looking for anything that they would need. The trip back to the wet planet was a short one. The Jeng moon hadn't gotten too far away from it yet. It was out of the system, but only by less than an hour's travel at the shuttle's full speed. The blue world spun peacefully below them, but somehow they did not find that all too comforting. Margaret plotted a course to the main continent and she nosed the shuttle in gently. She flashed the previous landing in her mind. She hoped that she would not have to undergo such dramatics this time. The buffeting started as the edge of the atmosphere starting dragging on the tiny ship and it deployed its stabilizers for atmospheric flight. Everyone was strapped in, so the trip was pretty much textbook. The shuttle zoomed in, dropping altitude at a ferocious rate, and then Margaret eased back on the controls and flared the wings to drop the airspeed and visually scan for a safe landing place. Fortunately this shuttle could land vertically, and that's what was required here. She picked an open patch of grass and eased the ship over the lush vegetation. The landing gear extended and the pads sunk a few inches into the damp soil as the gear took the shuttle's weight. Once down, Margaret killed the engines and started a battery recharge going. She didn't know how long they would be stranded on this planet, but she wanted power available when they needed it.

The crew unpacked their gear and took their hand-comps to the nearest rise of rock. They wanted to get set up in time to do some looking around. This was the first time any of them had actually visited the main landmass on this world. There was much to study and in the back of everyone's mind. That was the primary mission after all. This planet could still house a colony. They no longer had the expensive equipment for the archeologists, but now they didn't need deep surveys. That could be accomplished later. There was enough on the surface to keep them busy for quite a while. Plus they could use some of the Jeng runes to get to areas below ground that the instruments would have had trouble with. Quinn took the lead and they were soon face to face with solid rock. The group smiled at their fortune. It was not more than a few hundred meters from the shuttle landing spot. Quinn paged through his data and found the relevant rune phrase. He stood back and spoke the words. They sounded natural to him by now and the power flowed through the stone effortlessly. He had developed quite a knack for this type of technology. He wasn't quite sure why, but it felt right to him.

The stone began to turn fluid and reform. In moments, the opening was visible and soon the cavern behind it was fully formed. Quinn had altered the runes a bit and formed an opening in the roof that was retractable. When the group stepped inside, they saw the massive opening and Margaret smiled at him. He winked back at her and she left the cavern and headed back towards the shuttle. The archeologists simply saw the big skylight and continued to bring in the equipment in order to set up their camp. Quinn kept adding bits here and bits there by reading additional runes. He had made sleeping quarters and finally a lookout station to monitor the skies. After all, they were here to raise their best chance of rescue. Quinn felt exhausted after so much of the rune-speak and he laid down to take a nap before it was time to eat. He had just sat back when the roaring sound of the shuttle came from above. Margaret had flown it over to the hole in the roof, and was now bringing the shuttle down through the hole and parking it on the stone slab beneath. The archeologists were floored at the maneuver, but they soon recovered and finished their setup duties. The base, as it were, was now complete. Margaret shut down the shuttle again and she looked up to see the roof sealing back up. Quinn had read the appropriate runes and closed it up. "That man is really useful." She thought to herself, and she headed over to inspect the equipment that had been set up. Everything looked to be in order so she decided a bit of rest would do her some good too. The adventuresome life took something out of you, and she was more than a little nervous about coming back to this planet again. Of course, she didn't let that show to anyone. She had noticed her own white knuckles on board the shuttle and had taken the time to force herself to relax a bit. They would be eating soon, and she knew they would probably discuss what comes next then, so she had no problem waiting. Whatever it was, it would probably be brilliant. That was what was expected after all.

The Captain had watched his sensors when he got word from that Vorn character that they were leaving the system. Or course his equipment could not detect them, so he waited for a while to make sure that they were gone. Then the crew was put on alert. Ratledge was surprised by the move, but the Captain took it all in stride. He hit the switch on his command chair to broadcast his voice all over the ship. He sat proudly as he spoke.

"Today we move forward to realize a dream. We will accomplish this mission and earn all of us a tidy profit in the bargain. The planet below us has a vast amount of wealth on it. I cannot disclose what at this time, but know that it is enough for all of us to become rich. The only thing preventing us from realizing this goal is the lack of a full survey report. We can plant a colony here. I know this in my bones. The initial survey report also suggested the same. I am anxious to send the message that will draw the colony ship in, but I need hard evidence. Therefore, I am asking each one of you to do your best to see that this survey goes flawlessly. The Jeng threat is no longer here. They have left the system and the black squadron has just left as well. This means that we will not have to share our profits with them. We have a golden ticket to punch, and I intend to do so immediately. So remember to do your duty, and good things will come to all of us. Captain out." He finished and Ratledge simply looked at him like he was insane. If there was any pretense to the Captain's motives, it was vaporized now. He was obviously trying to enlist his own personnel in what basically amounts to the piracy of an entire planet. He wanted personal wealth and he saw no problem with exploiting a world that had no defense against his intrusions. Ratledge tried to figure out how to distance himself from this man, but saw no way until after he got off of this ship. They had been seen as being too close and he had to admit, that the idea of dramatic wealth appealed to him, although his duty was obvious here. He was not about to go gallivanting off on a treasure hunt of this magnitude. He decided to sit back and wait for his opportunity to slip away. There had to be a legal way to back out of a mission. The only way out he saw so far was the two-week deadline he had already posted into the logs. Hopefully this money hungry madman could not cause too much damage in that amount of time.

Admiral Vorn had separated his ships. He had returned to headquarters to file his official report. He had sent one ship on to shadow the Jeng moon and report back its position. He had left three ships in orbit around that ball of water to keep an eye out on the *Lincoln*. Something about her Captain rubbed Vorn the wrong way, and he did not trust the man any more than he trusted a mosquito not to bite. It definitely felt like something was up. He replayed his final moments of his tour by that insignificant planet in his mind, but he just couldn't see the problem. He knew it was there, right in front of him somewhere, but the answer eluded and frustrated him. It also drove him to desire the solution even more. He dispatched his message and waited in orbit for the reply. He knew that the troops he had out there would file reports in another day or so, and he would be anxious to see what was going on now that he had made a big show of leaving them alone. The Admiral was not a man of calculating and sitting around. He was a man of actions. He never much cared for politics, and headquarters was all about politics. He avoided it as often as he could. However, he was also honor-bound to do his duty. His work ethic had crowned him an Admiral. He had whipped other projects into shape, and this stealth project had been one of his most rewarding to date. The failure of his first mission in that unit was a heavy blow. He did not doubt the equipment; the new technology had obviously operated perfectly. The main problem was that his timing had been bad. Had the fleet been in-system a few days earlier, then they would have retrieved much more from the Jeng base, and thus made him a successful leader of men and women. As it was, he was the Fleet's most secret loser. Of course the secrecy issue saved him any public ridicule, but it also kept him from explaining any further than the review board was interested in. His side of the story would probably never be told. After all, facts were facts and he couldn't deny the factual evidence that had been presented. It had come straight from his personal and Captain's logs. It just hurt really bad to come out on the short end of the stick. He vowed never to have that happen again. He idly drummed his fingers on the console in front of him while he waited.

The committee considered the report and there were smiles around the table. This would be the disastrous mission that ended Ratledge's career. There would be much rejoicing, as the court martial would make certain that he was permanently out of their hair. Of course it was a shame that the Jeng had destroyed the base before anything useful could be obtained, but that had been a long shot in the first place. The fact remained that they were around. It had been believed that the ancient race was extinct, but it was now obvious that they were just in hiding. It was possible that they would run across another base later and maybe have more luck in procuring some of that fantastic ancient technology. In any case, it would be without a tiresome Admiral Ratledge underfoot. They hurriedly set a new set of orders for the black squadron and transmitted them out to the waiting ship in orbit. Of course they had to assume that it was out there. That pompous Vorn had not even de-cloaked in orbit around headquarters. He was too worried about security and there were no sensors on the surface that could detect the new stealth ships. The orders were simple enough. They would follow the Jeng moon under cloak and log where it stopped. Then they would monitor it for any space-bound activity. They could microburst the transmission back to headquarters with any details they needed to report. They could also dispatch one of the stealth ships back to report if the situation were serious enough. At least the black squadron would be away from the political people who mattered. It was difficult hiding their funding anyway. If the ships themselves were ever uncovered, then the political refuse would hit the governmental fan. Nasty words like "misappropriation of funds" would be used. It was all for the better to get that ship out of the system as soon as possible. Even if the odds were extremely remote that it would be detected if it did remain in orbit forever. The powerful men eyed each other speculatively and then they nodded as if in agreement and parted company. They had lives to get back to and this emergency session was over.

Vorn read the orders and sighed. He was being sent to nursemaid the Jeng moon and the orders expressly forbid him from contacting, attacking, or interfering with the Jeng and their activities. He was merely to shadow them and report what they were up to. He was getting the idea that they wanted to shuffle him away from the spot light of the political spectacle that headquarters was always swimming in. It was a big year for politics since half of the board members were up for re-election. There were also several bills on the docket about pressing for expansion in the fleet systems. This would facilitate more jobs, and more revenue for the fleet expansion. It also meant that they wanted to be more powerful in the face of the Jeng discovery. Of course that was not public knowledge, so the scheming would go undetected for quite some time, but the time for progress was upon them, and they needed him and his crew far away to do their dirty work. They were just out here to make sure that the Jeng did not become a threat before the committee was ready to admit publicly that they existed. On the bright side, he was being sent back out into space and he could stay away from the power hungry men in tailored suits and enjoy his work. He did actually enjoy it. He was one of the rare breed that could do his duty because it felt right, not because he had been ordered to. He sent orders to the helm and the Spearhead shaped hole in space that was a cloaked ship turned around and headed back to the Jeng moon. They were still receiving telemetry data from their stationed observer, and they adjusted their course accordingly. They should rendezvous in short order and Vorn was determined to provide every ounce of information that he could glean from these aliens. He was curious what type of people could sink an island like that. They would rather destroy it than let the enemy have access to the base. That was classic strategy in the past, but it was considered old-fashioned in this day and age. He pulled his mind back to the task at hand and he watched the navigational charts as they flowed across his terminal before the ship leaped forward into warp. In the back of his mind he owed them one, he just hoped the situation would arise that would allow him to pay the Jeng back in kind.

The Jeng commander was in a rage. The humans had actually come here! They had actually succeeded in getting aboard his moon and then they had even escaped. Of course they had help on the outside, but they never should have gotten that far. The guards and the warriors should have been able to contain the savages here, but that had not happened. What was worst of all was that Jeng technology was used in the escape. The pods had not even calculated that the intruders were so adept at using the runes. They had misdirected the automatons and escaped without firing a shot. This was going to make one of the worst reports of his career. It was pretty much a certainty that he would be replaced now. He didn't like the thought very much at all. Men who were replaced were usually not allowed to gain power again. They weren't killed for their incompetence, but a long life as an underling did not appeal to the commander. He now had documented proof that some of the Jeng knowledge was in the hands of these humans. The animals had not only understood the runes, they had used them effectively. That was something that many Jeng still had problems with. The ancient writings of power were a mystery to over half of the population. How had these aliens managed such a feat? It was beyond his comprehension. Still, he could not argue that they had done it. His power base would not be allowed to set up on the new target location. He ordered the moon to stop. He had to think, and think quickly. Was there a way to salvage anything here? His career and countless lives hung in the balance. The humans had become a threat now. They were able to use and add the Jeng power to their own. This was intolerable. If he could destroy the humans that possessed the knowledge, then maybe he could stop them from spreading the stolen power to the rest of the species. That had to be his next goal. The preservation of his own race demanded it. He still feared the outsiders, but now he hated them as well. He told the navigator to follow that tiny metal box they had escaped in. They needed to take that down first. Then he would decide how much damage had been done and what was needed to clean it up. While the preparations for the track were made, he began entering the report. He made each point and then added a bit about how he planned to minimize the effects of it with his new plan. Maybe some sympathetic eyes would read the report and commend him for the hardships he had already faced, and support his further efforts to maintain Jeng superiority. There was always hope. When the report was finished he dispatched a signal drone to transport the message far from the Jeng moon before transmitting it back to the Home Sphere. This would prevent the humans from detecting the drone's launch if they were here hidden somewhere. There was much to do to eliminate these humans. Unfortunately, most of it had to wait until he found them. His first order of business was to simply wait while the search continued. He passed the time fuming about his loss and hating the enemy. "When I catch up with them, they will be sorry they were ever hatched." He fumed to himself.

Quinn felt a tingle in the back of his mind. He did not recognize it at first, but something about it seemed familiar. He tried to concentrate on the sensation but it would flee his mind when he tried to focus. When he was relaxed it would re-surface into his mind on the edge of consciousness. It was like having a mental itch that disappeared when you tried to scratch it. He found it to be a bit maddening. He did not mention it to the others so that they would not think he had been on one mission too many. He could ill afford to allow them to see him go nuts just now. They were depending on him to get them back to their lives safely. He would not let them down now.

Night had fallen and Quinn would not be on duty for another two hours. They were working in shifts trying to finish their base and work on the transmitter to try and reach the *Lincoln*. Margaret had the shift ahead of him, and she would be too tired to talk when he came on duty. It had been like that for them since the new base was started. They each had secretly hoped to get more time together, but it had not worked out on occasion after occasion. They were both frustrated about the situation, but had to put their personal feelings aside for the good of the mission. The mission, what a joke it had turned out to be. They had been incarcerated and forgotten when the Jeng attacked. In truth, the mission had been over for them at that time. But his inability to give up had given them a second chance. They had managed to make contact with the mysterious ancient race. Of course the Jeng had duped them because they had trusted that any intelligent species would welcome human input in their lives. Quinn and Margaret had been sadly mistaken. In fact, Margaret would have classified the Jeng reaction as paranoid fear. They had tried to destroy the humans on this world with warriors bound by some ancient code of conduct. Their bonds cost them their lives against the cat-god they so feared and revered. Quinn had gained the creature's trust somehow and they were living with it in peace back then. Now they were alone on this god-forsaken ball of water. Margaret would be most glad when they finally reached civilization and she could at last relax. The constant worrying and fretting about survival got old after awhile, and she had definitely had her fill of it. Adventure and exploration was one thing, but being stranded and forced to live in an area under alien control was something quite different. She decided to check in on the progress of the two scientists before closing her watch.

The archeologists had completed their transmitter. It would now transmit a strong enough signal to reach anyone in system. Of course they could not direct it in a specific direction, but they could broadcast on a couple of frequencies and hopefully someone would monitor them. They started transmitting right away and were surprised to find the *Lincoln* was back in orbit. Hopes soared among the three personnel as Margaret had just walked in and overheard the first contact. The man stuttered into the microphone and the response came back with some static interference.

"*Lincoln* to lost sheep. Is that really you?" Asked the friendly voice on the other end. And Margaret smiled at the two men. They looked almost giddy in their enthusiasm.

Margaret took the microphone and waved the men to sit down and relax, they had done their job well. "Yes, this is Chief Shuttle Pilot Margaret Manning. We are on the main continent of the planet and request link-up for four people." She said into the mike and waited. The response took a few moments. When the answer came it was a question. "Are you alone?" She puzzled for a moment and then looked to the two men in the room. I am here with Tom and Roy, the archeologists we brought down to study this planet. Lieutenant Ramses is in another compartment. We are the only ones that I know of. Does that answer the question?" She replied.

The response was immediate this time. "Affirmative. It's good to hear that the two scientists were found intact. It will save the Captain the dirty business of writing the letters of condolences he was preparing to do. We will be altering our orbit to rendezvous with you in less than an hour. Estimated 30 minutes of flight time after that and you can kiss that water world good bye. The Captain wants a full situation report as soon as you're aboard as you might guess. Let me be the first to say Welcome home."

Margaret got a lump in her throat, but she pressed it down and responded with her full dignity intact. "It's good to be home and thank you *Lincoln*, survey crew out." She disconnected the line and looked at the two men sitting there, fidgeting with excitement. "Looks like our ticket out of here is on its way; you'd better get your things together. We're leaving this mud ball." Margaret left the two men in their busy packing to go and inform Quinn of the good news.

Quinn had been wrestling with the brain itch he was experiencing. It was growing in intensity and he was getting a little worried. He couldn't fathom what was happening and he was not sure he really wanted to know. He just wanted it to stop. Of course not knowing what the cause was would make getting it to stop quite challenging. He concentrated again and it slipped from his mental grasp. He had forced it back a few times that way. But each time it came back, it was stronger. He could feel it now a little bit even when he was awake and conscious. His troubles seemed to be linked somehow to this planet. He wished that they could just get off of this rock and back into space. Then he could forget about this nagging almost voice in his head.

Margaret walked into the room. She was smiling. That was something he had not seen for awhile, and he liked it on her. It made her whole face light up with youthful exuberance. She was dazzling when she was happy. She strolled right up to him and he could tell she had something important to say. She was nearly bursting to tell him something.

"What is it?" He asked, giving her the opportunity to get it all out.

The words burst forth from her in a rapid stream. "The transmitter was finished, and we contacted the *Lincoln* in orbit, and we are to meet them in orbit in less than an hour and a half." She finished and stopped to take a good deep breath. Her tension was easing a little, but it was obvious that she was still excited.

"I see." Quinn answered and he thought about leaving this world and returning to the *Lincoln*. It was like a dream come true, but something made him unhappy at the thought. The tiny voice rose to a scream. He could finally make out what it was saying, but it was only screaming one word. "NO!!!"

He jumped up from his bunk and startled Margaret. He looked around for a source, but there was nothing there to make the sound of the voice. He ran to the exit and stood outside. Sure enough, the voice was getting louder. He knew that he should pack his gear and get ready to leave, but something told him it was not the right thing to do just now. Instead he headed over to the beach. Margaret watched him go in confusion. Then she turned back to her quarters and began to pack her belongings. "Maybe he was just getting a good last look." She thought to herself.

Quinn reached the beach at a run. The shuttle had been moved here earlier to help with the antenna for the transmitter. He thought that the voice could be coming from it, but it was not. He thought about leaving again and the scream repeated again. This time it was much louder. He covered his ears to protect himself from the sound. But it did no good. The scream was inside his head. He was listening to another being's thoughts. Then it hit him. He was listening to the cat-god. It was trying to find him before he left. It was desperate to get to him and he was feeling downhearted at having to leave it behind.

Quinn gazed out into the water and a distant disturbance caught his eye on the horizon. It was the creature paddling for all it was worth. Who knows how far it had traveled to get there, but he could sense that it was tired beyond the mortal sense of the word. The effort it was making was beyond measure. Tom and Roy brought some cases to the shuttle and loaded them accordingly. They smiled at Quinn and went back to the base for more stuff to bring out. They puzzled over their leader's strange actions, but they were too excited to give it more than a quick thought and then they were off again. Both men were dreaming of being back aboard and returning to their comfortable lives. After a few moments of watching the two bungling around with another set of boxes, he looked out to the ocean and was startled by how close the beast was now. It was nearly close enough to see its eyes. It was still paddling madly and the water formed a mini wake behind it because of the forward progress the creature was making. It was most impressive. Quinn's mind was awash with exultation. The creature could see him now and it was relieved immeasurably. It felt the closeness of the human's thoughts. It detected the warmth that Quinn felt for it and it reciprocated the feeling and Quinn almost staggered at the ferocity of the emotions he was being pummeled with. He decided to sit down on the beach so that the others did not see his personal weakness. He felt drained.

His arms ached as if he had been the one swimming. The cat-god strolled onto the wet sand and eyed Quinn sympathetically. It then pulled some its mind back and Quinn immediately felt better. The link between them had been draining his energy to feed the creature the power to get ashore. Quinn was genuinely glad to see the creature. He had feared that it had drowned when the island sank, but he also realized that it was immortal. Maybe it couldn't drown like that. In either case, they were still linked and he knew that if it had perished, a piece of him would have died as well. He now knew that he could not abandon the cat here. He wasn't sure what the next move was. But the cat-god lay down next to him and nuzzled his ribs with that huge head and then laid a paw across his legs. There was no pressure or threat from the action, it was to comfort the troubled human and offer support for whatever was bothering it.

Margaret had finished gathering her meager belongings and she headed out to perform the pre-flight on the shuttle. The meeting was only thirty minutes away now and she did not feel like missing the boat this time. She took the now worn path to the shuttle and stopped dead when she spotted Quinn on the beach with the giant cat. They were almost intertwined and Margaret at first feared that it had attacked him. Then, she took a few steps closer and the cat raised its head and turned to look at her. Its eyes did not hold their red fire. She saw that it meant them no harm. She visibly relaxed and the cat responded favorably to her body language. Margaret stepped over to the two of them on the beach and she nodded at Quinn. "We need to cast off within the next ten minutes." She announced and the cat looked at her with a pure intensity that made her uncomfortable. Not threatening, but more of a probing sense of need. She didn't understand the emotion and it confused and frightened her.

Quinn looked up at her and shook his head. "I cannot leave the cat here." he announced in reply. "I will either stay here, or it will accompany us to the ship." Quinn said and Margaret's mouth fell open. She did not want to lose him now, but she saw no chance that the cat would survive on board the *Lincoln*.

"Are you crazy? That cat wouldn't get very far in space. It's too big to feed and the crew would mutiny in the face of sharing space with a killer like that." She held up her hands defensively. "I know you don't believe it's a killer, but the crew won't see what you see. They will feed upon their fears from our earlier reports. They were already nervous about the thing when they communicated to us. There is no way the Captain will allow us to take the cat aboard." She concluded and Quinn's jaw set. He had just chosen his path. Margaret felt a lump forming in her throat and tears welling up in her eyes. "Don't leave me now. I was just getting to know you, and I need you." She begged and Quinn stared at her with that same intensity that the cat had just done.

"You don't understand." He began and she backed a step away. "We are linked in a way that I cannot describe. I have no choice but to take it with or stay here. I have feelings for you as well, but the truth does not change. I need to stay here it would seem. You are welcome to stay with me. I hope that you will. But I cannot force you to. The cat likes you too you know. I think we would all get along famously if given the chance." He said and paused for thought and breath.

Margaret looked at him with horror on her face. "Can you hear yourself?" She retorted. "You were the one who brought us back here to be rescued. Now that the moment is about to come, you have changed your mind about rejoining our people. How do think that will look on your survey report?" She asked and Quinn looked away from her.

"You still do not understand. I am beyond choosing here. I have no interest in the survey report. I don't care whether this planet gets colonized or not. All that is important is the survival of the cat-god and my own proximity to it. I cannot be separated from it again. I wish you could see what compels me, but it just isn't possible."

Margaret went from shock to anger. The cat-god raised its head in defense and she stepped back, but her ire was still in full swing. "You inconsiderate, selfish jerk of a man. You know I need to get off of this world and get back to my life. I wanted you to be a part of it. Now I see that you are not the man I thought you were. So I will move on and leave you here. God only knows what I will tell the Captain. After all, he is eagerly awaiting your survey and will not be pleased by your dereliction of duty and your defection from the Survey Division. Let's not forget all of those people who are depending on you to find them a place to live. I mean that was the real reason for this colony planting run anyway wasn't it?" She bellowed at the implacable man on the beach.

Quinn thought for a moment, but the pull of the great cat was too strong and he could not resist it. "I - I'm sorry." He stuttered. "I cannot go with you. There is more here than I understand. I could only go if the creature could go with us. Don't think that I have forgotten my duties, they have just been superceded by something bigger and more important." He explained and Margaret seemed unfazed by his arguments.

"You haven't forgotten? That's amazing. Then how can you follow this course of action? That cat is doing something to you. I don't know what it wants, but I don't trust it. Please let it go and return with me. You are about to make history with the Jeng finds. How could you pass that up for mere companionship?" Then she turned to address the cat. "He has companionship with me. You are no longer needed here. Go away and don't come back." She ordered and the cat raised its hackles and bared its pointed teeth.

Quinn shot up and placed a hand on the cat's neck. "No, she didn't mean it. Let her go. She is upset at losing me. Don't worry, we'll be fine here." He spoke soothingly to the cat.

Margaret was floored at the compassion in his voice. If she had not known better, she would have thought that he was talking to a lover. "You are obviously confused right now. I don't know how long the *Lincoln* will stay in orbit, so I don't know exactly how long you have to decide your own fate, but we'll leave the transmitter here for you. We have to leave now though. Good bye, and I hope you come to your senses." Margaret turned and walked away to the shuttle. The two men shortly dropped the transmitter off out of the shuttle door and sealed the hatch behind them. Margaret applied the power and lifted the shuttle into the sky. She passed one more time over the beach and a tear welled up in her eye as she veered away to head for the rendezvous. She focused on the *Lincoln* and what to tell the Captain. The prospect was not pretty and she was soon crying as she brought the shuttle out into open space. The *Lincoln* was right where it was supposed to be and they were all relieved at the sight of the ship. They had successfully survived the toughest mission any of them had been on so far.

13

The Jeng commander had his moon following the trail of gasses that the tiny metal box left behind. They were heading away at first, and then they circled back to the water world that had been a Jeng world. He found the choice of destinations confusing, but his imagination thought the worst of course. They were after more of the secrets. He could just see them diving for riches under the freshwater sea. He had more weapons available at his command, and it would pain him to do so, but he could destroy that world all together. He had the vast collection of Jeng knowledge to pull from. That knowledge was ancient. It had been passed down from one generation to the next. No one really understood the runes anymore, but they knew what phrase did what. That was all that they needed to know. These humans had somehow cracked the ancient knowledge and were using it themselves. This was dangerous beyond anything the Jeng had faced in the last thousand years. If he could not stop them here, then galactic war was the only recourse. It was a thought that the commander hated, but he also felt it was eminent. He had to stop these curious creatures now. There could be no other way. Aliens were not to be trusted. The power they were on the verge of releasing could spell the end of the Jeng forever. The system came up on the viewer stone and he noticed the ship in orbit again. It was that same human ship he had taught a lesson once before. He thought that the ship had been properly motivated to stay away; obviously he had been mistaken. No matter, it was a mistake he would not repeat. He ordered the spires launched. The moon became visible as it launched a large barrage of immense spikes of rock towards the *Lincoln*. Unlike the attack on the shuttle, there were hundreds of them this time.

The *Lincoln* went on full alert. How had that moon just appeared again? This time the situation was worse. Telemetry reported hundreds of missiles hurtling at the *Lincoln*. "It appears that the Jeng are no longer interested in backing us off." The Captain announced dryly. "Helm can you plot us a course to miss those rocks?" He asked and the helmsman was calculating at a furious pace. The rock pieces were coming as if homing, and they were only two and a half minutes away. After a few tense seconds, the reply came.

"Sir, the only course I can see is directly astern. Run away long enough to outrun the objects. Any course change we might make will be accounted for. I don't understand how, but those things are being steered towards us. They have changed course twice to track to us already." The man answered shakily. He was obviously experiencing an adrenaline rush.

"Well, that's just brilliant. Run away. Do you forget that we are rendezvousing with our lost shuttle? How can we run away like that? We have to dance amongst these rocks and make them miss us. Then, when we have recovered the shuttle, we can blast our way out of here." The Captain told the crew.

Ratledge stood up. "Captain, have you considered that in our current position, we may be destroyed before that shuttle can link up with us? If so, then they would not have anybody to save them at all. Perhaps we should reconsider our options." He said and he hoped that he hadn't undermined the man's authority too much.

The Captain looked at the plot, there were now just under two minutes left. The blobs were converging into a giant mass on the screen. "Okay, tactical shoot those things out of space. Launch everything we have now." He ordered and the tactical officer hit a series of switches that readied and fired the weapons. Rockets and lasers shot forth-reigning destruction on the closest rock spires. The huge chunks of stone shattered. And now the *Lincoln* was faced with a wall of debris. This wasn't looking good to anybody on the bridge. The Captain even looked more than a little nervous. "Helm! Get us out of here full power!" He yelled and the helmsman sighed in relief. He punched the propulsion activation stud and shoved the lever full forward. The ship lurched forward and to the side in a high-speed turn then it got its bearing and shot forth at full power using both drives. Inside, the people were thrown into their seats as the massive power hurtled them forward. The debris wall followed them, but it no longer tracked to them. The *Lincoln* deftly avoided the center of the cloud, but it was so vast and spreading out so far that they could not miss all of the rocks. Meteor hits starting ringing off the hull all over the ship. Some rocks the size of marbles simply bounced off harmlessly, but a couple of chunks the size of passenger cars ripped through the side of the ship and destroyed part of the cruiser's defensive capability. A gash in the ship caused emergency doors to seal shut and several compartments vented off into space. Several crewmen were sucked out into the merciless airless void. The *Lincoln* lurched with the impacts as the shower continued. Further damage reports continued to ring in and the Captain knew they would spend quite some time repairing this if they survived this first volley from the enemy.

The Jeng commander jumped up and down in his control room. He had finally taken care of those blasted humans. Their ship was leaking. It would not be long now before it was empty and they would all die. He smiled at his own military conquest. He sent a second barrage after the wounded prey in order to finish them off completely. The massive launch of spires depleted his moon of some badly needed stone material, but he planned to excavate some from the planet below and refill his supplies. This would be the day that he would be remembered for. In his view he was personally saving the Jeng way of life and incidentally his career as well. He would be a hero among his people.

Admiral Vorn had rendezvoused with his designated shadow and they were both surprised to find the moon heading back to that water world. There must be something really important there to draw the Jeng back. Whatever it was, they were also surprised when they entered the system and the *Lincoln* was still in orbit. Vorn cursed himself for a fool. That man had known something was up on the planet and he didn't want to leave. Whatever it was, he now had more trouble than he could handle. The targeting officer called out for the Admiral's attention.

"Sir, I am tracing hundreds of projectiles heading towards the *Lincoln*." Came the excited report. "The Ship hasn't moved though. I don't know what they are waiting for." Came the speculation of the targeting officer. The confused man turned to face the Admiral directly. "Sir, they have done nothing at all, and now the spires are converging on them as if they are homing in on a target like a torpedo would a submarine."

The Admiral let the wet-navy reference pass. He knew that the man was a history buff. He also knew what the phrase meant and he had to agree. Looking at the screen, the huge chunks of rock seemed to be zeroing in on the hapless ship and its incompetent captain. He felt sorry for the crew, but he had been ordered specifically not to fire upon the Jeng. They did not want a war with these people. Of course if some of those rocks actually struck the *Lincoln*, then they would have technically drawn first blood. Then his hands would be untied. He had gathered his wing together. Ten stealthy ships were at his command. The enemy was not aware that he was even in system, and their attention was diverted elsewhere on the destruction of the *Lincoln*. The tactical situation was a green light. He just hoped that the *Lincoln* would survive long enough for him to save it.

Margaret brought the shuttle around to see what her sensor array was screaming about. There it was, in full glory, the Jeng moon. It was massive this close. Of course they had been much closer before. Memories of the first visit there caused her to shiver and she dove the shuttle away and back towards the planet. The shuttle was not equipped to go to war with the superpowers she was caught between. She started the solid fueled rockets and shot away from the conflict zone. It was a desperate maneuver to gain some distance before anything bad could happen. She knew that the moon had somehow followed them here. They had escaped using Jeng technology. According to Quinn, that had been one of the ancient race's base fears. She considered her options and came up empty. She had no options. She looked back at the two men in the crew seats. She saw the same realization on their faces. They knew that the planet was their only destination now. It was at this moment that Margaret most missed Quinn. He had always come up with some crazy plan to add options where none seemed to exist. His schemes were ones that worked more times than not. She wished that he were there or she wished that she could find a more palatable solution. But that just wasn't to be. She found the resolution inside her to do what she needed to do and veered the shuttle back into a re-entry path and hoped for the best. As the shuttle started buffeting in the upper atmosphere, the radar screen showed hundreds of blips heading towards the *Lincoln*. Her heart jumped into her throat, but the controls demanded her complete attention, and she had no choice but to worry about it all later.

On the surface of the planet, the Cat-god shared its link with Quinn and they both watched the goings on in orbit in their minds. Quinn saw the *Lincoln* in orbit, he watched as the tiny shuttle darted towards it, rocketing free of the atmosphere. He also saw in the cat's own vision that the Jeng moon was back. It was inching ever closer to the planet. He saw the angles involved and realized that the *Lincoln* would soon be visible to it as it came around to the sunny side of the planet. He bit his upper lip as he watched the Jeng moon change from smokey and hidden to sharp and completely visible. It meant that they had dropped their cloaking device. Then the horror started. The moon launched hundreds of sharp spires of rock at the *Lincoln*. This was no scaring off maneuver this time. They wanted the humans dead. His heart began to race and the cat seemed to be uneasy as well. They were sharing emotions as well as images now. Quinn thought for a solution, but none came. He was simply too far away to be of any help. His focus switched from the *Lincoln* to the small shuttlecraft, suddenly caught in the middle of the two combatants. Margaret was doing the right thing. She was running away from the fight. In fact, she was running back to him it seemed. The shuttle was heading back to the planet. He smiled at the thought of seeing her again. The cat got a bit worried at his emotional reaction, but it felt that it had a good hold of the human's mind. There would be nothing to worry about there.

As the two beings watched, the rocks continued to fly towards the metal ship. The ship was confusing, it didn't move at all. Then as a second thought it seemed; it launched weapons to attack the spires. The rocks were homing in on the ship; the missiles spread out and hit the entire wall of spires. There was a series of brilliant flashes and the problems for the *Lincoln* got worse. Now there was a wall of debris spreading out and encompassing the small ship. The cruiser would be pelted badly and some of those pieces were still pretty large. Quinn fidgeted as he watched the battle unfold. The *Lincoln* turned tail and ran. The debris field was still gaining but seemed to lose the ability to home in. They tried to skirt the wall of rock and missed most of it. They still got battered though. The ship was listing off to one side and it was bleeding air. Something moved and Quinn wondered what it was. It was something dark, like ten spearheads. They were that same smokey color the moon had once been. That meant that they were also cloaked somehow. Who else was out there? He didn't know. But as he watched, the *Lincoln* started to limp back into the battle, and the Jeng moon launched again! More than a thousand spires shot away and began to home in on the hapless little ship. Quinn knew that this would be the end of the *Lincoln*. It would be his first failed mission, and here he was using some sort of Jeng technology to watch it all happen. The Cat-god dropped its head and moaned at the pain that Quinn sent through the link. They were connected and sharing everything. The cat was not happy. Its tail twitched irritably, and its ears were folded back in anger. Quinn remembered that there were some bizarre Jeng runes that he had checked out only briefly; maybe there was something there that he could use. He left the cat lying on the beach and headed over to his hand computer and started rummaging through the files.

Admiral Vorn had ordered the tactical link initiated. It linked the computers of his ten ships so they all acted as one. Each order he would give would be echoed in all ten stealth ships. He was ready to go to war. His orders forbid it, but he was ready. The Jeng attack on the *Lincoln* demanded his intervention. Now that the first shots had been fired, he was free to respond in kind. The sensor technician brought up the display as a thousand more rock weapons launched from the enemy moon. It had visibly depleted itself of rock to launch this attack. The tactical analysis suggested that the *Lincoln* could not survive this attack unaided, so it was time for action. Vorn's face creased in a thin smile. His ships were poised to make history, and he was ready to take his place as a hero. He ordered his ships into a v pattern so that they could present a wider field of fire and clear as much rock out as possible. Then they all targeted the spires and opened fire in nearly continuous bursts. The rock spires were not up to the task of the new weaponry that was assaulting it. Vorn had unleashed a few of his anti-matter nukes and the blasts in space were colorful as huge sections of enemy fire vaporized in blinding flashes of warped space and time. The ten ships continued firing and the wave of force they were generating caused them to use their drive systems to remain in place to continue the onslaught. Within moments, the entire Jeng attack had been thwarted. Then Vorn turned his guns onto the Jeng moon itself. The brilliant explosions rocked the now diminished moon and tore chucks out of its heart. "The Jeng could not be happy over there." Vorn mused as his ships exhausted their ammunition on the largest pieces of the crumbling planetoid. The worst part of it for the Jeng is that the stealth ships never even dropped their cloak. They never saw the weapons that defeated them.

On the Jeng moon, The crew had seen enough! It was mutiny and the crew assaulted the Jeng commander. They had witnessed his previous attacks on the humans. They were ready to believe that he could destroy them once and for all, but now they were under attack from an unseen enemy. The wave of blasts destroyed their weapons and then started pummeling their world. The ground shook with each blast. They had suffered damage in most of their living spaces. This Jeng base was about to be destroyed. It was time to contact central command. They wanted to access the transport wall and evacuate the base before it was too late. The commander was in shock. He had not believed that the humans were this dangerous. His own command was now lost to them. This was unthinkable, but yet it was also true. His hatred burned inside him and he ordered the evacuation. The Jeng personnel began filing into the transport room and marching straight into the wall. It had already been set for the home sphere, and they were all anxious to get there before death came to take them. This left the commander by himself to contemplate his next move. He made the decision almost immediately. He brought forth the destructive runes and began the long phrase. This moon was sorely short of rock, but it still had enough mass for a decent impact. He read all of the runes except the last one. He took a deep breath and looked around. Then he spoke the last word and the Jeng moon erupted into a fiery ball of exploding particles. The blast shook the planet below as the shock wave hit it. The blast wave swept the stealth ships away like a hand swatting flies.

The *Lincoln* was farther away, but its wounded hull was hardly up to the task as the wave struck the weakened frame broadside. The sides of the hull facing the blast buckled and the ship would never go to warp again. Damage control teams scrambled to save the rest of the ship before it buckled in on itself. The Captain was knocked about because he had been standing on the bridge. Colliding with a control panel, he broke his arm and hit his head. He slumped to the deck as his crew watched helplessly. They had all been strapped in. Ratledge ordered a medical team to the bridge. Warning lights blared as emergency cut off systems were engaged. The ship was cracked at the core. The support struts had given under the pressure and she would never fly again. It was time to abandon the ship. The maintenance teams began to prepare what shuttles they had left. There was also one Lander craft that could hold about seventy personnel. The order was given by the XO and the *Lincoln* was abandoned in space. Its life was gone; it had served them well. Ratledge oversaw the evacuation of the Captain. No one was sure if it was to save his life, or to see that he came to trial for his negligence. Either way, the view of the drifting ship through a shuttle porthole had a numbing effect on the crew. The power failed aboard the ship and the magnetic containment dropped. A blinding explosion marked the end of the Navy's cruiser and the crew now had no choice but to head to the planet below.

Vorn's linkup had been lost. The self-destruction of the Jeng moon was a move that he cursed himself for not foreseeing. He had witnessed them destroying a base to prevent humans from getting a hold of it. He should have predicted that they would do so again. But the magnitude of the loss was staggering. An entire moon was just obliterated in orbit of a planet. If he weren't so busy trying to pull the pieces of his wing back together, it would have been a beautiful sight. A meteor shower the likes of which no one had ever seen was blazing its way through the upper levels of the atmosphere of the planet. The bright orange dots peppered the sky in a fiery rain that was causing waves of devastating size. Right now Vorn was more worried about his ten ships. They had been blown clear for the most part, but none of them were undamaged. In fact, what reports he did get from his other ships were sketchy at best. The cloak had even dropped on three of them. They looked like dull gray spearheads with chips taken out of them. They were listing badly, and the damage control crews aboard them were working feverishly to restore them to working status. Spare parts were going to be a problem. Although it is customary for a ship of the line to store spare parts for almost every system, these ships were prototypes and spare parts were not readily available. Each part would have to be fabricated for the repair. This would extend the maintenance cycle by at least three fold. Like it or not, Vorn would have to just sit in orbit for quite a while or abandon one or two of his helpless ships.

There was also the question of rescuing the survivors of the *Lincoln*. The sensor technician had observed life-craft leaving the ship prior to its obliteration, and they would have been forced to land on the planet. It would not be hard to find them since there was only one small continent, but they were in no shape to launch a rescue mission with all of their ships in some state of disrepair. The other thing to consider was the fairly dense layer of stone debris that was now locked in orbit about the planet. The moon had been broken into pieces even before it self terminated. There was debris almost encircling the ball of mud as its gravity locked them in place. It nearly made an impassable shield against normal vessels landing and taking off from the place. It will take a master pilot to get through an asteroid field this dense, and a highly maneuverable ship. That would preclude loading the ship with a lot of personnel, as the added weight would doom the flight to failure and destruction.

Vorn looked at his bridge. There was a lot of activity as his crew members were professionals, and they were coordinating efforts and making parts and operating at an efficiency that would make their drill instructors at the academy gleam with pride. He had handpicked many of the best people as he found them. They would find a way to salvage this blasted situation and get his command back in working order. He was fighting to remain positive. After all he had even lost his coffee supply as a particularly vengeful piece of space debris ripped through the galley of his ship. He felt that he had won this battle, but he also felt these that these cowardly Jeng warriors had cheated him of his final victory. He was itching for a rematch.

On the Jeng home world, the massive amount of arrivals drew the notice of Chancellor Drokin. Drokin was one of the ruling council of the Jeng. His tactical history had been the stuff of legend, and was now required reading at the training facility on the home world. The Jeng warriors that were arriving were each telling fantastic tales of this human race, and how they had been forced to destroy their bases to keep them from obtaining Jeng rune-talk technology. This story was not new. The Jeng had remained secret through its ruthless destruction of all evidence. That was widely known among the Jeng. But, a few of the warriors told of a small group of humans that had used the rune-talk to infiltrate and escape a Jeng moon base. That was something that chilled Drokin to the core. They could not have been around the runes long enough to study them and figure out how to use them. That would be a violation of the highest magnitude. There was definitely an investigation needed here, and he contacted the other members of the council and ordered the warriors to give testimony as to what exactly they saw.

The Jeng home world resides in a binary system so that they have ample sunlight from two stars. The orbit the planet enjoys brings darkness for a 4-hour cycle on a 27-hour day. Because of the ample sunlight, the foliage is immense and towering trees form a protective shell for the thick underbrush in the undeveloped areas. Most if the Jeng habitations are underground to avoid detection by outsiders, and that leaves the land untouched. A passing ship would not give their world a second thought, as it appeared to be water and thick vegetation only. In fact, many ships had been by and determined that the world was harmless. It was one of the ways that the Jeng enforced their barriers from all other life. The Jeng had long ago adapted to the short night, and it enabled them to remain active much longer without the rest most species required. There was always a cost though; the Jeng's immune system was weakened by the evolutionary changes. Many of them had died of disease over the last few centuries. Their numbers were diminishing. This coupled with the possible threat of the human race moving in on their territory spelled almost certain disaster to the ancient people. Fear was nothing new to these people; the Jeng were xenophobic of any outsiders. A sad point in their history was recorded when an insectoid species once crash landed a small ship on the home world and the Jeng burned it before it could open, roasting whoever was inside. The craft lay there in the sand for over a decade before the timid Jeng opened the vessel to find two Mantis life forms that had burnt to death inside their own escape pod.

The Jeng had no religion to speak of, but they had duties and honor. Fear of the unknown and outsiders guided most of their decisions as government went. Their isolationist stance was adamant, and they were ready to destroy whatever it took to maintain their way of life when these frightening aliens encroached upon them. They were like an unthinking hill of ants protecting their turf. They would dismantle and destroy any invader unthinkingly and then continue about their lives as before. It was a moral free environment. However, there were rules about honor. There were strict guidelines for battle. It was a code that formed the rigidity of their warrior caste. It was not for everybody, so the Jeng had formed classes for menial labor, combat, governing, and elite versions of all of these that taught the next generation in an apprenticeship type system. So, the Jeng maintained six basic classes that operated their vast empire over thousands of star systems, and tens of thousands of worlds. All without any other race realizing they were even there. The habit of destroying things as they moved on gave the illusion that the Jeng were an extinct, but highly developed race from the past. This was the adopted program that had been developed over a thousand years ago by one of the Jeng teachers and warriors. It had been a thought that had occurred to him more than once and finally he had spoken it aloud and it was adopted as law as soon as the ruling council got wind of it. Now it was the council that would hear how badly the contamination of humans had spread.

The council met in their palatial chamber. It was a perfectly round cave with clean corners and decorative stone inlays that depicted the history of the Jeng race. Any architect would give his right arm to get inside this masterfully formed room. But now though, it was the scene of tension that had not been felt in ten generations. The council members, of whom there were seven, were seated in tall stone chairs that elevated them a good eight feet over the level stone floor. They were positioned in a half-circle around the reviewing area in the center of the great room. In this center were several of the Moon-base refugees. It was time for the questioning, and the council deferred to Drokin to deliver the first question.

He observed the group of warriors and laborers and they began to fidget under his scrutinizing gaze. He turned to the man with the highest rank. It was a sub commander. The man would have been the third in line of the chain of command of the moon base. From his towering chair he studied the other man's face and caught a glimpse of fear in his eyes. He then moved in for the kill. "You have seen what drove the commander's decisions." He said matter of factly. "Was he justified in destroying the moon base, or was it just a cover-up for his earlier lapses in good judgment?" He asked, brutally straight forward.

The man's twitching became almost violent. He was torn between his loyalty to his chain of command, and his duty to defend the race as a whole. "Sir, the commander had several breaches of protocol that had caused him to perform the ultimate sacrifice. It was only this humble warrior's opinion, but I believe that earlier choices could have prevented the outcome of the engagement." He stated boldly, and Drokin's opinion of the man went up a couple of notches. There were murmurs in the crowd and then several nods of ascent gave credit to what was said.

Drokin looked at his colleagues, but they were content to let him continue with the questioning. "Very well sir, then could you list out for me the things that you think could have been done differently?" The council member prompted.

"First of all, sir, and this is said with all respect for my former commander, he underestimated the tenacity and ingenuity of the humans that had landed on the moon base." He started and Drokin cut him off

"What! He let them land inside the base?" He screamed in flabbergasted terror.

"Yes sir, he thought that he could talk them into leaving the planet with the island base and return from wherever they came from. I believe that he should have terminated them on sight as the standing order decrees. Instead, he sent them down to our base with an elite set of ten warriors. I don't know what his plans were, for he was always secretive in the ways of command, but it was commonly believed that he would have his warriors determine how much the humans knew and then kill them when the base was destroyed and hidden."

"I see, and this plan did not reach fruition, did it?" Asked Drokin, still too amazed that the commander saw fit to violate their mandates about aliens.

"No sir. The humans had set the Cat-God free when they stumbled into the base the first time. It was supposedly a joint mission to return the god to the vault. There it would remain harmless for eternity as was originally the intention of the Jeng ancients when they first imprisoned it there." The sub commander blurted.

Drokin cleared his throat. "I know my history soldier, I don't need your interpretations of what the ancients thought. But I am concerned that humans were able to get into a Jeng base and release a most dangerous god from our eternal holding cell. Do you have any knowledge as to how this had happened?" He queried.

The man shook his head. "Sorry sir, but the release of the god is what brought us to the base and by that time the humans were already inside and causing damage. What was worse, they were discovering our secrets. They seemed to grasp our technology and manipulate it for themselves. It was the one thing we hoped that they would not understand. It was most unnerving."

Drokin stepped down from his chair and paced back and forth in front of the terrified man. "So the next thing your commander should have done by protocol was to order the warriors to kill the humans and return the Cat-God to the cell. Was that what he did?" He asked almost painfully expecting the answer to be no.

"Actually, he did sir." The sub-commander responded and Drokin raised his eyes at the slight. The man saw the look and hurried into his explanation. "Sir the commander ordered the base dismantled, the humans slain, and the god returned. But there were complications. The cat-god took the warriors down one by one in ritualistic combat. The humans were somehow spared from the Cat-god's wrath. We still do not know how or why. In fact, a second team of ten warriors was dispatched to eliminate the humans and the Cat-god finished them off as well. By that time it appeared that the god was assisting the humans. They were living together peacefully in our base. The Cat-god struck our warriors with fear and they couldn't even enter the base. They returned in shame and were executed by the commander for their failure."

Drokin stopped pacing a moment and let that all sink in. "So he thought an example might prevent a future lapse in duty. Not bad I'd say. Then what happened with these humans?" He prompted and the sub-commander looked nervous again.

"Well sir, we used the Jeng Rune-talk to sink the island. It dropped the base into the ocean and sunk it forever. We knew that the humans breathed air, and it was assumed that they would perish in the base since we had also quietly jarred the entrance open so that the base would fill with water as it sank. The commander began to celebrate his victory over the humans and then we heard the alert sirens. The whole moon base sealed as per protocols. The drones reported later that the humans had returned to the base using the transport wall runes. They then made a tunnel, in fact several tunnels and returned to their small metal box. They climbed inside and sped away from the base. We now knew beyond a shadow of a doubt that they obtained some of the ancient knowledge. The worst part was that they seemed to understand the meaning of the ancient words. They understood the very knowledge that we have since lost. They employed the runes like masters of the craft. The commander ordered their box destroyed and spires were launched to take out the metal box before it could rejoin with their race. But before the weapons could reach the tiny box, some unseen enemy blew them out of space with a weapon we neither recognized, nor understood. The wall of sight saw no other enemies in the area, so we did not know how to proceed. The commander ordered us to track the metal box and it went back to the base-planet. We knew that was not a good sign. They should have been fleeing. We could not fathom what the humans were thinking. As we approached the system, it became obvious. The human's ship was there sitting next to the planet. Fearing that the humans had already rejoined their kind and the extraction of our ancient secrets, we had to destroy them. The commander ordered a few hundred spires launched and the human ship was hit and losing air. It was drifting awkwardly in space. A second launch was sent, this time with a thousand spires to finish the job. We had severely depleted our base of valuable rock and one of the subordinates mentioned that fact to the commander. He replied that we could always restock from the planet below so we figured that he knew what he was doing. But, the thousand spires did not make it to their target. That unseen enemy blew them up with some sort of anti-matter explosions. I had never seen anything as beautiful, or as frightening as their technology. When they finished destroying the spires, they turned their weapons on the moon base itself. The evacuation was called and most of us left except for the emergency crew. The captain sent the word forward that he was going to destroy the moon base and take the invisible enemy out with it. As far as we know, he may well have done that. The wall system cannot reach the moon base or the planet base anymore. It is widely believed that they were both destroyed. If they weren't however, a great threat to Jeng security exists and we must silence the new rune-masters before they can infect their population with our secrets." He finished and Drokin was really getting to like this sub-commander. A few more like this one and they would be able to handle any threat.

"I see. So where do you think that any more could have been saved. It sounds to me like your commander was simply overmatched by an unknown and unseen opponent."

"This is the part I was hesitant to express. In my opinion, he should have called in to home world for assistance when the Cat-God killed our warriors. He was already being beaten by a handful of humans by that time. The problem simply escalated from that point on and we lost two bases as a result."

Drokin turned to the assembled people of the Jeng and asked them as a group. "Does your experience coincide with the sub-commander's here?" There was an immediate response. The overall answer was yes, they agreed with the testimony as stated.

The council released the worried men from their bonds and sent them away so that the council could deliberate on the next move. Drokin was commended for his questioning procedure. It was nice to see such efficiency in a court like that and his public opinion was raised somewhat by his due diligence.

Drokin addressed the council first. "Good members of this ruling council, I implore you to accept the testimony with some small amount of skepticism. I see many places where this could be fictitious or even treasonable offenses, but the testimony is from a good man, and he believes what he is saying whole-heartedly. But the idea of humans becoming master rune-talkers is frightening beyond comprehension. I do not know what you intend to do about this threat to the security of our species. No, strike that. Our very survival is at stake! I would recommend sending a massive fleet to take out this troublesome little planet and anything that is left floating around it." Then Drokin seemed to calm down visibly. "That all having been said, I believe that we are lucky the commander of that moon base did what he did. We have enemies that we cannot even see. This is a dangerous situation beyond my simple comprehension. I will leave you now so that you may deliberate on the response we must release to the public. Good day sirs, and if necessary, good hunting." Drokin left the chamber. As the questioner, he was not allowed in the final decision, but he had done his job as well as anyone had expected. He had no doubts that they would be chasing down these humans once and for all. The stakes were too high to ignore this problem.

On the surface of the water world, Quinn watched with horrid fascination as the battle raged on. He watched as the Jeng moon erupted in a blinding flash of destructive force. He knew that there would be consequences here soon for all that mass hitting the atmosphere. He witnessed the destruction of the *Lincoln* and he felt a twinge of remorse. The Cat-god was still linked with him and it tried to console his worried mind. He had no way to bring reinforcements to defend his new home. He hoped that the same was true for the Jeng. There were several escape vehicles heading down towards him and he decided to prepare for their arrival. Using his hand-comp he brought up the appropriate Jeng runes and enlarged the living space to a colony size. Then he set to work forming fertile fields for food production. There was going to be a lot of mouths to feed soon. The cat watched him for a bit and then decided that he was not causing it any trouble so it laid down in the long grass to sleep.

Margaret brought her shuttle in on the desired path and landed safely on the beach. She noted her power reserves and that she would need more fuel to escape orbit next time. Margaret and the two archeologists left the shuttle sealed up and secure. They took the gear that had just been recently reloaded into the craft and headed back to the base that Quinn built. It was a lot larger now. Quinn had been busy it seemed. He was not in sight though. Margaret began to worry, but she caught a glimpse of the cat thing out by the fields. She decided to head over there before getting terribly worried. The walk to the fields was spectacular as the sky was filled with shooting stars. Pieces of the moon and the ship were falling into the planet's gravity well and the atmosphere was burning them up with immense amounts of friction. It was a glorious sight, like fireworks but spread across the entire sky. Sure enough, when she reached the fields, Quinn was there. He was enlarging the facility and filling the area with lush vegetation. There were many types of vegetables and he smiled at her when he looked up and saw her.

She felt a spark of interest when he paid her attention. She reprimanded herself for the momentary lapse of control and finished strolling over to him. Quinn was just finishing up a rune set and the fields looked to be growing new plants at a radically accelerated rate. Margaret also noted that he was no longer reading the runes off of his computer. He was speaking them from memory now. She wondered when that had happened. She decided that the topic could wait until the basic survival needs were met.

"How much room have you added?" She asked and he thought for a moment before responding. In fact he thought so long that she was beginning to think he had forgotten the question entirely. Then he spoke up and his eyes were far away.

"The new area will accommodate all of the survivors that are coming down now." He replied straightforwardly. "I don't know if those cloaked ships will join us down here, but if they do, we can accommodate them as well. He stood up and wiped his hands off on his pant legs. He had done this before and dirt marks on his pants were the proof of it. "We had better get inside, the meteors should be hitting randomly around us for awhile. It will be much safer inside during the storms that will follow." He said as if predicting the end of the world. He hung his head in sorrow and entered the base. Tom and Roy were there and they looked none too happy to be back. Of course Quinn didn't really care about them anymore. They were members of another species and they did not belong among his kind. Quinn stopped in his tracks. The thought had surfaced from his brain without prompting. "What did I mean by different species, and didn't belong among his kind? He shook his head and realized that his was not the only voice inside it. The Cat-god had somehow influenced him subtly. He felt a twinge of fear as he realized how much they shared in his head. The cat knew everything. How could he have committed so grave a security violation as that? He felt the cat's mind pulling him in and he tried to resist it. He planted his feet and held on for dear life. The Cat-god blasted him and his knees buckled. It screeched in his head alone and the torment was intense, but brief. The cat bounded up to the human kneeling on the floor. Quinn looked into the creature's eyes and saw that he had been under the influence of some mind-altering connection. Was it the runes? Or was it the cat itself? He could not tell. He decided right then to avoid contact with either and the cat hissed at him and bared its claws. It did not want to give up its prize now. It had almost gotten free of this blasted planet and it was ready and hungry to take its violence to other systems.

Margaret pulled out her hand comp and starting paging through the runes she had stored on it. She remembered something that might help now. She figured she would know it when she saw it again.

The cat-god stood up and showed massive paws to Quinn in an attempt to elicit his cooperation through the promise of force. It wasn't going to work. Quinn held up his hands and spoke a few syllables and the cat screamed in agony as a stone cage formed from the stone floor and entangled the beast. The tendrils of stone twisted and wrapped the cat limb by limb and then solidified so that it could not even move its jaw. Quinn had gotten his answer; the control came from the cat and not the runes. He felt his mind clearing as if he had been watching his own life through a mist floating above his body. He remembered everything, but it hadn't seemed real at the time. He realized this would not make a very good report, but he was determined to write it anyway, as soon as they could manage to get back to civilization. Then he realized, they might not have that long to wait. If one of the other survivors knew of a compatible stone wall, he could transport all of them to it with the Jeng spell. It was a good answer, and he was ready to be back. He just had a few things to attend to here first. He decided to encase the creature as it had been held before. He had the cage break from the ground and envelop the cat on the bottom side as well. Now it was held fast inside a ball of living stone. Quinn started rolling the beast down the corridors of his new base and he reached a point that the landmass sank deep into the crust of the planet. He spoke the words of the Jeng runes that formed the original vault and the same shaped room began to form before him as he spoke. The cat could not see the room, but it knew what was up. It cried out in anguish as Quinn set the door seals and rolled the stone ball into the opening. Then he stepped back through the doorway and spoke the sealing runes. The door sealed shut with the power of liquid stone. Then it solidified and the door faded away into the natural stone wall in front of them. The cat was forever sealed in. There were no opening runes on the doorway like there had been before.

Margaret looked at Quinn and saw his face sadden. He could still feel some of the creature's emotions and the trapped feeling was almost overwhelming. They chose to leave this area and head back towards the entrance. With the cat locked up, Quinn's true sight was gone. So when the survivors began to file in, it was a complete surprise to him. Duane was among the first to enter and he rushed over and hugged Margaret in a friendly embrace. He had been working on the runes and he thought he had a pretty good grip on the meanings, but Quinn quickly showed him some of the errors in his analysis and the depth of Quinn's understanding surprised Duane. The two men would have continued for quite some time, but there were other matters to attend to. The remaining survivors were filing in. The ship that had brought them was still functional, but it was a short-range vehicle much like Margaret's shuttle. In addition, it had no armament to speak of and no shielding at all. The power plant had been pushed to get them all here, but it would be fine. The life support scrubbers would need an overhaul though. Too many people were crammed into the ship for its system to maintain. They had been stretched beyond their programmed limits, but they still had an intact hull and the landing had been soft and by the book. All in all there were about sixty-five survivors now in the base. Quinn welcomed them as they came in, but he was not really paying much attention. The Cat-god still had some kind of hold on his mind and his thoughts kept creeping back to the trapped animal. It was the cause of much discomfort for Quinn, but he smiled to the crewmates as they were directed to quarters and divided up by specialties. This place would be well organized and they should be fine for a while so long as there were no hostilities from outside.

Duane looked around the base and found some differences from the Jeng base that they had explored. Most notably was the absence of control panels. No one had really figured out what they were for, so Quinn had not bothered to have them form when he used the runes. "Besides, they could be added later" Duane thought as he moved on to the next chamber. He continued exploring and noting in his personal log what he found. It wasn't until he reached the deepest regions of the base that he stumbled. The Cat-god's chamber was close. There were no markings on the walls, but the creature felt the inquisitive mind close by. It tried to reach out and touch that mind, but it was too distracted to be re-directed. Duane was checking out the foundations and found them to be solid enough to hold up much more than the base that was setting on the vast stone block. Of course the thing had formed from a Jeng Rune spell, not chiseled by the manual labor of some worker or servant. There were other major differences, and then Duane stopped in mid-thought. He could feel hate and sorrow close by. The Cat-god felt the link start to form and hungrily stretched out towards it. The resulting contact knocked Duane back and threw him to the cold stone ground. He shook his head and felt a trickle of blood running down his forehead. He figured he'd hit the wall or something on the way down. He stumbled around for a moment while he got his bearings back and then he headed back up the long shaft towards the main part of the base.

When he finally resurfaced, Margaret caught sight of him and gasped as she saw the wound on his head. He seemed to be oblivious to the damage and he was stumbling around dazed. She rushed over and sat him down. Then she brought out a cloth and stuck it into the wound. Duane was surprised when she dabbed another cloth and it came back all red. Then he looked back from where he'd come and there was blood leaving a trail behind him. "How had he gotten that hurt?" His mind searched for an answer but it was still not working under full power. The biggest problem right now was the blood loss. They needed to find a compatible donor and get some plasma into the man as soon as possible. Duane looked at his hands and they were a tinge of blue. He knew that was not a good thing and he lay down on the stone bed and tried to relax while Margaret looked for a medical technician to help with the administrations.

14

Admiral Vorn had his crews working around the clock trying to repair the damage that the Jeng moon had caused upon its destruction. The work was slow, but he watched as yet another system went on line and a green light flickered on over at his control board. He smiled at the professionalism of his crew, but he wanted revenge more than anything. He wanted these Jeng to feel the heel of human might. One of his ships had been dispatched to command central in order to get some reinforcements. The non-shooting confrontation with the Jeng was behind them now. They were at war, even if the government did not officially acknowledge it. They would soon enough. At least, they would before the Jeng could hit any civilian settlements. He knew the bureaucratic mentality. He despised it, but in his long career, he had become a master at manipulating it. It was a shame that the government was so inefficient, but he had to appease the right people to get things done. He was not above doing exactly that. He just wasn't sure which hand to kiss at the moment. He would send his own reconnaissance people in to figure out what the current political situation was, and then he would strike at the most opportune moment and accomplish his goals. He wanted to take these Jeng out, and he knew that someone would help him. He just had to find out who before it was too late to save humanity. He had to find a way to locate the Jeng headquarters before they could launch their final assault on his people. He watched the control panel as yet another system went on line and he smiled again. Each victory would lead to his inevitable place in history. He was ready to grab the beast of opportunity by the neck and squeeze the very lifeblood of success from its throat.

Drokin stood at the heart of an immense chamber. He had been called back for the counsel's decision on the threat of the human infestation. He eagerly awaited the orders he expected about launching a counter-invasion fleet to eradicate the upstart race that had infringed upon his people's space. Of course, he could do nothing without the council's support. He had no political power himself for he was simply a servant of the true people, as the Jeng referred to themselves. He hoped that his standing was enough to make sure that action was taken. It didn't even occur to him that he might not be the one sent to lead the fleet to victory and continued success in these violent times. He considered himself to be the best and only logical choice. His chin was held high and his eyes were steel-gray as he looked back at the counsel members and he was confused by their uncomfortable poses and gestures. He wondered just what was going on here. He decided to wait and hear the news from his superiors and then he could get on with saving his race from discovery and eventual extinction.

The procession continued and at last, the last counsel member was again seated in his podium and the meeting could continue. It started with a booming voice and the moment came that Drokin had been waiting for. He leaned forward and listened attentively as the words were spoken to him.

"We have decided that the humans are a negligible threat, and you are to relocate the forward bases to move them away from these curious people so that we may remain hidden from their prying eyes. A covert destruction crew will destroy the water world, and you are to be re-assigned for your bloodthirsty attitude into a less volatile position as a governor's assistant. You have nearly brought our proud race down with your war-mongering attitude, and the people deserve more from their leaders. We have existed for millennia by hiding and watching the various upstart races and making sure we are not discovered. We have never been so close to absolute discovery and thus destruction than we have been under your leadership. If it were not for one brave base commander doing his best to do his duty even under what we consider to be the gravest of circumstances, then we would already have been lost. The commander's family will be taken care of for the rest of their lives as honored guests of the counsel. Your name shall be stricken from the roster of the noble and you shall be dropped in class back to the servant level and the previously mentioned reassignment will take place immediately. You are also ordered without exception never to discuss this subject again. That includes any mention of the human race for the rest of your life. The penalty shall be summary execution. Is that clear?"

It had all been a lot to take, but now Drokin was in shock. He barely even noted that he was required to respond but he weakly spoke it aloud. "Of course sir, never again." He said and the spirit behind his eyes died on that day. He had been crushed. His political career had been destroyed, and his life was now going to be one of manual labor and servitude. He was contemplating killing himself, but he knew that he could never do that either. He had been raised to respect life, even his own. Guards came and escorted him from the chamber he was no longer allowed to enter. His reduced status would not even allow him to clean this room, let alone speak in it. He was hauled away, a miserable shadow of a man. Then the counsel switched to the next order of business.

"Would the protector please step up to the stand?" The moderator requested and a small Jeng man stepped up to the hot seat, but his demeanor was one of polished confidence. He was one of the few untouchable people in the whole Jeng Empire. Every one in the chamber knew that he was safe, and it created a relaxing hush over the room. The speaker nodded to the man in thanks for showing up at all. The protector nodded back and waved the man to a seat. The speaker quickly took the offered chair and tried to blend into the scenery.

"Gentlemen, it has come to my attention that this human contamination has reached a critical stage." He paused to make sure his words were getting through. The various nods and muttering around the room told him that they were. "I will go to this water world of yours and see to the damage. If the Jeng have been discovered, the complete removal of the infestation may be required. I have done this before; it is of no consequence to me, but if these people have somehow contacted their own government, it may be a messy thing when it is later discovered that they have all gone missing. That too has happened in our history. You all remember the accords of the Shasten. They were a people who had discovered, quite by accident, a Jeng outpost and were annihilated to the last being when they were discovered. We later found out that they were telepaths and were in constant connection with their home world. They brought great destruction upon our people. We were considered a ruthless savage race with delusions of conquest. Of course that was only their interpretation of our actions. But you can see it from their point of view and the facts are hard to argue against. We must avoid a re-occurrence of this type of event. Our race was hunted for centuries after that and we were spread far and wide by religiously crazed Shasten that even now tend to surface about every five hundred years or so to plague us again with their blood oaths and honor of their wrongfully dead. The human race and its adventuresome people have already claimed four times the space that the Shasten had when we encountered them. Their fleets are massive and some of their technology still baffles our brightest scientists. In my opinion as protector, we cannot afford to battle these creatures out in the open. A surgical strike is needed. If they do possess the Jeng artifacts and runes, then we must re-secure them and eliminate the people who know of their existence. This must be done delicately and quietly. It has also been reported in the questioning that the humans had somehow befriended a god. That union must also be severed. The god must be relocated, no matter the cost. It must not be set free again." He paused to get a breath and the counsel members were all in agreement based on their body language.

The Protector glanced around one last time then he began again. "I shall take my assigned vessel, the *Black Sword* and I shall fulfill the honor pact. The Jeng will be protected. They will not fall into the hands of the enemy, and I will return victorious and ashamed of what I must do. My duty is a sad one, and I do not relish the consequences of it. But, it is my sworn duty and I shall carry it out efficiently, and professionally. I bid the counsel good day. If all goes well, we shall meet here at the rising of the full moons. Live well and let the Jeng forever hide and prosper in the shadows of the galaxy." With that the protector stepped down from the seat of interrogation and the applause of the counsel rang in his ears as he strolled purposefully from the room. His robes flowed behind him like a flowing cape of fire and all eyes watched him until the doors closed and he was completely out of sight.

The Protector did not stop there. He headed straight to his personal ship and the *Black Sword* came to life. The ship was formed of polished obsidian and light would not touch it. It was the official ship of the protector. It was a position that was handed down from one protector to the next. Only the previous protector could choose the successor and no one knew what criteria the decision was based on, but it was obvious that the previous protector had known what he was doing. The Jeng race had always been protected by these ruthless followers of the strict code of honor the Jeng mandated millennia ago. Most Jeng only knew the three first rules of the mandate, but the protector knew all six. It was a code of conduct that all must live by, and their power was absolute in the carrying out of their duty. The grand ship pulled away from the Jeng home world and sped into the sky. Its dark silhouette traced a sword on the ground and it was known in the Jeng mythology to be the harbinger of death to outsiders. The protector's heart was saddened that he had been forced to intervene, but that nincompoop Drokin had almost brought the True People to open war, and that would violate two of the last three mandates. He sighed in resignation as he applied power to his ship and the Black Sword raced towards the distant blue dot that was the water-bound site of the sunken Jeng base.

The stealth ship *Amigo*, of Black Squadron, made its way into orbit around headquarters. The planet below looked peaceful enough, but soon there would be war. The opening shots had already been fired and the news was grim. Reinforcements were required and this boat had been dispatched to ask for exactly that. Admiral Vorn had enclosed sealed orders and these were to be delivered to the council directly. The ship's captain, Matthew Rayo, was preparing to personally go down to the planet and deliver the enclosed documents. He had already established communications with the government and they would allow him entrance into the chamber to be heard by the council. It was truly the first time that Matt would ever have been inside the seat of power of his people. It was a bit overwhelming, but not so overwhelming to make him forget what the Jeng had done out in space. He was set on following his orders and returning with the needed ships to preserve his race. He boarded his landing shuttle and the pilot closed the hatch and sealed the cockpit without prompting and as soon as he was strapped in, they were off. The shuttle danced about a bit as it was buffeted in the higher atmosphere, but then it angled in and approached the landmass they were looking for. Below them they could see flocks of birds and clouds as they screamed in towards the base and their possible mission. The green of trees and grasses was in stark contrast to the booming metropolis of gray and white they were rapidly approaching. Even the water sparkled and teemed with life as the shuttle slowed to a normal decent. Then they were crossing over the stone fences that bordered the city proper. They were now flying above a modern city of over three million people. The spaceport was on the far side, and they were in the lane for approach to it, just as they had been instructed to by flight control. The shuttle gleamed off of the sun as it rotated and set down gently on the landing pad. There was a moment before the gasses equalized and Matthew felt his ears pop as the cabin vented to the outside. The ramp was engaged and the motorized gears extended it down to the landing pad below. There was a scraping sound of metal on concrete and the motor sound died away, having been automatically cut off.

Captain Rayo advanced and trotted neatly down the ramp. The slope only gave him a momentary pause as he adjusted to the full gravity and rebalanced himself. His uniform was the black standard of the black squadron. His rank insignia had been well hidden by the lack of contrast in his uniform. The guards on duty simply ushered him into a land vehicle and they were soon off to rendezvous for the scheduled meeting.

The problem of Duane's administrations was further complicated by the fact that there were no medical personnel in the new base. The equipment they had brought along with them did not include a blood analyzer, so they couldn't even match the blood types. They could do nothing to help the man here, and he was sinking fast from life as his light started to fade. The cat-god writhed in agony below them as the link brought it nothing but pain from the human that had attempted to resist it. Duane's eyes flickered closed and his chest fell for the last time. The cat-god screamed in the agony of death, but it did not die. Instead, it fed energy through the link to the lifeless body of Duane. His eyes opened again, and the startled humans jumped back from him. Duane's body was changing. He was becoming less human. The cat-god's influence was becoming more prevalent. His eyes morphed into cat-eyes and his pupils turned into vertical slits. His body arched with anguish as his bones broke and reformed into another shape. Black hair started sprouting in tufts from his arms and legs. The body screamed in agony as the transformation completed. The cat-god was in front of them. At least a smaller semblance of it was. Duane was no more; there was no sign of his humanity anymore. His thoughts were of a primal nature. Without his will, the beast now had full control. What it wanted most of all was freedom, and then revenge. The hatred in its eyes burned bright red and it was looking for a victim to satiate the blood lust. This body was very low on blood, and it was hungry for it. There was plenty of it around, the smells of fear and blood mixed and nearly drove the animal into frenzy. The frightened humans were in shock at the horrifying creature before them. The shock was doubled by the notion that it was once a human being like themselves. Quinn had been away trying to find help when the change took place. The sight of the black cat creature did not paralyze him. The cat felt the danger and lunged for Quinn, knocking him back and drawing blood across his chest. Quinn righted himself and drew his hand up to point at the cat and spoke a few ancient Jeng words and the stone floor came alive and drew the cat into it. Bit by bit, the cat's struggle further advanced the hold the floor put upon it. Soon, the cat was buried up to the waist in the stone and then the rock re-solidified. It effectively pinned the wailing creature in place and bought a moment of rest for the stunned humans. Quinn stepped up to the cat, but realized that it was not the same one that he had been linked to. The link it was using he could sense, but it was different somehow, as if this was the receiver, not the broadcaster. He puzzled about it for a moment and then he finished the phrase that he had started. The floor continued its pull on the cat and drew it under the ground entirely and sealed up over it and the new cat would be a threat no more.

Margaret broke out of her stun first and ran to Quinn. She sobbed as she threw herself into his arms. She told him that the cat had once been Duane, and that the transformation had taken place just after he had died. She managed to convey the information between sobs. Now that it had been said, she broke down the rest of the way and collapsed into his arms in a fit. Quinn lowered her to the floor and held her for support. One by one, the others gained their composure and returned to whatever duties they could find just now. It was mostly to leave the two alone in their grief, but it was also an attempt to get away from the horror they had just witnessed. Quinn held her like that for a while and then Margaret grabbed some gauze to tend to Quinn's wounds. They both then headed back to the entrance to greet more arrivals.

Captain Rayo stood in front of the huge doors that allowed access to the council chambers. The doors themselves were made from real wood and were adorned with carvings from top to bottom.

They stood an impressive eight meters tall and the brass handles were polished to a high degree of brilliance. The guards on either side of the door were dressed in the finest of court regalia. Their uniforms were properly pressed and were perfectly tailored. The look was complete right down to the glass finish on their polished boots. Both men stood stone still and their faces showed no emotion of any kind. The two men did not even make eye contact with the nervous captain, but he knew they were there to prevent access if he didn't get the proper approval. All he could do was to wait.

Fortunately for the good captain, his wait was not a long one. The doors opened from the inside and the guards stepped back with parade precision to allow the door to swing fully. A small man in robes with elaborate embroidery on them signaled for the good Captain to follow him. So he nodded and followed the man into the vast space. He could feel all eyes on him as he strolled down the carpeted corridor in the middle of the room and stopped in the appointed circle. His nerves were nearly frazzled by the spectacle of it all, and he truly wished he were someplace else, anyplace else. Still, he had his duty to perform and he straightened his back and held his chin up before the rulers of his people. He took a good look at each one of the seated dignitaries he faced. He must admit that they were not an impressive looking bunch. He had pictured this room in his mind while he had waited, but the council failed to impress him. They looked like bored captured wolves. The spark had gone out of their eyes. They were merely puppets of a system now. He just hoped that they would be sympathetic to his cause. If not, he would have to resort to cruder methods of persuasion. As was protocol, he waited for the moment to speak. The small man in the robes announced him and he started at the sound in the otherwise deathly quiet room.

"Lords of the Just, Keeper of the faith, this is Captain of Space Navy Matthew Rayo. He has served in the Space Navy for six standard years and has been twice decorated for competency." The voice of the small man managed to fill the huge space and Matt was surprised by the simple fact. The speaker then nodded to him and Matt cleared his throat to begin.

"Sirs, I am here on the request of Admiral Vorn. There has been an incident and he has dispatched me to bring you this communiqué." He handed up the sealed documents to a servant and it was relayed to the podium and then copies were distributed to the various council members from the now open packet. Admiral Vorn must have enclosed the correct number of copies. Matt had to admit that the man really knew his business when it came to the court. Captain Rayo waited while the council read the document. He watched them closely for their reactions as he had been instructed to do. The expressions mimicked what Vorn said they would be. He almost snickered at the thought of them being so manipulated by a piece of paper, but protocol would never have allowed that sort of outburst from him. It was also true that paper was hardly ever used anymore. It had been obsolete for years and the fact that Vorn used it now spoke volumes to the council and they were heavy in their expressions when they all finished.

The old men looked at one another and then they seemed to come to an agreement of some kind. The podium directly in front of the captain lit up and the man behind it spoke. "You have brought us the gravest of news. You have engaged the enemy even though the orders were to strictly avoid contact. We are now at war with an unknown force, and we don't even know if our own security has already been violated. Then, we are also to understand that you need more ships to deal with this new threat, even though we will now need them to protect our very homes. This is all in addition to the simple fact that you already have the most technologically advanced craft that we possess." The old man paused as if to draw a deep breath to continue.

"Then you want to know if more ships will be coming after these have been given to you. There is much to do, I agree with the Admiral there, but sending more ships out where they will be seen by the enemy, unlike your cloaked ships, would simply waste them on the unknowns out there. We need to fortify our pickets here first. I am forced, therefore, to deny your request. There will be no more ships sent to that back water world and you are hereby ordered to bring those stealth capable ships back to headquarters and protect us. I will be transmitting orders to this effect directly to your ship. Do you have any objections to note in the log before we do so?" He asked and his old eyes took on a dangerous look. It was hatred and fear that were prominently displayed on the man's face. Matthew was in shock. He had not even dreamed that things would go so wrong.

"No sir, I understand the orders and I will transmit the return signal to Admiral Vorn. This way my ship already is available to you for defense. Is that acceptable?" He asked in return.

The old man nodded, he was obviously satisfied. "Very well, Captain. I will allow you to get back to your duties. This meeting is adjourned." He announced and the robed figure escorted the dazed Captain back out of the chamber and out to the ground vehicle that had been waiting for him outside of the government building. He still didn't know what he could have done to make the outcome different, but it was now obvious to him that Vorn had miscalculated in a bad way. The man was going to be furious with him when they finally met up again. He could just see his own career spiraling out of control and him dying a lonely death as some lowly ensign in his later years. He gulped as the vehicle sped off to the landing pad. The transport whizzed along the ground and pulled up next to the ramp to the small ship he would use to get back into orbit. He was dreading the next transmission he had to send, but there was no way around it, so he might as well get it over with. He strapped in and the ship sealed and arced to the sky. He rode in silence to his fate.

The protector had seen alien races invade Jeng territory before. It was nothing new to him. The historical records of the Protector line showed time after time where another race briefly found out about the existence of the True People, and were then silenced into ignorance. He was still en route to the water world that had claimed two Jeng bases, but he had some pretty advanced technology in his ship. He was already looking at the system to see if he could see this so called enemy of the people. He tried several of the rune-sets and found he could reveal nothing about the planet at all. That was definitely strange as no one there could have the power to prevent him from seeing. If there were no one at all, he would at least see empty beaches and plenty of water. But even that vision had been blocked. It was yet another mystery around this unfathomable world of ocean. He gave up his attempts and waited for the ship to actually reach the system before he would try again.

The small colony of refugees on that same water world was busily making a temporary home for themselves. There was much discussion about a suitable target wall for the Jeng runes to transport them back to one of the human worlds. At this point, they didn't even care which one. They just wanted to rejoin their people and tell their stories. The loss of the *Lincoln* was a stunning blow. The loss of a colonizable planet was even worse. Now the loss of their freedom was beyond reason. They were not mad at anyone specific; they were just frustrated by the twist of fate that had stranded them here. In fact, most of the hatred seemed to focus on the destroyed Jeng base. Had that not happened, then maybe the chain of events would have been broken and they would be on their way home, or even to the next target planet. Either option was better than simply waiting for a rescue here. They understood that they were in enemy territory. The thought did nothing to quell the fears of the people. At least the threat of the cat or god or whatever it was seemed to be past. The beast was one less trouble that they had to deal with. Quinn had asked around for anyone who could remember a wall of stone, and they were coming up surprisingly blank. In fact, Quinn tried to use the runes for long-sight, but found that they did not work. All he saw was a black shroud of darkness. The sight was eerie and he discontinued his attempt. They kept asking around and Margaret felt up to the task of helping out. She continued the questioning after Quinn was exhausted. Of course, no one really understood why they were asking about memories, but when they found one, it would all become clear. At least they hoped it would.

Deep beneath the ground, the cat-god stirred. It had been buried and then it had found a link. It sent all that it could through the link, but it had been painfully severed. It put up a mental block to prevent detection. The dark shroud covered over half of the planet and was growing with the creature's rage. Many of the ancient Jeng runes would not work now that the shroud cancelled their power. The beast had used this tactic only once before. It had nearly destroyed the Jeng race once and for all when it brought the mighty ancients down. They had become almost gods themselves. The attack it had thrown at them humbled the entire race. since then they lived in perpetual fear of outsiders. But it was a god's duty to lower mortal beings that try to go too far. It was an instinct of control that felt quite satisfying to the mythical beast. After all, what good was it to be a god when mortals tried to take your very secrets and elevate themselves to god status? The image of the cat caused fear in the hearts of all the Jeng. The dark cat-god bided its time and collected its strength. The pressure of the unforgiving stone contorted it almost impossibly, but the angry beast could not die. It would eventually get free and it would wreak havoc on whoever was around. It knew that its day would come again, and it was ready to taste the flesh and drink the blood of its enemies. Its mind could still feel the presence of the humans. There were more of them now then there ever had been on his planet. He could slowly tap them for additional strength. It was not an easy task, but the cat-god had the patience of an immortal, and it would succeed. There was already enough power to shift some of the nearby stone. The problem was that the runes that had buried it had been also instructed to drag the god down into the depths of the planet. That meant that the amount of rock to move was colossal. It was fortunate that neither food nor sleep was required, and time was not really an issue. It would eventually get free and terror would follow in its wake.

The black squadron hovered over the water world and they were still a ship down. But they were up to speed in the formation that remained. The repairs were at long last completed. Admiral Vorn looked out of his viewscreen and he watched as the ball of water below glistened with the rising sun's reflection. It was actually an astounding sight, but his mind would not even allow those types of thoughts to penetrate his hatred. He was interested instead about getting some of the personnel from down on the planet and bringing them up to replace some of his lost crew. There had only been minor casualties aboard the wing, but they were already a skeleton crew due to the secrecy surrounding the project as a whole. He could use a few good people manning some stations that were spread too thin just now. He could then increase his efficiency and decrease his response time to any threat. He turned to his communications officer and the man looked back a little nervously.

"Get a message down to the planet." He ordered. "I want as many volunteers as will come until we are fully manned. If too many answer, then make sure we get the best-trained people that are available." He said and the communications officer pressed a few buttons on his control panel and spoke into a tiny microphone that was on his headset. He repeated his call a couple more times and then he switched off the signal.

"Sir, there is no answer from the planet. We are either too far away from the base, or no radio equipment survived when the *Lincoln* was destroyed." He offered and the Admiral was not amused.

"That's nonsense! They have working ships down there. Each of them had radio equipment enough to communicate with us. Get them on the horn now!" He bellowed at the man who flinched back impulsively.

"Yes sir, I'm on it." He said as he reactivated the circuit and tried again.

On the surface, the survivors were establishing themselves and placing equipment in the various parts of the control center. Everyone was so busy that no one noticed the flashing light on the communicator. They assumed that no one was out there, so why monitor a piece of useless equipment?

The signal stopped and then it started flashing again. A maintenance technician from engineering who was dropping off a couple of crates noticed the flashing light and picked up the headset. The voice on the other side cracked with strain, but it repeated a simple message. "Is there anyone down there?" The man excitedly responded and the relief in the speaker's voice was obvious. "This is the flagship of the black squadron. I have been ordered to request replacement personnel for the wing. We need volunteers from your people to complete our staff." There was a pause and it was obvious that an answer was expected. The technician did not want to speak for everybody, so he put the man off a bit.

"I will pass on your request to Lieutenant Ramses and we will see who wants to go with you." He spoke clearly into the set and switched off the connection. Then he left to find Quinn.

The Protector entered the system and found the water world looking quite normal. It was strange that he still could not pull up any images of the surface, but he was unconcerned about it now. He would just have to land and look for himself. The black ship hovered in and entered the atmosphere. It left a vapor trail behind it; otherwise it would still be invisible from the ground. Of course it could be seen from space with the blue backdrop of water behind it. But the Protector had seen nothing in the system to suspect that he might be observed. He expertly guided the ship through entry and he veered towards the sight of the sunken base. He had to make sure that no traces of it still existed to be found. This would require a dive and several hours of investigating, but he was ready for it and his gear was primed to go. The black stone ship looked like a giant floating sword, hovering above the water a mere dozen meters. He commanded a hatchway to open on the bottom of the ship and fully equipped, stepped out and fell into the water. He took an initial survey and was pleased to see that the bottom was quite a ways down. That meant that the sinking process could have been completely successful. He hoped that it was so, for it would shorten his time under the accursed water and get him back into the comfort of his ship. He spotted a piece of something projecting up from the bottom and he swam towards it.

Ratledge and the Captain had landed on a small outcropping of sand amidst a huge ocean. They were far enough away from the mainland, that there was no hope of their meager radio equipment getting through to anyone. That was assuming that anyone would be listening in the first place. The Captain was still badly injured. He had taken a serious blow to the head and a broken leg from the landing on this miserable world. That was in addition to the injuries he sustained aboard the *Lincoln* before Ratledge had pulled him out. It was not lost on the Admiral that if he had left the man, he would have blown up with the ship, as competent captains were expected to do. But the two men were alive now. He couldn't say for how long though. They had no provisions and they were a long way from any sort of help. The Captain kept floating in and out of consciousness. His injuries looked worse each hour they spent here. The Admiral wanted to do something, but no opportunities presented themselves. He had watched several small craft entering the atmosphere and they had all gone west of his position. He basically surmised from this that the main landmass was in that direction. The area they were sitting and lying on was only about forty feet across and the waves rose and fell enough to submerge it for a little over an hour at high tide. It didn't submerge deeply, just a few inches, but if Ratledge was not careful, the water could wash the Captain away in the night. There was a sonic boom and Ratledge looked up to see a black ship cruising into the atmosphere. It was substantially larger than the escape ships he had viewed earlier. He knew that they were an insignificant spec at this distance, but he waved anyway. The ship continued in under a controlled and powerful angle of entry and it cruised south of their position. He continued to wave until the ship was out of sight, and then he sat back down on the wet sand and fell into a depression. He then remembered the radio, and ruffled through his things to retrieve it. A moan from the Captain told him that the man was currently awake. The radio was dead when he retrieved it and his spirits sagged even further.

"What... what was that?" He asked weakly and the Admiral propped the man up a bit to try and get him to eat some of the seaweed that had washed ashore on this glorified sandbar in the middle of a huge ocean. The weed was bitter and the Captain tried to spit it out, but Ratledge continued to stuff it in and told him to chew. With a final soft whimper he chewed and swallowed with a great effort. Then he looked at Ratledge and his eyes were clear and focused. "What was that?" He asked again and Ratledge looked to the sky before answering.

"It was some black ship. It was long and thin and it went to the south of here. I don't know who it was, but I tried to signal them to no avail." He replied and the Captain surprised him a bit.

"That is the direction of the sunken Jeng base. It's obviously not one of ours then. Our people would go to the main landmass and settle in while they waited for rescue. There's nothing left of the base to draw our people there. My guess is that it's a Jeng ship and you'd better not try to signal it again. I'm pretty sure they are not completely happy with us just now." He finished and his eyes took in the Admiral's reaction. The man actually smiled and then his eyes fluttered shut again. He was gone to this world again for a time. Ratledge made sure he was still breathing and then he sat back to think.

☆ ☆ ☆

The Protector was pleased with what he found when he reached the sight. He had uncovered the piece of wreckage below the surface and knew that it was a downed spacecraft of some alien origin. The base was nowhere to be seen. His instruments told him that it was over a mile down. "That should discourage anyone from trying to find it." He mused to himself. Then he marked it off on his checklist and headed back to his ship. He called it down to the surface of the water and then he climbed aboard. The warm waters were fresh water, so the automatic cleaning jets had little trouble spraying him off and testing for contaminants. In moments, he was back at the controls and this time, he headed the ship towards the northwest and the main landmass. If the humans had survived, that was the most likely place for them to be. He sighed again at the loss of the two Jeng bases, but he set his jaw and kicked the ship into flight as it gradually gained altitude, the long shadow of the ship fell away from the black sword along the ground, and he watched it as it danced along behind him on the watery surface below. As he watched, the shadow crossed a couple of beings stuck on a tiny outcropping of sand. The Protector blinked and looked back, but the speed was too great and he could not verify what he had seen. He slowed the ship down and veered around to see if it was what he actually thought it was he saw.

Admiral Ratledge had sat back and watched as the Jeng ship sped away from him. It dropped close to the horizon and seemed to freeze there for quite some time. He kept an eye on it, but it was not doing anything that he could tell. Of course he had to admit that the distance was far too great to make out any real detail. He didn't want to lose sight of the craft though, so he exercised his patience and continued to keep watch on it. After some time, he estimated about three hours based on the travel of the sun, the ship began to move. He watched closely and it turned. He could only just make it out now. It had either turned towards him, or directly away. He decided to watch it until it disappeared. He counted one hundred and thirty heartbeats, and then he realized it had not disappeared yet. In fact, it looked a little larger now. He got excited and stood up to try and signal the ship. He knew that his chances of survival were pretty low being captured by the Jeng, but right now the Captain's chances were about zero of surviving until the new dawn came. The ship drew ever nearer and the Admiral could see swells of water on either side of the ship. It must have been traveling pretty fast. Then, all of a sudden, it swept overhead. From below it looked like a giant sword of the darkest black stone. The shadow of the craft swept over them a fraction of a second later and Ratledge waved and shouted for all he was worth. The ship sped by so quickly, and they were such a small target in the vast ocean of blue water, he was pretty sure that the ship had not seen him. But his fears turned to wonder as the ship slowed down and started to circle back. His hopes began to lift and he tried to wake up the Captain. The injuries were bad enough, but the man was getting terrible sunburn on top of it all. Ratledge cringed a bit at the man's cry of pain as wakefulness took him.

"What is it? Why do you wake me to this hell? Are we about to die, or something? He asked. He tried to see past the man and just over Ratledge's shoulder he saw a gleaming black sword of immense size. His memory of mythology classes convinced his addled mind that it was an omen of death and he smiled at the possible release from his agony. He actually got the strength to sit up and watch as the ship hovered in and lowered to just over their heads. The Admiral was busily trying to straighten his uniform up, but it was beyond hope. It had been ruined somewhat in the crash landing. It had been frequently wet and re-wet in the relentless ocean waves, and it had been rolled about on a block of sand that was their only lifeline for several days. Suffice it to say that he would not stand up in any official events in his current attire.

As the two men watched, a hatchway opened up and a strong yellow light poured over them. Their skin tingled, as the beam seemed to pass through them somehow. Neither of them knew what it was, but they did not feel any fear from it either. Then the light faded and a Jeng looked out from the opening to stare down at the two humans. They made eye contact and the alien man appeared to be more curious than angry, so the Admiral felt that there was a chance they could survive this encounter. Then the alien before them surprised both men; he spoke.

"I am the Protector of the True People. You are on our property, as we have claimed this planet. I am therefore required to remove you from it and place you in the nearest neutral position I can find with due expedience." Then it cocked its head to the side and paused. Then it spoke again. "Do you understand?"

The two men knew that they were expected to reply, but both were still in a bit of a shock at hearing perfect speech come from an alien being that they thought they were at war with. "Yes, sir, we understand." Admiral Ratledge finally managed to blurt out.

The Protector nodded their acceptance and lowered a platform down to them. It was obvious that they were to climb onto it to be elevated into the ship. They did so with the Captain almost passling out from the pain. They were lifted and the platform became one with the floor. There was not even a seam left when the movement was complete. The Admiral looked at it and whistled. The alien stepped up and looked at his mouth. Then it formed an "o" with its mouth and tried to duplicate the sound. It did not really work. It came out more of a sputtering and the being gave up and returned to his post.

The interior of the ship was a lot like the exterior had been. Everything was black obsidian, and the lines in the room were all ramrod straight. It looked rather sparse. There was one chair at the head end of the room, and a console in front of it with all of the controls just as black as the wall they were set into. It was as if the ship had been chiseled out of one solid piece of stone. In fact, he could not feel the throb of a motor or conventional drive system. There were no metal decking plates, and there were no displays or video screens of any kind that he could see. He wondered how the thing could move at all, or even how it was controlled. The room was a little short at about two point one meters, but it was a good 10 meters wide. The sword appearance it sported outside made the floor and ceiling taper in as you edged away from the center of the room. The sidewalls were a mere two point five meters high. There were no seams anywhere. The stone was polished to a reflective sheen. Even in black, it reflected like a mirror. The stone had a thin gray vein, like the darkest marble and the whole thing seemed to suggest power.

Ratledge stood up and stepped closer to this being who called himself the Protector. The Jeng paid him no mind at all; he didn't even turn to face the humans as the Admiral approached. Ratledge stepped as close as he dared. Then he cleared his throat to try and get the Jeng's attention. The alien being looked away from the flat glossy panel to stare at the human. "My colleague needs medical help. Can you help him?" He asked with some skepticism.

The Protector looked back at Ratledge, and then he cocked his head to the side like a dog might when you told it something it didn't understand. The Admiral pointed to The Captain and repeated his request.

"This man needs help, can you help him?" He said, this time with a little impatience flavoring his tone. He watched as the Jeng looked from one human to the other. It seemed like he did not understand the question, even though he had spoken plainly with them earlier. It was a little confusing. The Admiral's patience was thinning as the seconds ticked by.

The Jeng stood up and walked over to the man on the floor. He lifted a handheld device from his belt and waved it over the Captain and watched as a little readout displayed symbols that Ratledge could not make out. The box made a whirring noise with an occasional beep, and the scanning process took about two minutes. The Captain groaned a bit and the Jeng jerked back from him.

The Jeng turned to Ratledge and spoke. "I cannot help him; your physiology is too different from ours for my tools to be of assistance. But we can lock him in place until help can be found. It is not the best solution, but it is the only one that I can offer you." He said and then he waited for Ratledge's response.

The Admiral did not know what to expect, but he believed that the man would die without some sort of intervention, so he agreed to the locking procedure. Then he stepped back to allow the Jeng Protector to do whatever he was about to do. The Jeng stepped over to the wall and waved a hand over it. A console formed in the very stone and the Jeng touched it in several places quickly and the area of stone around the Captain became liquid and pooled up around his body. It swept over him like a black stream of water and then it re-solidified and the Captain was encased in living stone. Ratledge drew in a sharp breath and then he whistled again. Again the Jeng made the "o" shape with its mouth and attempted the maneuver but its sputtering just didn't match the whistle it was trying to reproduce. He made a gesture like shrugging his shoulders and then waved his thin hand over the console and the wall returned to its former smooth state. "It is done; he will be protected from additional harm until help can be found."

Ratledge looked at the Jeng and asked a fearful question. "Are we considered to be your prisoners?" He queried a little nervously.

The Protector thought for a moment and decided to hold his response for a moment. He checked their course and he checked the speed. He was still on target for the next leg of his mission. Then he returned his attention to the expectant human in his ship. "You are here for removal from our world. You are not allowed to roam freely due to security issues, but you are not locked up either. You can roam this room only. Facilities will be made available to you, as they are required. I still have a mission to fulfill. If there is any interference in that duty, I will terminate both of you immediately. I have to function for the good of the True People. It is a calling above all others and I will never shirk in my duties. Have I made myself abundantly clear to you?" He asked and Ratledge nodded.

Ratledge got a serious look on his face. "You must also understand that I must act to preserve my race. If I see that you are attacking my people, I will kill you where you stand. I understand that you could have left my companion and me on that little patch of sand and that we would probably have perished. But I feel you deserve to be told where I stand, and what I will allow. I must also tell you that many of the survivors of our ship have probably come to this planet. If they need to be removed, it will not be by all-out slaughter. They will have to be returned to my government. If your goals are consistent with mine, we will get along just fine."

The Protector was hard pressed to believe what he had heard. These humans were a forward people, of that he was certain. But this man seemed honorable enough. He had taken no negative action since boarding the ship. He had detected no weapons on either of the beings, but he somehow believed that they could kill with their strong hands. He decided that caution was called for here. But the logic of the human's statement reflected that of his own. It would appear that the Jeng Commander's assessment of these people was somewhat lacking. He had called them unsophisticated savages. Yet this man had requested aid for his comrade. He had done nothing that would violate a strict personal code of honor, and he was also willing to resort to violence to protect others of his kind. It was more or less the same as the True People. This whole mission was becoming quite instructive for the Protector. He only hoped that the humans could learn as much from him as he was learning from these two specimens. "I see no problems between us, other than your presence here on our world. I will of course act honorably, and you must do the same to earn my trust. Do you find this acceptable?" He asked the towering human.

"Yes, I too believe that we have an understanding. It would be good if we could work together to accomplish our goals. It may be possible to reunite with my people without bloodshed if I can talk to them briefly before you show yourself. I can warn them about your coming, and they would not be so frightened." He added trying to be helpful. He didn't come out and say it, but Ratledge feared the possibility of being trapped inside the living stone like the Captain was. He was ready to become as genial as was necessary to avoid that fate.

"Your plan sounds reasonable to a degree. I would not allow you to re-enter your society simply to warn them of my coming. The potential for disaster in that plan is inherent and obvious. You could simply tell them where to expect me and they could have their weapons trained on me before I ever saw them. No I am not in that much of a hurry to die. But I can allow you to talk to your people with me already there. That way they could see you and me together and know that we are not fighting each other on a personal level. Then maybe we could convince your people to abandon this world and move on to another. They must also leave behind the True People's technology. That is the only thing that would appease my people and make amends for the loss of two of our bases here. It is the best way to preserve peace between our peoples." The Protector finished with a flourish.

"If your thoughts are of peace, then I believe I will trust your plan and do what you ask. I know that our people don't want to be on your planet. They lost their transportation off of this world. They are just stranded here. If you are willing to move them, then I am most certain that they will leave this place without much argument. It is also a good thing that I outrank anyone down there. I can order anyone who isn't thinking along those lines to leave and that will be the end of the resistance." Ratledge boasted boldly.

The Protector looked at the strange human again. "You have a command structure too?" He asked and Ratledge nodded affirmative. "I did not know that your people were so advanced. I see them using these metal boxes, but sophisticated actions speak much louder than sophisticated toys." Then the Jeng man changed the subject. "We will be closing in on your people soon. The mainland is rapidly approaching. I am detecting several of your small metal boxes on the ground, and there seems to be a lot of your people here. There may be too many to transport with my ship. We may have to work on a new plan to evacuate your people." The Protector stated blandly.

Ratledge rubbed his chin. The action seemed peculiar to the Jeng man. "I guess we will just have to play that by ear." He said and the Protector looked at him as if he had switched languages in mid-sentence.

"I don't understand your remark." The Protector replied and Ratledge looked a little embarrassed.

"Sorry, what I meant was that we will have to see what is going on, and then plan accordingly. We can't decide here, because we don't have enough information yet."

The Jeng nodded, it was a habit he had picked up from this

human already. "I think we can get more information now, we are over the beach and heading towards your people right now.

The *Black Sword* swooped in low and brushed the tops of the trees as it came in and lowered to just above the level of the tall grass outside of the new base. There were several humans about and they were all pointing and yelling at each other. The ship lightly touched down and the Protector made the ramp extend to allow access to the ground. The Admiral followed him out of the ship and down to the wet grass. There were even more cries as people pointed to both of the beings and yelled to someone inside the doorway. The Protector walked proudly up to the entrance. The humans that were there were backing away from him as if he had the plague. The entrance was clear when he reached it. The Protector tried to cross the threshold, but it was as if a force stopped his movements. He pressed on again, and found the doorway to be impenetrable. He looked back at the Admiral who was confused by the alien's halt.

"I cannot pass through." He announced and Ratledge looked surprised. The Protector backed away from the doorway and Ratledge stepped into it. He stepped through the threshold and turned back from inside.

"I don't see a problem." He said as he shrugged his shoulders. He stepped back outside again and stood next to the Jeng man. "Anybody in there in charge?" He yelled into the doorway and Lieutenant Quinn Ramses stepped forward with a smile on his face.

The young officer looked at the Admiral and the Protector pacing in front of them. He had been under some immense strain of late, and his hair was beginning to gray at the temples. His demeanor was one of a cat prowling in front of a cage of mice. "How may I help you gentlemen today?" He asked and he managed to do it without showing favoritism to either man he addressed.

The Protector was steaming inside, he was being held back and he felt the threatening stare of this human. He stepped forward and met with that same preventive force again. His indignity flared. "I am here to remove you humans from the True People's world and restore our rightful property to the empire." He stated boldly.

Quinn stopped pacing; he squared off with the alien being. The Jeng was shorter by a good six inches, and he was also thin and wiry next to the powerful looking survey crewman. He locked eyes with the Protector, as if trying to see if he were telling the truth or not. "I am not interested in your mission. I am interested in getting my people home. Right now our options are very thin. I believe that if you are here, then you must have a ship that can transport us away." Then Quinn paused in thought. "Well, at least some of us. We have been trapped here since the fight in the skies. I don't know what kind of people you are, but I personally am tired of all of your supposed higher morals and smug superiority. I have learned the ways of your runes. I admit that they are truly remarkable, but they are only tools. You have been allowed to use them for centuries, perhaps millennia, and you have done nothing but hide and skulk. I will not subject my people to this type of lifestyle. If you want to have this world back, then you can have it. But I need my people taken safely back to one of our planets. I also need assurances that your people will not attack mine. I have already been double-crossed once and I don't think you want me to be your enemy, so I suggest you keep to the straight and narrow. I want you to make the arrangements as soon as possible." Then he closed the distance between them until they almost touched noses. "My terms are not negotiable. What do you say?"

The Protector was shaken. Never before had he been addressed with such potential venom. This human was dangerous. He walked like a predator. He had the confidence of a god, and he was obviously familiar enough with the runes to make the force fields he had constructed at the doorway. He tried to talk and the fear choked him a bit. "I am willing to talk to my people about leaving your people alone. But I must insist that you drop the aggressive stance that you have assumed. I am not the one to be intimidated by your flamboyant boasting and posturing. You are mistaken if you think that the Protector of the True People can be pushed around like some other domesticated animal you might care to produce. We have a solution for you, but it will require some sacrifice on your part. You are hereby ordered to vacate this planet and leave behind the Jeng technology you have stolen. If you disappear from our territories, then we will have no reason to pursue any further hostilities against you." The alien paused to collect himself and then he continued. "I believe that we can help you with the problem of getting your people off of this planet. Are you willing to give up the runes?"

Quinn looked at the alien in surprise. "Of course not, it can advance our society by leaps and bounds if properly researched and manipulated. You cannot expect me to simply turn my back on the possibilities that the knowledge presents us." He waved a hand in front of the Protector. "Are you sure you're feeling all right? Maybe the sun has been too much for you." Quinn turned and walked back into the doorway. "Come with me, we'll get you some refreshment and let you sit down for a while."

The Protector did not see any difference in the doorway, but he stepped forward anyway. He was startled to find that the barrier had been removed. He stepped through without incident and he was shocked at his next vision. The room was vast; he had expected that. But it was not of a Jeng design. This human had made this base. It was a violation of the Jeng mandates and he knew there would be repercussions from this for quite some time. The human was stepping over to a working waterfall in the corner of the chamber. He pressed a stone goblet into the stream and captured the fresh water and handed the sloshing cup to the Protector.

The alien warrior took the proffered cup and sniffed it. The smell of the water was sweet and clean. In fact, it was clean. It had bubbled up from hidden springs locked away beneath the island. The Jeng cautiously tasted the water and found it to be cold and refreshing. He downed the rest quickly and smiled at the human. It was better than any water source that the True people had installed in their various bases. He was impressed. "I did not believe that this sort of thing was possible with our runes. Can you show me how it is done?" He asked and Quinn looked at the man suspiciously.

"You just told me I have to leave these runes behind. I don't think you know what they can actually do. I could never forget what they are capable of. Maybe your people can teach us how you use them so that disastrous mistakes can be avoided." He suggested and the Protector looked like his eyeballs were going to pop out.

He raised his thin chin indignantly and retorted. "It is not the way of our people to share our technology with lower forms of life." He said in a most arrogant tone. Then he saw the reaction on the faces around him and he added. "Of course, we have not evaluated your species to determine if you are indeed lower than us. There would have to be some testing to prove that one way or the other." He finished weakly.

Quinn sat down on a stone bench that had been formed into the wall and he motioned for the Protector to do the same. The Jeng complied and sat down next to the human. "I believe that we have gotten off to a bad start. But I also believe that both of us are civilized enough to overcome our prejudices and reach an equitable solution to our dilemma." Quinn started ticking off points on his fingers. "First of all, you need us off of this planet. On the other side of the coin, we would like to plant a colony here. I have made this fortress for just that. It is our first major point of contention. But I think we can negotiate and solve this one." The Protector nodded.

Secondly, you want us to forget that you even exist, or at least to not tell anyone else that you do and stay away from the rest of our race. This is not truly feasible. Even if we had the technology to remove memories, we would be loath to do so since meeting your people has been exciting and informative. From our point of view, you are a lost civilization that we can interact with. Our need to grow and accumulate knowledge would not let us pass up an opportunity like this one easily. I understand that your usual solution to that problem has been some sort of genocide on the aware aliens. You must know that your warriors tried several times to attack us just to be thwarted by your own technology. I believe that option is no longer available to you. I would suggest that you attempt to seek peaceful relations with us. If our lifestyle is sufficiently good, no one will miss the rest of our race. But you must know that sooner or later, we all feel a calling for others of our kind. It is a common emotion to all advanced beings. In fact I would guess that you feel it somewhat even now as we speak." He finished and he looked at the Jeng expectantly.

The Protector nodded slowly. "What you say is true. Our people have killed before to protect our own security. It is also true that we feel the need to rejoin our own people. As Protector, I have the sometimes-sad duty of remaining outside of the normal workings of my people. My duties take me away from my people often. I am quite happy when I get to return on those rare occasions. I did not realize that it was a common feeling. The need to belong is one of the strongest natural emotions."

Quinn smiled at the man knowingly and continued to his next and final point. "I also understand that you wish us to forego the use of your technology. In truth, the Jeng runes are only a part of the power. You must be able to ask for what you need to make the runes do their job adequately. I think that is what you have lost over time. It is possible that we can help each other here. You could allow us to keep your valued technology in exchange for our description of how that technology actually works." He rubbed his hands together as he watched the alien man think over what had been said.

Quinn took a deep breath and continued again. "I believe that your people have been in hiding for far too long. It would probably help them dramatically if they joined the galactic community. I happen to be a representative of a community just like that. You could petition for membership in the group and then you would be granted rights and probably financial gains for your trade of technology and artifacts. This is in addition to the possible benefits you might well collect from our advanced medical community. We are learning how to prolong our lives and make ourselves sturdier for rougher environments. Such advances could be made available to you as an active member of the Fleet." Quinn raised his hands as the Protector began to protest.

"I understand that it is a lot to take in, just try to think about it and we can talk again tomorrow. In the mean time, feel free to look around and if there is anything you need, feel free to ask." Quinn stood up and walked away from the confused little man. He had been genuine and honest throughout the entire speech. Of that the Protector was certain. This man had given his own plight some serious thought and the solution seemed so reasonable. It was surely a sign that something was amiss in it. No one was this serving without being somewhat self-serving in the process. Whatever it was he was after was still a mystery. The only things that he was sure of were that the humans would not give up the runes and they would be hesitant to leave this palace of a base.

His people would also not want to be a part of this galactic group. They had spent so many years hiding in the shadows. More than one race had been obliterated to secure the knowledge of the Jeng existence. It was not something that the Protector was particularly proud of; it was simply a fact. He had hoped that a quick sterilization and a few bombs could solve this quandary, but it now looked as if the humans had settled in to stay. There were too many of them already for him to handle alone. The hazards of calling in reinforcements were obvious. If he brought in more ships, then there would be more to clean up afterwards. No, he must seek another solution with these people.

That is what they were, too; people. They were not animals or creatures as the commander at the destroyed base had recorded. These were thinking, reasoning, and honorable people. Their uniqueness was hidden by their similarities to the True People. They had the same goals. They wanted a good life and the ability to procreate and further their own race among the stars. The only major difference seemed to be that they did it out in the open. They didn't hide behind broken artifacts and ancient legends. They also did not originally have the runes. They did have their own technology though. It was different, but it was strong. It had allowed them to colonize vast sectors of space without the use of the mighty ancient runes. These people had been forced to figure out their own solutions to the problems of space travel and they had done it. The Protector had to admit to himself that these people were remarkable. They were so alive. They were busily bustling to feed and house themselves. Everyone's needs were being met as a collective effort. It reminded him of a hive. But the difference here was that the one in charge, this Ramses character, was not a queen. He was not responsible for the continuation of his species through direct procreation. But he would not hold that against the younger human. The Jeng warrior decided to take a walk around the facility and see just what kind of differences the humans had put into this fortification.

15

When Quinn left the Protector, Ratledge took the opportunity to corral him to the side. "I have been amazed at what you have accomplished here. You have done the service proud with this base you have constructed." He started off in a pleasant voice. But then he lowered his volume and huddled in closer to the Lieutenant. "We have more problems with this Jeng man than you may know. He has the Captain aboard his ship still. I saw him encased in stone. It was a temporary measure to set him aside until his medical needs could be met. Now that we are back with your group, we should negotiate his release as part of any deal struck here. I don't know if anyone will be out to rescue us. Headquarters knew where we were, but we were unable to get a signal off before the ship blew up. No one knows that the *Lincoln* is gone. There have been regular transmissions received from HQ about every two weeks. Based on that schedule, we will be missed in about three more days. From what I see around here, you can hold out that long easily enough. It would take a ship a couple more days to get here, assuming it was sent when we were reported missing. My best guess would be at least a week."

The Admiral took a breath and sighed. "Furthermore, this Jeng has a ship nearby. It couldn't hold many of us, but it is usable. Of course, I don't know how he flew it, he never touched any controls. It could be used by the Protector to escape. I don't know if things will deteriorate that far, but you should be aware of the possibility. As long as he feels safe, there should be no reason to think that he will run off on you." The man looked a bit uncomfortable. "Lastly, you should consider putting a guard on him or something. That man can be dangerous. He freely admits that a cleansing would have been his first option if it had been available. I don't like the sound of that, and I would guess that you don't either. Suffice it to say that I don't really trust the man. Just keep him under close scrutiny. God knows what sort of mischief he can get into inside a complex like this."

Quinn looked at the Admiral after the lengthy speech and shook his head. "I appreciate your views on this. I didn't know that the Captain was still alive. I will have him released right away, but we are very limited on our medical staff. We have wounded as well. Not everyone managed to get to safety when the ship blew up." Quinn looked around to see if anyone was paying them any attention. No one was. "Don't worry about security. The man could not do anything in this complex that I would not know about. I built it and I run it. I am connected to it. I am responsible for every nook and cranny, and the building knows it. We are quite safe inside here. In fact, it is this sense of safety that is the hardest thing for the Jeng to let go of. If I can convince them to abandon that security for the security of the league, then maybe we will have a new member to our society. If not, we may have a new enemy. Either way, this crisis will have been long past." The two men continued to walk away and Quinn suggested that they get some food. Ratledge could not disagree since he was starving from his ordeal out at sea.

Vorn had gotten his ships in working order. The reinforcements he had requested from HQ had not arrived. In fact, he had been recalled by radio message. His messenger would not return. The missing ship had been reassigned to watch over headquarters and defend the home world. He knew that the fight was out here, not back at the home world picket. He knew that he could do little to help if he returned with his tail between his legs. It stuck in his craw that the higher-ups didn't have the confidence in him to handle the situation out here. Of course he had to admit that the situation had not gone well so far. They had lost the *Lincoln*

and damaged the black squadron. But the enemy had lost two bases, including one the size of a moon. Something had to be said about that. The biggest problem was that the enemy was still a big mystery. He didn't know where they came from. He didn't know how many of them there were. He didn't even know if any had survived the battle he was engaged in. It was a big question mark that bothered him.

But there were questions he had answers for. He had seen that there were survivors of the *Lincoln* that had managed to get down to that accursed planet. There was a need for rescue down there. He didn't know how long they could survive on the planet unaided. He hoped that they were resilient enough to make it until he could get down there. He had been in contact with the surface and he had requested personnel to complete his crews. But he still hadn't heard back from the people down there. He was a little upset at the delays. Did they not understand what kind of vulnerability undermanned spacecraft created? He was pretty sure that they were more worried about their own survival down on the alien world, but the black squadron was all that protected them from anything coming from space. He finally decided to go down to the surface himself. It was the only real way to get to the bottom of exactly what was going on down there on that strange planet. He needed answers fast. He had to do something quickly before he was forced to return home empty handed.

The Protector took some time and looked around the facility. He had to admit that these humans had used the runes to perfection. The layout of the base was logical and even allowed for the proper movement of air from chamber to chamber. The place was organized better than any base he had ever been in, and he had seen most of what his people had to offer. He was now convinced that his people could benefit from what these humans, especially that Quinn fellow, knew. In fact, he knew that his people could benefit greatly from the thinking process of a fresh mind. Their civilization had stagnated over the past several thousand years.

He now saw that as a liability, not the comfortable place it had always been for him in the past. He got the feeling of being left behind. But it was not just him; it was his entire race. It was most unsettling. But he also knew in his heart that his people would be deathly afraid of the kind of change that this situation seemed to lend itself to. He made up his mind to try. But he felt that a good talk with this human would be necessary to hash out the details. All he knew for certain was that any changes would have to be made in council on the home world. He tried to envision Quinn Ramses standing before the council members and demonstrating his knowledge of the lost arts of the Jeng Rune speak. He knew that they would at first be appalled. He also knew that they could not ignore the human threat anymore. There was just too much at stake here. There had to be some middle ground in which the two peoples could unite and coexist. At least in his mind, he understood the problems now. His mission was no longer to "clean up" the human mess. It was to pull his people forward and allow the race as a whole to grow in a fresh new galaxy where other races knew of their existence and everyone worked together for mutual benefit. It was a shocking new vision for him, and it was exactly what this Quinn was suggesting. He was beginning to develop a deep respect for this man from another people. He hoped that he wasn't being deceived.

He decided to try some of the foods that they were offering. It was simply plants from around the area. His people have eaten plants for as long as he could remember, so he didn't find it strange. He was handed a flat round device and was told to fill it with the things he would like to try. There was quite a variety on the table before him. Each container had something different in it and each substance had its own serving utensil sticking out of it. He took several things that he could not recognize and placed them neatly on his disk. Some of the things were hot, and some of them were chilled. He wasn't sure why, but he thanked the young lady for the food and went over to a table to sample it. As he walked away from the buffet, he was convinced that there were not that many kinds of plants on this whole planet. He wondered why they went to such great lengths to prepare food different ways. He sat down at an empty table and prodded the various foods with his fork. At least he was told it was a fork when the lady handed it to him. It looked like a miniature farming implement. It had prongs for stabbing, presumably. He tried to stab a yellow substance on his disk and found that the consistency varied throughout the substance. His stomach turned at the thought and he tried to set the food back down. It was stuck on his fork. He shook the arguing implement and the food was still stuck on it. He finally used his finger to push the offending food item off of his fork and he then wiped it clean with a piece of paper material that had been provided with the disk. His motions had not been lost on the humans.

Quinn sat down across the table from the Protector and smiled. "Don't like the potato salad huh?" He asked and the Protector looked at him with a blank stare.

"What is potato salad?" Asked the Jeng man with a slight slurring of the words due to his alien accent.

"Well, a potato is a root vegetable that is peeled, cut up, and boiled in water until it is a little softer. Then other things are added to it including mustard. That's the yellow stuff throughout the dish. Then the whole dish is chilled and served. I haven't tried this batch, but I have heard that this is some of the best you will ever find." Quinn informed him and the Protector stabbed the piece again with his fork.

He timidly brought the piece to his mouth. He smelled the piece and it smelled tangy. Then he popped the piece into his mouth and then extracted the fork. An explosion of flavor assaulted his mouth. It was creamy; it was tart; and it was wonderful. His eyes closed, as he tasted it again and again. As he chewed it the textures made sense. He was lost in the moment and when he reopened his eyes, Quinn was smiling at him. "I have never had anything like this before in my life. I did not know that my mouth could sense so many things at once. Our food is a paste made from specific plants to provide us the exact nutrition that we require. It does not taste like this." He proclaimed.

Quinn looked at the plate. "You seem to have a pretty good mix there. Go ahead and feel free to try anything you want. You can refill your plate when that's all gone. I will leave you alone to your sampling." With that Quinn got up from the table and smiled again. The he headed back into the crowd. He was gone in a matter of seconds. The Protector looked through the crowd in a useless attempt to spot the man, but he had already vanished.

Vorn's spearhead ship arced across the sky on its decent to the water planet. The basic design was aerodynamic and the craft made atmospheric entry without any mishap. The crew was well seasoned in space, but this sort of piloting was completely different. The Admiral smiled at the training he was allowing his crew to experience. He would have ordered the whole wing down if they weren't in enemy territory against an enemy they couldn't even see, much less count. He sorely missed the crewmen that should have been in the missing slots. His men were doing their best to make up for the shortage, but it was a near thing at best. What was worse was that he was short a ship that wouldn't be coming back. He had been ordered back to headquarters to protect their precious hides from these alien invaders. Of course these "invaders" had been here first, and by no small amount of time. They had simply been in hiding for all of humanity's expansion through the cosmos. An indicator light blinked and broke the Admiral's train of thought. The pilot switched it off before he could even tell which one it had been.

The pilot must have felt the stare from behind him because he remarked. "Sir, that was only a hull temperature warning light. It wasn't calibrated for our new skin. We will be in no danger on this flight." He announced in a tone that suggested he might be trying to convince both of them. The navigator looked on and tried to remain unnoticed on the bridge. The thin black ship crossed the seemingly endless water at a low altitude. The shadow mimicked the great wedge as it glided effortlessly over the waves. It even made a spray off of each wingtip as the airfoil did its job and kept them aloft. Within moments, the main continent came into view. It looked like a ridge of color on a blue background. The sky was clear as far as anyone could see and the sun was bright and cheerful. It also meant that there would be no stealthy approach. Vorn shrugged his shoulders at the thought and resigned himself to being seen. He had gotten used to being cloaked and undetectable. It somehow made him feel more vulnerable that he could be seen from the ground so easily.

The great ship descended into a clearing and crushed many of the crops that Quinn had just finished accelerating into full growth. The people were trying to wave him off, but the pilot landed right in the middle of the fields. The landing gear had been extended and they pressed the soil down a good eight inches as the weight was distributed into the ground. The black squadron commander was down. He stood proudly at the top of the ramp as the motor slowly lowered the platform to allow a graceful exit of the ship. He strode out onto the walkway and strode purposefully down it. At the end of the ramp, he looked back at his ship. It was really the first time he had seen it in the light of day. It was still a magnificent sight. Its sleek lines and lethal appearance was the stuff of dreams. At least they were the dreams of those seeking conquest or power. Of course the Admiral was one of those that craved both.

He tore his eyes from his own ship and stepped up to see who it was who was greeting him. Several workers from the *Lincoln* were there, and they were not happy to see their work destroyed. After all, food was survival when you were trapped on an alien planet. The colonists encircled the Admiral and he got the notion that he might not be too welcomed here. His ego was such that he could dismiss these ruffians out of hand and he pressed his way out of the circle and marched towards the entrance without so much as a shove from the small crowd. They simply watched him with their mouths hanging open. Then they shrugged and went back to work trying to salvage as much of the plant life as they could from around the mighty ship.

Vorn stepped up and into the doorway to the base. A strange

sight met him there. Quinn was talking with another Admiral.
He thought for a moment and then he realized it must be that
Ratledge that had been sent from Headquarters. Of course he
would have survived and taken command of the base. Vorn's
purpose now had a focus and he walked straight up to Ratledge as
he put on his best diplomatic smile.

"Hello gentlemen." He greeted them and they broke off their
conversation to look at the newcomer. "I am glad that you have
both survived your ordeal. I am sure that we can come to an
arrangement that will be satisfactory to both sides. I need some of
your personnel to man my ships. Without them, I may not be able
to hold this system you are currently settling into. In exchange,
I will inform headquarters of your whereabouts and I am certain
that a rescue operation would then shortly ensue. What do you
say? can I have some of your people?" Vorn asked and he looked
to Ratledge for a response. He was startled when it was Quinn
who answered him.

"I can ask for volunteers, but I don't think you'll get any." He
explained. "People around here seem to have given up on the
violence and hatred. They are willing to make their new life here
and forget about the government-sponsored war that you seem to
be driving for. Peace is a more equitable solution for us now. We
are even negotiating for a lasting peace now. You can stay for a
couple of days, that should allow everyone ample time to consider
if they want to leave or not. But after that, I want you gone."

Vorn looked at the man incredulously. "You can't be serious!"
He bellowed. Vorn held himself for a moment and his face burned
red with rage. "I don't care who you have impressed in the past. I
am the only thing protecting your sorry hide from alien invasion
on this backwater little world. This utopia of yours is an illusion.
You will all fall before the might of the Jeng before it is all over. I
am the only one that can help you. I don't see how you can just
dismiss me like that. I outrank you more than a little. If I order
you to send me the people I need, then you will comply or face
a court martial. That is if I don't shoot you on the spot. I will
not tolerate any insubordination from you or anybody. You will
prepare your people for my selection. Then I shall draft any that

I need to complete my crews and you will be free to rot here once I have gone. Until then, I am in charge of this base and my word is law. "Is that clear?" His stare could have cut Quinn in half, but the survey man didn't even flinch.

"Sir." He began. "You have no power or authority here. The only place you do is aboard your ship. That is unless we requisition it from you. I would watch your tone or you will find yourself in one of our new civilian cells. My guess is that you will find it less than hospitable. Enjoy our food and drinks here and I will pose your request to the people. Another threat to our authority here and you will find yourself under arrest. Is that clear?" He asked and Vorn looked ready to explode.

Vorn clenched his fist. His entire being wanted to pound the upstart's face in and bathe in his blood afterwards. But he held it back and formed his next question. "What gives you the authority to rule over a colony?" He looked around. "Especially one that was never even properly planted. These are not colonists; they are survivors of a shooting war that took place above this miserable planet. You have no rights here, except those given every citizen." He finished and Quinn stood tall before him.

"I have claimed this world for the government, and am currently acting as an ambassador in the negotiations of peace with the Jeng. This gives me full executive authority over all things on this planet. When negotiations are complete, I intend to step down. But for now, I am the source of power here. According to regulations, you have the right to protest my authority in this situation, but you must do so at headquarters. Since you have already been recalled there according to our radio specialists, I suggest you head there right away. If you so choose, you can wait the two days to see if anyone is willing to join you. But make no mistakes; we will not tolerate interference in my duties, or in the duties of the other personnel who have decided to make a home here. Now go get something to eat and leave me alone. I tire of your militaristic attitudes, and I wish not to be disturbed for the remainder of the day by you. Good day sir." Quinn simply walked away and the Admiral stood there in shock. He knew there had to be something more he could do, but he was unsure what it would be. In his mind, this Quinn was an egomaniac with little more than delusions of grandeur. There was also the safety of the other survivors to think about. The man had even convinced himself that he was negotiating peace with the Jeng. What utter lunacy. Still, there was always hope that someone that far from reality would make a serious mistake and allow the opportunity to be dethroned by the ones who were willing to look for the option. Vorn began his plotting. He had two days to find a weakness in Quinn's armor. He would be very careful about how he proceeded. After all, this man did seem to have the public support.

The rest of the colonists left the newcomer alone. The Admiral had gone up against their leader, and found that he was not up to the task. It actually served to solidify Quinn's position in their minds. He had stood toe-to-toe with the military and won out in a battle of wills. Surely he was chosen to be a leader. Vorn decided that he actually was hungry. He headed over to the food area and found a decently stocked buffet. He had not seen such an elaborate offering since he was back on the home world. His supervisor had given him a proper send off and the spread was luxuriant beyond his means. There didn't appear to be any meat here, but the many dishes were festive and eye-catching. He picked up a plate and started to fill it. He grabbed a fork and headed for the tables. He stopped in his tracks. Sitting alone at a table was a Jeng warrior. His mouth dropped open and he nearly lost his tray. He caught himself and set the tray down on the nearest table. Luckily it was an empty one and he sat down behind the tray. He simply stared at the being that was consuming dish after dish and he was savoring every bite. He couldn't believe his eyes. Could that Quinn have been telling him the truth? Could he really be negotiating with the Jeng? This one seemed harmless enough, but looks were more often than not deceiving. He made a show of eating for a while. He had lost his appetite, and he was more than a little curious about this Jeng man.

Finally, the creature seemed about through with his plate of food. It was amazing watching him taste one thing after another. Each experience looked to be better than the last. The body language was unmistakable. Then the being got up and brought his plate to the line again. Vorn couldn't believe his eyes. Where did that small frame put all that food? No matter, his curiosity got the better of him and he moved to the Jeng's table while he was off for another load. He figured a good conversation could shed some light on Quinn's motivations. At least he hoped that it would.

The Protector had a fresh new disk filled with some other types of foods. The human that was serving had smiled at him and offered him something called dessert. The food smelled sweeter. He was certain that it had some sort of glucose in it. He decided to taste it and find out for sure. He returned to his table and found a human seated there. He looked for an empty table, but there was none, so he shrugged his narrow shoulders in a very human gesture and sat down where he had been before, across fiom this newcomer. He made eye contact with the human and the intruder looked at him like a predator would at prey. It was a little uncomfortable, but the smells of all the sweet foods brought his attention back to that magic refillable disk. He sampled a few choice bits and savored them as the heavy looking human male watched him closely. After about half of the food was gone, the man spoke to him.

"I see you have enjoyed the dessert tray. How do you like the food?" He asked, trying to make light conversation. The questions burned in his mind, but what could he ask without offending this representative of a new alien species.

The Protector swallowed the morsel he had been tasting reluctantly in order to speak. "Yes, it is quite good. We have nothing like this among my people. We have bland food that is only just palatable by our standards. This food is remarkable. That Lieutenant Ramses of yours was quite right to send me down here to try it all out." He finished and he forked a heaping bite of apple cobbler into his mouth and his eyes rolled back into his head in the explosion of pleasurable flavor in his mouth. It was almost indecent to watch.

"Yes, that Quinn is a good man." The Admiral lied to the alien before him. "In fact, we are thinking of promoting him to teach others how to talk to people like yourself. I could take his place as negotiator for you when he leaves." He added, and the Jeng man looked concerned.

"I don't think that would be wise. Quinn's dream is the inspiration for the talks in the first place. It will be difficult enough to convince my people that we must coexist with you. If you take Quinn away, the chances of success drop drastically. As you said yourself, he knows how to talk to us in a way that we can understand."

Vorn leaned back for a moment. "I may have no choice, the decision is not mine to make; it comes from above my level. My superiors would like his talents re-employed rather quickly. I am sure that you can make do with me. After all, I am a military leader of sorts. In addition, I can speak with the authority of my race. Quinn has to double check everything with his bosses back at headquarters." The Admiral shifted his weight uncomfortably as he lied to the small man. The body language he was putting off sent warning signals to the Protector. He was instantly suspicious.

"If all of that is so, then you may have to accompany me to our home world and address the council there. Do you know how to use our rune-speak?" The Protector asked, trying to trick the human in with his bloodthirsty eyes.

Vorn did not know what rune-speak was, maybe it was some sort of language used only in counsel. He was pretty sure that he could pick up enough of it to get by. If nothing else, the Jeng man here could tutor him a bit during the voyage to their home world. "No, I must admit that I am not familiar with your rune-speak language. But if you help me out with it on the way, I am certain that the meeting with your counsel will be most rewarding." He replied and the Jeng man stood up.

"If you will excuse me, I must be going now. I have duties to attend to. This is not a vacation for me. Be sure to thank the man for the food. It was most educational for me." And the Protector left before Vorn could get in a word edgewise. He scratched his head as he watched the alien drift off into the crowd and vanish. He was unaware that Quinn had done the same thing to the Jeng about an hour and a half before. Of course, he would not have cared if he had known.

Back at headquarters, plans were moving forward in the defense initiative the council had ordered. A picket of warships was in system now, and they were roughly thirty-five strong. It was not only that simple fact that brought some peace of mind to the people, but also that some of these ships were the latest technology that humanity had produced. It was true that the rest of black squadron had yet to return. It was also true that Admiral Vorn was on the brink of career suicide if he delayed much longer. But they were not the only squadron with those miraculous advancements in starship design. The government had made three such squadrons. Each went through the same maneuvers and tests without the other's knowledge. It was a triple blind test to see if the ships performed up to expectations. It was always the council's opinion that one shouldn't put all of their eggs in one basket. Blue squadron and Gold squadron were each ten strong and they were all circling above the heads of the well to do on the home world. According to policy, they still didn't know of each other. Each group had been given their orders individually, but they were acting as a team now, and didn't even realize it. The main project on the minds of the council at this time was the automated defense platforms. These were portable missile platforms with sophisticated tracking and stealth capabilities. They were not a new concept, but there had not been a threat to the home world for so long that they had gone slack due to disuse over time. Now the need seemed urgent and crews were dispatched to bring the old platforms up to speed. The electronic signatures of the home world and its systems were coming on line and everyone there would soon breathe a big sigh of relief. They would be secure in the knowledge that nothing could get to them without them seeing it coming. After all, this was war.

While his people prepared for war, Quinn was focused on peace. He had laid out plans on what to say to the council of the Jeng people in order to underscore his points. He had a pretty good idea of how to proceed, but he wanted to pass it by this Protector and see if he agreed. The man had disappeared though. Quinn had asked around and found out that he had gone into hiding after talking to that Vorn character. Quinn was a bit upset over that, but he resolved himself to get to the bottom of it and stomp any possible rebellion that the military man was trying to cause. He knew in his heart that peace was the only equitable solution and he was prepared to see it through. This colony he had started would survive, but he had to ask the people if they wanted to join this Admiral Vorn. He decided to hold a meeting. It would be the first town meeting they had since settling in here. He spread the word and summoned his people to the vast chamber in the center of his base. The high stone ceilings were perfect acoustically and the speaker at the front would be heard by all like in an amphitheater. Once the word was spreading, he went to the chamber himself in order to watch the people arrive.

The room was vast, as the original had been in the Jeng base. Its stone ceiling sloped in towards a dome cap far above their heads. The height was almost dizzying. But the details didn't stop there. Quinn had envisioned a mighty church cathedral when he spoke the runes. So ornamentation was covering the walls for the first forty feet up. There were elaborate statues of humans in various poses. There was one woman, dressed in robes, reaching out to a stone bird and it landing on her finger. There was a space pilot with full gear, standing beside his aircraft before a significant battle. There were statues of all walks of life. Doctors and mechanics were equal citizens with politicians and generals. Each was on a marble pedestal that seemed to erupt from the intricately carved stone floor. Of course the stone was not really carved; it had reformed into the pleasing shape. But the thought did not spoil its beauty. There were rows of seats like church pews and a raised platform on which sat several high-backed stone chairs. The room could hold about five hundred people. There was also a speaker's podium in front of the rows of seats and it was currently empty. He strolled over and looked out at the assembly. People were trickling in from both of the rear entrances and he was getting a good idea of just how many people had survived the destruction of the *Lincoln*. He knew that all of the inhabitants could not have gotten off in time. But he felt that most of them had. It lifted his heart a bit at the realization.

The assemblage got noisier as it formed and several of the people decided to declare themselves ushers and helped people get into their seats. The volume was easily amplified by the acoustics in the room. Quinn made a mental note to change some of its aspects later. But for now, it would simply have to do. When the last trickle of stragglers finally got to their seats he held up his hand for quiet. It was not immediately successful. But he was patient and soon the murmurs died down and he felt confident to continue.

"Good people of the good ship *Lincoln*. I address you today as the founder of this new colony of the human race. We are representatives of our people and we have among us a couple of noteworthy additions. First of all, many of you have already seen the Jeng warrior called The Protector. He is here on behalf of his people to sue for peace with us here at this base." He said with authority and the crowd erupted in riotous applause. After about thirty seconds, he held his hands out in a quieting gesture and the applause died out. "Furthermore, I intend to go with him to their home world and address their government about arrangements to keep this planet for colonization. If all goes well, we could be helping them to use their rune technology in exchange for the rights to this world." He said and again the room erupted in supporting applause. This time he let it go a little longer. He needed them in a good mood.

"There is more news than this though." He said in a foreboding manner and the crowd quieted down more quickly than before. "You may also know that Admiral Vorn is here. For those who do not know who he is, he is the leader of the Back Squadron. They were on assignment to investigate the Jeng threat alongside the *Lincoln*. Most of the members of the squadron are still up in orbit. He has brought his one ship down to ask you for volunteers. His crews are evidentially short-handed and he would like some replacement personnel. I have authorized him to ask you for those volunteers. I have not, however, authorized him to shanghai anyone and he cannot press you into service. But if you ever dreamed of becoming a part of a military fleet, then this is your chance to realize that dream." Quinn's tone was serious and the people took notice of the subtle shift. "He intends to pursue a hostile attitude towards our potential allies, the Jeng people. I have already told him that I disagree with his point of view, but every citizen is entitled to an opinion. I have promised that I would pass on his request for volunteers, and I have done so. The choice is now completely up to you." Quinn stepped back from the podium and the people began to raise points for and against the issue like a debate team. On one side, some of the people did not trust the destructive power of the Jeng. They had destroyed the island base and an entire moon just fighting one ship. It was horrendous tactics considering what could laughably be called 'acceptable losses'. On the other hand, there was fear that if peace wasn't achieved; they might have to give up this new home. For some with relatives back in civilization, that wouldn't be too bad. But many had already begun to think of this wet planet as home. Even those with off-world friends and relatives agreed that this home was too good to just let go of it. Once regular transportation was established, many of its down sides would be academic at best.

The arguing raged on and on and it was becoming obvious that most of the people wanted to keep this base and their new home. Quinn stepped back to the podium and the yelling and arguing stopped abruptly. Quinn cleared his throat for emphasis and then he addressed the people in a charming and pacifying tone that calmed the nerves of more than one of his guests. "I can hear both sides of this argument, and both sides have valid points. There is no shame in wanting to go and there is certainly no problem with wanting to stay. In either case, the decision must be made on a case-by-case basis. We do not have to decide as a group here. Those who want to join up with Admiral Vorn can be at his ship's gantry-way at 0730 hours tomorrow morning. All of those who would rather stick it out here simply stay back during the ship's departure. There will be no hard feelings either way. This base is not a monarchy or a dictatorship. You are all still citizens of the league and I will not attempt to interfere with your individual rights. I believe that this meeting is officially over and I thank all of you for attending. It is good to see so many faces here. I hope that we can continue in this supportive and cooperative manner all of our days." With that he left the podium and the crowd cheered and applauded again. Quinn left the platform and the applause continued. Margaret had met up with him at the meeting and she was making her way towards the popular leader. But the crowd was simply too thick and she was frustrated by the throng of bodies also seeking an audience with Quinn. He shook hands and nodded and waved as he headed through the crowd like a knife to the exit. He was tired of being the center of attention and he needed a little quiet time. The people followed him for a bit, but he was not going to say anything else exciting so they eventually lost interest and headed back to their duties or quarters to make their final decisions.

Admiral Vorn had watched the meeting from the wings. He was pretty sure that the Jeng man was also here somewhere, but he could not see him anywhere. How could somebody so different blend into a crowd of humans like that? He wasn't sure but it only served to heighten his suspicion of the man and his race in general. He had heard the man was called 'Protector.' That meant he was some kind of policeman or something. Vorn could deal with a man like that. They all thought basically the same way. There were ways to appeal to that type. He began plotting his next encounter with the alien.

Aboard the *Black Sword,* the Protector watched the meeting with great interest. He had been disillusioned at the attitude of that Admiral and he was ready to leave the planet and write the human race off. Something about that Quinn character though, made him stay behind long enough to see what was going to happen next. He was truly interested when the meeting started and Quinn started by disagreeing with the Admiral. In the military of the Jeng, he would have been killed for publicly renouncing a superior officer like that. Still, these humans were a bit different. It was true that they were not the Jeng. They were too bold for the lifestyle his race had adopted. The Protector found that he respected their initiative and their drive. He was singularly impressed with this Quinn fellow. The man handled authority like the best of them, even when that authority was suspect. He seemed to make rational decisions even when placed under pressure. Then he listened as the clapping calmed down and Quinn surprised the Protector. He said that he would have to go to the Jeng home world to address the council. Although he agreed with the assessment, he had not even brought it up with the man. His appraisal of the human raised a couple of notches, and it was pretty high already. He opened the hatchway and left the ship. He felt the need to talk with this man as soon as possible. His only concern was that Admiral fellow. He had to avoid that one at all costs. The man looked at the Protector with the eyes of a jackal. The feeling of being the prey was more than a little unsettling. He decided to simply go straight to Quinn's office and wait for him there. If the two humans disagreed that much, then maybe the Admiral would not be allowed in Quinn's office.

Quinn finished, leaving the crowd behind. He gave a handshake here, and a hug there. There were many people to meet with, and he was physically exhausted by the end of the ordeal. He decided to rest in his office and seal the doors. He knew the right runes to do the trick. It should allow him the chance to rest. He hadn't realized he had been awake quite as long as he had until the pressure of the public relying on him to secure their future weighed heavily upon him. It was a burden that his short career in Survey had not prepared him for. But it was also one that no one else could hold, so he felt a little trapped by it. Still, all was going pretty well so far. Once conditions were patched up with these Jeng people, then the threat of attack from the skies would be eliminated and he could rest easier. He also did not want to have Admiral Vorn around any longer than he had to. If he had been in charge of the man, he would have taken him off of that black squadron and put him in a safer position. One in which his rashness could not start a galactic war. But he was not in charge of the man. In fact, his position was quite tenuous just now. If peace talks eroded away, then his authority would become null and void. The vindictive Admiral would not let the opportunity pass by to make an example of him if that happened. Quinn felt like he was hanging from a thread and swinging madly to reach a ledge somewhere to get to safety. Problem was, he didn't know where the ledge was, and he could see nothing but air in all directions.

He reached the entrance to his office and he stepped inside and spoke the words. The doorway sealed up with molten rock and re-solidified into a solid surface as if the door had never existed. He heard a gasp behind him and turned to the sound. The Protector was seated there, his mouth hanging open. Quinn stepped forward with a surprised look on his face. "I didn't know you were in here." He said simply and the Protector stood up.

A moment of indignation swept the Protector. "You use our ancient technology to close your door?" He asked a bit miffed at the prospect. The Protector shook his head at the implications of everyday use of the runes.

Quinn started a bit at the change in attitude of his Jeng guest. "I only did it to seal the room so that I could rest undisturbed. It may have been a bit over the top, but I assure you that the runes were not damaged in any way, and that the rock will reform itself without any difficulty." Then Quinn stopped and turned back to where the door was. He spoke the door rune and the doorway reopened and the rock solidified into its former position. "There, is that better?" He asked and the Protector stared at him incredulously.

"You have taken something sacred and mysterious to us and made it your play thing. You cannot know how much of a slap in the face that is to us. The True People's pride is tied to their ancient technology, and here you are flaunting it to simply lock your door. I thought you were different than that military oaf that accosted me earlier, but you have not taken my people's fears seriously." The Protector was obviously upset; his face was turning a shade of purple that looked rather unpleasant.

Quinn held up his hands in surrender. "Whoa there, you don't completely understand the situation here. I may have overstepped my bounds with your beloved technology by locking my door with it, but I am by no means taking that technology lightly. It is a tool, much like any other tool, its true value is in its uses. I believe that you and I can learn a lot from each other. But we must get past certain issues first. If you are going to hold onto this image of your technology as some sacred thing handed down from your ancestors, then we are going to have a problem. I understand that they are a part of your culture, but from what I have gathered your populace doesn't even use them. Is this true?"

The Protector stood back a second from this human who spoke with undeniable power. "What you say is true. Only the most sagely of our scholars have memorized the runes. The instructions we have handed down from scholar to scholar only tell what a certain rune does. That is different from what you have achieved here. You have altered the runes to suit your needs. Deep down inside, the distorting of our sacred runes sickens me, but another part of me is pleased to know that they can be tailored to a specific purpose. I don't think that the idea has even been brought up among my people. You must understand that all of my people hold the rune-speak in high regard. It is our sole basis for our lifestyle and existence. We have that, and a code of honor. Neither can be addressed in my government without offending someone. You must get it through your thick human head that you cannot flaunt the power you possess in front of my people. They will be hard pressed to take your words at face value, but if you throw away caution and attack their system of power and religion, you will meet with more resistance than even you can handle." The Protector paused, obviously thinking about what to say next.

"You have given me things to think about that no one else has even dreamed of. I believe in your vision of peace. But even though I believe in it, I am frightened of a botched attempt at realizing that dream. The thought of going to war has become repulsive to us. We fear all outsiders, and your race seems to have gotten a foot in the door without our prior knowledge. That is also frightening to us. You will have to walk a very fine line to impress my government and secure the peace you seek." The Protector looked at Quinn again; he seemed to be sizing the human up. His unblinking stare was a little unnerving to Quinn, but his resolve was still unshaken.

The self proclaimed ruler of the new colony of man sighed. "I am willing to see your people. I believe that if we do not secure this peace, there will be no one left to grieve for us when we are gone. Both of our races have powerful armaments and military forces. There is no easy way to end a war once it has started. The best way is to avoid it in the first place to secure a brighter future. The educational process of your people is one of my first priorities. I realize that it will be quite a shock to many of your people, but it is also necessary to make sure that the peace can last. There can be no hiding of thoughts and motives. All of the playing pieces must be in the proper places and the proceedings must be honest and honorable." Quinn sat down and let out a big sigh. "I don't think the next few days will be easy, but they are necessary to accomplish this goal. We need to talk to your people, and then we must also talk to mine. Are you willing to meet with the ruling council?"

The Protector started at the question. "You mean your people also rule by counsel? That is the way of the True People. It would appear that we might have more in common than I originally thought. I agree with the idea of truth being the catalyst for peace. In this vein, I must admit that there is a human Captain in my ship. He is damaged and I have isolated him in a stone case to keep him from deteriorating any further. When we go to see this council of yours, we should probably transfer him to one of your advanced medical facilities. I doubt very much that you have one hidden here. He would surely die if the casing is not opened in a good environment for medical treatment."

Quinn smiled at the emissary from the True People. "I already knew about the good Captain in your custody. Admiral Ratledge told me about him. I figured that you would tell me about him when you were ready. With that out of they way, I think we can move forward in this venture and go see your people. I have prepared a small speech for them and I think that it is about time that they heard it."

The Protector nodded his agreement. "I can take you there without too much trouble. My ship is close by and we can easily be there in under a day from here." Replied the alien being that held the future of his own people in his hands.

"That close?" Quinn startled. "I didn't know we were practically on top of them like that. That might explain why they were unwilling to give up this rather useless base when we first landed."

The Protector shook his head, no. "You fail to understand what I said. We can be there in under a day, but it is still a long way away from here. We will be traveling outside of time for a bit and that allows us to re-enter at a point in time that we choose. This is valuable to our people because we can be in many places when we are needed. Of course there are restrictions on it and we cannot share this technology with you. The use of the runes must be enough because it is the only technology under negotiation."

Quinn smiled. "I think we have an understanding then. Besides, if one gets too greedy at the table, then one will usually fail to accomplish their goals. Later we can negotiate for anything more based on whatever we have that you need." Quinn stood up and crossed the room towards the seated Protector. "When can we leave, time is of the essence here. We can ill afford to let the military men push the galaxy into war before a peace arrangement can be reached."

The Protector rose to meet the human. He stretched his neck as far as it would go and nearly met the man eye to eye. "We can leave at once. I too am interested in the preservation of lives. Your people are not dangerous to wipe us out, but you are not to be discounted beyond that. I fear that if our peoples went to war there would be no empire left for either one of us to enjoy. It is better that we continue upon your path to peace than to trot blindly off to war. Are you ready to depart now?"

Quinn did not hesitate at all. "Yes, let us go and meet this council of yours. I understand that fear is our greatest enemy at this time, so I will remain calm and collected to the best of my ability. I trust in you to make the right moves to help me reach my goal. I will be in your arena after all. I am relying heavily on you for support in this venture. You did mention that your voice held a lot of weight in your government. That may be all that saves us in the end."

The Protector nodded his agreement. It was still a wonder to him how this human understood so many of the intricacies of the True People. He would be a formidable enemy if it came down to that. As it looked so far, he could become a formidable ally. Time would be the true teller here, but he was sure that they could sway the council to accept the radically different legislation they were proposing. It just needed to be shown in the proper light to make them see the truth in the words, "We shall leave for my ship then. You may want to bring along a witness though. Jeng procedings usually have a witness for important personal matters."

Quinn thought for a second. "Okay, I know just the person to accompany me. We can find her near the shuttles." He said and then he bolted for the door. The Protector followed closely behind, his stride quickened in an attempt to match the human's speed. He cursed his shallow gait inwardly as he huffed and puffed behind the longer strides.

Margaret was cleaning an air filter for the scrubbers when Quinn came up in a hurry. She saw under his arm that the Jeng man was in hot pursuit and her initial reaction was one of fear and defense. But Quinn's look was not one of someone being chased and he belayed her fears when he stopped next to her and grinned at her.

"I need you to come with me on a trip." He said and she cocked her head to the side a bit to signal him to tell her more. He took the hint and continued. "I need to go to the Jeng home world and put forth my plan for peace with their governing body. The Protector will accompany me, but he says I need a witness with me for important meetings such as this. I can think of no one better suited to be my witness than you. There is the added comfort of having you by my side when I need the moral support as well. Will you go with me?"

Margaret thought about it for a moment. She had strong feelings for Quinn but he hadn't given her the time of day since he founded this blasted colony. She understood some of it that he was just so busy. But if she were that important to him, then he could have made some time. She was a little bitter over it. But she looked into his eyes and she knew that she wanted to be with him. It was an honor to be asked to such an important and potentially historical meeting. She decided to give him another chance. "I'll go with you to this meeting. I'm not sure what I can do to help, but the potential is too great to ignore." She replied and Quinn's smile broadened. He looked almost cartoonish with that silly grin. She fell for him again at the sight. She didn't even bother to curse herself inwardly for the weakness.

The Protector stepped up and smiled his best too. The effect was somehow lost on his curious features. But at least he was trying to learn. That was more than they could have hoped for from a first contact situation. The trio left for the ship. The Jeng man led the way, as he was the only one that knew how to enter the sword ship. They marched off behind the alien heading for their place in history, or at least they hoped it was.

16

Admiral Vorn had received several votes of confidence from the people of this newly established colony. He was quite happy with the type of people that were on his side. Engineers and diplomats, they were some of the more highly trained personnel on the planet. He greeted each one amiably and asked them to meet with him at his ship at 2100 hours. He intended fully to leave the god-forsaken planet behind him and seek out these Jeng warriors. He still had some revenge to find and the additional crew would bolster his chances quite a bit. He had received a communication earlier from his other ships in orbit that things were all green. He had a fully ready squadron and he was prepared to use it as effectively as possible. He had his men target the sword ship that was landed here at the colony. If it moved, he was to be informed. Then, if he so chose, it could be blown from the sky at a word. It was his most reassuring ace in the hole in this turbulent situation. But he knew from his training that a good leader always had back up plans. He had several in mind, and he hoped that they would not be needed. A swift military strike now could end the war in victory for the human race and restore him to popularity on the home world. He was already envisioning the statue they would erect in his honor.

A chime on his communicator brought the Admiral out of his dream and he shook his head to clear it of the cherished vision. "Yes, Vorn here. What is it?" He asked in a burley tone.

The device crackled a bit as if there were some sort of interference, but the next words came through loud and clear. "Sir, the ship is on the move." Vorn did not have to be told which ship.

He had been waiting to take on this sword ship himself for some time, but now it looked like his chances were slipping away. The lucky ones were the crew in orbit. They would have to engage this threat to human security. He held the mike with all the dignity he could muster.

"Blow that ship away. I want nothing left of it. I don't even want the scrap yards to find anything valuable." He ordered in a cold as ice tone that sent chills through the communications officer's spine.

"Yes sir. Orders understood." He acknowledged and the comm. line was cut. Vorn could picture the ships in formation bearing down on the hapless Jeng vessel. He wished he were up there. He would have savored the moments before the strike came. Watching the unsuspecting ship close in on his radar and then sending a complete salvo against it with no reaction time for a decent shield wall. It will be a glorious victory. He smiled and stared at the sky. The sword ship was a tiny dot now and the stealthy black squadron was invisible to the naked eye. Of course, they were invisible to most systems as well. He watched even as the dot disappeared into the distance and his mind's eye brought to him the valiant struggle of an overmatched alien and the final demise of the sword ship and all who were in it. His intelligence said that the lowly Lieutenant had been aboard before it took off so that would rid him of two problems at once. This was certainly turning out to be a good day. He sat down and waited for the communicator to beep and tell him the news he was waiting for.

Eight ships waited as the sword ship cleared the atmosphere. Its sleek design allowed it to slice through the turbulence with only the slightest of bumps. Quinn felt the satisfaction of the clean ascent as the ship powered its way out into the blackness of space. The formation of cloaked ships did not read anywhere. They were essentially unrecognizable blobs to the radar. As such they were not even reported to the humans and the Jeng man on board the ship. There was a moment's pause as the sword ship crossed its own path to adjust to the new destination. Then all hell broke loose. The order to fire had been given and the Black Squadron was at practically point blank range. The missiles screamed out and started accelerating. They didn't have much time to accelerate before they impacted on the obsidian hull of the sword ship. The shock wave threw the passengers from their feet and spilled them unceremoniously onto the floor.

The Protector was able to track the missile's course back and he sent a few rock fragments their way. There was an explosion as one of the stealth ships blew up under direct fire, and then the whole wing materialized in front of them. The damage to the sword ship had been mostly superficial. After all, it was made of solid stone. But even that could be broken off into small fragments. A dozen missiles had hit home and the ship was listing off to the side. The propulsion, whatever it was made of, was not balanced anymore. The Protector swung around and glared at the humans. "Was this some kind of a trick?" He screamed at them. "You lure me into an ambush above your stinking colony. I should kill you both right here and now!" He screamed and Quinn spoke quickly in the ancient Jeng Rune Speak to form a wall between them. He needed time to think. The wall he had just made had taken valuable stone from the hull and he wanted to put it back intact as soon as possible. Margaret was mostly in shock. She didn't think that Vorn would order such an attack. It had to be his people. Those ships were unique as far as she knew. The black squadron had them in their sights now. She was simply waiting to be finished off by the next salvo of missiles. Quinn had other things in mind. He dropped the wall again and the Protector was startled into inactivity. He had been looking for a way to drop the wall himself. His familiarity with the runes was not as advanced as Quinn's.

Quinn stepped up to the man and looked him straight in the eyes. "You will have to trust me on this. That force out there is not the enemy. They are following that blind fool Admiral Vorn. I think we can stop them from attacking without destroying them, but it will be a near thing. I will need to use some of the stone of this ship as a weapon though. Do you give me permission to do so?" He asked, fully expecting to be denied. But something in his tone got through to the alien before him.

"Do what you can; we are still interested in acquiring a peaceful existence between our peoples. If your miracle will do the trick, then I shall not intervene." He said and he lowered his head. He had just abdicated protection of his people to an outsider. Only future history will be able to properly judge his actions.

Quinn looked out of the window and concentrated on the spearhead shaped ships as he launched a single glob of molten stone at each of the targets. He was still speaking the runes out in a pattern that no Jeng had ever heard before. Quinn was using combinations of runes to try to achieve his goals. The ritual was most complex. Sweat beaded up on his brow as he continued the speech. Syllable after syllable, the runes became more difficult to say and he almost stuttered at the difficulty.

The acting commander of the Black Squadron had watched as his missiles tracked in and struck the enemy ship. At first it looked like the missiles had no effect on the enemy ship. That strange sword design was still intact. There were no readings of leaking oxygen into space and there was practically no debris. Yet he had witnessed at least a dozen direct hits. He got a sinking feeling in his gut as he watched the ship list to the side a bit. There had been some damage, but his own ship could not have withstood that same onslaught. He knew then that he was overmatched in this battle. What's more he knew that he had struck the first blow while the enemy was unaware of his position, or maybe even his existence. The element of surprise was now lost. The field was almost even now. He ordered his crews to reload the missile tubes and he started plotting a solution to the target. The enemy ship was so close he might have been able to fire and hit without solutions plotted, but why take the chance when he had the time? In any case, he was now worried about running up against these ships. His hardware was state of the art. But the enemy had different arts and he may well be in over his head. His wing reported in that they were ready when a series of stone projectiles formed from the outline of the ship and launched at them. The squadron was still under cloak, but the stone spears came rushing in straight at them as if they were painted some highly reflective paint. The commander gripped the arms of his chair as the spires zeroed in. All of the projectiles hit and he was rocked in his seat as the damaged areas lit up on his status display. He had only been hit by one of the pieces, but his ship would not be able to give chase if the enemy were to break off and run. His engineers were reporting loss of one of his engines completely. The missile launcher was damaged beyond repair, and they had lost another four crewmembers when a bulkhead buckled just fore of the launcher ring. He sighed heavily as the reports were still coming in from the members of his wing. Of the eight ships, only two could now move under their own power. They were still trying though. The formation was still together, mostly from the momentum before the impacts. Then the unthinkable happened. The cloak dropped. They were now sitting ducks in front of the black sword shaped ship that seemed to be turning back towards them.

The commander asked over the com-link if any ships still had firing capabilities. Six ships reported that they did, but there would be problems with loading. All of the ships had been hit in or around the missile launchers. The firing was too accurate to have been random. Then the reason occurred to him. The enemy had been physically watching as the missiles came for them. They had simply plotted reverse courses and sent their attacks back to the hidden vessels. It was simple and ingenious at the same time. He nodded to the enemy ship. They had obviously survived his treachery, and now they would most likely destroy his entire command before moving on. After all, it is what he would have done. Never leave an enemy stronghold intact. The sword ship finished its turn and now it faced the black squadron. The commander simply waited for death to come. Then it started; pieces of the ship began to break off and melt. These new blobs began to streak over towards the spearhead of ships and the general alarm sounded. The commander sat back down and gripped his chair tightly again. "Brace for impact!" He ordered.

Quinn finally reached the end of the rune-speak and when the final word was spoken, the blobs splashed onto the fronts of the black squadron's ships. The whole front halves of the vessels were covered with the molten rock. Then it solidified and the vessels were disabled. Weapons, view screens, scanners, and even communications antennas were coated with a fairly thick layer of obsidian rock. The ships hung there in space. They were now deaf and blind and their crews shut down the engines so that they wouldn't run into each other in the tight formation they were now in. They were no longer any threat to the dark stone ship. Quinn turned to the Protector and bowed. "I believe that we are free to resume our course for your world and the governing body situated there." He announced and the Protector leaned back and eyed the human.

His eyes blinked twice and then he addressed the human in an even tone that failed to hide the emotion behind his words. "I have never seen anyone use the runes to such a degree. Our masters of the scholastic arts would like to get a hold of you. Of that I am most certain. You used words that I have never heard before. Surely you used them in a way that no one had ever imagined before. Your solution was non-violent as well. If you can talk as well as you fight for this peace, then I am sure we will be successful on this mission." He turned back to the wall and waved his hand over it. The ship resumed its course.

Quinn felt pretty much drained, and he settled back into the ship to rest. Margaret caught the subtle change in body language and was ready to catch him as he fell. She laid him out on the stone floor and made sure he was not in an awkward position that would be counter-productive to resting. Then she left him alone and headed back forward to the Protector. He had watched the whole display and he looked a bit concerned.

Margaret shook her head at him. "No, he is not injured; only tired. Your rune language draws a portion of its power from the individual speaking the words. The set he just spoke was long enough to tax his system a bit. He will fully recover soon. You mentioned that it would take about a day to reach your world, he should be back to normal before then." She diagnosed and the alien man seemed to relax a bit. The motion brought Margaret's mind into focus. This Jeng man really did count on Quinn to do all of the tough negotiating. She sort of resented the fact, but it did not change it. Besides, Quinn was probably honored beyond most reasoning to be held in this regard by the Protector of the *True People*.

The sword ship targeted the home world and the sleek design lended itself well to the acceleration that commenced. Neither human passenger was prepared when it actually happened. The front of the ship had been turned transparent by some command that the Protector spoke to it. The lights of the stars streaked into lines and then they crossed and refracted into the different colors of the rainbow. Then the red plasma masked the whole thing as they jumped out of time. The black ship was now caught in a limbo state of non-time. If this had been a conventional ship, the gauges would have had nothing to display. They were currently outside of the normal laws of nature. The effect was memorizing and then the sky went completely black. The lack of details was startling. The Protector noticed the confusion and explained that light could not penetrate the veil of time so there would be no view until they dropped back into normal space.

Since they had about a day until they reached their destination, the Protector set up some comfortable quarters so that some rest and relaxation could take place. Then he offered some refreshments. He brought forth a pitcher with water and some food that looked like cake, but was bland and had a stale metallic aftertaste. Both of the passengers ate it, but they did not ask for seconds. These people had a lot to learn about food. Quinn practiced his speech on Margaret and the two of them kept busy until the Protector announced that they would soon be able to see something outside. They both headed to the front of the ship and watched as the blackness burst into full colors of streaking rainbow effect. It was quite dazzling. Then the lights melded back into streaks of white and finally, the stars solidified back into dots. Centered in the vast view before them was the Jeng home world. It was similar to Earth. There were major continents and vast oceans. The difference was that the dark side of the planet had no lights scattered throughout it so it looked unihabited from orbit. The black ship cast its shadow on a floating chunk of rock nearby. The world was situated in a field of asteroids. But something looked a bit unnatural about them. Quinn's mouth dropped open when he realized what they were.

"Those are defense platforms!" He exclaimed. Margaret looked at him in surprise. Then she looked out of the view port and tried to see more of the asteroids. There were little specks of rock scattered all over the area. There had to be thousands of them. They formed a protective belt around the planet. Margaret thought about the scale of the project that had put them there and was instantly impressed. These people used their resources in ways that humans had not thought of. Still, they were here to find a peace with these same people. Hopefully, there was enough common ground to understand each other. The obvious problem of getting out of here alive if something went wrong was of the utmost on her mind. Quinn had no reservations about the future. He was ready to embrace it and his courage would hopefully be infectious on his friend and witness.

The sword ship crossed the threshold of night and day and sailed unerringly towards the capital city. The Protector was allowed to land immediately even though several other craft were waiting in a landing queue. There was a group of guards in ceremonial garb waiting for the crew as the ship landed in the underground hangar. The two humans and the Protector were led away and up to a grand palace of intricate stone. The stonework was of course made from Jeng Rune Speak, and Quinn could see similarities to this one in the ruins that he had seen on file in the archeological archive. There were grand staircases and towering ceilings. The pillars of solid marble were holding a vast stone block above the entrance to the immense building. The trio was ushered into the building proper and brought to a waiting room that was furnished with plush chairs and carpeting woven from something that neither Quinn nor Margaret had ever seen before. If they hadn't known any better, they would have guessed that they had been woven from spider's web. On second thought, they didn't really know better. In any case, they were woven in bright patterns that contrasted greatly with the people that they were made for. The Jeng guards were nondescript. Their features were average at best. They were almost clones of each other. The uniforms destroyed any sense of individuality that they may have thought of displaying. They both stood by a tall wooden door. The wood stood out from all of the stone construction. Quinn felt that this door was different somehow. It had not been formed from the stone as everything else had been. The looks on the guards made him a bit nervous. They kept sneaking glances at the two humans. It was obvious that neither had ever seen one before. It was probably even more confusing that these two humans were of different sexes. The visitors had yet to see a female Jeng. Of course their walk had not exposed them to hardly any Jeng. It was as If they were being kept secret from the general population. It was a little unnerving, although great pains were taken not to offend them. It was as if they could minimize this disturbance and get back to business as usual around here.

A small Jeng man in ceremonial robes stepped into the room and ushered the group over to the door. The Protector was called in first. He nodded to the messenger and strode purposefully into the hallway beyond. The messenger stood there watching him for a couple of paces and then he turned to Quinn. "You and your witness may proceed in a moment. I will signal you from the other end of the hallway when it is time. The Protector has told us that you wish to address the council. This will set a precedent for such visitations from other races. Basically the only thing that had kept you alive to this point is the Protector's reassurance that you are not a threat to the council. You must be advised that there will be armed guards present and any hostilities will be dealt with quickly and fiercely." The younger Jeng admonished and he looked at the two humans trying to determine their level of understanding.

"I am not here to start or prolong a war. I am here to secure peace from your government. One could not expect to get their cooperation through violence. You will have no trouble from us on that count, let me assure you." Quinn replied in his most supplicating tone. The messenger seemed to be satisfied and he left them standing there as he hurried down the exposed hallway. The guards turned to make sure that the visitors did not follow him prematurely. They needn't have wasted their time with the display. Quinn was quite content to wait his turn in line to save his people from conflict. He watched as the messenger reached the far door and slipped through it. There was the faint sound of arguing from the chamber beyond, but the distance was too great to make out any specific details.

It was about fifteen minutes later when the messenger leaned out of the far door and waved them forward. They practically ran the first couple of steps, and then they calmed down a bit and composed themselves. By the time that Quinn was at the door, both he and Margaret were ready to enter it. He wondered in the back of his mind if that mental transformation hadn't been the architect's intentions when the room was designed. He didn't know, and at this point he really didn't care. He stepped into the room. Room was too little of a term to describe the magnificent chamber that they had entered. This was a grand cathedral of a room. There were statues along the walls, and stone benches lining one of the walls as some sort of grandstand area. The Protector was still in here; he was seated in a chair off to one side of a row of podiums that were arranged in a line across a raised platform. The various Jeng council members were seated behind their respective podiums and they all tracked to the two new occupants of the room.

Quinn stepped up to the speaker's platform. It was a bit lower than the podiums, so he could still be looked down upon. He knew that most nobility liked to distance themselves from lower castes, so he was prepared for the disparity in positions. In fact he was comfortable with it. Let them look down on him as long as they listen to him carefully. Margaret took a seat in the first row of stone pews that filled the central area of the room. The Protector fidgeted as the humans entered the chamber and approached. Quinn was uncertain how to take the action. If the man was that nervous, maybe there was something more to be nervous about that he did not know of. Still, whatever was going to happen would happen. All he could control was his own role in the whole affair. He solidified his resolve and gripped the speaker's podium on both sides.

"Distinguished members of the True People. I have come as a representative of the human race to sue for peace with your ancient and honorable civilization." He began in a most regal tone and then he watched for reactions among the group. It was like staring at living statues, there was not a flicker of interest among them. He brought up his arms to encompass the whole assemblage. "You are in a unique position to write the history that future generations will learn about. A union between our peoples could advance both sides much farther than they could achieve individually." He announced and again there was no reaction from the group. The Protector was fidgeting even worse now. He even occasionally shook his head.

"You have come to a position where some sort of action is required. The way I see it, you have been in hiding from all outside races for millennia. This system has worked for you in the past, but it has also cost you a great deal. Your heritage has been stained by your own people's inability to use your inherited technology to its fullest." Quinn stated flatly. He finally got some sort of reaction, but it was one of fear and hatred among the assembled panel. He felt the room grow colder as the hatred flowed from the men before him. He swallowed and stood firm. "I can help you to achieve the dreams that your forefathers had envisioned. I know the Rune Speak language, and I can help your scholars to understand its intricacies and thus help your race as a whole to step forward. Your people have stagnated in the disuse of their creative potential. I believe that we can help you to accomplish more than you may have ever dreamed."

One of the men at the raised podiums stood up and pointed angrily at Quinn. "You blasphemy in our sacred council chamber! Outsiders should never have access to the Runes, since they are meant for the True People alone. Uncivilized people such as you should not have the power. It is dangerous in the wrong hands. You will be cleansed of this knowledge and then returned to your people. We will continue as we have always done and your people will be wiped from our planets and then we shall disappear back into obscurity. That is the way of things for the True People. How could you, an outsider, ever understand the complexities that are the Jeng Horde? What is worse, you have somehow infected our Protector. That means that a new one must be appointed, and he is unwilling to name his successor. You have caused this council more trouble than any other race has ever done. I hope that you are satisfied, because we intend to erase your meddling and get back to normal around here." The pompous man finished accusingly.

Quinn stood there for several seconds. His neck turned red with the anger that he was holding at bay. "Sir. You are out of line as I see it. I have the floor, and your comments are counter-productive to the discussion at hand. First of all, we have access to your runes. That is now a matter of fact that cannot be changed. I shall not be 'cleansed' as you put it because if something happens to me, then my people will come to war against you. This is not a threat so much as a warning. I am here to prevent such an activity from taking place. My people are already preparing for war with you. Now as to the Protector, I believe that he has opened his eyes and his mind much better than you have. You have decided that we are not able to help you even though you have not allowed us to even try. This does not sound like good leadership to me. Perhaps you should reconsider your hard line stance and rethink the issue before you. I believe that you need us badly. Do you realize that your people have not advanced in the last several thousand years? Do you want to spend the next thousand the same way? You may find that my people will advance beyond you by the time we meet again. It is a real and possibly scary possibility. Perhaps you should ask your Protector what he knows that you do not. Maybe then you would understand what I am offering you here." Quinn finished and stepped down from the podium.

The Protector stood up and slowly made his way to the speaker's platform. He looked up at the intimidating podiums and the even more intimidating men sitting at them and he swallowed visibly. "The human speaks the truth. His race is dangerous, and he is here to prevent them from coming after us." He stated shakily and the council gazed at him with the same hatred that they had displayed for Quinn.

The same troublemaker stood up and screamed at the Protector. "What do you know that makes it all right to bring this filth into our chambers? These savages are dangerous. You both have told us this. Does this mean that he will attempt to assassinate us in our own court? I could find a hundred reasons to liquidate both of you now, but we need a new protector and by our laws, you must name him."

The Protector tried to hold his ground, but he was visibly shaken and Quinn could see his shoulders twitch under the strain. "You have asked me what I know. It is a simple thing to read my mind and find out what I know. So let me not bore you with that. Instead, let me tell you what this human knows. He knows how to make our runes work for purposes that we haven't even imagined. I saw him disable eight of his own vessels with rune-speak to allow us to come here. His motives are honest and just. He is probably confused now with the treatment that you are affording him as I have told him that the Protector has the final word in all matters concerning the outsiders."

The man behind the podium turned dark red; he was obviously building up some decent anger. "You cannot speak for everyone concerning the outsiders!" He screamed at the Protector. "What gives you the right to make changes that will affect the entire race?" He asked with fire in his tone.

The Protector stood tall and lifted his chin towards the council. "I am the Protector. By the mandates that I must follow, I have absolute authority over all things concerning the outsiders. I am personally charged with the well being of the True People. It is not a charge I take lightly. This man here has proven that he has something to offer us as a species that will break us out of our complacency and the stagnation of our technology base. On top of that, his people know of our existence, and the cleansing you are so fond of would be impossible without raising the attention of their government. The news has already traveled too far to contain the situation through the normal means. Your hands are tied in this matter. Stop your blustering and think about your people. You know as well as I do that we have remained the same for your entire lifetime. Is that what you wish to pass on to your sons? Life without change is less than a full life. You could personally doom our entire species to an eternity of darkness by simply shutting out this light." The Protector had used most of his energy fighting the indignity of the accusation and he slumped a bit after having said his piece.

Quinn stepped back up to the speaker's podium. The Protector moved gratefully aside and allowed him the floor. "I do not fully understand your reluctance to embrace change. But I do understand that the life you have led up to this point has forever changed. I have come a long way to help you. My people are at this moment gearing up for a fight. If I am to go to them and sue for peace on your behalf, I must know that it is wanted on this side. Only you can determine what is right and what is wrong. That is the responsibility of all leaders. The great leaders can do this without thinking about it first. The right answer is the one from the heart and they know it without question. Perhaps if you took a moment to consider what I am offering, then maybe you would see that I don't offer much, just coexistence with us. Is that any more or less than you want from us?" He asked and the Protector stepped back up to the podium and Quinn stepped aside to allow his access.

"These people have a bonus to offer us. You have not tried their food. It is amazing. There are different textures and flavors to boggle the mind. You must sample some of what they have to offer." The Protector pulled a few mints from his pocket. "These were served after a good sized meal. I was saving them for later, but I think you should try them now." He said and he held his hand out in offering.

The council was obviously not expecting this and the reactions were mixed. On one side, they were afraid of the small pills. They could be some form of poison. On the other hand, The Protector has already eaten some and was ready to side with these humans after having tasted it. It must be something special. A few of the council members stepped down from their posts and took a mint from the Protector's hand. They sniffed them and the smell was different than anything that they had ever consumed. Then, one by one, they popped them into their mouths. The explosion of mint froze them in place. Their tongues were afire with the cold blast of flavor. One of the men spit it out right away. The rest of them watched as the others savored the taste and began to 'bliss out' on the sensation.

The angry council member pointed an accusing finger at the Protector. "You have drugged them. I'll see you hanged for attempting to circumvent the security of the council. The mints were getting smaller in the mouths of the Jeng, but one of them grew impatient and a loud crunch was heard as he bit the candy and it broke into pieces in his mouth. The others turned to him in curiosity. The smile on his face told the story and they all were soon biting and crushing the candy in their mouths. The ones that had not tried the mints were now being offered some by the ones that had. Soon they were all crunching the mints, even the begrudgingly angry man. He was the least impressed by the flavor, but he had to admit that it was like nothing he had ever eaten before. He actually found the crunch to be quite rewarding. His demeanor started to soften a bit.

Quinn took the podium again. "Those are simply after dinner mints, they are made from a plant extract with sugar added. Sugar is another plant. These foods are just a small sample of what we have available for consumption for you. Of course there is also Rune training available. All that I am asking is the willingness to follow a peaceful solution. What do you say?" He asked and many of the council members nodded their appreciation enthusiastically. Then others joined in and finally, the angry councilman caved in and supported the initiative.

The speaker stepped down and the Council addressed the room as a whole. "I have to announce that we are to consider peace with the humans. It is in the best interest of the Jeng race, and we are behind this initiative fully. We shall have a cultural exchange in which many of these exotic foodstuffs will be brought to us and our people will be taught their preparations. In addition, we will offer access to the Rune-Speak by approved personnel in exchange for training in the new methods of use for those same runes." The man looked at Quinn directly. "Go now, and tell your people that we are ready to talk peace with them. If you can avert this coming war, then you will be considered a hero to the True People. We are considering you the Protector of the Human Race with all of the privileges and duties thereof."

The Protector was surprised at the ruling, but he was quite pleased as well. It meant that Quinn was now his brother, sort of. He could think of no one else that he would trust with such a designation. The trio left the room after thanking the council for its time and following the exiting procedure as directed by the messenger. Once outside, Quinn took a moment to let it all sink in. It had been a close thing, and he was quite tired. But, the work was not over yet. They had another such council to convince as well. They headed back to the sword ship and boarded the ramp. Margaret had watched quietly as the meeting progressed. Now she was looking at Quinn with new respect. He really was the messiah of peace he tried to be.

Clearance for their departure had already been arranged by the time they asked for it and they were soon clear and into open space and on their way before anyone could change their minds. The feeling on board was positive, almost to the point of giddiness. Quinn put a hand on the Protector's shoulder. "That was some thinking you did back there. I had no idea that food could be so persuasive. You definitely know your people better than I do. I hope that we can work together for a long time. I have much to learn from you and I hope that I can return the favor."

The Protector looked at the human and judged that his tone was sincere. "I am honored to be your brother. Fellow Protectors are all brothers. I am happy for you and I am also happy for myself. It has been quite lonely being the only recognized Protector. Now I can talk with someone that has the same interests and that lives by the same rules as I do. It is a most exciting time for me. I do not know where your home planet is, but if you'll give me the coordinates, then we shall go there straight away." He said and Quinn smiled back at the man. He had never had a brother of any sort. The closest had been his instructors at the academy. But this bond was a lot different. He really did feel kinship with this alien being from another race and his heart was lighter at the realization. He supplied the coordinates and they went back into that blackness to spend a couple of days travel.

Admiral Vorn had finished his time on the planet and he rejoined his wing in orbit. He was surprised to find that all eight of the ships had been disabled. They were still alive, but EVA crews were chiseling rock off of the hulls. Communications were restored just as the Admiral re-boarded the lead ship.

He headed for the commander of the wing, and he was not pleased. They had obviously let that alien ship go and now they had to get under way. The only place they could reasonably intercept that Quinn fellow now was at headquarters. It was coincidental that his current orders were telling him to return to that planet anyway. It looked like fortune was smiling on him and he was ready to get on with it just as soon as he tore a piece of this man's rear off in a fit of righteous rage.

Shortly after the scolding and the following redoubling of the repair efforts, the wing headed back toward the home world. He was certain that he could still gain that hero status if he could just get there in time. He had no idea how long he had until that Protector reached home. He just knew that they needed to be blown from the skies before they could infect the minds of the council. He got preliminary reports of the fleet around the home world, and his smile broadened. There was a lot of hardware in system. The likelihood of the Sword ship making it to the planet was pretty remote. His own forces would only solidify that position and he could not wait to get them in place to do their part.

The two Protectors sat together and Margaret watched from the side. They were sharing a coffee and some talk. Quinn was mostly interested in the argumentative Jeng councilor, and the Protector had a lot of information on him. It seems that the man had gone through a troubling childhood and been denied the chance to go through the military training due to medical reasons. Then, he was forbidden to participate in three other career choices before he finally got into the council as a last minute entry. He carried a lot of grief around with him, and he held a particular grudge against the Jeng military division. That explained some of his reluctance in the first place. There was much more, but they didn't have time to continue. The Protector got up and went over to the control panel. He waved his hand and saw that warships surrounded the planet. He brought it up to Quinn and they both watched as the sword ship sailed into the system with the heaviest picket that Quinn had ever seen between them and the planet. More specifically, it was between them and the council. That meant that they had to get through warships to sue for peace. It was not a pleasant thought. The sword ship dropped out of warped space and the ships all came to life around them. Weapons went from standby to ready and target locks kept pinging off of the sleek black stone ship. The situation was touchy to say the least. Quinn stood in the middle of the black ship and formed a clear barrier around him in some form of mica. Then he rose through the hull of the ship and the bubble allowed the fleet to see the human standing on top of the sword ship. His personal communicator beeped with several ships trying to contact him.

He reached for his communicator and the beeping stopped. He pulled the piece to his ear and the many voices were too much to be heard clearly. "Hold it people, one at a time." He shouted into the pickup and the chatter died out completely. "As you can see, I am human. I am Lieutenant Quinn Ramses of the survey crew and I am en route to the home world in order to bring a peace initiative to the council. Stand aside in the name of peace for the human race." He ordered and the ships did not budge from their blockade.

A voice rang out clearly from the communicator. It was the voice of authority. "I am in charge of this fleet. I am Admiral Horniczek, and I request that you come aboard my ship for questioning before anyone goes down to the planet. I cannot allow such a security risk to go down to our protected government installation untested."

Quinn smiled and looked at the various ships. He knew that many of them had a visual of him, and they were wondering what his reaction would be. "I understand your need for security. But I must also tell you that I have security issues of my own here. I have a duly appointed representative of the Jeng race with me and we both need to get safely to the planet to present our proposal to the council. If you can personally guarantee our safety, we will both submit to your questioning before heading down to the planet. Is this satisfactory?" He asked, thinking that it all sounded reasonable enough.

The Admiral thought for a moment, trying to see if there was a loophole or clever escape attempt in the works here. He could not see one, so he responded. "That will be satisfactory. I shall expect you within the hour aboard my ship. The other vessels will back off and allow you easy access to my flagship. I look forward to meeting the famous Quinn Ramses, and his guest."

The transmission ended without so much as a request for confirmation. The Admiral was not being very forthcoming. He had a lot to worry about. Not the least of which was a possible alien spy going down to his own government's sacred chambers.

17

Admiral Vorn had just entered the formation when the sword ship dropped into the system. Alarms went off all over the ship. Sensitive scanning equipment picked up the intrusion instantly and the crew responded with practiced efficiency. His first reaction was to warn the planet about the new arrival, but he was thwarted because someone had a jamming field and no one was going to speak to anyone down there. The jamming field was strong. It was too strong for even his transporter beam to penetrate. That meant that there were some other ships out there with advanced technology. He became suspicious. But the moment demanded his immediate action. He attempted to contact the other ships of this fleet and he was ordered by an Admiral Horniczek to stop trying to use his communications equipment. He was not authorized to use it during negotiations with the alien ambassador.

"Alien ambassador!" Vorn screamed into the pickup. "That man is not an ambassador; he is a stinking Lieutenant of our own Survey Crew. He was assigned to the *Lincoln* before the Jeng battle moon destroyed her. He also started an unregistered colony on the Jeng owned planet and then he disabled eight of my wing ships to leave the system on this delusion of grandeur of his. I will have him up for court martial as soon as I can get him into custody!" The admiral shouted to this Horniczek fellow. "As soon as he boards your ship, lock him up. I want him held for me and I will take custody." He demanded and there was a moment's pause before the other man answered.

"Sir." Horniczek began. "You are in no position to demand anything. You are not in charge here, I am. I will do as is proper given the circumstances that I perceive once I meet this Lieutenant Ramses of yours. Furthermore, you are to refrain from using the communications airwaves as I have already instructed you. If you do not maintain radio silence until otherwise ordered, I will have you placed under arrest and then we shall see who goes to the chopping block. Do I make myself clear?" He asked in a dangerous tone that the distance of space could not diminish.

Vorn swallowed some of his rage and bit back his first response. Then he picked up the mike again and there was cold steel in his voice when he spoke again. "You have not heard the last of this. When the Jeng have conquered us, history will record you as the one who brought the human race down. I will be here when you need me to bail you out of the mess you are destined to fall into. Vorn out." He cut off the communications equipment and pulled the mike from its cord, severing the cord and making another repair necessary for his maintenance crew. Then he stepped over to his scanner technician.

"I want you to find a hole in that scattering field. I need to beam over there with a rifle squad. If that idiot over there thinks I'll stand idly by while he gives away the home world, he is sadly mistaken." The scan-tech nodded that he understood and he began cross-referencing the scan data, looking for holes in the snarling electronic web they were caught in. Vorn turned towards his operations officer. "Walter, I want a squad of men ready to board that vessel as soon as we have access to it. We need to move fast or all will be lost."

All over the ship, preparations got underway and Vorn sat in his command chair brooding. His temper was being held in check, but only just. He was ready for some real fighting action. He hoped that he would be the one who got to Quinn first. It would make his victory all the sweeter.

Margaret and the two Protectors readied themselves for interrogation. At least they prepared as well as they could. It was assumed that it would be an ordeal, but neither man was ready to turn back. There was too much riding on this mission and its hope of success. The future of hundreds of systems and thousands of worlds hung in the balance as the power struggle started to play out. Of course they were unaware of Admiral Vorn being in the system, or of his plans. They were blissfully unaware of his threats and preparations. Not that it would change the reality they were currently facing. They still had to deal with the forces in orbit before they could advance to the planet and attempt to secure a lasting peace with the ruling council down below. The sword ship drew up slowly and was dwarfed by the Admiral's flagship. It was one of those new top of the line dreadnaughts and it was loaded to the teeth with armaments. It was over two and half kilometers long and its missile launchers were numbered with three digits. The impressive sensor clusters were spread neatly across the hull and afforded an electronic barrier to missile locks and communications equipment for most of the technology in service today. The black sword ship nestled in alongside the massive cruiser and was almost lost in its shadow. Meter by meter it edged in and finally made soft contact with the hull of the larger ship. A soft seal was linked to the stone ship and the trio left the safety of stone and crossed the threshold into metallic confinement. There were several men on the other side of the airlock. They were wearing hazardous material suits. They secured the environment from the wearer. Quinn wondered what they were worried about. He was not similarly adorned and he was fine. Maybe they had some doubts of that, or maybe it was just protocol on first contacts aboard the flagship. Either way it did nothing to instill a sense of calm for the invited guests of the Admiral. The Protector looked around and settled down considerably when he noticed that the men were not armed. This meant to him that they were worried about viruses or bacteria, and not the potential violence from the people themselves. The three were ushered down a service corridor and placed in a sterilization chamber. Bright lights burned away their clothing and the outer layer of skin. The most surprising part was that other than being embarrassed, they were completely unharmed by the cleanser. Even the Jeng man thought that the machine was well designed. Fresh clothes were available in the next compartment and they even had something for the Jeng who was considerably differently built. Someone was going to great lengths to ensure that he was not upset by the proceedings. Then the three of them were taken for identification screenings. Retinal patterns were recorded. Quinn and Margaret's pattern matched the one on file for them and they were both cleared immediately. The Protector's pattern was stored on file and he was issued a badge stating his identification. It seemed a little unnecessary to him since he was the only member of the True People on board, but he complied with the request to attach the badge on his chest.

Finally, they were ushered into a conference room. It was huge. On board a ship this size, Quinn guessed they had too much space to find things to put in it. The room was bigger than the bridge had been on board the *Lincoln*. There was a long tapered table stretching an impressive 25 meters down the middle of the room, and Quinn noted that it was made of real wood. So were the thirty or so chairs that were evenly space around it. At the head of the table was a high-backed chair that was facing away from them. As they noticed it, it swung around and a balding man with Admiral stripes smiled at them. He was withered looking and his chair looked to be permanent. His skinny wrinkled hand hovered over the controls and he brought his chair around the table and rolled it over to the three space-people.

The man eyed the three of them closely, and then he smiled. "Please forgive the decontamination process. I am susceptible to almost all of the known diseases, so I must take precautions in order to prolong my life." He spent an extra few seconds, eyeing Margaret up and down. He nodded appreciatively and then turned his chair around for the trip back to the head of the table. "Please have a seat." The gravelly voice said. They wondered how he had sounded so forceful on the communications line if he was this failing in health in person. As if he heard their thoughts he spoke up. "I use an interpreter when communicating with others. It helps to make my authority stick. Now if you will do me the courtesy, please tell me what your business is down on the planet."

Quinn stood up and the Admiral looked at him sourly and he sat back down. Then the old man looked straight at the Protector. "Well young man, out with it." He ordered and the Jeng warrior stood up nervously. "Well sir, we are here to ask your government to agree with our government that war is too expensive for both of our sides. We feel, as does your man Ramses here, that trading and mutual respect would far better serve both peoples. We can offer you the power of our Rune-Speak in trade for food preparation secrets and training in some of your technology." He said and the old man nodded that he had said enough.

"Very well. Lieutenant, what do you have to add to all of this?" He asked and there was a twinkle in his eye.

"Sir, I have very little to add. My feelings are the same as the Protector's here. I believe that peace is the best way for us to proceed and to grow. I would also add that later trades of technology could greatly enhance our relationship in the future. Each race has something to offer the other. It is a symbiotic relationship of equals. We have needs, and so do they. If they are fulfilled together, we become the stronger for the effort we put forth today." Finished, Quinn sat back down and the Admiral made a "Humpf" sound and leaned back a bit.

He looked at Margaret and it was obvious that he now wanted her input as well. She stood shakily and then she took a deep cleansing breath and spoke. "I believe in Quinn. I agree that war is the least profitable ambition that we could undertake. Quinn is the only one that suggested that we do otherwise. He has a vision of the future and the peace he wants for it. I trust in him and I trust in that vision. I have also met with this Jeng Protector here. He is an honorable man and I believe in him as well. He holds the same ideals as Quinn does. Although he did not realize this was so at first. With both men, their primary goal was the preservation and advancement of their own species. They each saw the pro's and con's of going to war and the con's outweighed the pro's by no small margin. They each then made a commitment to prevent this war at any and all personal costs. Now they stand before you, and they hope to soon stand before council as they did on the Jeng home world and plead their case to the highest court available. My belief stems from the determination that I know they both share and the righteous goal they have embraced. Won't you let them accomplish this mission and save both races from needless killing and destruction?" She finished and the Admiral looked at the woman with a new respect. She was obviously a professional. He had read her file. She was a decorated pilot and a good commander. She was also in love with Quinn. That much was obvious from the start. In fact, he also knew that Quinn loved her back. They seemed to not have noticed it together yet, but he knew that it was only a matter of time. He envied them a bit, but they were still on a mission, and he needed to make a decision. He sat there for a moment more weighing the visual cues they were offering him. At last he made the decision and he smiled at the trio before him.

"Sirs and madam." He began almost regally. "It has been my great honor to host you here in my humble ship. I wish you all success on your mission, and I wish you all continued long life and happiness. He pointed at the humans, especially you two." He said with a smile. "I hope that when you are in front of the council that you can put in a good word for me as well. It would be nice to be remembered for something other than battles at the end of an illustrious career such as mine." He said and his smile faded for a second and was quickly restored. "You may return to your ship now. I will clear the way for you to descend to the surface next to the government building and you will be shuttled to the chamber, as I'm sure you have been before. This is not the first time I have heard about you Quinn. You impress me, and that is saying something. I am glad that one such as you made this first contact. A lesser man may have bungled it beyond peaceful negotiations. I will stand in your way no longer." And he waved them all off.

The door opened on the far side of the chamber and several space marines with assault rifles piled into the room screaming for everyone to halt. The Admiral screamed in rage as unauthorized personnel were boarding his ship. He hit a red button on his chair and alarms sounded all over the ship. He hoped that his crew was more prepared than he was. The four people in the room had not moved and the rifles were leveled at the two Protectors. Margaret stepped in front of Quinn and told the men not to shoot. Quinn shoved her back to the side. He couldn't lose her now.

"What is the meaning of this?" Quinn asked and he used a driving authority in his voice. "What ship are you from?" He asked in a dangerous tone.

The marine was ready to fire at the first sign of resistance, but talking was not effective resistance so he held his trigger. "I am a member of the black squadron." He said noncommittally. "You are under arrest pending court martial for starting an illegal colony and impersonating an ambassador. You will follow us to Admiral Vorn's ship." He said and that was the card that Quinn was waiting to hit the table.

Quinn started to speak up again, and Admiral Horniczek cut him off. "Admiral Vorn." He said with distaste. "Does not have the authority to board my ship. Nor do you. I suggest you put away those weapons and return to your ship or I will be forced to place you all under arrest." He said and as if to underscore the statement, several other marines came up behind them with weapons drawn and ordered their surrender. The well-trained men knew that they were impossibly bottled in. One of their objectives had been to disable the electronic dampening field before snaring the quarry so that they could be beamed out, but they had stumbled across the traitor first. Now they were stuck like rats in a maze. They dropped their weapons and knelt down on the floor with their hands interlocked behind their heads. It is the position that they were about to order Quinn into and he recognized it right away.

The Admiral commended his men for their timing and efficiency then he turned his chair back towards the trio. "You'd better get going. It seems history is not going to wait much longer for your peace. I suggest you hurry up now." He admonished and they exited the conference room and were led at almost a run to the airlock door. They left the dreadnaught without further discussion and sealed the sword ship quickly. They were traveling away from the gigantic ship and breaking the first edges of the atmosphere in record time. The way was indeed clear as Horniczek had claimed and they were pleasantly surprised when the ground shuttle was there as promised. They were hustled into the main corridor. The Protector noted that it looked much like the one on the Jeng home world. He wondered if the humans even knew that they had lived such similar lives. He thought not. They were brought through two massive wooden doors and they entered the main chamber. Just like the Jeng council, they were arranged on raised platforms and a speaker's podium was set in the middle below them. The similarities were almost eerie. Of course one major difference was that the men at the higher podiums were all human instead of True People. But that was as he had expected it to be. They marched all of the way up to the podium and this time, it was not Quinn who stepped up to the podium; it was the Protector. The Jeng man placed his hands confidently on both sides of the podium and spaced his legs comfortably apart.

When he spoke, his voice carried through the chamber like a symphony hall. "Esteemed members of the human ruling council. I am here on the request of your survey crewmember, and that of my government. I am here today to ask you to consider an alternative to fighting between our peoples. I am certain by the number of ships in orbit that you already know how our two races met each other, and the catastrophic results that came of it. If you do not, then I will elaborate on that. I was not there, of course, but I will tell you what was reported to me by my people, some if which were there." He paused and the faces were eager to hear the next words he had to say.

"One of our older bases had been planted on the water world that your ship, I am told the *S.S.F. Lincoln* was sent to check for possible colonization. A survey crewmember attempted to take his survey but was shot down by the automated sentinels placed at the entrance to the base. This was unfortunate, but it was also unforeseeable. No one had been to this planet according to our records for over a hundred years. It was assumed that you had found nothing valuable and had left it untouched. Since that is the way we wanted it, we did not interfere any further. Anyway, this new ship was shot down and splashed into the ocean. It was considered lost by us. Your ship, however, dispatched a shuttle to discern what had happened to the first ship. It was also attacked.

It made a crashed landing on the island containing the Jeng base. Shortly after that, your Quinn Ramses broke many of our laws. Not the least of which was accessing and using Jeng technology. At first, the commander that had been summoned did not find anything troublesome about the little world. When he sent a team down to the planet, a god that was on the planet slaughtered them. It had been held in a confinement facility on the planet and was opened by Quinn. He later apologized for the incident and he recaptured the animal and placed it back in the cell."

"Being able to accomplish that, however, alerted the commander that the humans on the planet had been accessing and using our Rune-Speak. That is forbidden by one of our oldest laws. Still, the problem was not solved when another landing team was dispatched. Instead, the god was freed again and it slaughtered more of our warriors. This became an incident and the commander wanted to avoid the council stepping in and taking command from him. He tried to scare away the *Lincoln*. While it was away, he ordered the island to be sunk into the ocean. That would accomplish the task of securing our technology, and removing the human infestation at the same time. I know that this sounds harsh, but you must understand that our people have lived for millennia in hiding from all outside races. One of our laws is that no one shall know of our existence. But additional problems arose when the *Lincoln* came back and there was a battle over the planet. The *Lincoln* was destroyed and the Jeng moon base was self destructed as some cloaked ships attacked it from somewhere unseen. It was later reported that the cloaked ships belonged to Admiral Vorn. He has tried to prevent peace from the beginning. It is believed that this is due to his loss of the Jeng base on the planet. He does not handle defeat well."

"With the loss of two bases, I was dispatched to determine what needed to be done to restore the system to peace. This usually requires the extermination of the intruders and the total destruction of all artifacts so that the Jeng people are not discovered. However, when I arrived on the planet, I found a thriving colony on the main continent of the planet and Quinn Ramses in charge of it. It had been built using the Jeng technology and I was shocked at how well he understood the runes. He met with me personally and told me of his plan to keep the planet for his colony and to trade his knowledge of our runes for it. I was doubtful, but we went to my government anyway for him to present his case for peace. His conviction won them over, mostly. Food had something to play in it as well. Then we traveled here to beseech your aid in the pursuit of peace between our peoples."

The Protector took a deep breath and steadied himself for the next part. "My people agree to let humans use the Rune-Speak technology. If you don't yet know what it is, Quinn can explain it for you better than I can, at least from a human perspective. Secondly, we will allow you to keep the planet with your colony on it. What we ask in exchange is small in comparison. We ask for training from Quinn. We also ask for your diversity in food preparations skills. Our people have not embraced food as you have. You would be amazed what flavor would be like if you had not had it all of your lives. This also opens the door for further negotiations on future technologies. But the most important reason of all to accept this offer is the cessation of hostilities between our peoples. There will be borders and boundaries, and there will be fleets. We could join your fleet as a member. We could trade our goods for your own. There is so much to learn. But it all begins with you. Your decision today determines whether or not this remains a dream that Quinn and I both share, or does it grow to fruition in our lifetimes. The future is up to you." The Protector sat down next to Quinn. He was obviously exhausted, but he held his head up high. He was the only Jeng man that these humans had seen, and he was determined that they would see the best that a Jeng could be.

There were several moments of quiet in the vast chamber. The Protector's last sentence kept ringing through the minds of the council members, "The future is up to you." It was a most apt phrase. Everyone in the chamber felt that history was being made here. But what history was it going to be? Quinn crossed his fingers and Margaret put her hand on his shoulder for support. The moments dragged on a bit longer and one of the councilmen clapped his hands together loudly. Then he did it again. Then he started clapping faster and soon, the other members started applauding too. Within moments, the entire room was lifted into high spirits. The head of the council held up his hand and the clapping died out.

"Sir. I have heard speeches delivered in this hallowed hall many a time. But I have never heard anything so true as the words that you have been spoken here today. A simple message with a simple theme, delivered honestly. I commend you for your initiative. I also commend your comrades. They have chosen their friends well. The man you are with is not unknown to us. Lieutenant Ramses has distinguished himself before us on more than one occasion. It only brings you credit that he is behind you in the endeavor. We can let the lawyers of both sides hash out the details. That is not important at this time. The most important thing now is that we have an agreement." He paused and looked at his fellow council members. There was not a headshake in the place. "I believe that you have that. I want you personally involved in the details young man. It is the least I can do to reward you for your efforts on our behalf. Do you have something you would like to say?" He asked and Quinn stepped up to the podium.

"Sir, I thank you for your wisdom in this chamber of power. I would like to commend those that have helped me along the way. First of all, the Captain of the *SSF Abraham Lincoln*, who is at this time in stasis due to injuries he sustained. Secondly, I would like to thank the XO of the *Lincoln* who really ran the ship. Next is the Protector himself. Without his help, I probably would not have convinced the Jeng that peace was the answer for them as well as us. Finally, I would like to thank Admiral Horniczek for allowing me to come down here with my esteemed colleague to present our case to you. He has asked to be remembered for suing for peace, rather than for his military battles. I would like to honor his request." Quinn turned back to Margaret and she blushed. "Finally sirs, I would like to thank Chief Pilot Margaret Manning for her endless contributions of support and her unblinking dedication to honor and duty. She is a professional beyond reproach and I am honored to have served with her." He squared up his body and saluted her with a crisp salute that raised a couple of eyebrows in the chamber. "I am ready to undertake the further negotiations that you would have me do. The Jeng people have named me a Protector of my people. It is an honor I do not take lightly. I thank you for the opportunity to carry it out."

The council was interrupted by the sound of a mechanical motor. The rear doors opened and Admiral Horniczek rolled into the room. His smile was genuine and the council waited for his chair to make the long journey to the podium. He rolled up to the platform and stopped just short of the podium. It had never been designed for a figure of his stature, but he was not concerned. "I have an announcement to make." He said in his gravelly weak voice. The words still carried throughout the huge room. Admiral Vorn has been caught trying to prevent this hearing. It is a matter of treason. It is believed that he is guilty of more crimes that we are as yet unaware of. We are currently interrogating his crews. I believe that this will clean up a particularly nasty obstruction for the Lieutenant." He said triumphantly.

The head of the council tapped his microphone. "Actually, your statement is partly mistaken Admiral." The man said and all eyes shifted to him in concern. "You are addressing *Captain* Quinn Ramses. He is to be given a fast ship so that he has access to both heads of government for his negotiations. I will expect that he would like Margaret to remain by his side, so she is hereby promoted to Lieutenant commander and is assigned to the same ship as pilot/navigator for the duration." He said with a smile and a wink. "Congratulations son, make us proud." He said and the room exploded with applause again. The Protector was leading the clapping this time.

Quinn strained to be heard over the ruckus. "Thank you sir, I'll try."

THE END